The Nature of Magic

EDGE CASES 2

The Nature of Magic

Silver Linings

Podium

To everyone who wants a little more magic in their lives
And also to my cat

All rights reserved. No part of this publication may be reproduced, stored in a retrieval system, or transmitted in any form or by any means electronic, mechanical, photocopying, recording, or otherwise without prior written permission from Podium Publishing.

This is a work of fiction. Names, characters, places, and incidents are either products of the author's imagination or used fictitiously. Any resemblance to actual events, locales, or persons, living, dead, or undead, is entirely coincidental.

Copyright © 2024 by Christopher Seck Choa Hong

Cover design by Cosmic Croissant (Toast)

ISBN: 978-1-0394-3658-9

Published in 2024 by Podium Publishing, ULC
www.podiumaudio.com

The Nature of Magic

CHAPTER 1

ROAD TO ELYRA

[**Alright. You know what to do. *Don't* screw this up.**]

Xothok flicked his gaze one last time over the traveling caravan, slitted eyes narrowing slightly. There were indications that this was a diplomatic envoy—the Guild emblem imprinted on the side was a telltale giveaway—but this was a diplomatic envoy from the *Adventurers' Guild*, and so while it wasn't anything to be taken lightly, he had no reason to believe he and his twenty-strong troupe would fail to take them down. There couldn't have been more than six people in the caravan. He was low Silver, and most of his men were at least mid-Bronze, if not higher.

He sniffed once. His stomach growled, and he hissed low in displeasure.

They had food. *Good* food, too; maybe a diplomatic gift to Elyra, considering the trouble they'd had with food lately. But Elyra wasn't the only one having troubles with food, and Xothok wasn't inclined to care about the troubles of that bunch of stuck-up, pretentious assholes. It wasn't like the food would ever reach the mouths of the needy.

[**You sure we can take them, boss?**] one of his men questioned, messaging through the system, and he held back a sigh.

[**I'm sure. Guild or not, they're not likely to have more than one rare class. They're about to make camp, so wait for them to split up and then target them one by one, like I said. *Don't* let them call for help. We have silencing scrolls for a reason.**] His tone would have been short and clipped if he had been actually speaking instead of sending through the system—these were all things his men should already have known but it seemed to satisfy them nonetheless.

He kept a close eye on the adventurers as they began to set up camp. There were four major threats that he could see; likely, the one in full armor was the one they needed to worry about the most. Clerics had next to no capability in combat. The rogue had a dagger and so probably wasn't specialized against long-ranged attacks.

The entire party didn't really seem to be geared toward handling long-ranged attacks. Xothok smiled in a grim sort of satisfaction. Part of him felt sorry for them. A mage was the strongest counter to their group, and even then, they had the scrolls needed to disable wizardry; they were expensive, though, and he preferred not to use them if he didn't have to. This was perfect for them.

[**Bet that armor's gonna sell for shitloads of gold,**] one of his men sent. [**I call dibs.**]

[**I don't know what a dib is, but absolutely not,**] Xothok replied bluntly, and he heard the man mumble something rude. He gave him the finger. [**And don't fucking say anything out loud when we're preparing an ambush, idiot.**]

Not that Xothok blamed him, really.

Banditry was, contrary to what some people expected, a good deal of . . . *waiting*. He trusted his men, but he knew full well that they didn't have the training to survive a fight with four battle-hardened adventurers; if they *could*, they would've become adventurers themselves. It paid better than this nonsense. That was part of the point of the Adventurers' Guild, he'd heard.

They'd tried to join, even, over in the Elyran branch of the Guild, but they'd been turned away. So here they were, and these adventurers were the unlucky sods that would suffer.

[**They're splitting up, boss,**] someone reported. Xothok glanced up. The armored fellow was staying by the camp they'd set up, and the other three were heading off. In different directions, no less. The half-orc seemed to be heading toward the river, and the cleric and rogue looked to be going in opposite directions to gather firewood.

[**Follow them,**] he ordered, even as an odd feeling of discomfort pooled in him. This felt . . . too convenient. But the adventurers had shown no sign that they knew anyone was following them. [**But be careful.**]

Xothok stayed at the camp. At low Silver, he was stronger than the majority of the upstart adventurers out there. He wasn't stupid enough to think he could take what was obviously a rich adventurer decked out in enchanted armor on his own, but the group that fought him would need his help.

And then he waited.

[**Sneak**], at least, was a common skill. He'd made every one of his men max out its grade for situations exactly like these—ones where they needed to follow and wait until the group they were targeting was far enough apart that they couldn't just regroup. The way the skill worked at max level, their odds of getting spotted were less than one percent per hour; with those odds, he wasn't worried about getting spotted.

Time passed.

The sun began to set, casting shade down into the forest. Purple-black wood began to stand out amongst the more vibrant reds that the leaves began to shift toward; the Sunlit Forest was precisely known for this particular phenomenon. Luminescent gold began to light up the central veins of each leaf, and the armored man below them looked up, as if admiring the slow change in color—and then he glanced out at the rest of the woods, as if wondering where his friends were.

It was time. Xothok gave the signal.

[**Go.**]

Byrrhon smirked. He was hoping he'd get one of the easier marks—and the way he saw it, the lizardkin mark was the easiest of them all. Five on one, the little fucker didn't stand a chance. Few rogues were equipped to handle crossbow bolts, let alone five of them, and all this one had was a little dagger. It was pathetic, really.

He was almost tempted to attack before Xothok's signal. If it weren't for the fact that the lizardkin would probably kill him . . .

He licked his lips, ran his finger along his crossbow, then eyed the lizard below. He wanted the dagger, he thought. It looked like it had some fancy inscriptions on it. He'd keep it for himself, hide it when Xothok asked for the loot—say the rogue had thrown it and it had gotten lost, or something. It wouldn't be too hard to lie, and none of the men in his team would dare contradict him.

The signal came. He and his men fired their arrows all at once, aimed directly at the rogue's back; he wouldn't even have the time to see it coming—

—the air rippled, and the bolts pinged off an invisible barrier.

Byrrhon froze.

The rogue turned around, and Byrrhon found himself almost insulted. The lizardkin looked *nervous*. Nervous but determined; he drew his dagger and began to cut a rune into the air.

Not a rogue, Byrrhon realized. And it was worse than that—the wizard had known they were coming. How had he known? They'd all been under [**Stealth**] the entire time; the odds of them being spotted were—

He didn't have time to finish the thought. A wave of heat rolled over him, the sheer density of magic distorting the air, but it ... wasn't a [**Fireball**]? The heat soaked into him, eating up his energy; he felt his consciousness practically being dragged away from him, though he fought it as best he could.

The last thing he saw was the ground rapidly approaching. The last thing he *felt* was anger that a pathetic whelp of a lizardkin had managed to best him.

—⚏—

Two—he didn't really have a name beyond the number, which represented him being Xothok's second-in-command—crouched up in his tree and waited. He was patient. Xothok had taught him to be patient. Xothok had taught him everything he knew, in fact, as far as he could remember. Two didn't remember any life other than this one, but to be fair, his memories didn't go very far back.

Below, the priest-cleric or whatever he was hummed to himself, gathering firewood and tucking it beneath an arm. Mostly, he was picking up loose branches and dry leaves, kindling to build into a bigger flame. Two remembered that from Xothok's teachings.

The people he had with him were used to his more reticent nature, and none of them grumbled about waiting, which he appreciated.

The signal came. Three of them fired crossbow bolts at the priest's back; two dropped silently to the ground, wielding their daggers. Closer to rusted knives, really. The priest seemed to jerk backward at the sound of the crossbow, and Two allowed himself to feel a brief flicker of satisfaction. If he was reacting like that, then he wouldn't be prepared—

—but the crossbow bolts passed through him, and he seemed fine.

Two frowned.

He threw himself at the priest, together with the other man he had with him—the long-ranged fighters would have trouble hitting him with them in the way, he knew, but crossbow bolts didn't seem to affect the man anyway? He would fight, then.

And then he realized what the problem was.

It wasn't that the bolts didn't do damage to him. They *did*. His knife was cutting into the man too. But either he had far more health than anyone should have, or he was healing back from every hit dealt to him.

The worst part of it was his eyes.

The priest wasn't worried. He wasn't scared. He just seemed *sad*, and Two didn't particularly care for the look of pity he was giving him.

He was so distracted by the look in the priest's eyes that he didn't see the prepared spell in his hands. The flash of light was so bright it blinded him.

But even blinded, he couldn't stop himself from seeing those eyes. Those pitying, gentle eyes.

―⚎―

Morkar's legs ached.

He hated waiting. He hated all of *this*, really, the fact that they'd been reduced to preying on random adventurers and merchants just to make sure they got the food they needed to keep going. He'd made an argument that they could just try to steal the food from the caravan and leave before anyone noticed, but Xothok had shot that down; trying that would get them noticed and hunted down.

If they took out the adventurers, they'd have time to leave before the Guild realized anything was wrong. And Xothok was *right*, at least as far as Morkar could tell—he wasn't particularly strategically minded—but he still hated it. And waiting to ambush someone didn't sit right with him.

Also, his legs were cramping. Because he was crouching in a fucking tree. That made him grumpy.

The orc—or half-orc; Morkar really couldn't tell the difference and didn't care to learn—was in the river, washing some of her equipment. She hummed to herself as she scrubbed away at her mace, taking more care of that single weapon than Morkar had seen any of their band take care of their own bodies. Thankfully, the men he had with him refrained from making any disgusting comments. Gods forbid Byrrhon's people were here.

The signal came. Morkar dropped out of the tree with a grunt, his tail helping to counterbalance his weight as he fell. Three bolts shot out of the trees towards the half-orc—

—who *vanished*.

Morkar blinked once.

"Um," someone said. One of his men. Except there was someone else with him, too. The orc's hand was gripped firmly around the crossbow's firing mechanism, preventing the bolt from firing. Pressed against his throat was a faintly glowing sword.

No one moved. The orc grinned at them. "'Sup," she said. "Wanna try fighting fair instead? Ambushes are for suckers."

Morkar paused.

And then despite himself, he grinned. He hefted his axe.

"If that's what ya want," he said.

―⚎―

Xothok didn't waste any time himself. His [**Enhanced Hearing**] caught the *twang* of crossbows as his men attacked all four adventurers at the same time, split as they were—but even as the bolts shot toward the armored man, he leapt out of the tree he was perched in, using a [**Charge**] to give him some forward momentum. Xothok felt the skill take hold, carrying him forward at incredible speeds just behind the rain of bolts; if the adventurer survived the first wave, Xothok's sword would strike directly toward the gap between the helmet and his torso, straight into his neck for a critical hit.

His sword struck true.

The bolts that hit the armor deflected and scattered, bouncing off the dark metal like it was nothing; Xothok wasn't too surprised. Enchanted armor was often reinforced against basic attacks like that. It didn't mean the attacks wouldn't carve off chunks of his health. Xothok himself held a look of grim determination on his face as he kept his sword in the adventurer's neck, counting the seconds. The longer he held it there before the man moved away, the more health it would drain, and the more the pain would put him off-balance...

...except the man wasn't moving back.

"What are you doing?" the armored man asked him curiously. He talked like it was *normal* to be able to speak with a *sword inside his throat*. Xothok jerked his sword back like it was on fire and stared, trying to suppress the fear bubbling up in him.

This man was a threat. His senses were screaming a warning at him. [**Danger Sense**], which hadn't gone off until now, was suddenly blaring in his ears. Even if it hadn't, he had years of instinct honed from fighting in the streets and then for his life as a bandit.

Every bone in his body told him to *run*. He jerked, trying to make himself move, to force down the panic suddenly bubbling through his body, the certainty that he was now about to die. He glanced up and around—maybe if any one of his teams had succeeded, they could hold someone hostage...

A searing wave of heat flashed over his scales, coming from the direction the rogue had been wandering in.

A bright flash of light seared into his eyes from where the cleric had gone.

From the fighter's direction came a loud shout. It didn't sound like any of his men. It didn't sound like a shout of pain, either. It sounded like a shout of triumph.

Xothok stared at the armored man in front of him, who was staring back at him in what seemed like mild curiosity instead of anything approaching anger. He swallowed back his panic.

"...I surrender?"

CHAPTER 2

NO FREE LUNCH

There were several things the Guildmaster had warned Sev and the others about before allowing them to leave for Elyra. The first, of course, was the possibility of bandits—the routes they normally took didn't often have bandits on them, given they were rarely traveled to begin with, but the path to a Kingdom was always ripe for the picking. Bandits knew how to choose their targets, of course; they wouldn't attack anyone that seemed too powerful, or anyone with too large of a delegation, or anyone who seemed like they didn't have anything worth stealing.

The other warnings she gave were for dealing with Elyran politics in general. Vex had some idea of what they were like, and he nodded vigorously to every one of the Guildmaster's points. Don't make jokes at the expense of any noble. Don't call them out in public. Don't interfere with anything they're doing.

She had sighed and cut herself off midway through the explanation, because absolutely none of them looked like they were planning on taking her up on her advice. Except for Vex. And even he was starting to look a touch rebellious after a quick glance at Derivan.

"If you *do* run afoul of Elyra's politics," she had said, and then she'd hesitated, eyeing all of them carefully as if to figure out how much trouble they were going to get the Guild in. Then she just sighed. "We'll back you up. The Guild's been trying to make some changes in Elyra for a while, but it's hard to participate in a system without being influenced by it in some way. We rotate the people that work in the Elyran branch every so often, and even that's only *mostly* successful. Some things still slip through the cracks.

"And on that note: if any of the problems you see are with the *Guild* . . . report them to me. But you're also authorized to deal with them directly.

You're a Silver-ranked team, and I'm giving you Gold authority. Make use of it."

So that had been nice.

Back to the problem of the bandits, though.

They'd decided almost immediately after the meeting that they would make themselves targets intentionally. They'd make their caravan look weaker than it was. They'd leave a symbol of the Guild on the side of the caravan, to show that it might have something worth stealing.

If there were bandits en route to Elyra, then they wanted to do their part in making that route safer.

To that end, they'd spoken to Max about their plan.

"It *might* work," she had said thoughtfully. "As long as you don't get in over your heads. If you keep an eye out and make sure you spot them before they spot you... then sure. They'll expect a diplomatic envoy to be guarded, but the standard guard team is one Silver-rank and three Bronze-ranks. Just make sure they don't hit the food and remember that they might decide not to attack you anyway."

Which was fine. They weren't looking to intentionally pick a fight, and they didn't have the time nor the skills to chase down bandits that they didn't know for sure were there. But if they were targeted, they would be prepared, and they would have a plan to lead the bandits into their own trap.

Even with all that preparation, though...

―᙭―

Sev hadn't expected things to work out quite so well.

Vex had been the one to notice the bandits first—the lizardkin wizard spent most of his time observing the movement of mana anyway, when he wasn't working on one of his sketches or on a runic formula. It hadn't taken him long to notice that the ambient mana was avoiding a patch of trees farther into the Sunlit Forest, and although he couldn't see any actual *people*, the mana had been a rather obvious tell.

From there, they'd quickly worked out a plan. [Endless Echoes] could work out, roughly, what sorts of skills the bandits had; Misa insisted they use that to make sure they wouldn't be caught completely by surprise. All she had to do was find a few versions of herself that had hopped out of the caravan to challenge the bandits to a fight.

According to her, those versions of herself had been rather embarrassingly easy to find.

They'd learned from there that those bandits weren't really a threat to them at all, so they decided to wait it out. They'd get attacked by the bandits sooner or later, but the bandits were clearly waiting for an opportunity, for them to drop their guard; they'd planned out several possible scenarios in the safety of the caravan, messaging each other using the system.

If they were attacked before they made camp, they could deal with the bandits in short order—Misa had confirmed that.

If they were attacked *while* they were making camp, they would try to lure the bandits out. [Endless Echoes] came in useful there, too; they tested making camp a few times in simulated alternate timelines, and while Misa's information-sharing capabilities were somewhat limited, the fact that the fights rarely lasted more than five minutes... helped.

As a result, all four of them knew pretty much exactly when they would be attacked, how they would be attacked, and how long the fight would take. Misa cautioned them not to be careless, though; this was exactly the sort of thing that might lure them into being overconfident, and everyone had quickly assured Misa that they would take the ambush seriously when it happened.

It was just...

"I can't believe that just took us two minutes," Sev said plainly, looking at the others, then at the carefully restrained bandits. Max had provided them with a set of particularly durable, enchanted ropes for exactly this purpose. Misa grinned at him, looking just faintly smug.

"Told ya," she said, folding her arms.

"Yeah, yeah," Sev chuckled. He turned his gaze to their captives, staring bemusedly at the large array of men and women that were bound up in front of him. "What are we going to do with you," he muttered with a sigh.

The lizardkin he presumed was the bandit leader opened his mouth, and Sev raised a hand to forestall him. "No, I wasn't asking *you*; don't you start talking."

Xothok snapped his mouth shut again, looking disgruntled. Farther in the back, an infuriated bandit—Byrrhon, Sev vaguely remembered—tried to yell at him, and mostly failed through the [**Silenced**] effect Vex had placed on him.

Just him. He was the only one that would not stop talking and kept insisting that his being defeated was a fluke. He'd basically turned purple when Vex [**Silenced**] him and was in the process of doing so again now.

"I was not aware humans could turn that color," Derivan said mildly, watching Byrrhon with interest.

"We usually don't." Sev massaged his temples. He could feel a headache coming on.

"Do all organic species do this?" the armor asked. "Can lizardkin scales change color? I feel I have seen Vex do this, though it has always been too subtle for me to be certain."

Vex yelped a little when his name was mentioned, took a step as though to hide behind Derivan, realized Derivan was the one teasing him, and then promptly hid himself behind Sev instead. The cleric blinked once, glanced at Vex, and then stared at Derivan. "I—" he started. "I'm pretty sure that's something else?"

Sev was abruptly reminded that lizardkin claws were in fact rather sharp, and while Vex's talons were almost certainly not digging into his wrist on *purpose*, they were also not letting go. He wiggled his hand a little until Vex loosened his grip, then took the opportunity to pet their resident wizard on the head.

"Max said she'd pick up any bandits we caught if we found them, right?" Misa asked, taking pity on Vex.

"She didn't really tell us *when* she'd be picking them up, though," Sev grumbled. "For all we know, we have to drag them all the way to Elyra."

"We could just send her a message," Vex piped up. His voice was pitched a little higher than normal.

"Right, right, I'll ask," Sev said, pulling up the system—

"And do *we* get any say in this?" bandit-leader Xothok growled out now that there was a lull in the conversation. Sev was honestly surprised that he'd bothered to wait to speak at all, but...

Perhaps he shouldn't have been. More than anything, the lizardkin man seemed *tired*. All of the bandits were quiet and sullen, really, save for Byrrhon; Sev didn't miss the way a lot of them were looking to Xothok like they were expecting him to get them out of this somehow.

"You're bandits." Misa was the first to respond, and her voice was startlingly cold. "We're probably not your first targets. You approached us ready to kill. So how about fucking *no*."

Xothok didn't back down. "And what's this Max going to do with us?" Xothok asked, ignoring Misa's words. There was a thick sort of bitterness in his voice, and he spat his words out like they were venom lodged in his throat. "Slaughter us? Sell us into slavery?"

"What the fuck?" Sev sputtered. "*No!* Obviously not. I can't say I know the exact procedure, but I'm sure Max will. If I had to guess, you'll be provisionally hired into doing community work for the Guild and paid a fair wage. And carefully watched so you don't go doing shit like this again."

Xothok stared at Sev. "We are *bandits*," he said, and his voice was cold; Sev realized with a start that the bandit didn't believe him. "If you are to execute us, tell us now, so that we may make peace with our deaths."

"Uh, boss," one of the other bandits said. "I think you misheard them? And also that sounds like a good deal please don't argue the point."

Xothok just glared, ignoring the other bandit. "We *tried* to join your damn Guild," he said. His voice burned with anger and the smallest hint of something *else*; Derivan stepped forward, concerned, but otherwise remained silent. "They kicked us out. Wouldn't listen to a *damn thing* I tried to tell them. You expect me to believe that after all that, the Guild wants to *help*?"

Sev frowned. There *had* been some mention of problems with the Elyran branch, but from what the Guildmaster had told them, it shouldn't have reached the point where the Guild would turn away people that wanted to work for them.

"Do you know how many of us have died?" Xothok asked. "Just to get here. Do you know how many of us starved? How many brothers I've had to bury?"

"And how many innocents did *you* bury?" Misa asked, her eyes hard. "You didn't react when I mentioned other targets earlier. You *have* hit others. They didn't survive, did they?"

"None of us have restraining skills, believe it or not!" the bandit leader's voice shook. "What do you want us to do? We barely have any food to eat. There's nothing to hunt. The monster corpses all disappear if we kill them. It's us or them. If we can steal the food, we steal it, but if we *have* to go through someone..."

Xothok's tail lashed angrily behind him.

"Tell you what." Sev spoke as calmly as he could manage, though he felt a strange, foreign anger coiling in the center of his chest. He wasn't certain what that anger was directed toward; not Xothok, he didn't think. "Max says it'll be a couple hours before she can make it here. Why don't we talk over dinner?"

"Are you trying to mock us?" Xothok glared. "I *will not* watch while you gorge yourselves in front of us."

Sev decided that the time for words was over.

There were no words that could fix this. There was too much hurt there. But a warm meal would, if nothing else, be a start.

Cooking for something like twenty-five people would have been more of a chore if the caravan's food supply hadn't included an absolutely enormous amount of bread—something about bread was, apparently, far more amenable to spatial compression magic than most other foodstuffs. Probably all the air. The same thing applied to most pastries and baked products, according to a *very* enthusiastic Vex's lecture... several moons ago.

So dinner was bread and a *massive* pot of stew, the pot itself conjured out of the earth and sterilized with fire. That part was easy. The more complicated part was figuring out how to feed people that were being restrained with ropes.

But Misa checked with [Endless Echoes], and it seemed that none of the bandits were particularly inclined to run away from the offered food, or even take off running *with* the food. Not when they could smell the rich, fragrant aroma of it nearby and were told they could ask for seconds. Nor were they particularly inclined to fight, after the rather one-sided way they had been taken down to begin with.

The only real problem was Byrrhon, who refused to eat, or indeed admit that they'd lost the fight.

"Leave him be," Xothok said when approached with the topic. "Just... put some bread near him or something. He'll eat it when no one's looking."

"Has he always been like that?" Sev asked curiously.

"No," Xothok said, but he fell silent and didn't seem to want to elaborate further.

Xothok had been angry and snappy with them, right up until the part where they'd actually started feeding his men. He hadn't believed a word they said until then. The moment they'd *untied* his men and given them food, however, his face had gone carefully blank.

It remained just as blank when they untied his arms, all the way up until the moment Sev quietly handed him his own bowl of stew along with a hearty helping of bread.

Sev could see him struggling with himself. He could see Xothok trying to figure out what he wanted to say, trying to figure out *how* to say it—

"What the fuck is all this?" Xothok asked bluntly. He didn't sound angry anymore. Instead, there was a certain kind of exhaustion coiled up into his voice, like a tension that was only just starting to unwind.

"Food," Sev said, trying for a joke, and when Xothok glared at him, he backpedaled quickly. "I'm not making fun of you. But you're hungry and we have food. I don't think it needs to be more complicated than that."

He meant it, too.

Xothok looked down at his plate for a moment. He grabbed his bread, dipped it into the stew, and took a bite, all in lieu of responding.

When Xothok finally spoke, he did it without looking at anyone.

"Fine," he said, his voice a little softer. "But don't think this changes anything."

CHAPTER 3

PICKUP LINES

There was a ritual of sorts that Sev, Derivan, Vex, and Misa had started. They'd started it ever since they'd learned that the night sky was *wrong*—ever since they'd learned that it had once been scattered with brilliant stars.

They'd tried to tell others, of course. Max, the Guildmaster, Misa's mother and the villagers of J'rokksur. But no one else had been able to retain any information they tried to share, no matter what combination of skills they tried. Whatever kind of infolock this was, it seemed different in some way from the ones they'd dealt with before.

Even now, after removing the lock—if that was indeed what they had done—they could feel the knowledge slipping out of their minds again. It was so easy to look at the sky and think that everything was normal. That the expanse of darkness above them was all there ever had been.

But it wasn't.

And so, every night, Derivan would cast the skill that was clearly meant to be [**Starry Night**], though the name of the skill hadn't fixed itself in the system. They would watch. They would grieve. They would try to remember, though the world clearly wanted them to forget.

This was just the first time they would be doing it with an audience.

The bandits had all been restrained again—most of them hadn't put up much of a struggle, surprisingly, though a number of them had certainly *tried* to run when they went to restrain them. They didn't make it very far before Misa appeared in their path, wielding her mace threateningly, and it didn't take much more than that for them to be cowed. It was one of the little tricks they'd figured out before heading out on this trip. Vex could fire an invisible [**Mana Bolt**], and Misa could block that attack, looking for all the world like she could teleport freely. Another layer of misdirection that was proving itself to be useful.

It helped that the bandit leader, Xothok, seemed resigned to whatever would happen. He didn't *trust* them, explicitly, but he wasn't fighting them, either. He was just . . . watching them, something unreadable in his eyes.

"Any idea what he's feeling?" Sev asked Derivan quietly. "He's just staring."

"He is . . . worried," Derivan said, glancing at the lizardkin. There was a brief flicker in his eyes. "He cares about his men. He regrets some of the things he has done, even if he feels he had no other choice. He feels hope, but he is angry he feels that hope, because he has been burned on hope before. And . . . a small part of him feels fear, I think. He worries that if we are correct, then the crimes he has committed will have been for nothing."

"Physical Empathy is doing well for you," Misa noted, a hint of surprise in her voice.

"I am not completely certain, of course," Derivan admitted. "There are many small details. I can feel the way his heart beats. His posture is guarded. The stat helps me interpret these things, but my own views are still imposed on them."

"It sounds about right to me," Sev said with a sigh. "We're going to need to look into what he said about the Elyran branch of the Guild. They shouldn't have turned them away like that, not if they were looking for a job. Or there's some information we're missing on what these guys did . . ."

"Sometimes Elyra overprioritizes its nobles," Vex said, looking down. "They have to look like the best and the brightest. Nobility in Elyra is earned—it's not exclusively a right of birth. But the side effect is that the nobles hate it when someone that isn't a noble ranks higher than them."

"That sounds kind of fucked," Misa said with a frown, and Vex just shrugged, withdrawing into himself slightly. Derivan watched him with concern, moving over to take a seat next to the lizardkin.

"Perhaps we should move on," the armor offered after a moment. "We will have to go to Elyra and see what is happening in the Elyran branch for ourselves; further speculation now will always be incomplete."

"I'd like to move on," Vex said quietly. Sev glanced at Misa, and both of them nodded.

Derivan cast [**Starry Night**].

Once again, that deep-blue fog began rolling in from the edges of the clearing, past the slightly alarmed cries of the bandits; more than one of them pulled their limbs back from the tendrils of fog, though Derivan made sure not to let the fog conceal any of them. Instead, he focused the spell upward, allowing the fog to blend almost seamlessly into the night sky.

A rather unique point for the Sunlit Forest, however, was that the bioluminescent gold of the leaves shone right through the fog like it wasn't even there. They glittered in the breeze, looking for all the world like someone had painstakingly painted the veins of every individual leaf on a canvas.

Small, flickering fireballs began to appear within the fog. Derivan kept the dial on the size small, as he always did; instead, he began to make more and more of the stars appear, until the fog was littered with countless tiny specks.

A breeze blew through the clearing, and the leaves rustled, swaying in the fog. The stars stirred, swirling within the confines of the spell.

Just for a moment, the painting came to life.

Even the bandits had gone largely silent, where they'd previously been talking with one another, worried about what might happen to them. Now they were all just staring at the canvas in the sky that Derivan had created. Xothok, in particular, seemed taken aback by the sight.

Vex was the first to let out a breath.

"I never get tired of seeing this," he said quietly.

The others nodded silently. They watched it for a moment more, with only Misa sparing an occasional glance at the bandits to make sure none of them used the moment to try to escape, but none of them did—they all seemed equally enamored by the sight.

Even Xothok, who seemed enraptured by it. Sev glanced at him briefly, then did a double-take and focused more carefully on the bandit leader; he looked like he was *crying*.

"Why the fuck does this seem *familiar*?" The words were hissed out, and Sev was fairly certain that none of them were supposed to hear them. The half-memory seemed agonizing for the lizardkin; he stared into the sky with gritted teeth, straining to remember something that was no longer there.

They'd tried showing this skill to the Guildmaster, too, exactly like this. Her reaction had been remarkably similar to Xothok's—bewilderment, and a certain frustrated anger. There was wonder there, too, but there was a deeper sense of pain. Some part of her seemed to recognize that she'd lost something precious to her.

It was the closest they'd been able to get to explaining to her what they'd discovered.

She didn't *understand*, per se. But she understood that something important had transpired, and promised to leverage all the Guild resources she could to uncover the truth. Velykos, the stone elemental priest—they'd made sure he was using [**The Walls Have Ears**] too, when they spoke to the Guildmaster about it. It was the best they could do.

Xothok's reaction was even worse than the Guildmaster's, if anything. His pupils were dilated, and his breathing came rapidly.

"What do you mean, *it seems familiar*?" Sev asked, half to distract the lizardkin from whatever destructive spiral he was in. Xothok whipped around, as if he'd forgotten that there was anyone else there with him.

"Exactly what I said." Xothok rapidly regained control of himself and turned his tear-stained gaze into a glare. "Did you do something to me? Was that a mental spell?"

"It was not," Derivan said, though he seemed concerned that that was the first conclusion Xothok had jumped to. "It was a visual effect. A reminder of sorts."

"What the fuck kind of a reminder was that?"

There was a short silence. Derivan observed Xothok for a moment and then spoke. "You are angry because it made you sad?" he said, cocking his head. "And that made you feel vulnerable."

"Like hell it did."

"Derivan," Vex said awkwardly. "That's one of the things we don't say out loud."

"Oh." Derivan blinked, eye-lights flickering in his helmet. "My apologies."

Xothok didn't answer him. He stared off into the distance instead, stubbornly refusing to meet any of their gazes. Sev sighed, glancing through his system and noting a few new messages.

"I don't think we can get anything more here," Sev said tiredly. "Max says she'll be here in the morning. It's been a long day. Let's get some rest and set up a night watch. Derivan, you okay with taking the night shift again?"

"Of course," the armor said. "I do not need to sleep."

"Yeah, but that doesn't mean you should always take the full duty," Sev muttered.

"I'll stay up with him for a shift," Vex volunteered. "Um. It's only fair. And I'm used to staying up late, anyway. And lizardkin don't need that much sleep."

"You only needed that first sentence," Sev said, amused.

"I appreciate it," Derivan said, chuckling.

And with that, they retired for the night.

—⚜—

Max arrived in the early hours of the morning, just as the glow began to fade from the leaves of the Sunlit Forest. She grinned and waved when she caught sight of Derivan standing guard over the bandits—Vex was next to him, having curled up onto the rock at some point, with a blanket pulled over his body.

"Did he fall asleep out here?" she asked, glancing with amusement at the lizardkin.

"He was very sleepy, despite his insistence on not being sleepy," Derivan said with a chuckle. "It is not the first time he has done this. Did you know he cast a [**Sleep**] spell on himself once by accident?"

"I did not know that," Max said brightly. "But that's kind of great. Are these the bandits I need to pick up?"

"Yes," Derivan said. "Twenty-one of them in total. We have some concerns we wanted to share, however..."

Derivan quickly briefed Max on the situation. She'd heard a little bit about what happened from Sev, apparently, but hadn't gotten all the details over the system; she frowned when she heard about the Elyran Guild apparently rejecting these bandits, and about the particularly stubborn one that was Byrrhon.

"Really?" she asked. "That's... It's weird that we haven't heard anything about that. All the reports from the Elyran branch have seemed normal."

"We will be investigating," Derivan said with a nod. "It seemed strange to us, too."

"Well, let the Guildmaster know what you find," Max said. "Or let me know. Either-or. We're trusting you to handle things in Elyra."

"What will you be doing with the bandits? Can you handle them all by yourself?" Derivan asked curiously. Max grinned.

"Trust me," she said. "I have my ways."

—⚎—

Max did not, in fact, have her ways.

It wasn't that she couldn't handle the bandits by herself—she was pretty sure she could do it with her eyes closed, if she had to, though she didn't particularly want to test that theory.

It was just that this was an *escort quest*, functionally, and she hated escort quests. She got bored! It was so much travel and not enough teleportation. She knew, logically, that [**Right Place, Right Time**] cost her more the more she used it; she knew that she should be using it less, despite how convenient the skill was.

But still, she'd gotten used to teleporting around, and now mundane travel made her bones ache. And she wasn't even thirty yet!

Bah. Whatever. There were other ways to entertain herself on the trip.

Max sidled up to Xothok, who stared back stoically at her, looking only the faintest bit disgruntled. "So," Max said cheerfully. "Tell me about yourself!"

"Do you think we should feel bad for the bandits?" Sev asked conversationally.

"What?" Misa stared at Sev. "Why? Max is awesome."

"She is," Sev acknowledged. "But she gets bored easily. It'll take like two seconds for her to get bored here."

"What does she do when she's bored?" Misa asked curiously. Sev grinned.

"*Really* aggressive friendship. Trust me. She'll have their barriers down in no time."

CHAPTER 4

A NEW JOURNEY

The earth was quiet today.

Often, Velykos would be able to hear echoes of emotion from the earth, through his connection with Nillea. Sometimes it was fear, like there was something big coming and little could be done to change its course; sometimes it was anger, like there was something truly wrong and the earth was shaking in its desire to fix it. More often, it was smaller—gentle, happy trembles, or sad little quakes.

It had been most active when those strange adventurers were here—the odd priest, the little lizard, the protector, the fighter. The earth never seemed silent at all when they were around, not even when they left for that dungeon of theirs. It was only when they left—*truly* left, on their diplomatic mission to Elyra—that the earth settled. And that was . . . strange.

It left Velykos wondering what their significance was. Or perhaps it was not them that was significant? Perhaps it was something else that was following them? Whether that something was a light or a shadow . . . only time would tell.

As for him, it was time for him to leave on his own journey. He had been enlightened, in a manner of speaking; something truly important to him had been changed, and Velykos would not allow it to stand.

First, though. The Guildmaster wished to speak with him. And he suspected he knew what she wished to talk about.

"I am here," Velykos said into the air. It was where the Guildmaster had said to meet her, and he had no doubt she was there, only hidden.

A woman was indeed standing near him. He didn't jump—he simply turned and bowed his head respectfully. "Guildmaster."

"Velykos," she said, returning the greeting.

Neither of them spoke for a moment. Velykos turned his gaze toward the sky. It was night, of course, which meant only the light of the moon shone down on them, and [**The Walls Have Ears**] told him there was something deeply wrong with that fact. The Guildmaster, too, was troubled—he could see it in her posture.

"There's something wrong with the sky, isn't there?" the Guildmaster said. She sighed. "I could glean that much. They tried to tell me more, but I couldn't retain anything. I'm not used to being on the other end of that kind of magic."

"There is," Velykos rumbled. Stone and pebble rained down his chin when he spoke; he wished it wouldn't, sometimes. It gave his voice a gravelly quality that many found intimidating. "Something is . . . missing."

"Missing," the Guildmaster echoed, and she stared into the sky. Velykos felt her heartbeat, slow but steady. He felt the beat of her emotions, too; there was a weight pressing down on her, a certain sadness. A small part of her recognized what was missing, just like he did.

"I trust those four to keep figuring things out on their end," the Guildmaster said eventually. "But I'm getting a lot more reports of errors cropping up in the system, for old and new adventurers alike. They're not *significant* errors, by any means, and it's possible I'm just getting more errors because I'm asking for them to be reported. But there's a definite trend."

"And if what they said about the gods is true," Velykos said, "then we may be running out of time."

"We have decades, as far as the gods are concerned," the Guildmaster said. "They don't get erased that quickly. Honestly, we're lucky that the four of them have figured out this much on their own, and they're on their way to get more answers. But that doesn't mean we're going to do nothing with what they've given us."

"No," Velykos agreed, though he was at a loss on how they would explore more on their own. "But what will we do?"

"Research, mostly," the Guildmaster said with a sigh. "The Guild is going to leverage its contacts to find out what the Kingdoms have managed to uncover about the history of this world. They know more than they're saying, but I don't think they know the stakes."

"And yet we cannot tell them what the stakes are," Velykos said. "Or have you tried already?"

"I've tried," the Guildmaster said. "They promise to help, and then they forget as soon as we stop speaking. The only way to get their help is to not tell them at all, and without that leverage . . ."

She didn't need to finish her words. Velykos understood that mortals were strange creatures; many of them cared so much about things he did not. Gold, for instance, was demanded for nearly any service that could be provided, and many seemed eager to get their hands on as much of it as they could. No doubt the Kingdoms desired an abundance of coin to render their services to the Guild.

"It is strange that those four can remember and we cannot," Velykos mused.

"If we knew why, we'd be a lot closer to understanding the crux of this problem, I think." The Guildmaster frowned slightly. "I've spoken to the J'rokksur leaders about this. Misa's parents—Charise and Orkas. They think it has something to do with the reality anchor Misa holds."

"And what do you think?" Velykos asked curiously.

"I don't know," the Guildmaster admitted. "It's an easy answer, but it doesn't explain everything. We know *how* they got their reality anchor, so we could try sending in a team to get one, but . . ."

"It is dangerous," Velykos said, and the Guildmaster nodded.

"The conditions they were able to get their anchor in are rather specific," she said. "And I don't have a good feeling about sending people into a random dungeon break. Max already tried teleporting into one, and the fact that she didn't manage it is a bad sign. It might not be survivable outside that specific circumstance."

For a moment, they were silent. And then the Guildmaster looked at him. "What about you? What are you planning to do?"

"I must understand in more detail what is happening to the gods," Velykos said. "I have some idea now of what might have happened. Of who I might have met, and what might have changed in my past. But I cannot know for sure. I think, perhaps, if I travel back to the quarry that I originally came into being in . . ."

"Would that work?" the Guildmaster asked him, and this time it was his turn to go silent for a while.

"There are traces left in the earth, always," Velykos said eventually. "They are difficult to track, even for elementals such as I. But it is not impossible. Not with divine assistance, and assistance from the system."

"I'm not sure I would be so quick to rely on the system."

"I do not think the system is evil," Velykos chose his words carefully, seeing the doubt in the Guildmaster's eyes. "But I do believe it is . . . unchecked. It appears to be a solution to a problem we cannot see."

"It's not a very good solution," the Guildmaster said, still doubtfully. Velykos nodded.

"That, I agree with," he said. "It is incomplete. Perhaps it was rushed. Or perhaps the problem at hand cannot be solved. We cannot say until we know more."

"And we won't know more until our efforts bear fruit," the Guildmaster sighed, and then she looked up at Velykos again. "I know I've asked before. Are you sure you don't want me to send an escort with you?"

"An escort would be difficult for me," Velykos explained, though not unkindly. "My needs are not the same as that of most mortals. I do not need to pause to rest or eat, and while I could accommodate them, I feel it would only slow me down."

He could take care of himself. Stone elementals were hard to hurt to begin with, due to some of the passive buffs their species had. And more importantly, this was something of a personal journey for him; he understood and appreciated the Guildmaster's desire to make sure he was safe, but this was something he felt he needed to do alone.

"Actually," the Guildmaster said. "I have a new team that might be perfect for you, there."

"Oh?" Velykos tilted his head curiously.

"They're a veteran team made of Skeletal Warriors," the Guildmaster said. "They don't need to eat or sleep, just like you. But they're all still . . . adjusting. The change from mortal to immortal has been hard on them."

Velykos had many questions about that, but he focused on what was the important detail to him. "You believe they need help adjusting."

"Yes. And I think you'd be a good guide for them."

Velykos hesitated. ". . . This journey I wish to take is personal," he admitted, and then he considered it some more. "But not so much that I cannot bear company, I think.

"Thank you," Velykos added, though the words weren't strictly necessary, and the Guildmaster gave him a nod.

They stared at the sky for a moment more, in a moment of strange solidarity. Different as they were, Velykos thought that the Guildmaster was perhaps one of the few here that might understand how he felt; both of them understood that something had been stripped away from them, and their best efforts had yet to yield any real results. There was too much they still didn't know, and they couldn't rely on Sev's team to find out everything.

But even for someone immortal, there was only so much time that could be spent on quiet moments.

"I will let you know anything I find," Velykos said, turning to leave.

"I'll do the same," the Guildmaster agreed. "I'll have the new team meet up with you shortly. Give them about an hour."

Velykos nodded.

—⁂—

It took precisely forty-eight minutes for the team to arrive. The five of them came dressed in heavy clothing, obscuring all but the most prominent of their features; simply put, they looked vaguely humanoid, and nothing else. Velykos couldn't help but wonder if this wouldn't be suspicious to other mortals.

"Eh, it ain't more suspicious than showing our faces," the team leader had told him when he'd asked. Herald, his name was? Or perhaps it was Harold? He'd never gotten a handle on human names. "Just gotta be careful around people, is all. Will we be goin' through a lot of cities and the like?"

That was a good question. Velykos hadn't actually kept up to date on the development of villages and cities. "I do not think so," he said. "I am merely headed for the quarry I was born in, to find traces of an old friend. There is a town nearby, but it is on the other side of that quarry, I think."

"Good," the captain said. "Less complications that way. You ready to get goin'? I gotta say, it'll be nice to have a healer on our team for once."

Velykos took a moment to watch the five of them, curious. They were quite different from what he'd expected, when the Guildmaster had first mentioned fresh immortals that needed to adjust to their new lives—but he supposed he had no frame of reference for how a mortal would act after the transition. Perhaps there wouldn't be a difference at all, until years and years had passed, and they had accumulated the same sort of experience a typical immortal had.

The captain was the most at ease in his new form, if Velykos was reading his body language correctly. He could never really be sure, and he was missing a lot of the cues he normally had; no heartbeat, no temperature, no strange distributions of blood for him to make inferences with. But he seemed relaxed and at ease, with just the slightest bit of tension when he spoke.

Two lizardkin-shaped individuals seemed the next most well adjusted. They stood close together. Siblings, perhaps? They glanced at one another occasionally, and Velykos could feel the way they would tap their feet nervously against the ground every so often, or the way their tails would touch the ground and then jerk back, like they didn't want to be reminded of the new, strange weight.

There was an orc—Velykos was pretty sure the largest figure was an orc, though he could have been wrong—who seemed not to care too much about his new status as a skeleton. His discomfort seemed to be with something else; he moved like he expected everything to be *heavier*, and it bothered him that it wasn't.

And the last one . . . That poor man would need Velykos's guidance the most, he thought. The Guildmaster had spoken to him before about this one. The human wasn't coping well. His body felt like it didn't belong to him, the way Velykos understood it, and it was causing him no small amount of mental distress. In a way, he could sympathize—stone elementals were very much the same way, in that they were always sculpting themselves into a body that better suited them—but he understood that the young man's situation was fundamentally different.

In the not-too-distant past, he would have asked Nillea for guidance. But now . . .

Now he wondered. Sev had given him ideas. Perhaps he could try something different.

CHAPTER 5

THE FIRST QUEST

Derivan sat in the back of the caravan, considering their journey thus far. The bandits were still the most exciting thing to happen to them—there were no monster attacks, no mysterious dungeons appearing in their path. It would take a few more days of travel still to reach Elyra, and that was without considering the requests the Guildmaster had asked them to complete. She had marked out two in particular that the Guild didn't have the spare adventurers for. The first was located in the village of Fendal and had been marked as *suspicious* and *urgent*, which was . . . concerning; the second was a simple request to help an Elyran noblewoman harvest the alchemical reagents she kept in her garden.

"I am still unsure as to why this first request is urgent," Derivan admitted, looking over the form they'd been given for the third time. It seemed relatively simple—it was an extermination quest of sorts. At least, he assumed that was what the "handle an infestation problem" part meant.

"Guildmaster priority," Sev said with a shrug. "Something weird happened with the receptionist that took down that quest, and the Guildmaster wants us to make sure that everything's on the level."

"Doesn't she have other people she can send to help with perception bullshit?" Misa folded her arms. "I dunno about you, but I feel like we've dealt with more than our fair share of perception-related problems."

"I think that's exactly why she wants us to handle it," Sev said. "Nothing beats experience, and we've handled more infolocks and broken system boxes in the last week than most people do in their entire lifetimes."

"It makes sense for us to handle it," Vex agreed quietly.

Derivan glanced over at him. The lizardkin had stayed mostly silent throughout their trip—he had been most animated when they were dealing with the bandits, and Derivan had hoped that whatever malaise had overcome his friend had been resolved. But the moment they got back on the road, it had returned, and he spent most of his time just silently staring out of the caravan's window.

Not for the first time, he tried to approach the topic gently. "Are you all right, Vex?"

"I'm... fine," Vex said, managing a small smile at Derivan. He held that smile for a moment before it crumbled, and he let out a sigh. "Or not, I guess. I don't know. I know it's some time before we actually reach Elyra, but I'm not... looking forward to going back there. I didn't plan on doing that for another year or so."

"You said before you wanted to wait until you were ready to talk about it," Sev said. "I don't think any of us want to push you, but if you think it'll affect you..."

Vex looked down, conflicted. "It won't," he said. "I handled the bandits fine, didn't I? And I'll tell you before we reach Elyra. I promise. It's just, we've got these two other quests to handle, and I feel like if I tell you all now, it'll just be a distraction. Let's handle these other quests first."

"If you say so," Sev said. Derivan simply placed a hand on Vex's back, and the lizardkin looked back at him, an unspoken gratitude in his eyes.

"Let's go over the quest again," Misa said. "See if there's anything we're missing."

Derivan hummed. They'd all looked at the form multiple times, of course, but he thought he understood Misa's change of subject for what it was—a way to let Vex gracefully escape the conversation they'd found themselves in. Sev pulled out the sheet of paper that the request had been written on.

To say that the request was strangely worded was an understatement.

To the Adventurers' Guild:
The town of Fendal requests a Silver team to handle an . . . infestation. Further details will be given on arrival. Please come to the town hall and ask to speak to Gensen.

As a rule of thumb, the Guildmaster had explained, the Guild didn't accept vague requests like these—they'd learned that lesson a long time ago. The Guild had standards as to the kind of requests they would take, both as a politically neutral party amongst the Kingdoms and because they were positioning themselves as a constructive power rather than a destructive one. People had tried to get around it with vague requests like these, and the Guild had responded by banning these types of requests.

In certain, limited circumstances, however, vague requests could still make it through—typically requests that were too embarrassing to be publicly listed. In those cases, the one making the request would still have to disclose the details to the receptionist, but the listing itself was allowed to be vague.

Except the receptionist that was noted on the submission form didn't remember being given the listing, nor did he remember putting it up.

This had, of course, immediately garnered the Guildmaster's attention.

It was still very little information to go on. Derivan wasn't certain what they would find there—as he understood it, the receptionist that had accepted the listing had almost certainly heard out the request, agreed that a Silver team was necessary, and then put the request up before having his memories stolen away.

What kind of infestation required this level of secrecy on top of a Silver-ranked team to handle it?

"Nothing more there than the last dozen times we looked," Sev said dryly. "Unless one of you can magic something out of there."

Misa groaned. "We're just going to have to wait until we get there, aren't we," she grumbled. "I *hate* waiting. Also this stupid caravan."

"I think the caravan is kind of nice," Vex offered.

"It's *nice* but it smells fuckin' weird and it makes me nauseous." Misa sighed, kicking at the metal floor beneath her feet. The rumbling of the caravan had apparently been getting to her. "Don't get me wrong, though. The Guildmaster's an amazing woman for getting all this together for us. Just wish there was a faster way to get there."

"Can't say I don't feel the same," Sev said, glancing out the window. "The caravan reminds me of Planeshifter technology. It's just...weirdly familiar, in a way I can't really remember anymore. And that's uncomfortable, let me tell you. At least the scenery's nice."

Derivan agreed silently. They were still passing through the edges of the Sunlit Forest even now, as the sun began to set again and the colors of the forest began to change; this time, he was able to enjoy the change of scenery in relative peace, watching in quiet wonder as gold light began to bloom across the leaves. Vex climbed up to the seat to watch through the window with him, and Sev and Misa followed suit with their own windows, each of them slowly taking in the evening view.

In that quiet moment, Derivan considered that for all the adventures that he had been on with his friends, it was times like these that settled deep into the memories of his soul. These were the moments he felt he would never forget—*could* never forget.

There was only one more incident that night. Right as they passed out the border of the forest, Derivan felt a strange chill ripple through him. He frowned, sitting up and asking the others if they had felt anything similar.

They had. But though they talked about it, there was nothing further they could glean from the event; it seemed to be a simple, odd coincidence.

And so the night passed, with Derivan keeping watch through the night as usual.

The next morning saw them arriving just on the borders of Fendal. Derivan noted with some curiosity that the town was set up quite differently from Misa's home village of J'rokksur. He supposed part of that was because Fendal was directly supported by Elyra, and so had the funding to build all the infrastructure they wanted; the town was packed with buildings of wood and stone, polished and painted to perfection. The roads were surprisingly smooth, too, made of a flat, hard stone that allowed their caravan to move without constantly bumping them up and down.

"Oh thank the fucking gods," Misa muttered as soon as the road smoothed out. "That was giving me a headache."

"Need me to work some magic?" Sev offered. Misa pointed at him and gathered just enough energy to scowl.

"We know how your healing works now. It's not actually healing if you're just taking it from us, you fuck." Misa paused. "I appreciate it, though."

Vex laughed a little at their antics, swinging his legs and peering out the window at the town of Fendal with some combination of fascination and discomfort.

Derivan, for his part, was busy carefully observing the townsfolk. They were a diverse crowd, to be sure—there were several species of being he'd simply never encountered before—but what was stranger to him was that Physical Empathy couldn't read most of them. He would get the occasional glimmer from one or two of the more nervous-looking individuals, but those ones just hurried along and tried to interact with others as little as possible.

Concerning, Derivan thought. None of the townsfolk seemed aggressive, but there was a lack of life here that disturbed him to his core. He'd gotten used to the bustle and laughter of J'rokksur whenever he visited, or even the raucous arguments and cheering that could occasionally be heard echoing through the halls of the Guild. What he had *not* gotten used to was . . . silence.

The residents here spoke in quiet murmurs, the volume just low enough that the sound didn't carry. They exchanged goods without saying a word to one another—not to barter, not to bargain, not even in simple greeting. Derivan wasn't even certain if the few merchants he could see were counting the gold they were receiving, and *that* seemed off compared to every other merchant he had met.

"This place feels off," Misa said with a slight frown. "Can't pin it down, but it's real uncomfortable. I'm not the only one gettin' that, right?"

"You're not." Vex hesitated, his tail waving nervously behind him. "It's really quiet. No one's talking?"

"Maybe they're all just introverts," Sev suggested. Everyone else stared at him, and he raised his hands in surrender. "Right, right. Bad time for a joke."

"Are you not fairly introverted yourself?" Derivan asked, mildly curious.

Sev folded his arms. "No calling me out," he said. "Seriously, though, I'm getting this too. There's a clear spot just a few feet up ahead. Let's just stop there, secure the caravan, and get to the town hall on foot. I'm not sure I want to be trapped in a tiny space surrounded by people who might be compromised."

"You think so too, huh?" Misa glanced back outside the caravan, and her hand fell to the hilt of her mace. "... I hope we don't have to fight."

She meant it, too. Derivan saw the tension in her shoulders—as much as she enjoyed a good fight, she didn't relish the thought of fighting townsfolk.

Neither did he, really.

It didn't take long for them to get the caravan situated. Sev snapped open a Guild-provided scroll and flicked a drop of system-provided mana into it; the runic system embedded in the scroll flared to life, establishing a series of barriers that would keep their gear and cargo protected.

"Incoming," Derivan said, and Sev tensed, looking up quickly—only to relax almost immediately.

"Don't use that word when we're being *approached*," Sev complained. "I thought we were being attacked!"

"My apologies," Derivan said politely. He rather thought that the lack of urgency in his voice would have communicated that, but humans were strange at the best of times. Or maybe it was just Sev?

The two guards he'd spotted—both human and both sporting spears as their weapon of choice, one significantly taller than the other—finally finished their approach. The taller of the two spoke in a gruff voice. "State your business," he said.

Derivan thought it odd that the guards only chose to talk to them once they left the caravan. If they wanted to know what visitors were doing in their village, surely they would have been approached immediately?

"Hi, we're new here," Sev said. "We're on an urgent request from the Guild posted by someone named Gensen. We were told we might be able to find them at the town hall."

"I see," the guard said after a moment. "You here for the quest?"

"Yes . . . ?" Sev blinked.

"Good," the guard said with a nod, then pointed. "Town hall's over there."

Without waiting for a response, he marched off with his companion. Derivan stared after him, slightly bewildered by his behavior.

"Okay," Misa said. "I'm calling it now. There's some sort of mind control involved."

"I don't know if it's anything so direct," Vex said with a small frown. He was squinting at the air, as if only just noticing something strange; Derivan followed his gaze, amplifying his own [**Mana Sight**] to see what the lizardkin was seeing. "The mana here is behaving weirdly, too."

"It looks like it normally does," Derivan said cautiously. He watched the semi-playful ambient mana dancing around, as active as ever. "Are you seeing something different?"

"No," Vex said. "It's the fact that there's ambient mana here at all. It usually avoids towns. It prefers gathering in natural places."

Sev frowned. "Keep an eye on it," he said. "But let's get to the town hall and see what Gensen wants, first."

Derivan nodded in agreement. Fortunately, the town hall was rather conveniently close to where they had parked—the only problem was that it was a relatively nondescript building that blended in with all the rest, and if the guard hadn't explicitly pointed it out, they might have walked past it without noticing. As it was, they only realized they were at the right building because of the tiny letters emblazoned on the *handle* of the door to the town hall, of all things.

Even the inside of the town hall was remarkably plain. It was sparse and barely decorated, save for a red carpet lined with gold, a couple of pillars holding up the upper floor of the hall, and then a desk at the far end of the room.

Just in front of that desk stood a tired-looking elderly gentleman with his arms folded behind his back. He watched as the four adventurers filed in, not saying a word.

"Er . . . we're looking for Gensen?" Sev tried once they were within speaking range.

"Then you're just in time," the old man said with a small, weary-looking smile. "I am him. Why don't you have a seat, and we can have a chat?"

CHAPTER 6

PLANS AND LEARNING

Vex couldn't help but feel anxious.

Something about Fendal felt off to him. Where the presence of mana was usually a comfort, this time, something about it felt... dangerous. Like it was a warning. He wriggled in his seat, slightly annoyed by the fact that the chair was tall enough that his feet didn't even touch the ground.

Derivan wasn't having any problems with his seat. The armor sat ramrod-straight in his chair, paying polite attention to the old man that was apparently in charge of this place. Gensen, apparently. Vex watched Derivan for a moment, distracted, and then jumped when Sev spoke.

"You said in your request that there was an infestation," Sev said. "What kind of infestation?"

"Let's not speak of such things to begin with," the old man said, though not unkindly. The exhaustion seemed to vanish off him as he spoke. "You must be tired from your journey, surely. Perhaps I can get you a spot in one of our inns?"

Sev blinked. "That would be... nice? But I'd really rather you tell us what's going on first."

"If you insist," Gensen said.

Vex wasn't paying attention to what the old man said. He watched the mana instead—it was drifting through, even in this building, and wasn't *that* strange? It didn't move the way it usually did, though; there was nothing free-spirited about it.

It moved with *intent*.

The lizardkin wondered if there was someone controlling it with [**Mana Manipulation**] or a variant thereof. He'd never seen mana moving with such purpose before. It almost made him want to try to reach out with his own

[**Expert Mana Manipulation**], to see if he could touch on it—or maybe do what Derivan had done before, and just *ask* the mana—

"Vex?" Sev said, and Vex blinked.

"What?" he said, and when he saw everyone was looking at him, he coughed awkwardly. "Um, sorry. I wasn't paying attention."

"Apparently there's a goblin camp nearby," Sev said. "They raid Fendal every so often and take the mana crystal stores sent by Elyra, among other things. Gensen wants us to help . . . clear the camp." He said the words with a noticeable amount of distaste, though it was masked for Gensen's benefit. Vex was just used to reading his friend by now. "You're the resident tracking expert, so I wanted an estimate of how long you think that might take."

Vex absolutely wasn't the tracking expert, but he *was* the "rogue"; if Sev wasn't being upfront about it, then he didn't entirely trust the old man. A quick peek at the others told him they all shared the same sentiment—there was a certain tension in the air.

He frowned, contemplating the question. Gensen's story didn't add up. It didn't explain half the things they'd noticed were wrong with Fendal, and the others felt the same way, he was sure, given the looks on their faces. Misa had her brows drawn together skeptically, and Sev was controlling his expression so tightly Vex was worried he was going to pop a vessel. Derivan's helmet allowed him to keep the best straight face out of the four of them, but Vex could sense his armored friend's concern radiating out of him anyway.

"Um," Vex said, mostly to stall for time. He wasn't exactly sure what Sev wanted from him, so he slid his gaze toward him, waiting for a sign. After a moment, he saw Sev shaking his head just slightly—*delay*, he interpreted the gesture as—and then folding his left arm over his right, two fingers twitching at the end of the gesture. *Two days.* "We'll need some time to investigate, of course. Find out where their camp is, what kind of numbers we're looking at. I'd say we'll have a plan of attack in two days or so."

"Of course," Gensen said with a nod and a kind smile. "Shall we settle your lodgings, then?"

"Please," Sev said with a nod, and the old man hobbled off.

It was strange, Vex noted as they waited, how *empty* the entire town hall was. Surely a town hall would have more people working in the building. They could all have been out of sight, but the mana signatures here told a different story: Gensen was the only living person within these walls.

Which was a weird and slightly morbid thought. Vex grimaced a little, cursing himself for adding the word *living* to that thought. It made him think of corpses.

A moment later—though sadly not nearly enough time for the four of them to discuss what they thought was happening—Gensen emerged from the side room.

"All right. There's a room waiting for you at the Sleeping Bird inn. It's south of here, two blocks down and to your right," Gensen said kindly, presenting them with a set of keys. "The room is the fifth door to the right on the second floor. It's quite a spacious room, and you'll have food available both in your room and in the lobby below. I hope you enjoy your accommodations."

... Why were there keys to a random inn just hanging out in the local town hall?

Vex opened his mouth to ask, and stopped short just before actually speaking when Sev gave him a warning glance. He pretended to yawn instead, using the motion to trickle some power into [**Advanced Mana Sight**] as he did so. A fun fact about mana sight: its use didn't actually require you to keep your eyes *open*.

Which was both a blessing and a curse, if the mana around was particularly bright. Vex used a small stretch to eye the room Gensen had just emerged from, keeping his eyes closed so that the glow of his intensified mana sight wouldn't be visible—but besides the presence of ambient mana, it all seemed normal. No traces of magic, and no traces of strange behavior from the mana, even.

Vex followed Sev and the others somewhat mindlessly as they were escorted back out of the town hall and toward the inn, his gaze flicking over the details of the town and trying to pinpoint exactly what it was that felt so off about the mana here. Nothing struck him as particularly out of place. The townsfolk were going about their days, picking up the bread and produce they needed from the open market just a few yards outside the Sleeping Bird. There were a few more expensive-looking shops that had their own fancily decorated interiors and entire lines of customers, and Vex counted at least one alchemy shop and one exotic-looking bakery among them.

It was all very ... normal.

Well, except for the part where no one waiting in line was fighting or fidgeting. *That* was strange. Vex had never seen lines this polite, not even in the so-called commoner districts in Elyra.

(The noble districts were far worse about queues. Vex had never seen a noble stand in line patiently. He even remembered his older brother throwing a fully powered [**Fireball**] at another noble family once, although in Helix's defense, they'd had their bodyguards threaten him first.)

The mana did seem to gather more in some places than others—there was a florist selling a variety of beautiful, purple-blue flowers that the mana seemed to love. It twirled around that shopkeeper and his flowers, seemingly excited every time someone purchased something or even just looked at the flowers. The sight comforted him. It was the most "normal" behavior he'd seen from the ambient mana in Fendal.

"Do those flowers interest you?" Derivan asked him curiously.

"Huh? Oh! Uh, they're very pretty, but I was more looking at the way the mana's moving around them." Vex felt embarrassed, for some reason. The flowers *did* look nice. "It's acting differently around different people, see? It's kinda hard to see, but it looks slower and more... sickly... near the guards, and it's a lot livelier around the children. Kind of hard to establish a pattern, though—"

Vex caught himself as he began to ramble—but Derivan didn't lose interest, like most others did when he began to talk like this. The armor's expression was one of genuine interest—

At least until it changed to one of concern. Derivan reached for him, grabbed him by the shoulders, and physically placed him about a foot to the side in one smooth motion that left Vex blinking in confusion. It took him a moment to realize he'd been moved right before he would have walked into a wooden lantern pole. "Oops."

"Perhaps you can share your thoughts once we are inside?" Derivan suggested with a chuckle. "We have arrived."

The inn that Gensen had mentioned—the Sleeping Bird—was a large, three-floor building, if rather plain on the outside, with pale-blue walls and round windows decorated with smaller versions of those purple-blue flowers. Its only unique feature otherwise was a sign that featured a rather crudely drawn bird sleeping in its nest, which Vex thought was charming.

Sev pushed the door open, and Vex followed just after him, expecting to find a lively inn full of people.

The building was empty.

Sev blinked. "Uh... maybe that's why Gensen gave us the key instead of telling us to get it from the owner?"

"So he can get us to stay in an empty inn?" Misa raised an eyebrow. "Smells more like a trap to me."

Sev frowned, considering the possibility. "You don't see anything strange in the mana, do you?" he asked Vex.

"I've been keeping an eye out," Vex said, shaking his head. "The ambient mana in this whole town acts a little weird, but this place isn't trapped or anything. Not that I can tell, anyway."

"This building's too big to not be staffed." Sev tapped his fingers on his staff, glancing at the floor and at the tables. "Nothing's dusty, so it's been recently cleaned. You can't sense anyone else in the building?"

"Nope," Vex said, suddenly feeling a lot more nervous. He'd thought the empty inn was *weird*, not that it might be dangerous, but with the way Sev and Misa were acting he was starting to second-guess himself. "You think there's people hiding here?"

"I mean, probably not, if you can't sense them. [**Triage**] doesn't spot anything either, and it should ping on anything living." Sev took a few cautious, light steps farther into the inn, like he was worried the floorboards would snap beneath his feet.

Misa stared at him, then shook her head. "If it ain't a trap, then let's just get to our room," she said, sighing. "The empty inn lobby is kinda fuckin' creepy."

"We *could* just stay in the caravan," Vex suggested, glancing around the lobby nervously. Was that shadow moving? It was probably just his imagination.

"We'd have to explain that to Gensen if he comes around to check in on us," Sev said, making a bit of a face. He began the climb up the stairs to the second floor, and Vex trailed behind him, trying not to jump at every shadow. "And I think we have better odds of figuring out what's going on if we're staying here. It's pretty obvious the problem isn't a goblin camp, but I don't know why he'd hide the real problem from us."

"Maybe his head got fucked by whatever's messing with the rest of the town," Misa grunted. The wooden stairs creaked dangerously under her.

"It is a possibility," Derivan said. Unlike Misa, he strode up the stairs with no concern for whether he would damage them. Vex was half-certain he'd leave footprints behind in the wood. "I am not sure that he believed what he was saying, and what is particularly strange is that he did not seem frustrated by the raids he mentioned, only mildly concerned."

"Yeah, he didn't really *act* like there was any kind of emergency," Sev said with a frown. He approached and opened the door to their room—the fifth door to the right was at the end of the hallway and led to a room that must have occupied half of the entire floor. It was also almost certainly spatially expanded in some way. The accommodations were better than even what was provided by the Adventurers' Guild, considering it came with a small kitchen and smaller, sectioned-off rooms.

"I changed my mind. I don't want to stay in the caravan," Vex announced. Misa snickered at him.

"This place is pretty nice," Sev admitted. "Must cost a pretty penny."

"Eh, as long as we don't have to pay, I don't care." Misa threw herself back onto one of the couches, ignoring the way the entire thing rocked back with the force of her weight. She groaned with pleasure. "Fuck, I'm grateful to the Guildmaster and all, but it's really nice to have an actual *seat*."

"No kidding," Sev agreed. He sat much more politely in one of the unoccupied armchairs. Vex sat himself in the last couch and wiggled into his seat as Derivan took a seat beside him, though Vex huffed a little at the way he had to curl his tail around into his lap. Most seats just weren't really built to accommodate lizardkin.

It was a small gripe, though. Misa took barely a second to switch gears again, changing the subject and leaning forward, her expression serious. "But let's talk about this. What's up with Gensen? Think he's setting up some kind of trap?"

"I don't think so," Vex said, taking a moment to realign his thoughts. "It's definitely a possibility, but I think it's too early to jump to that conclusion. We *should* keep in mind that he might be compromised while we investigate."

"I'm inclined to agree," Sev said. "I'm not sure I believe the story about the goblins at all, though. The people here don't act like they've been raided recently."

"If he is not compromised, he could be lying," Derivan suggested.

"Why would he lie, though?" Misa frowned. "*Someone* put in a request with the Guild and told us to get in contact with him. There has to be a reason for that."

"He's either pointing us in the right direction, or else he's a lead himself," Sev concluded. "Either way, I think it's prudent for us to investigate things besides the goblin raids."

"I can look into the raids," Misa said. "Some of the guards are pretty good at tracking. I can summon 'em, ask 'em to help. That kind of thing."

"Then I'll talk to the people and see if I can get them to talk about the raids that have supposedly been happening," Sev said.

"I want to look into what's going on with the mana here," Vex said. "I've never seen ambient mana so active inside a town. Too many skills and spells being cast pretty much all the time—mana doesn't typically like that. Derivan, I'm thinking maybe if you try that new method of casting you've got here, we might see different results."

"New method of casting?" Misa asked curiously, and Vex nodded vigorously.

"I still haven't figured out how to do it yet! But he found a way to cast spells without relying on the system *or* on runic constructs," Vex said, his tail moving to wag almost without him being consciously aware of it. "I've been trying to learn how, but it's slow going on my part. You wanna show 'em, Deri?"

"I will try," Derivan said, a faint hint of fond amusement in his tone. He reached out again, and Vex watched him with bright eyes, following the movement of the mana. The abundance of ambient mana made it easy to cast here, at least—the new brand of spellcasting Derivan had acquired would not, he suspected, work as well in normal cities. The ambient mana in them was too dead and lifeless to cast much of anything; it could serve only as fuel for the system.

Motes of mana gathered curiously around Derivan's hand as he prodded it gently with [**Mana Manipulation**], guiding it into the right shape, the right flow. The process was still far slower than system-assisted spellcasting, but there was a certain ethereal beauty to it: the way the lines of color danced as they moved, slowly assembling themselves into just the right shape, then melting into the form of the barrier spell he had uncovered . . .

For a moment, the barrier hovered there, shining pristine. Vex almost reached out to touch it. He took a step forward—

—and the barrier abruptly flexed and shattered.

There was a small silence.

"This has never happened before," Derivan said, his voice concerned, and Vex couldn't help but echo that concern.

Because he was watching the mana move in the aftermath, and it was agitated.

Worried.

Angry.

CHAPTER 7

KITCHEN LIZARD

"It was *angry*," Vex insisted. It was hard to explain exactly what he'd seen—hard to explain why it was so strange to see the mana behaving this way, when his companions had never seen mana move with intention at all. "I don't know if it was angry at me, or at Derivan, or at something we can't see, but the mana here is definitely angry."

"Okay." To his credit, Sev didn't question what Vex believed he'd seen; he cut straight to the point instead. "Do you know what that means for us, exactly?"

Vex shook his head. "I—I'm not sure," he said. "I've never seen mana behaving like this." His tail swished about anxiously behind him. Without prompting, he felt Derivan's hand slip down and wrap around his own, squeezing lightly as if to comfort him—and he froze, feeling his heart beating a little faster.

Bad timing, Vex, he tried to tell himself, but it wasn't like he could stop his heart voluntarily. He didn't dare speak, afraid it would spoil the moment; his nervousness and anxiety were all but forgotten.

Until Derivan spoke, anyway. "Perhaps Vex and I can investigate this problem," he said. Oh, right; that was what they were talking about. Derivan didn't seem to notice the small existential crisis Vex was in the middle of having. "I believe I may be able to coax more information from the mana. And even if I cannot, there is a pattern in the behavior of the mana we may be able to trace . . . There are people and places that it seems to prefer. If nothing else, that is something we can investigate—perhaps it is trying to tell us something."

There was a small silence. Misa looked at the remnants of the barrier that Derivan had cast; fragments of mana still remained, quite unlike the normal usage of a spell provided by the system. She shook her head after a moment.

"I don't really know much about this mana stuff," Misa admitted. "I gotta take your word for it. But I'm pretty sure this isn't about fucking goblin raids, so that's our biggest lead right now."

"Well, we probably aren't going to be chasing after goblins tonight," Sev said, glancing out the window. Vex followed his gaze. Outside the inn, the sun was beginning to set, and the town of Fendal was cast in the dim, orange hues of the sunset; many of the townsfolk were heading back to their homes, and the stalls they'd seen earlier were beginning to close. Even the mana seemed less active, drifting about the streets in a lethargic, sagging manner.

"Let's just have dinner and turn in for the night," Sev said with a sigh. He wore a slight frown, and his gaze kept darting back toward the window; Vex wondered what was on his mind. "I don't want to stay in Fendal longer than necessary, but it looks like whatever's going on here isn't going to be *simple*. We'll take whatever time we need to figure this out properly. I'll keep the Guildmaster updated."

"Something up?" Misa asked, raising a brow slightly. "I mean, I know we're in a hurry, but you're a little anxious."

Sev hesitated for a moment, like he wasn't sure if he wanted to talk about it, and then he sagged. "It's mostly Aurum," he said, sighing. "He doesn't say much these days, but he's always very worried. His angels are scouting the celestial planes to try to find out if a new god is being targeted, but we don't have any news so far. I think the lack of news is getting to him."

"Can't say I blame him," Misa muttered, then shook her head. "Right! Like you said, time for dinner. Whose turn is it to cook?"

"Vex's, I think," Sev said.

"Yup, it's my turn," Vex agreed. He didn't move from his seat. Derivan was still holding his hand, after all. Misa stared at him for a moment, then her eyes landed on where Derivan's hand was placed over Vex's, and she snickered.

"You two are going to need to sort that out eventually," she said.

"What do you mean?" Derivan asked curiously. Misa just shook her head.

"They're hopeless," she said conversationally to Sev. The cleric grinned. "I can do it if you'd rather stare at Derivan for a bit longer."

"I'm— That wasn't what I was doing!" Vex protested. It was totally what he was doing, but he wasn't going to admit *that*.

"I do not mind," Derivan said, with what Vex thought might have been a touch of protectiveness.

"Don't *encourage* her," Vex groaned. He got up and out of the couch, stumbling a little when he realized his tail had wedged itself between the cushions. Derivan reached out to steady him, and he made sure he *didn't* pull away abruptly, even though that was his first instinct; instead, he gave Derivan a grateful, embarrassed smile, and made his way to the kitchen while trying desperately to pretend that the other three weren't staring at him.

Dinner was an enjoyable affair, at least.

The kitchen in their room was surprisingly well stocked—Vex had expected to have to pick up some ingredients from their caravan, but that wasn't the case at all. Small preservation runes lined the cupboards, and exotic meats that Vex didn't even recognize were stocked in about half of them.

"There's no way this is a room they give to ordinary adventurers," he muttered, staring at the breadth of ingredients.

"No kidding," Sev said, making Vex jump; the cleric was watching over the kitchen counter, having apparently decided his time was better spent watching Vex cook. The lizardkin stuck his tongue out at his friend, getting only an amused grin in response, and began pulling out ingredients . . . mostly at random, really.

A lot of his favorite spices were available. There were leaves from an herb he didn't really remember the name of, but he knew was grown exclusively in specially cultivated gardens in Elyra; peppers that were spicy, in the sense that they actually converted part of your personal mana into fire-aspected mana; fresh five-point—*star* fruits. Berries, rabbit meat . . .

Vex paused.

"Isn't Elyra dealing with a food shortage?" he said quietly, looking from the contents of the pantry and then back to Sev. "Why do they have so much food just . . . available here?"

". . . Huh. Why indeed." Sev frowned. "Maybe they just left it here and forgot about it?"

"Maybe." Vex wasn't convinced. Something about that answer didn't sit right with him, and Sev didn't look like he believed his own words either. "But this is a lot of food."

"I'll ask around about the food situation when I'm out tomorrow," Sev suggested. "We're only going to be here for a day or two, hopefully, so if people need food . . . I mean, this is all technically ours, right? They don't know how much we eat. We can just give it away."

Vex blinked, then grinned slightly. "You're not *wrong*."

And with that, Vex got to cooking.

It wasn't all that long ago that he didn't know how to cook at all. His life as a noble had been pampered, in that sense—he'd never had to prepare his own meals, not when their family had a personal chef that would prepare all their food for them. He'd been a little curious about it once, but all it had taken was one instance of being chased out of the kitchen for him to lose any interest he had; why learn to cook when there was *magic* to learn?

Of course, then he left his home, and he'd had to survive on his own. It hadn't taken him long to regret not knowing how to cook. All he had to eat most of the time was stale bread or oversalted stew, the latter of which happened every time he gathered the courage to make something that wasn't just bread. Stew was simple enough, he told himself!

It turned out it was not.

He'd only actually learned how to cook when he'd joined Sev and the others. The rotating cooking schedule meant that he had to be the one to cook for the party every so often, and none of them were willing to let him get away with serving up badly cooked stew every single time it was his turn. None of them let him go about it alone, either; Sev and Misa had made it a point to teach him, and he'd gotten reasonably good at it.

Derivan... well, Derivan had no idea how to cook and was exempted from the schedule. He'd made an attempt once or twice, and still expressed a desire to try, but the results were still a disaster so far. Maybe when they had a day to fully dedicate to teaching him.

In that time, Vex had learned to enjoy himself cooking. There was something calming about it—the process was easier once he knew what to do, and [**Dagger Proficiency**] actually helped him when it came to cutting meats and vegetables. Who would've thought!

Well, Misa had. But that wasn't the point.

He glanced up and over at Misa and Derivan just to see what they were doing while he was grilling rabbit meat. They'd found some sort of board game in one of the cupboards, and Misa was spiritedly arguing with him about the rules of that game. Sev was watching them too, faint amusement painted on his face.

"It's nice to actually have a room to ourselves again," Vex commented as he plated up three plates—almost four, before he remembered Derivan didn't eat.

"You have no idea how hard it's been not to bitch about sleeping in the caravan." Misa laughed. "Getting a room to ourselves is great, even if there's some weird shit going on."

"Or even if it's haunted," Sev added.

"... is this room haunted?" Vex asked, suddenly worried.

"I'm *pretty sure* it isn't. But you never know!"

"*Sev*," Vex said with a sigh, but he wore a faint smile. "All right, come on, the food's ready."

Vex carefully balanced all three plates as he carried them out to the couches, using his tail to secure the one balanced on his forearm—a perk of being a lizardkin. Derivan couldn't eat, of course, but he participated in conversation right alongside the rest of them. Vex resolved to figure out that one skill that allowed Derivan to share in another person's taste. He wanted the armor to be able to try his food, dammit.

It was a good night for the four of them.

—⁂—

The next morning started with chaos.

Vex woke up in the early hours of the morning, as he usually did. He started going through the previous day's notes, also as he usually did. It didn't strike him that something was *different* until a particularly loud *thump* shook the walls of the Sleeping Bird and made him jump.

There were *sounds* now. Sounds of people talking and laughing amongst themselves, the clacking of mugs and the hiss of food being cooked; Vex could even smell a faint but delicious starchy aroma drifting up through the doors of their room. It sounded like what a full tavern sounded like.

But Vex was relatively certain that he hadn't heard anything when he'd first woken up. He hadn't heard any doors opening, either. The building had been empty when they'd first arrived, and the fact that it had been filled with people without any of them noticing was alarming.

Vex went to Derivan. The armor never slept, after all.

"I had not noticed it before you mentioned it," Derivan said, a hint of concern seeping into his voice. "But I believe you are right. I heard no sounds of people entering. Perhaps we should investigate."

It was early enough in the morning that Sev and Misa were still fast asleep; Vex sent a quick message to them through the system, to keep them apprised of what they were doing, and he and Derivan went down the stairs together. They both stopped at the foot of the stairs, briefly stunned.

The inn was *full*. The lobby functioned as a tavern, and it was full of people of all kinds, from other lizardkin to orcs and even an elemental or two; every one of them was laughing and talking with one another like it wasn't *four in the morning*, and Vex couldn't help but wonder briefly if he was dreaming.

At least, until he saw the mana. He froze. The mana was thicker and denser here than he'd ever seen in Fendal—and it was dancing and twirling, like it was partying right alongside all the people in the inn.

"Are you seeing this too?" Vex asked, just to make sure. Derivan nodded, and Vex stared.

Strange.

CHAPTER 8

BREAKFAST

Vex didn't have all that much time to contemplate the behavior of the mana before he was accosted by what he assumed to be the owner of the tavern; a large, portly woman smiled brightly at him as she noticed him coming down the stairs, and immediately walked over to greet them, a smile on her face.

"You must be the new guests!" she said cheerfully. "I'm Anyati, owner of the Sleeping Bird. I heard about you from Gensen. I didn't think you'd be up so early, though! I hope we didn't wake you up? I might have to replace the sound enchantments, if that's the case . . ."

"Uh," Vex said, a little taken aback and wishing very desperately that Derivan would take the lead. "I'm Vex. We didn't get woken up; don't worry. I just wake up early." *And Derivan doesn't need to sleep*, he thought but didn't say.

"You must be starving, then!" Anyati said, and she took Vex by the arm immediately, leading him over to a conveniently empty table that the lizard-kin could almost swear wasn't there before—though he was frazzled enough that he couldn't really tell. "Sit, sit, I'll get you two some warm porridge."

"We don't need . . ." Vex started, but the woman was like a whirlwind; she'd no sooner sat them at the table than disappeared into the kitchen, leaving Vex staring awkwardly after her. He blinked once, then turned to Derivan, who was sitting politely in his seat with his arms folded across his lap and looking vaguely amused. "Was this table always here?"

"I believe so," Derivan said, his voice warm with laughter. "Though this Anyati could tell me that it was not, and I imagine I would believe her. She does not leave much space for doubt."

"You got that right!" someone over at the next table yelled. The two companions she sat with flinched away from her and gave her a half-hearted glare.

Vex exchanged glances with Derivan, a little surprised that they'd been heard over the noise in the tavern at all. "That's our Anyati!"

Vex was honestly starting to feel a little overwhelmed.

Derivan seemed to recognize this, however, and took over for him. "If I may ask," the armor said curiously, "where did you all come from? The inn was empty when we came earlier."

"What kind of a question is that?" the woman responded, grinning at him. "You're the ones from out of town! Where are you from?"

Derivan seemed thrown off by the question. He blinked once, eye-lights flickering within his armor as he considered the question. "We are from the Guild," he settled on saying after an awkward pause. "Though we have spent most of our time housed at the outer Elyran branch town, between Elyra and Anderstahl."

"Y'all need to name your towns," the woman snorted, but she grinned at him, reaching out to shake his hand, then Vex's. "Good to meet you, though. I'm Hanna. My friends here are Visyen and Noram."

She gestured to the two people seated at her table—one of them an orcish woman who greeted them with a half-wave-half-salute, and the other a young lizardkin that was not unlike Vex, though he had blue scales instead of green. He was taller, too, though he also seemed to be trying to sink into the wall.

"Noram's shy," Hanna added with a conspiratorial whisper, winking at them both. Her lizardkin companion managed to muster up a half-hearted glare.

"I am not," he said. "I just . . . don't handle taverns well. You know that."

Indeed, Noram was clearly more anxious than either of his two companions; Vex felt a pang of sympathy. His tail was stiff and coiled around the leg of his chair, and he'd pushed himself back as far as possible so that his back was against the wall.

"I am Derivan, and my companion is named Vex," Derivan said, inclining his head politely.

Vex's attention, on the other hand, was on Noram. "Are you all right?" he asked. He was all too familiar with the panic that being in a crowd could cause. Noram's gaze darted to him before he relaxed by a fraction. He sighed and nodded.

"I'm fine. It's just . . . taverns are loud," Noram said, shaking his head slightly and looking into the air. He let out a frustrated sigh. "And you won't understand this, but the mana here is behaving strangely."

"He's been going on about that for weeks," Hanna said with a laugh and a shake of her head. "Poor guy. He's the only mage around that thinks the mana's acting weird. We think he caught something on our last outing. We're adventurers too, you know, or we're going to be. Just need to sign up."

Visyen finished her drink and placed it delicately down on the table before offering them both a smile. She was some sort of mage class, too, judging by the flow of mana around her robes. "There's no mana here," she said. "We don't know what's up with Noram. It's possible he inhaled some blueweed gas on our last dungeon expedition."

"I did *not*," Noram insisted, looking upset.

"Um," Vex said. He looked around at the rest of the people in the tavern—they were talking amongst themselves and not really paying attention to the group in the corner, though they did get curious looks every now and then. He paused awkwardly, trying to figure out how to explain that he, too, could see how the mana was behaving.

"I do not think he is hallucinating," Derivan offered, seeing that Vex was getting a bit stuck on his words. Vex shot his friend a grateful look. "There *is* mana here, and it is behaving strangely. Both Vex and I can see it."

"What?" Visyen frowned, then double-checked; her eyes glowed blue for a moment as she channeled more power into her own version of [**Mana Sight**], and then she shook her head. "I don't see anything. Same skill variant, right? [**Mana Sight**]?"

"[**Advanced Mana Sight**]," Vex said.

"Intermediate," Derivan added, foregoing the full name. He'd unlocked it while practicing with Vex during one of their many midnight studies as they traveled. Visyen frowned and glanced at Hanna, who shrugged; she didn't seem to care. Noram, meanwhile, looked absolutely vindicated.

"I *told* you I didn't just forget my blueweed cloth!" he said.

"I'm sure you didn't," Visyen said placatingly, though it was dismissive enough that it made Vex frown. "But that doesn't explain the discrepancy here. I don't see a drop of mana in the air. And I've got the intermediate variant as well, so it can't be the skill. Are you sure *you* two didn't inhale some blueweed?"

"I do not—" Derivan began, and Vex—realizing what his friend was about to say—quickly interrupted.

"Neither of us have been near any kind of blueweed," he said. "And some of our skills that rely on ambient mana are acting up, so it's definitely real."

"Huh," Visyen said, her brows furrowing slightly. Then she shrugged, calling for another mug of beer. "Well, it's fine, I'm sure. I can't imagine it matters. Maybe our skills are malfunctioning."

"It's probably not that much of a problem, right?" Hanna said, her tone almost apologetic. Noram, meanwhile, was looking increasingly upset.

"Something's *wrong*, I'm telling you," he insisted, and then he looked pleadingly at Vex and Derivan both. "They don't usually just dismiss me like this. You gotta reason with them. We need to look into it or *something*."

"Noram," Hanna said, a note of warning in her tone.

"He's right," Vex said suddenly and louder than he intended, surprising both himself and the others at the table, judging by the startled looks they all cast him. Derivan's surprise quickly turned into a soft, encouraging smile, the kind he gave through the gentle glow of his eyes and a slight squeeze of his hand on Vex's shoulder. Feeling emboldened, Vex continued. "I don't think we should be ignoring mana fluctuations like this. This is the kind of thing you only see when..."

Vex paused mid-sentence, suddenly struck, and Derivan glanced at him in askance. Vex narrowed his eyes, thinking.

"This is the kind of thing you only see during things like dungeon formations," he said, finishing the thought.

Derivan paused and stared at him. Noram's eyes went wide. Hanna and Visyen both didn't react, save to look slightly confused.

It didn't make sense. There couldn't be a dungeon formation event happening here—the system sent notifications when a dungeon was forming, and they formed only from Mana Nuclei to begin with. A formation event happening here would necessitate that Fendal was sitting on top of an undiscovered Mana Nucleus, and that was an absurd thought.

Maybe something similar, then? A similar process, though Vex couldn't think of anything else that led to this sort of behavior in the mana from all the literature he had read; there were some esoteric monsters that could cause similar fluctuations in ambient mana, but none on this scale. As far as he could tell, the strange behavior was present all throughout the town.

"We can't be in the middle of a dungeon formation," Noram argued, frowning. "We're not on a Nucleus. That's not how dungeon formations work."

"I know *that*," Vex said. "But it doesn't have to be a dungeon formation. Just something similar."

"You guys are being ridiculous." Visyen snorted, rolling her eyes. Hanna looked a little more apologetic.

"I think maybe my team should get some sleep," she said. "We had a pretty long night, you know."

"No, I want to talk about this. I *need* to talk about this," Noram said, and then he focused intense eyes on Vex. "You two can go sleep if you want. I need to figure this out."

Hanna frowned at him, then sighed. "Can't force you to do anything, I guess," she said. "You coming, Vis?"

"I am," Visyen said, finishing her second drink and placing it back down onto the table. Vex blinked, realizing that there were at least five other empty mugs on the table that were probably hers. She grunted, looking over at Vex and Derivan. "I think you will be wasting your time," she said bluntly, then hesitated. "But it was a pleasure to meet you. Let us know if you find out something important."

Noram's brows had furrowed a bit as Visyen spoke, but he relaxed once she continued; Vex could sympathize. He'd been expecting a fight of some sort. He'd seen that many times with . . . his siblings. With his brother's tendency to get into a fight with his father, especially.

Vex shook his head to clear his mind of those thoughts. He didn't want to think about it.

CHAPTER 9

DUNGEONS AND DRAWINGS

Vex was, fortunately, pulled from his thoughts when Noram spoke.

"They're usually a lot more reasonable," Noram said apologetically, glancing up at his teammates as they retreated up the stairs. He walked over to sit at their table, though he kept his distance from the two of them.

"They seem nice," Vex said, and he meant it. Hanna had been nothing but pleasant, and Visyen hadn't needed to add that last part; she'd done it only because she realized she was coming off as rude. Beside him, Derivan nodded, and Noram let out a relieved chuckle.

"They can be a little overbearing," Noram said. "But they're kinda like my older sisters. I love them. It's just, I've tried to talk to other people about this, and no one else wants to, so . . . I don't have anyone to talk to about it."

Vex exchanged glances with Derivan. "Sounds like an infolock."

"I am less certain," Derivan said, then hesitated. "But . . . perhaps. The signs are similar."

"What's an infolock?" Noram asked, confused. Vex took the opportunity to explain, and when he was done, Noram's face was considerably paler.

"That's an existential crisis waiting to happen," he muttered, then frowned. "But why would I be an exception?"

"I don't know," Vex said.

"The rules are still unclear to us," Derivan added. "But it seems that you are excluded from the lock if you are involved in some way in its creation."

"I— But I didn't do anything!" Noram said. His eyes flicked left and right nervously, though. Vex frowned—a lie, then?

"You may not have realized it," Derivan said, his voice gentle. Vex relaxed. Physical Empathy was much better than he was at interpreting other people. "Your friends mentioned your last dungeon expedition? When was that?"

"It was weeks ago," Noram said, but he looked stricken. "And this started happening after we came back... I didn't think anything I did was related, I swear."

"Did something happen in the dungeon?" Vex asked, worried. The timing—a few weeks ago—that was around the time they'd "broken" the dungeon they were exploring. There were messages sent out too, about how fragments of that dungeon had been scattered into existing ones.

"No," Noram said quickly, and then sagged a little bit. "Yes. Maybe? I don't know. It was weird. I got separated from the others at one point, so if what you're saying about infolocks is true, it has to have happened then. But nothing *weird* happened. I just opened a door, and then I was back with the others."

"No system notifications?" Vex asked.

"None." Noram was looking around anxiously, in a way that felt rather painfully familiar to Vex. It reminded him of himself in the early years, before his little brother had been born. "Do you think all this is my fault? Some people are acting weird. I don't know if the mana changes caused it, but..."

"You opened a door," Vex said, shaking his head and trying not to think about his little brother. Not now. He offered Noram an encouraging smile instead, though it felt like it was paper-thin. "We don't even know what that did yet, if it did anything. But maybe you can—"

"Porridge!" Anyati announced, the innkeeper bustling over and startling both Vex and Noram; Derivan was as stoic as ever. Two heavy bowls of porridge were slammed onto the table in front of them; it smelled heavenly, and Vex's mouth began watering just from the sight of it. It came with crunchy pieces of fried dough on top and thick slices of meat, sprinkled with just the right portion of greenery—

Noram was staring too, and he looked like he was starving. Vex hesitated, but before he could say anything, Derivan noticed and spoke up.

"My armor negates the need for food," the armor said. "Would you like my meal instead?"

"I—I couldn't do that," Noram said, but he looked like he desperately wanted to. "I mean, are you sure? It's not like I haven't eaten; it's just I'm still hungry, and I don't really know why..."

"I am sure," Derivan said, and nudged the bowl over to Noram. Vex couldn't help but smile slightly at the sight.

It didn't take long for Noram to begin devouring the bowl like he was starving. He took the first bite like he was being cautious of his food, but the next ones came more and more rapidly, until he was practically shoveling porridge into his mouth; Vex took more polite sips of his own meal in comparison.

It *was* delicious. But he wondered if it meant anything that the food Noram had eaten apparently hadn't been filling.

"Maybe you can show us where the dungeon is," Vex said, continuing his earlier thought as they ate. "It's not very far, is it?"

"It's not," Noram said, pausing for a bit so he could wipe off some of the porridge that had gotten on his nose. "Uh. It's pretty close. It's a small, low-level dungeon. Doesn't usually give much in terms of rewards; we just use it to try to level. Not much success so far, either."

"What level are you?" Vex asked curiously, then blanched a little as he realized the faux pas he'd made. "Um, you don't have to answer that. I was just wondering."

"We're around level twelve," Noram said with a slight shrug. He didn't seem embarrassed about it or bothered by the question. "We figured we wanted to at least get past ten before applying to the Guild, you know?"

"The Guild doesn't really have a level requirement," Vex said. "You don't *have* to do that."

"I know," Noram said. He looked down slightly. "We just wanted to prove to ourselves that we could do it too, you know? The other jobs around here are all farming and taking care of the town, and those are important, but we wanted..."

He trailed off a little bit, looking embarrassed, and dove back into his porridge. Vex exchanged glances with Derivan.

"You do not want glory," Derivan said, cocking his head slightly. "But you want... something more than this town?"

"Yeah, exactly," Noram said. He sighed—he'd finished about half of his food at this point and was finally starting to slow down. He looked around, as if to check if anyone was listening to them, and then lowered his voice and spoke again. "And Fendal is low on mana crystals, too. They won't admit it, but the supplies from Elyra are dropping. We're going to need more, and we want to try to help farm more."

"Why not just farm at a Nucleus?" Derivan asked.

"It's normally less dangerous than a dungeon," Vex added.

Noram grimaced a little at the question. "There aren't any nearby. We'd have to travel further out, and there've been attacks lately. Monsters and bandits. A low-level dungeon is actually safer."

"The bandits shouldn't be a problem anymore, at least," Vex said, but he frowned a little at the mention of monsters. "When you say *monster attacks*, do you mean the goblins that have been raiding Fendal?"

"Among others," Noram said with a nod. "The goblins are just the closest ones. There are some slime-insect colonies further out that are almost Silver-ranked. Elyra said they would send out one of their Elites to take out the colonies, but we haven't heard anything about that since."

"That is . . . concerning." Derivan glanced at Vex, who sighed.

"It's not unusual for Elyra, I don't think," Vex said uncomfortably. "I don't like it, but if one of the noble houses called in to use the Elites, they'd get priority."

"It doesn't matter," Noram said. Vex opened his mouth to argue—it very much *did* matter—but the younger lizardkin looked . . . *tired*. He shut his mouth again. "Let me help you guys out. I know I must be pretty low-level compared to whatever you guys are at, but . . . I want to help. Please. Especially if I caused this."

There was a small pause there while Vex considered the danger and the pleading look on the young lizardkin's face. Noram had even stopped eating his porridge.

"If the dungeon is low level," Vex said slowly, "and we make sure we don't get separated."

"I promise it is. All the enemies are less than level ten. I can handle them," Noram said. "And . . . I want to know more about how professional adventurers do things. I think it's important."

"What about your friends?" Derivan asked. "Would they be coming as well?"

"I . . . can talk to them," Noram said. "But I don't know if they will. They think chasing this is a waste of time. And experience gain is really bad if you're with high-level people, so . . ."

Noram sighed and went back to finishing his porridge. Vex was still only about halfway done, and surreptitiously channeled a bit of fire magic back into his bowl to warm it up a bit.

Noram's tail was still wrapped nervously around the leg of his chair, and he was tapping his foot; it was like what Vex himself did when he was nervous, he recognized. Heck, he was nervous right now, and his tail had already subconsciously begun to curl around the leg of the table—

Derivan seemed to recognize this and reached out again, calmly placing a hand on Vex's once more, and the lizardkin felt heat rising to his face. The armor's hand felt warm against his own, though he was just made of metal; he wasn't sure if that was his imagination . . . But what Derivan was doing worked, and his tail relaxed and spooled down onto the floor instead.

"Can we . . . change the subject?" Noram asked, oblivious to what was going on between the other two. He'd finished off the last of his food and now was tapping the spoon on the edge of his bowl. "I want to know more about adventuring. Um. If you don't mind. What kind of adventures have you had? Did you fight any crazy monsters?"

Vex blinked.

He hadn't expected *that*. But Noram's eyes were bright and interested, if a bit nervous; he'd wanted to ask this question from the beginning, but he'd only mustered up the courage after being treated like an equal.

He smiled a bit. "We've had some pretty crazy adventures," he said. "So crazy I think I should start with one of the tamer ones."

"What!" Noram seemed to forget his nervousness for a moment; he leaned forward and made the most pleading eyes Vex had ever seen a lizardkin manage—

—except for his little brother. Vex swallowed back the sudden swell of emotion and managed to smile at the younger lizardkin. Riss was fine, he was sure. He had time to get him out.

"—*please*," Noram was saying, and Vex blinked and refocused.

"Fine, fine," he said, injecting just a touch of playfulness into his voice, and he could swear that the other lizardkin *wiggled in his seat*.

. . . He did the same thing, sometimes, so he supposed he couldn't really judge.

"There was this one time I convinced my team to go explore some old ruins," he said, his voice low and soft—he leaned in like he was trying to keep a secret, and Noram leaned in too, almost instinctively. "You know how there are all those ruins about, right? The ones that are said to have ancient magical secrets?"

"Yes," Noram said, nodding rapidly; he looked like he was holding his breath. Vex couldn't help but chuckle.

"The one we went to was trapped," he said. "We didn't know what we were dealing with at the time. But have you ever heard of runic circles coming to life?"

"They can do that?" Noram asked, his eyes wide. He was a mage himself, so he no doubt was imagining what that meant—his hand tightened around his wand, like he was getting ready to defend himself.

"They're not supposed to be able to," Vex said with a chuckle. "But they could *there*. We still don't really know why. The ruins were littered with runic circles, and some of them were designs for new spells—but some of them, if you tried to draw them and channel mana into them? You'd be attacked by a living manifestation of mana."

"Whoa," Noram said. Vex blinked, holding back a laugh. When had the lizardkin gotten out a notebook? "How did you beat them?"

"I figured out how they worked," Vex said with a grin. He was genuinely proud of this particular story—neither Misa nor Derivan had been able to fend off the circles, since they were largely ephemeral things, creatures of mana that followed them around and blasted spells at them. "They were slightly modified versions of the spells they could cast. There was a sort of runic program attached to it; the circle as a whole resists mana manipulation, but you can still tear apart that attachment point."

"But you said it doesn't work outside the ruins?" Noram asked, still scribbling notes.

"Believe me, I tried," Vex said with a chuckle. "Derivan will remember it."

"He would not stop complaining about it not working," Derivan agreed, but his tone was fond and affectionate. "It was cute."

"It was *not!*" Vex complained.

"We all agreed," Derivan said whispering conspiratorially to Noram, who nodded seriously and *switched to taking notes on this—*

"You're not actually taking notes on that, are you?" Vex asked, groaning.

"'Course not," Noram said, laughing. He seemed more comfortable with them, at least—he grinned, and flipped the notebook around to show them. It was just a list of notes about the ruins, and a small diagram for what he thought the runic circle might look like.

It was astonishingly accurate, actually.

"I've got notes on what the circles looked like," Vex said, trying to gather himself. "I can share them with you, if you like."

"I would love that!" Noram said. He said it maybe a little too excitedly—some of the other tables turned around to look at him, and he blushed and sat back down in his chair. "I mean, I would love that. Thank you."

"He is giving you quite the honor," Derivan said gravely. "To this day, Vex will not show me his notebooks."

Vex squeaked. "I have a good reason for that!" he argued, though he really didn't. He just couldn't let Derivan see his notes.

... Or Misa. Or Sev.

He couldn't let *Noram* see his notes, now that he thought about it; he'd ask questions about the sketches.

... He could copy the circles out. That would work.

"I am sure," Derivan said, sounding amused.

Vex groaned.

CHAPTER 10

INTERMINABLE INTERVIEWS

"Huh," Sev said, glancing through his system messages. He glanced at Misa—they were having breakfast together in the room, having decided that the suddenly crowded tavern downstairs was not for them.

Well. More accurately, Sev had decided that the crowded tavern wasn't for him, and Misa had opted to eat with him so he didn't have breakfast alone. Which was a gesture he appreciated, really.

"Looks like we'll be splitting the party?" Misa asked, glancing through her own messages, and Sev nodded.

Vex had sent him an update through the system in a series of rapidly conveyed words that he'd evidently rushed to type. Sev wasn't sure what to make of it. The fact that only one mage could see the mana behaving oddly in town was strange enough, but...

Then there were the other things. The mention of a dungeon, albeit a low-level one. Vex's concerns about the behavior of mana. The potential for it to be connected to the dungeon they had broken weeks before. Vex had added that no one had technically actually answered the question of where they'd come from overnight—even Noram, when asked, seemed to frown a little bit and then said he couldn't remember. Everyone else deflected from the topic.

And then there was *still* the matter of food, and how Noram had said he'd remained hungry no matter how much he ate until he ate with Vex and Derivan.

That part in particular, Vex had noted, was strange—but it was a minor sort of strangeness, and he didn't know what it could point to. Sev didn't either, but he made sure to cast a quick [**Purify Food and Water**], just in case.

"Any idea what's going on?" Sev asked, raising a brow at Misa. She shrugged and shook her head.

"Not a fuckin' clue," she said. "But I'm thinking my mom might. I sent out a couple messages so she can get a few people ready to help me scout out these goblin raiders."

"Meanwhile I have to get ready for a day of socializing," Sev grumbled, and Misa grinned at him.

"Consider it training," she teased.

"I'm already the leader of the party!" Sev complained. "I don't need diplomacy training!"

"Funny, you're whining like you do."

"*Misa*," Sev huffed, and Misa laughed.

"You'll be fine," she said, giving him a more-genuine smile. "You always get worried about talking to people. We picked you as the party lead for a reason. I get too aggressive, Vex is too nervous, and Derivan doesn't like using a lot of words and doesn't really follow most customs."

"So you *admit* you're too aggressive," Sev said. Misa narrowed her eyes playfully at him.

"Don't push it."

Breakfast was a simple affair—Sev cooked up some pancakes with the ingredients in the pantry, and after breakfast, he and Misa split up to do their respective parts of the investigation. Vex and Derivan, he was sure, would be fine; the two were headed out to a low-level dungeon with company. Sev told them to call on him if there was any trouble and healing was needed, though, and he made plans to head over once he'd finished questioning people about the goblin raids. That wouldn't take *too* long, he figured.

How very, very wrong he was.

The problem with a task like "go and ask people questions" was that "people" turned out to be a pretty large variable. The first person he decided to ask about the raids was Anyati—and he *still* hadn't managed to extract himself from the conversation.

"And they broke all my good pans!" she complained. "Can you believe that? Came into the inn and smashed them right up. Didn't even take anything. What's the point of that!"

She was bustling about the kitchen while she was talking, cooking meals for the surprisingly many hungry customers outside—not all of them even looked like they were from Fendal. There was a table of water elementals sitting in the corner, their thin, wavering forms splashing harmlessly against the wood. Elementals were a rarer sort, so Sev was surprised to see a number of them apparently traveling.

And the rest of the tavern's visitors... well, there were plenty of the more-common species he'd come to expect—lizardkin, orcs, humans. But there were some of the rarer species, too. Some of them he'd never seen or heard of before, even.

There was a table where a lone crystal floated above a seat, very occasionally making a *ting*, which appeared to translate into a request for a drink—Sev wasn't sure how they were drinking, exactly, except that alcohol seemed to vanish within a certain vicinity of them.

There was a table where a man that appeared to be made entirely out of plants and vines was sitting. He was devouring, perhaps a little frighteningly, a plate that was stacked high with steak—the vines and petals on his head opened up to reveal razor-sharp teeth and an interior maw that led straight into a dark void, and the steak disappeared into it, with the plant-man barely chewing. Not for the first time, Sev wondered about the food shortage and how bad it really was.

There was yet another table where three kobolds were chatting animatedly between one another, which wasn't particularly unusual except for the fact that kobolds were generally considered a "monster" by the system. No one was giving them a second glance, though, and Sev mostly wanted to meet them, because *good god*, they were small and cute. He was glad he'd never faced off against a kobold—he was pretty sure he'd refuse to fight them on principle.

"And!" Anyati said, and Sev blinked; he'd forgotten she was still talking. "One time, they raided the town just to scream really loudly in the center of the town! They were ranting about... eh, I don't know. But it was very disruptive," she said, huffing.

"That doesn't seem... *bad*, though," Sev said, phrasing his words carefully.

"It's terrible!" Anyati complained. "How am I supposed to get business done with goblins yelling outside my inn!"

Sev decided that he wasn't going to get anything that was actually useful out of her and moved on. She hadn't seemed explicitly *angry* about the goblins, at least; frustrated with the raids, certainly, but she'd never mentioned any great harm that they'd done and didn't really seem to care about them beyond wishing they'd be less disruptive when they raided.

But that didn't really match up with what they'd been told. Gensen had mentioned the goblins stealing from the mana crystal stores; Anyati had mentioned nothing of the sort, only that they'd been loud and disruptive.

And that trend was consistent, he would come to find. Or rather, it was consistently inconsistent.

He asked a man at a flower shop what he thought of the goblin raids, and the man had immediately launched into a full-on rant, just like Anyati. He was another one of the plant-people that Sev had never seen before, and his complaint was that the goblins would always raid in the middle of the night; they were the stealthiest creatures he'd ever seen in his life. He'd wake up in the morning to find his flowers half-chewed-on.

"I can just grow them back," the man, whose name was apparently Seed-Planter—Sev didn't comment on the name—said. "But it's a waste of mana! And I shouldn't have to do it in the first place."

"We're going to try to figure it out," Sev said, trying to project reassurance into his voice. "Have you heard anything about them stealing from the mana crystal stores? Or being loud and disruptive?"

"What?" Seed-Planter frowned at him. "No, I didn't hear anything about that. I didn't even know we had mana crystal stores."

"So they just . . . sneak around at night? And chew on your flowers?" Sev asked a little helplessly. Surely that wasn't the only thing Seed-Planter knew they did.

"Yes," the plant-man said, apparently still very convinced that that was, in fact, the primary goal of the goblins.

"We'll figure out what's going on," Sev said with a sigh. "You take care, all right?"

"Are you sure you don't want to buy some flowers?" Seed-Planter said, leaning forward. He brandished a single flower that looked a little bit like a rose, though the center of it twisted off into several smaller roses. They were a pale blue, matching the color of his robes remarkably well. "These ones would look great on you. They match your eyes."

"My eyes are black," Sev pointed out, amused.

"They're a very dark brown," Seed-Planter said, acting affronted, but he seemed to grin in his own strange way—the petals and vines on his head spread open wide, revealing the same razor-sharp teeth that he'd seen back in the tavern. "And I happen to think pale blue matches very well with dark brown."

"Or it happens to match my robes and you're just trying to sell me flowers," Sev commented with a laugh. "But I'll take it."

And he did. Seed-Planter was kind enough to pin the flower on his robe for him, too, a small burst of magic causing two thin thorns to grow out of the flower and stick to the fabric of his robe; it wouldn't *actually* damage the fabric, he was assured, although Sev was a little doubtful of that claim. It didn't really matter, though. Sev wasn't particularly attached to the integrity of his robes.

The florist-merchant waved him goodbye after extracting a promise from him that he'd return, and Sev began to search for the next person to question.

The pattern remained the same. Everyone *knew* about goblin raids; none of them seemed to agree on what the goblins *did*. They all agreed on the time, but never on what the goblins did or where they were. On top of that, they all seemed to have very specific, personal grievances when it came to the goblins; it was never that it disrupted the *town*, it was that it disrupted some aspect of their personal lives, or their personal business, or else just something they cared about.

Which was . . . certainly a pattern. Sev wasn't sure what to make of it. He was almost concerned it was all just some sort of very elaborate prank, but he couldn't imagine the sort of skills that would be needed to fool nearly everyone in a town.

The next step, then, was to speak to someone with a skill that could pierce illusions. Intuition-type skills, like Misa's mother, or various forms of observation and mildly precognitive skills often given to people with classes centered around protection.

Sev went to look for the town's guard captain. Hopefully, whoever they were, they'd be all business, and he could get the interview over with quickly so he could join Vex and Derivan and whoever it was they'd brought with them to the dungeon—

"Oh, I'll tell you about the goblin raids, all right," the guard captain told him when he finally found the man. He was an older man covered in heavy plate armor, in sharp contrast with the light leathers that his men wore. Sev couldn't even see his face. "Let me tell you, back in *my* day—"

Sev sighed.

CHAPTER 11

A PATH THROUGH STONE

Misa was, compared to Sev, having a far more interesting day.

The first thing she'd done was use her [**An Anchor of Heart and Home**] skill—or her [Anchor] skill, as she liked to think of it, since that was much shorter—to call a copy of her mother and two of the guards over, ones that specialized more in tracking and hunting than necessarily in guarding the town. She gave them a chance to acclimate themselves to the strangeness of having two bodies while she spoke with her mother, who was having no such problems.

They were still in the privacy of the inn, anyway, so the two guards could bump into the walls all they wanted.

Though it *was* pretty funny.

"This place *is* strange," Charise said, her brows furrowing slightly. She ran her fingers over the wood of the walls, frowned, glanced at Misa, and took a step away from her. Then she tapped on the wood again, her expression contemplative. "It doesn't feel entirely here, but it's more solid in some places than others."

"The fuck does that mean?" Misa asked, earning a scowl from her mother, and she raised her hands in surrender. "I'm just worried!"

"I am too," Charise admitted. "But I don't think it's bad. It just feels . . . different. It's going to be hard to say until we know a little more about what's going on."

No answers yet, then. Misa was forced to accept that with a nod, though it was a little tense. For all that there wasn't much they could do with that information, a part of her still worried . . .

But no. She was going to trust that the others could take care of themselves and focus on her own task.

Which was tracking down the goblin raiders.

"Are you guys set up?" she asked, glancing at Volaro and Juni—the two guards her mother had brought with her. Juni was a half-orc woman like herself and was grinning at her as she bounced up and down on her toes; Volaro, on the other hand, was a surly-looking older man who mostly seemed eager to get this over with.

"This is *so cool*," Juni said. "Can we do this more often?"

"Any idea where we should start?" Volaro asked politely, pointedly ignoring Juni's question.

"I don't actually know," Misa said. Sev hadn't been able to find out, either, though she'd been periodically messaging him—so far, his interviews hadn't yielded much information. No one had actually seen the so-called goblin raiders coming and going from any particular direction. Misa was starting to question whether they were even goblins at all.

"Then we'll have to circle the town," Volaro said, letting out what sounded suspiciously like a long-suffering sigh. "If we're lucky, we'll find something the goblins left behind. We have some skills that will help, but they might not be enough, depending on how long ago this was."

Misa raised an eyebrow, interested. "What kind of skills?"

Volaro gave her a *look*. "I know your reputation. Not today, Misa."

Her mother smirked at her, and Misa did her best to scowl in response—though she couldn't help the slight grin that edged in on her lips.

Surprisingly, it didn't take them too long to find something once they got out of the inn. They'd barely walked out of town when Volaro stopped, frowning.

"Something's pinging my skills," he said, hesitant.

"Already?" Charise glanced sharply at him.

"It's not usually this good." Volaro frowned slightly, glancing into the air like he was staring at his status screen. "[**Tracking Instinct**] is supposed to just accelerate the process of me spotting things I would normally spot. This is the first time I'm getting *directions*."

"I mean, that doesn't sound like a bad thing," Juni said brightly.

"It's different." Volaro folded his arms. "And different can be dangerous."

"Bah," Juni scoffed. "Point me in the right direction, old man. I'll find the thing!"

"I'm not—" Volaro sighed, accepting defeat midway through the sentence.

While they walked, with Volaro leading the way, Misa gave her mother an amused raise of the brow. "Are they always like that?"

Charise smiled. "Volaro's practically adopted Juni," she said. "He just won't admit it. And Juni's going to keep calling him 'old man' until he does."

It was still early in the morning, and so they had plenty of time to find what they needed. Misa wouldn't have minded if they'd taken much longer; the plains that surrounded Fendal weren't exactly interesting, but it had been a long time since she'd been able to just go on a walk with her mother.

And yet, right as she was about to strike up a conversation . . .

"I found something!" Juni pointed excitedly at a clump of bushes that looked identical to all the other bushes nearby—even Volaro looked confused, although Misa noted that he seemed quite certain Juni knew what she was talking about. He just wasn't seeing whatever she was seeing. "There's an underground passage here. *Very* well hidden."

Juni pushed the foliage to the side, revealing . . . ordinary dirt, as far as Misa could tell.

And then Juni poked her foot at it, and the dirt collapsed into a passageway.

"What the fuck," Misa said flatly, and then she stared at Juni. "Was that a skill? Or was that just hidden by magic?"

Juni grinned. "You sure you want to know?"

"Yes," Misa said bluntly, and Juni laughed, sticking her tongue out at her.

"Yeah, I figured. It's just hidden by a [**Minor Earth Illusion**]. I'm surprised they have that kind of magic at all. Minor elemental spells have some level of physical presence; most monsters just have the standard [**Minor Illusion**] variant, and those are pretty easy to spot."

Misa blinked. "That's very specific."

"I learned it at tracking school."

"We didn't have a tracking school."

"She learned it from me," Volaro said tiredly. "Can we please just go? The goblins are clearly hiding in there. We can go in, clear them out, and be done with this."

Misa frowned. "Probably *not* how we're going to do things," she said with some authority. For one thing, she wasn't practiced with fighting with Volaro and Juni, and certainly not with her own mother; it was always Orkas that had trained her, even if Charise was formidable in her own right. For the other, it didn't feel right to do this without her own team. And besides! The information they had was still *incomplete*.

But not for much longer.

The inside of the tunnel was dank and musty—and the worst part was that the tunnel was poorly lit at best. There were torches, certainly, of the everbright variety; Misa recognized the rune from the various times Vex had tried to show off the spell—but those torches were few and far between, and set so far into the wall that the light they cast into the tunnel was barely a speck of light in what felt like a very long trail of darkness.

And the worst part was that the passageway was small, forcing Misa to bend down to avoid scraping her head against the ceiling. There was something strange about it, too; she couldn't pinpoint what it was, exactly, but this didn't seem like a place that was built for goblins. Too many strange edges in the tunnel, no sign of any tools left on the ground, and there was the strangest sensation of goosebumps on her skin, like something here was *wrong*.

The four of them walked along the tunnel in a single file, mostly silent except for the occasional grunt of irritation from Misa and her own mother's tinkling laugh, which made Misa grumble even more. They expected the path to begin branching out, as it always did in goblin dens like these, but...

Nope. It was just a straight passageway.

They took a few more steps forward, and Juni suddenly frowned. "There's some kind of magic here," she said, stopping in place. Misa almost bumped into her, then froze, narrowing her eyes slightly.

"Hostile?"

"No," Juni said, but she hesitated for a second, sniffing the air. "I don't think so. It feels like spatial magic. It's... spatial compression? I'm pretty sure it's some variant of spatial compression."

"Hang on," Misa said. "Are you *smelling the magic?*"

Juni grinned. "It's a skill. [**A Nose for Magic**]. Managed to learn it using some tips from Volaro. Pretty cool, right?"

"I didn't even know that was a thing you could do." Misa paused. "I don't even know if *Vex* knows that that's a thing you can do."

"It's a common skill in that it's technically easy to get it, but not a lot of people actually get it," Juni said. "Skill rarities are weird! But it's pretty useful if you're a tracker and you don't have [**Mana Sight**], like me."

"You'll have to teach me sometime," Misa said, and she meant it. Having a new skill could only help expand her repertoire, and the fact that it was a different way of detecting magic might mean she could cover for things that Vex didn't spot—

"You might not want to learn it," Juni said, interrupting her fantasies of skill exploitation. She looked a little embarrassed. "If there's any strong magic around, it's usually impossible to stop sneezing."

Oh.

That made things a lot more awkward, didn't it?

"Anyway, let's keep going," Juni said, quickly getting over her own embarrassment. "We're not too far now, I don't think. The magic smells stronger ahead."

Nothing about the pathway had physically changed, but both Volaro and Charise seemed to agree, so Misa prepared herself for a potential confrontation. [**Guard Stance**] flickered into activity around her as they ventured carefully into the depths of the tunnel.

And then they hit a dead end.

Except it *wasn't* a dead end, of course. Juni reached out to tap it, and it crumbled away just like the entrance had; this time, when it crumbled away, Juni hissed and pulled back, because the light from the tunnel was spilling into a massive underground cavern in a way that was really quite obvious—

But no one seemed to notice them. Obvious as it was, the tunnel they were in was just one light amongst many—and there were many other entrances that all spilled into this enormous cavern dug deep into the middle of the earth. Below them, small enough to look almost like the specks of stars, glittered the lights of a bustling city.

It was enormous. It was undeniably beautiful, too. Above the city floated what looked like a river suspended in the air, raining gentle, glowing trails down into the city below. She couldn't quite make out what it *did*, but it was an awe-inspiring sight.

"What . . ." Misa began, and then stopped; her voice carried much farther than she wanted into the enormous cavern ahead of her. More quietly, she spoke again. "What *is* this?"

There were *buildings* down there. Buildings of stone, lit with the light of everbright torches and sophisticated mana lamps. Small figures ran around in crystalline streets, and a thin precipice of a path just outside the tunnel led down into the city proper.

Misa didn't need to look closer to be able to tell that goblins were far from the only species in this sprawling underground city.

"Perhaps we won't be clearing them out," Volaro said, and Misa gave him a deadpan look.

They were here to scout. *Only* scout. She wanted to figure out more about what was happening here, but she wanted Sev and Vex and Derivan with her, too; this was too big for them to explore on their own, and her villagers didn't have the levels to back her up. Because there was something else that Misa was noticing about the citizens down below—

All of them were monsters. Every single species she saw, she knew the system categorized as a monster.

And yet... not a single one of them had a system label. No level. No species indicator.

Nothing.

[**Guys,**] Misa sent through the system. [**I think you need to see this.**]

CHAPTER 12

DOORS

Vex stared at the dungeon that Noram had led them to. "Are you sure this is it?" he couldn't help but ask.

It was a dumb question. The system had it labeled. It was just so . . . dinky-looking.

Noram's dungeon was just a hole in the ground. It sloped downwards, opening up into a cave of some sort, but it didn't change the fact that it was one of the least impressive dungeon entrances Vex had ever seen—and that was amongst even the low-level dungeons he had visited before.

Those usually at least had a *door*.

"Yup," Noram said, sounding a little embarrassed. He even kicked a bit at the ground. Vex wasn't sure why he was so embarrassed—it wasn't like he'd been the one to design the dungeon. "I know it doesn't look like much, but it's pretty big on the inside."

"Does this dungeon have a theme?" Derivan asked, which was probably a more practical question than what Vex wanted to ask. What he wanted to ask was closer to *Can Derivan go inside the hole first?*, which would mostly have been embarrassing.

"Doors," Noram said. "The main room is just a hallway of doors. Every door inside leads somewhere different, though, and sometimes just touching a door will teleport you inside the room. That's why I didn't think too hard about opening one back when I got separated from the others. We got pushed into different doors by a trap."

"I can't believe it's *door-themed* and it doesn't even have a door for the entrance," Vex complained, and Derivan chuckled, ruffling the frills on the back of Vex's head. The lizardkin maintained his huff for as long as he could, which was a grand total of about two seconds, before he whined. "*Derivann.*"

"Yes?" the armor asked him, his voice teasing.

"I can't *complain about things* when you do that!"

"I believe complaining about things is Sev's job," Derivan said, still sounding amused. "Perhaps it would help you to know that there are mana signatures coming from the doors within?"

Vex perked up, his dismay about the entrance to the dungeon immediately forgotten. Noram snorted out a laugh.

"You're really into magic, huh?" the other lizardkin asked.

"Aren't you?" Vex asked, blinking a few times. "You're a mage."

"Well, yes, but . . ." Noram trailed off, and this time he looked a bit upset. "Actually getting your hands on spell scrolls is pretty hard if you're not apprenticed or part of one of the noble families in Elyra."

Vex winced, but Noram didn't seem to notice. He continued. "It's hard to really get excited about magic when all the good stuff is locked away from me. I'm hoping I can learn more when I join the Guild, though! Maybe I'll find some cool stuff in ancient ruins, like you did."

Bah. This was the same sort of thing! Dungeons had secrets too, secrets that could be harvested for *more magic*. He was being a little too dismissive about his ability to learn, Vex decided. He could do some learning now.

"You can learn a lot from dungeons, too, not just ruins," he said, his voice taking on a familiar, lecturing tone.

"From dungeons?" Noram looked a bit skeptical. "I don't know about that. Aren't they all about, I dunno, challenges and traps and stuff?"

"Sure," Vex said with a shrug. "But that doesn't mean there isn't anything you can learn from it. A lot of the time . . . Actually. Let's go in. It'll be easier to show you."

With that cue, they made their way into the dungeon. Derivan insisted on leading the way, of course, just in case.

True to Noram's word, the dungeon seemed like it was just one long hallway, with an array of different doors alternating with each other on each side. Every door was unique, though, both in mana signature and in appearance. There were the standard doors made of wood, along with heavier-looking doors made of metal. There were doors that were barely doors at all, made of straw or clumped-together grass that was barely holding itself into the shape of a door, for all that it held the appearance of one.

And some of them were distinctly *traps*. It was obvious from the runic imprint on the doors, but that wasn't something Noram would be able to see without the advanced version of [**Mana Sight**]; he would have to look at the flow of mana around it instead . . .

Which made this a good opportunity for teaching Derivan, too, actually. Vex flipped his own [**Mana Sight**] to the basic version, allowing the runic inscriptions to fade from his sight, and guided both Noram and Derivan to the first trap he spotted.

"This door's a trap," Vex said. "Do you see the way the mana's flowing around it?"

"It doesn't look that different from the other doors," Noram said, frowning.

"I am unsure," Derivan said. "There is a confluence of mana at the center of the door, like with all the other doors, but this one has... There are more streams of mana leading into it than out of it, compared to the other doors."

"Exactly!" Vex beamed, even as Noram frowned and peered more closely at the door. "Even if you can't see the runic inscription directly, you can still read how the mana flows to get an idea of what the door is doing. This one is storing more mana than it's releasing—it's basically an explosive trap. If the rune gets triggered, it blows up like a shockwave."

The non-trapped doors, by contrast, usually had the same number of "input" and "output" streams of mana. The visual noise was enough that it had never been outright obvious to Noram, but his interest seemed piqued. "I can use this for my own spells, right?" he said, making a connection.

Vex grinned. "Exactly," he said. "When the system generates a runic circle for you, look for more inputs than the default. You can change your spells that way."

Noram actually looked excited about this. He grabbed his notebook and began scribbling, and Vex pumped a fist in the air. Success! *Magic.*

Ahem.

"Can you show us to the door you mentioned?" Vex asked.

"The doors rearrange every time we come in here," Noram said, hesitating. "I can *recognize* it, it's pretty distinct, but... This place is a maze. It was a few corridors in, the last time."

Noram reached out, and—after a quick glance at the flow of mana—pulled open one of the glowing white doors; it led down into another hallway. The doors, Noram quickly explained, worked like this: the white doors were doors into new corridors, and the other doors either were traps or would lead to challenge rooms of some sort. They'd never encountered a monster in the hallways themselves.

And so, for the next while, they just wandered the hallways. Vex kept track of which doors they went through, though Noram said that going backward would always land them back at the entrance. Keeping track was a safety measure to keep his anxiety at bay, and to prevent him from having to think about . . . other things.

He kept in contact with Sev and Misa, too. Sev told him about who he was talking to, and the strangeness that was meeting all these species that he'd never seen before. He spoke about the sheer, strange concentration of magical beings in Fendal. Misa talked about the tunnel they were navigating their way through, and her mother's suspicions about Fendal being not all there. Vex wanted to ask more questions, but right as he was about to—

"Found it!" Noram called, sounding excited.

A small part of Vex had been worried they wouldn't find the door—that opening it had triggered some condition that would erase it from the dungeon's memory, or something like that. He'd heard of similar things happening in other dungeons. But no, this was definitely the door, and Vex knew it without a shadow of a doubt before Noram even pointed it out.

Because the door had the symbol of the Ashion House on it. The symbol of his family.

It was empty of any mana signature that he could detect, though, even flipping his [**Mana Sight**] back to the advanced version. As far as he could tell, it was magically dead.

"The door looked like this the first time I saw it, too," Noram said. "No mana to speak of. It was one of the other reasons I was so sure it was safe. And nothing seemed to happen when I opened it . . ."

"But something did happen," Vex said softly. "You recognize that symbol, don't you?"

"It's one of the noble houses in Elyra, I think?" Noram said with a slight frown. "I don't pay much attention to the nobles, sorry. Too stuck-up for me."

"Right," Vex said, opting not to tell Noram who he was, exactly. At least not yet. Maybe if it turned out they had to keep working with him, but that was a can of worms he didn't want to open now, or preferably ever; without realizing it, he clenched his teeth slightly. It was subtle, just the smallest subconscious flinch.

And yet Derivan noticed his discomfort. A metallic, surprisingly warm hand slipped into his own and gave it a gentle squeeze. Vex stilled a little, and let out a small, relieved breath; somehow, even in the smallest way, this was enough to push away the memories of his family.

He would need to confront it eventually, he knew, but for now, this was . . . nice. Being near Derivan was always comforting. Vex leaned in, almost subconsciously, to Derivan's presence.

And Derivan didn't seem to mind at all.

Anyway. They had a door to think about, and Vex had a suddenly fluttering stomach to ignore.

"I think..." Vex paused, trying to gather his thoughts.

The door seemed like it was related directly to him. He remembered the name of his bonus room; it was <A World Without a System>. He remembered the way the spell had malfunctioned when Derivan had tried to cast. The people Sev had spoken to, the majority of which were magical species...

Vex reached out for the door, and sure enough, a box appeared.

> **<NOTICE>**
> **Activation of bonus room <A World Without a System> has failed. Insufficient data at this dungeon. Insufficient units of <ERROR>. Safeguards failed. Rollback failed. Partial activation of bonus room <A World Without a System> initiated within the limits of region H-72.**

"Noram," Vex said, and the other lizardkin perked up a bit on hearing his name. "Is there a trend to these doors? What kind of challenge rooms do they usually open up into?"

"There isn't *really* a pattern," Noram said cautiously. He could sense something was wrong, clearly; Vex had no doubt that his face was a little pale, and Derivan seemed to be coming to his own conclusions, from the way he was looking at the doors. "They're all... rooms, I guess? Like most of the time, they're all places that doors would lead to. Except the weird ones."

There was a door a little farther back that he'd noticed seemed familiar—the memory came rushing back to him now. He sprinted backward, to both Derivan and Noram's startled surprise, and they shouted as they ran to keep up with him. Vex was mostly hoping that he was wrong, because he wasn't sure what he would do if he was *right*.

There was a door back there that looked a little bit like the door to their room at the Sleeping Bird inn. It wasn't a trapped door, either. Vex pulled the door open—

—and stared at a nearly perfect replica of the very same room they lived in, down to the dirty dishes they'd yet to wash. Except... Vex caught a glimpse of someone there. A human man holding a crossbow?

He vanished into the wall before Vex could say anything about it, and Vex blinked, wondering if he'd imagined the whole thing.

But that wasn't what was important right now.

"The theme of this dungeon is *doors*," Vex said. "These doors lead to any place that a door might lead to. But when you opened that door..."

"What is it?" Noram asked, looking worried.

"It was a door to another dungeon's bonus room," Vex said. The words felt heavy, maybe heavier than they should have been, because he was now considering that all of this might be *his fault* instead. <**A World Without a System**> had been seeded off of *his* class, his skills, his personality. "I think... I think this dungeon copies doors and the places they lead to. This door leads to another dungeon's bonus room, bypassing the usual trigger conditions. But it couldn't copy that bonus room completely. It just *tried*."

"It could not create a world of its own," Derivan said out loud. He glanced sharply back toward the door. "You are saying that the dungeon is creating an effect that is removing the influence of the system from this town."

"Pretty much," Vex said heavily. "And—maybe a bit more. This still doesn't explain the stupid goblin raids."

"But—that can't be right. Everyone would've gotten system sickness," Noram said, his tail flicking at the ground nervously. "Right?"

"They might not," Vex said. "Not if the room makes it so that the system never existed in the first place. Not if it makes it so that the system doesn't *need* to exist. It explains all the magical creatures, and the reason the magic is so upset with us: we're not from this town. Our link to the system is stronger."

Specifically, the barrier Derivan had created had fractured only when *he'd* stepped closer to it. His link to the system had angered the mana. Vex felt a chill settle in his stomach.

"But I still have access to the system," Noram protested.

Vex glanced at him. He wasn't so sure. "Do you?"

Noram frowned. And then he frowned harder, scrunching up his eyes, and Vex felt his heart sink.

"Fuck," Noram said after another moment passed, miserably.

A message came in through the system.

[**Guys,**] Misa had sent. [**You need to see this.**]

Vex wondered if it was just his imagination or if the box was paler than usual.

CHAPTER 13

A CITY OF MAGIC

Vex followed along behind Derivan, glancing cautiously at the walls of the tunnel around them. The system messages from the dungeon had been their cue to leave and meet up with Misa; they exchanged a few messages to make sure they were all on the same page, and Sev had been thrilled to finally have an excuse to extricate himself from all those interviews.

Noram wasn't here, and neither were any of Misa's people. Without the overlay of the system, there was no easy way for them to gauge how powerful the monsters down in the cavern were, and while they weren't necessarily expecting *hostility*, given the nature of the raids...

Vex's friends were still the ones more equipped to deal with danger.

He did have to promise Noram that he'd keep in contact, though.

It hadn't been long before they found themselves in the tunnels Misa had mentioned, but Vex had to admit that he was feeling uncharacteristically nervous.

The mana was acting strangely when it came to spellcasting. Derivan's barrier spell had failed. Their prevailing guess was that it was Vex stepping closer that had caused the reaction; Derivan's system was broken, and Vex's was not.

So they had decided to test it.

But if the reaction had been angry when Derivan had cast, then it had been outright hostile when Vex made his attempt. It was a good thing they hadn't encountered any monsters down in the door dungeon, really, because Vex's spell had outright exploded in his face.

They were prepared for the possibility, so the spell he cast to test had been a weak one, and even then Derivan had to catch the lizardkin as he stumbled from the resulting explosion. Vex's expression had been ashen. He'd always been close to magic. To have it actively fight against him...

Distressed was a mild way to put it. But Derivan assured him that they would find a way to work around the problem, and he felt his unease fall back to the wayside, replaced by a warmth in his chest.

The animosity between mana and the system, though... He'd never considered that possibility. It explained why ambient mana was so abundant in nature and so sparse in towns and cities; it explained why natural mana fled if he used a skill.

So many little things were clicking into place. He'd been searching for the answer to this for years. He itched to write all this down in his notes, and after a moment's hesitation he did, in fact, pull out his notebook and start scribbling.

He was still scribbling when they approached the end of the tunnel, where Misa and Sev were already waiting. Vex only stopped when Derivan grabbed him to stop him from falling right off the ledge and into the city below; he yelped, dropped his notebook, caught it, dropped it again, and then caught it a second time.

Then he stared out into the underground city ahead of him.

The sight of the massive cavern with a whole underground city was awe-inspiring, to say the least. Vex couldn't stop himself from gawking at the sight for a whole minute before he eventually gathered himself, and a little bit of his nervousness leaked back in.

"Are you sure you want to do this?" Misa asked. She looked worried—part of her knew how badly Vex wanted to explore this new city, but she also knew Vex didn't have his magic. His [**Chromaturgist**] class was useless if he couldn't make any runic circles at all.

"Yes," Vex said with some trepidation. "I know I can't cast magic right now, but I won't be a burden."

"I'm not fucking worried about you being a burden," Misa said with a sigh. "You pull your weight in more ways than just magic, you know? You don't have to prove yourself or anything."

Vex hesitated. "I know," he said softly. "But anti-magic exists. This is a danger I'm going to have to deal with at some point. If it gets too dangerous down there, then we can bail, but I can still protect myself a little."

He gripped his dagger. Derivan looked at him, something like concern and protectiveness flickering in the lilac-purple light of his eyes, and Vex tried to ignore the way his heart fluttered. Misa was probably right in that it was past time he talked to the armor about his feelings...

... Not now. Not yet.

"Let's go," he said instead, though Derivan looked at him curiously, like he'd noticed something. Misa sighed but nodded, no doubt resolving to use her blocking skills to make sure Vex stayed safe. She took the lead, as she always did, one hand resting on the hilt of her mace.

[**Guard Stance**] was not active. They were all a little cautious about using skills at the moment, though less because they thought it wouldn't work and more because Vex suspected it would make the mana react to them and make their presence far too obvious.

Vex followed right after Misa. He felt the slight sting of a thin, almost-invisible barrier of illusory mana he hadn't noticed, felt it pass over his eyes—

The moment he stepped through, the whole cavern burst into multicolored light. Vex stared, stopping in his tracks and almost making Sev trip over his tail.

Misa hadn't mentioned the amount of *mana* here.

Presumably, she'd never stepped past that illusory barrier. She wasn't quite as starstruck as Vex was, but she'd stopped when the lizardkin did, using the opportunity to take in the sight. Outside the cavern, they could see the river of magic that floated above the city; *inside*, it became clear that the river split off into distributaries and tributaries, flowing through the city like a tree of light. Independent streams of mana split off to dance and weave among each other, and even they had so much density that Vex was sure they were visible to even those without [**Mana Sight**]—

"Whoa," Sev said, confirming his thoughts. "Is that *mana?*"

"Yes," Vex said. He toned down his own [**Mana Sight**] with a wince as a particularly brilliant stream drifted right past his eyes; the skill was making things a little too bright for him. "I've never seen mana this active. Not even during dungeon formation events."

"Perhaps this is the natural state of mana," Derivan suggested. "If the system did not exist."

"I'm thinking more and more that *all of this* is," Vex said with a sigh. "Which makes me wonder what the *point* of the system is. It's clearly manipulating mana, dungeons are at the center of that manipulation in some way, it's outright harvesting gods . . ."

He glanced at Sev, who shrugged. "Aurum is quiet today, and we're not going to find anything out from standing around," he said. He hesitated for a moment. ". . . I'm a little worried about the guy, but there's not much to do about it. It might just be that this place makes it impossible to commune with the gods."

"Let's get going, then," Misa said, waving them forward impatiently.

The sheer concentration of mana diminished somewhat as they headed down the path set into the stone; it circled around the cavern, leading them on a curved route down toward the central city. There were dozens of other paths that were the same too, cut into the rock like a set of spirals leading down. Vex wondered if those paths led to other towns—surely not. They would've gotten a lot more than just a report from Fendal, had that been the case.

Then again, the whole town was clearly under some kind of infolock, so...

"There aren't that many towns around here, are there?" Vex asked, worried. Sev glanced at Vex, then followed his gaze to the paths circling around the walls of the cavern.

"No," he said cautiously. "But the path here had spatial magic in it, right? So this is pretty far away from Fendal."

"We're going to have to do so much walking to check that out," Misa groused.

"We could also just ask," Derivan said calmly. They were approaching the floor of the cavern now, which meant that they stood on the outskirts of this magical city. Vex barely had the time to wonder at the arrangement of magical lights, many of which looked nothing like the runic inscriptions Elyra used to fuel its own lights—there was *some* kind of rune painted on the floor, but the language was entirely different, nothing like the detailed circuitry Vex was used to—before Derivan approached one of the many so-called monsters that were going about their days.

"Excuse me," he said politely, and the cockroach-like man he'd spoken to turned back to him, startled.

"You talkin' to me?" he said. His voice was low, bordering on gruff; he hefted the groceries he was carrying onto a ridge on his hip.

"Yes," Derivan said. "I was wondering if you could tell us where the other paths lead. We are new here, you see." Derivan indicated the other spirals cut into the wall, and the other man peered at him, antennae dipping low over his eyes in a curious impression of a squint.

"They don't go nowhere," he said gruffly. "Roads are sealed. No one knows why."

"We're here," Misa pointed out.

"Roads are mostly sealed," he corrected himself with a sigh; the plating on his body chittered strangely, vibrating. "Go to the city hall if you want to talk about it. I ain't the scholarly type. Got some mages there trying to figure out the Roads. And take a shower. You guys stink."

With that, he started to walk off. "Thank you," Derivan called after him, trying to be polite, but he looked baffled. He turned to the others. "Do we... stink? I do not believe I am capable..."

"I can't believe he just said we stank," Misa said, looking offended.

"Let's just go to the city hall," Sev sighed. "Again."

Vex frowned, looking around. The lights in the city were reminding him of something—he remembered the version of himself that Misa had summoned, casting off meteors with a brush.

The symbols on the ground weren't runes. Not as he knew them. They were more like miniature paintings in themselves...

He was walking forward before he even realized it.

"Uh, Vex?" Sev asked.

"Just give me a second," Vex said. "I wanna look at some of the lights. Did you see them? The runes they use down here are totally different. If there's a whole new method of spellcasting I can use... maybe it'll work better than system-assisted spells."

Sev raised an eyebrow, but he didn't protest as the lizardkin scurried over to one of the so-called lamps—poles of solid light that extended out from an image painted on the ground. Vex examined it closely, though there wasn't all that much to look at, and he felt Derivan approaching him as well to stare curiously at the symbol.

"The material looks similar to the mana your [**Splash of Mana**] skill generates," Derivan noted. "Do you think you can still use that skill?"

"Probably," Vex hedged. He wasn't actually sure. "System skills are still working properly... Skills and spells are differentiated by mana usage colloquially, but they're more nuanced than that academically. The ones that generate runes are the ones that are actually considered spells; everything else is a system skill that happens to cost mana. [**Splash of Mana**] doesn't generate a runic inscription, but I'm still kind of worried..."

He trailed off a little. Derivan was *right*, though, in that the rune he was looking at looked like it was painted out of mana, the exact same way things had looked when he was creating material to work with using the [**Splash of Mana**] skill.

He grabbed a notebook out of his tailpouch, making a quick sketch of the rune. It was nothing like the painting he'd made with Derivan, so many nights ago, modeled after his [**Starry Night**]. But there was still a certain beauty to it. It was made of long, swooping lines that looked almost like wings; the mana flowed into it from the sides and up through the center, filling out the rest of the image in a prismatic sheen before forming that glowing light pole.

A part of him was half-concerned that his pencil sketch would be enough to trigger whatever magic there was here, but the mana stayed thankfully dormant—he didn't want to accidentally burn a hole through his notebook or anything.

"That explains some of the things I was confused about," Derivan admitted. "Do you think you can use these to cast, with the system disabled?"

"I need a brush," Vex said. "I think I should limit my use of system skills as much as possible, just based on what we've seen so far. Even if I can get away with using Splash to generate the mana paint, using [**Delineate**] to paint it might be a bit much."

"There are supply shops nearby," Derivan said, glancing around; his eyes alighted on a particular ramshackle hut with a dangling sign just outside. "Perhaps we can look in those?"

Misa sighed and glanced at Sev. "We're gonna get sidetracked by a shopping trip, aren't we."

Sev chuckled. "But look at Vex. He seems pretty happy."

Vex, for his part, playfully flicked his tongue out at Sev.

And yet... he couldn't deny it. This was new. This was *exciting*. This was why he'd come out to adventure in the first place, or at least a *part* of the reason he'd done so. This was also new magic! It was the thing he'd been after for most of his life, the thing he'd spent years researching, and the one thing that might help him with...

Vex pushed his mind away from the thought. His siblings could wait. He couldn't do anything for them still.

The lizardkin took Derivan's hand and outright dragged him toward the shop that he'd seen catch Derivan's eyes earlier. All the nearby ones looked mostly the same, anyway. They were slightly dilapidated and old-looking; the stone they were made of was worn and chipped, and the paint had peeled, but *dammit*, they were *magic shops*, in a world that seemed to use a completely different system of magic.

There was so much here to learn!

Vex paused a second before he stepped into the shop, the chipping and peeling paint suddenly striking inspiration within him. Was that why some of the light-lamps were weaker than others? They weren't all the *same*; some were dimmer than others. Maybe, like the paint on a shop wall could chip and peel, the runes could...

He needed a better name than *runes*. The system was completely different. *Glyphs*?

"I'm gonna call these non-runes *glyphs*," he decided, and then scribbled down a note about it in his notebook so he wouldn't forget.

"Glyphs?" Derivan asked, and Vex beamed at the question.

"Look," he said, throwing himself practically entirely off course to drag the armor to a nearby failing lamp instead of the shop he'd been about to walk into. Sure enough, he was right—the glyph was damaged, the paint partially peeled. "The glyph is damaged, but the light's still working; it's just a bit weaker. Regular runic inscriptions, circles, circuits—whatever you want to call them—they don't work like that. Any damage either breaks the spell or alters its function, usually in a very predictable way."

"But glyphs remain functional," Derivan said, and Vex nodded excitedly.

"It could change the face of enchanting," Vex said, and then he frowned slightly. "Although I'm not sure... Hmm. Glyphs look like they function using ambient mana, and outside of dungeons, runic inscriptions usually have to be powered by personal mana or a mana crystal. Normally, I'd say that saves on mana, but most cities don't have that much in the way of ambient mana..."

He frowned, starting to mutter to himself. Derivan chuckled.

"Perhaps we can worry about that later?" he offered. "There was a shop you wanted to go to."

"Right!" Vex brightened again, grabbing Derivan's hand to pull him into the shop.

"Wow, I think they completely forgot about us," Misa laughed, staring after the two in amusement. "Which one do you think is going to confess first?"

"Hard to say," Sev mused. "Derivan's got Physical Empathy, but I don't think he understands what Vex is feeling, and Vex..."

"He's still got some demons, huh?" Misa's smile turned a little sad.

"He'll tell us about it when he's ready. Come on; let's go after them. I want to see this otherworldly magic shop too."

CHAPTER 14

THAT ONE MAGIC SHOP

There *was* a small part of Vex that knew there were bigger things here to worry about. They had some of the answers, but they didn't have all of them. The idea that a dungeon had tried to copy his bonus room, of all things, and that that had somehow leaked into Fendal and created an entire underground city—it explained the mana's reaction to the system, the appearance of so many magical creatures that had been thought to be long extinct, the system itself no longer being accessible to Noram and presumably many others.

It didn't explain how strangely some of Fendal's townsfolk were behaving, or the nature of the so-called goblin raids, or the issues with food.

And even then, none of that told them how they could *fix* the situation. Maybe the only way to fix it would be to go on ahead to Elyra and complete the dungeon there, where the real bonus room would be.

Maybe.

But there was *new magic* here. Magic he'd never seen before—magic he'd never even heard of. The glyphs he'd seen were nothing like the runic inscriptions he'd been taught, and they were nothing like any mage used to cast spells, as far as he knew. He was reminded of the glyphs he'd painted into the sky, back when Misa had summoned a copy of him. He wondered what path he would've needed to take to learn about them so much earlier in his life.

New magic was important. If he could understand this form of magic, he might be able to change everything. His family would have to listen to him, then, and he'd be able to pluck his little brother away from them; all of his siblings, even, if he could convince them to listen—

"How may I help you?" a light, polite voice sounded, and Vex blinked as he glanced up at the shopkeeper.

Quite literally *up*, actually. The shopkeeper was almost as tall as Derivan was, and even taller if you counted the feathery antennae. They were lithe and slender, but their true build was hidden in an enormous amount of fluff, and Vex resisted the desire to ask to pet it.

"Can I pet it?" Vex asked, having resisted his desire for all of five seconds.

The shopkeeper tilted their head slightly. "You know," they said. "That is strangely not the first time I have been asked that! Perhaps dinner first would be appropriate?"

Vex let out an embarrassed cough. "Uh, sorry. Reflex. I'm looking for... I want to know a little more about how you cast magic? I saw the symbols that were painted on the floor outside, and I wanna know how that's done. And if you have any tools for doing that. Like, hypothetically, a giant paintbrush."

Vex's voice trailed off. The shopkeeper's expression stayed amused, or... at least, he hoped they were amused.

"You are seeking to learn magic!" they said. "But this is not the best place to learn. One of the academies deeper in our city could assist you, perhaps."

"I'm just looking for some tools," Vex said quickly. The idea of an academy for learning magic was absolutely far too attractive to him, and if he spent too much time thinking about it he would cave and try to get into one. And they *definitely* didn't have the time for that. Probably. "Do you have any suggestions?"

He glanced around the shop as he asked, taking in the haphazard shelves and custom-carved statuettes and plaques, all delicately painted with different symbols. The gentle glow of an orange, sun-shaped glyph painted everything in the shop in all the hues of the sunset.

For all that they were still on the city outskirts and the shop seemed old and unremarkable on the outside, it was warm and cozy within.

Part of it was that the magic here was warmer, somehow, in a way that was comforting. It wove in and out, dancing between the items in the shop. And the shop seemed to have almost everything—Vex had chosen this one because Derivan's gaze had landed on it, and hadn't expected it to be particularly special, but it *was*.

Even besides those statuettes and plaques, there were all kinds of what were clearly minor artifacts. There were small, complicated-looking mechanisms whirring on the shelves, some threatening to tip off. There were a colorful, sparkling variety of gems packed dense with mana. There were even small pieces of weapons and armor, though those were more limited in quantity and seemed more decorative than not.

The shopkeeper was watching him patiently. "If you are new to magic," they began, and then they paused, waiting patiently as Vex jumped, startled.

He'd completely forgotten he was in the middle of a conversation. The shopkeeper wore an amused smile. "If you are new to magic, I would recommend a basic magelight. It will channel mana into the correct shapes for you."

"How does it work?" Vex asked eagerly. "I've never seen one before."

"Ah! Are you a visitor from the Roads, perhaps?" The shopkeeper gave Vex a friendly smile. "I suppose I should have guessed. Things must seem quite different here. Your magic does not work the same way, if I understand correctly?"

"Yeah!" Vex perked up slightly, though a part of him wondered how the shopkeep could possibly have known. "We use runes, but they look different from yours. What do you call them?"

"There is some nuance to it," the shopkeeper said with a chuckle. "Most frequently, they are called glyphs, as you must know? They are a self-perpetuating idea, to a degree."

"I thought I made it up," Vex said, his eyes wide. The shopkeeper gave him a friendly smile.

"It is instinct to know what they should be called, strange as it may sound. All glyphs hold their own inherent meaning, and the root of that is that they are glyphs. But there are certain, special glyphs that we call Signs, though that particular part of magical theory is rather complex. I would teach you a small lesson in magic, but alas, I have been told I must charge for that, and that it is 'bad business' to simply teach."

"I could pay," Vex said hopefully.

"If you are from the surface, you cannot," the shopkeeper said, though they spoke kindly. "We trade in mana slivers here—fragments of mana that are deposited when any great act of magic is performed. We give to the mana, and it gives to us in return."

They paused, then chuckled. "Though perhaps that was not its intent when it first began awarding them."

Vex had *so many questions*. "What kind of great acts of magic?" he asked, almost tiptoeing so he could lean in closer.

"Now that would be telling." The shopkeeper managed to smile with a sort of flourish at the end, sweeping their head forward so their antennae dipped down in a makeshift bow. They glanced to the sides, as if checking to see if anyone was watching, and then leaned in to whisper. "New paintings, usually, or great new works of art. Sometimes it's the discovery of new glyphs, or simply two existing glyphs being combined in a new way . . ."

"You can combine them?" Vex said, his eyes wide. He flipped open his notebook again and began scribbling notes. "How?"

"Everyone has their own methods," the shopkeeper said with a light, airy sort of chuckle. "And the results are always slightly different. Some practitioners believe there exists an innate talent within people, but I think that is rather foolish. Whatever magic you create is *yours*; the biggest problem, I believe, is that people try to copy others.

"Magic comes in two parts. One part in the mana in the air, yes, the source of all things magical—but the other part comes from *you*. Your own interpretation of what magic is. What mana is. There are always rules, but the rules are yours and yours alone."

There was a small silence after the shopkeeper spoke, where their words hung in the air like the stars in the sky; the way they spoke had a certain enchanting quality, a quiet but firm belief. It resonated with the mana in the air, almost, like it was about to begin coalescing into a spell.

"That's a beautiful thought," Vex said softly, but he was watching the mana in the air. "Do you cast with your voice, then?"

"Do I?" The shopkeeper laughed. "Ah. Perhaps I have revealed too much."

"I'll come back and pay you some slivers when I get some," Vex said, determined, and the shopkeeper seemed to grin at him.

"Confident," they said cheerfully. "But I like that kind of confidence. Perhaps a free gift, to get you started on your journey? Or perhaps we could call it an investment, if you can truly gather slivers with your magic."

The shopkeeper walked purposefully through the shelves, their steps surprisingly light; despite their size, they didn't make a sound on the admittedly creaky wood of the floor. They scanned the shelf of magelights carefully before selecting one and presenting it to Vex with a flourish.

It looked remarkably like a paintbrush. The end of it glowed faintly, and Vex could almost sense the tiny mana well within that would seep into the brush when he began painting. The handle was beautifully intricate, carved with a glimmering image of a deep-sea whale, and when he took the magelight from the shopkeeper—carefully, reverently—the tip of the brush shone even brighter.

The reason it was called a magelight, no doubt.

"I will skip the spiel about how it is ethically sourced," they said cheerfully. Vex blinked.

"Do I need to worry about . . . ethically sourced magelights?" Vex asked, shaken out of his reverie by a sudden anxiety. He hadn't even known that was a thing he needed to worry about.

"Not when the Roads are down," the shopkeeper said with a wink, to Vex's relief. "Take your time and experiment. It may take you weeks to understand what glyphs are like, and even longer to get your first slivers. But if you truly love magic, you will find your path, just like I did. And do not worry if it does not work for you! Not all mages use magelights. I certainly do not, as you know."

"I'm not sure we have *weeks*," Sev commented, and Vex almost jumped again, having forgotten that Sev and Misa were there at all. He didn't even know when they'd entered the shop.

"If you are from the Roads, then I should let you know that time does not work the same way once you cross the boundary," the shopkeeper said helpfully. "You will have plenty of time to do whatever you came here to do . . . Well. I suppose with most of the Roads not operational and one barely functional, that time displacement is less of a guarantee . . . But that particular function remains, to the best of my knowledge."

"What do you mean, *barely functional*?" Misa asked, looking up from the small statuette of a cat she'd been peering at.

"The remaining Road only works some of the time," the shopkeeper said with a small shrug. "It is inconsistent and sometimes deposits visitors far away from their intended destination. Sometimes, it leaves those walking it as . . . mana-ghosts, shall we say. It is what happens when we cannot be properly translated into the lands beyond the Roads, and can only exist as manaforms until they return."

"What?" Misa asked. "Is that going to happen to us?"

"You are here, are you not?" the shopkeeper said with a light chuckle. "You can be translated as much as you need to be. So no, it will not. I would not worry overmuch; those that are mistranslated often make their way back, soon enough."

"I guess that explains the raids?" Sev said, uncertain. The shopkeeper cocked their head in curiosity.

"What are these . . . raids . . . you mention?"

"We came here from a town called Fendal," Sev explained, exchanging glances with the rest of the party briefly. Vex shook his head; he didn't have a problem with explaining to the shopkeeper what they were doing there. "They had complaints about their stores being raided . . . amongst other things. We were investigating the problem when we ended up here."

"Hm," the shopkeeper said. "I believe we have had similar issues. Perhaps it's best you find our mages; they will be able to tell you more. The city hall is near the center of the city, if you are in need of directions."

"Thank you," Sev said with a slight bow of his head, and he glanced at Vex. "You ready to get going?"

"Yeah," Vex said, then glanced at the shopkeeper. "Thank you for the magelight," he said, as sincerely as he could manage. He clutched it tightly, deciding it was now his most precious possession. "And for all the advice about magic."

"Practice your glyphs diligently," the shopkeeper said with a wink.

"I will." Vex mustered up the most diligent nod he could.

Sev led the way out of the store, with Vex the last to emerge; he kept looking back longingly into the store, spotting a few magical artifacts he wished he could afford to purchase for later study. Once he had earned a few slivers, he told himself—though he was quickly distracted by Sev talking.

"The time-displacement thing," Sev said. "It feels a little . . . convenient, doesn't it?"

"I'm not complaining," Misa said with a shrug.

"There was a time displacement in <**The Village's Last Defense**> as well," Derivan said. "Perhaps it is simply another symptom of the bonus room leaking out?"

"The shopkeeper mentioned they're having similar problems to the raids here, too," Sev said thoughtfully. "But the way they explained it didn't really feel the same . . ."

"Oh!" Vex realized, and when everyone looked at him, he blinked, scratching his frills in embarrassment. "Um. I just realized I forgot to ask for their name. I'm gonna go ask real quick."

Vex ran back over to the door and poked his head into the store; the chimes over his head rang again as he pushed open the door, and the shopkeeper raised a single fluffy brow at him. It was really so ridiculously fluffy. "Back again already?"

"I forgot to ask for your name," Vex said, embarrassed. "You helped me. I want to at least know your name. I'm Vex."

"Ah, of course," the shopkeeper said with a chuckle. "You may call me Anyati."

CHAPTER 15

FRIENDSHIP

Vex's tail coiled tight as he walked, a symptom of his nervousness.

"You said their name is . . . the same as the innkeeper in Fendal's?" Sev frowned.

"It might not mean anything," Vex offered hopefully, though he didn't really feel like that was true. "It probably doesn't mean anything, even! Two people end up with the same names all the time."

"I think we have the experience now to say that it's *probably* dungeon fuckery." Misa scowled. "Or system fuckery. Or both."

"Maybe," Sev hedged. "*Convenient events* aren't uncommon in dungeons, especially in bonus rooms. It's a part of the narrative the room is trying to establish, usually. The first shop you wander into happening to be a shop with a shopkeeper that just gives you the tools you need to learn magic for free . . . That's about par for the course, I think. The name thing is weird, though; dungeons are usually more creative." Sev glanced to Derivan. "Any thoughts there?"

"I do not know," Derivan said with a light shrug of his shoulders. Vex relaxed a bit, looking at him; if Derivan didn't seem too concerned, then maybe he didn't have to worry too much, either. "It is best we speak to the mages that the shopkeeper spoke of, however. Perhaps they have made progress in understanding the problem."

"I just worry that it's my fault," Vex said softly; he saw Derivan reach for him, and felt an armored hand pet the back of his head, in a soothing, gentle movement. He leaned into the touch, allowing the sensation to settle him.

Derivan knelt in front of him then, and Vex froze, for they were so close he would have been able to feel the armor's breath, had he needed to breathe at all.

"It is not," Derivan told him firmly. "You spoke to Noram and told him that it was not his fault for opening the door. The same applies to you. It is perhaps not even the system's fault, for the system has been failing around us ever since that dungeon first appeared. Do not spend your time worrying about who to blame. There is new magic here to be discovered, and a solution to be found; is this not the exact sort of opportunity you wished to have when you first began your journey?"

Vex blinked. "That . . . was the most you've said in a while, I think," Vex said with a slight chuckle, trying to ignore the way the intensity of Derivan's eyes, the *certainty* in them, made him feel. ". . . It is, yes. Thank you."

"You should do speeches more often." Misa whistled.

"That was barely a speech," Derivan said, shaking his head as he stood back up, and Misa just grinned at him.

Vex did feel better about it all, though.

Not completely. But better.

The party made their way through the city, leaving the more worn-down outskirts behind; the city grew stranger and more sophisticated as they made their way farther in, with the architecture getting progressively more fantastical in a way that hadn't been visible as they'd made their way down the path into the crater.

They knew already that the river of mana above split off into tiny, smaller streams; now they could see that it filtered down through the sky and fell onto the homes and shops like slow-falling rain. Some buildings seemed to have special, purpose-built filters to capture this rain, little funnel-like structures built of magic that drew mana in like some sort of sinkhole; others were built to allow the magic to flow off of them in patterns, the almost-liquid energy etching glyphs deeper wherever it went.

Vex was *fascinated*. Here was a city built like the city of his dreams. Elyra had mana crystals everywhere, albeit enchanted and protected, built to empower all the various devices they had created to support daily life. But this? This was a city that was built to live in synergy with the mana—there was no taking here. They accepted what the mana was willing to offer and no more. He wondered briefly if something similar would be possible for Elyra, in time, but . . .

. . . the system seemed to make that impossible. Mana never gathered in this abundance, not even in the wildest or emptiest places he'd managed to find.

"Excuse me," Sev was saying, and Vex blinked himself back to paying attention. "Could you tell us where the city hall is? We've been told that's where the mages are."

"Of course," the woman he spoke to replied—unlike many of the other creatures down here, she seemed to be almost entirely human, save for some unearthly etherealness about her. She inclined her head closer toward the center of the crater. "Just look for the tallest building there. You can't miss it, really. The city hall functions as a mage tower."

Well, that explained the massive building stretching up high enough to reach the mana river.

The odd thing was that the building simply hadn't been visible until they'd known about it being a tower—and now that they did, it was impossibly obvious. Some more obfuscation magic, perhaps? Vex was beginning to think he needed to put more of a focus toward learning magic like that; the privacy it would give him was unparalleled.

"Thank you," Sev said, and the woman gave him a gracious nod before walking away.

"*City hall* seems like a weird name for something that's a big fuckoff tower," Misa remarked, staring up at the tower. Sev and Vex both snorted out a laugh, and Derivan chuckled in amusement.

"Maybe it's a translation thing?" Sev offered. "It *is* weird that they speak the same language we do."

"It's not that uncommon in dungeons, though," Vex pointed out. "There's almost never a language barrier in a bonus room, unless that barrier is part of a challenge the dungeon intends, or something."

"I still think it should just be called a big fuckoff tower," Misa said.

"A naming scheme common to mortals, I am sure," Derivan said, amused. "Perhaps they wish to be more welcoming to visitors. They have mentioned that there are usually many more Roads open than this one; I am sure they are used to strangers. It would make sense, then, to name the tower something its visitors would know to look for."

"And yet it doesn't even show up until you know it's a tower," Misa said with a dramatic sigh. "Classic wizards. And when did you start calling us mortals? Did Vex show you a weird book?"

"I sometimes choose my own books, I will have you know," Derivan answered.

"Hey," Vex said at the same time, glaring at Misa in a mock huff, and she smirked at him.

"You booby-trapped your sketchbooks. You absolutely fall into the same trap of doing unnecessarily complicated shit."

"I do not," Vex grumbled, though there was absolutely no heat to it.

"Don't worry," Sev said with a grin. "We'll build you a tower one day and let you cast whatever spells you want on it. Maybe some decorative lightning? That would be pretty cool."

"I will help," Derivan said, suddenly perfectly serious, and Vex buried his snout in his hands.

". . . I want a wizard's tower so badly now."

"But you want to adventure with us more, right?" Misa grinned at him, elbowing him in the side. Vex pretended to frown at her for a moment more before he broke into a smile of his own.

"Maybe I'll just have to put *legs* on the tower. I'll even give you all your own rooms."

"Now you're talking," Sev snickered.

"I'm not sure Derivan needs his own room," Misa said, teasing. "Maybe he can share with you?"

Vex felt his face warming up with a blush beneath his scales, but he kept up an appearance of haughty dignity, though he could practically feel Derivan's curious gaze piercing into him.

"I would not mind," Derivan offered, perfectly seriously. And then, a hint of a joke: "Though I am a bit concerned for my safety. The last time I touched one of his notebooks . . ."

Both Misa and Sev burst into laughter, and Vex tried very hard to make sounds that were more coherent than vague grumbles—but for all that he protested, he felt a small warmth growing in him. That small ember of his remaining worries didn't go away, exactly, but it was shielded from him by a reminder.

No matter what this "bonus room" was doing or what was happening with the system, it wasn't a problem he had to solve alone—and as they joked and bantered all the way to the doorstep of the tower, he found himself smiling.

Sometimes, he let himself forget that things weren't the same as they had been with his family in Elyra. Sometimes, he felt that he had to tackle his problems alone, to prove himself and hold himself to some invisible standard he could never quite reach.

But not here. Not now. *Not anymore.*

Vex stepped into the tower after Sev and Misa, with Derivan right at his back.

Vex hummed.

The city hall—and it felt strange calling it a city hall, when Misa was right, and it was indeed just a "big fuckoff tower"—was about exactly what they expected on the inside, which meant that it looked nothing like a city hall at all. There *was* what seemed to be a makeshift desk made of piled-up stones and stacked with official-looking paperwork, and that was the only thing that made it city hall-like at all.

The rest was . . .

Well, there was what Vex was pretty sure was an otter sleeping on the desk, for one thing. Planeshifted Earth animals weren't unheard of, but this was particularly strange, considering it was in a bonus room—or at the very least a mockery of one. For another, magic swirled all around in gleaming patterns that were visible to the naked eye; the walls were painted with complex glyphs that were almost complete paintings in and of themselves.

And right at the side of the tower were stairs. A long, frankly unsafe-looking series of wooden planks leading up to the upper levels of the tower.

". . . I guess we climb?" Vex said, uncertain. Sev blinked, looking around the tower for anything else.

"Might as well," he said. "I don't see a bell we can ring or anything."

He was the first up the stairs, but he'd barely taken a few steps before a low, gruff voice stopped them. "Hey!" it said. "Where do you think you're going?"

Vex glanced back. "Um," he said. He didn't see anyone there. Some sort of [**Invisibility**] spell? But he should have seen the traces in the mana, if someone was invisible. "We're going to find the mages. We were told there are problems here, and we wanted to see if we could help. And we wanted to get some help in turn."

He had no idea why he was speaking for the group. This was Sev's thing! But the cleric seemed more than content to allow him to speak, and he'd already started talking, so he'd sort of trapped himself in this position.

"Want to see if you can help, huh?" the voice scoffed, and Vex peered closer, trying to figure out who was speaking—

. . . It was the otter, wasn't it.

The otter stood up, folded his little arms, and glared a little glare. "The upper floors are off limits. If you want to petition for an audience, you need to do it here, with me."

"We didn't know that," Vex said, a little helplessly. He glanced to Sev for help, and the human seemed to finally take pity on him.

"We apologize if we were rude," Sev said. "We're pretty new here, and we're still getting used to everything. We came here from the Roads—the town we're helping is being raided, and according to them, they're being raided by goblins . . . but the story is very inconsistent. We were told you might have more information."

The otter narrowed his eyes in a way that looked remarkably human. "We *might* know something," he said. "But you should tell us what *you* know first, and then we'll tell you what we know."

Sev stared at him. "You don't know anything, do you."

"Of course we do!" The otter puffed out his chest, which was a bit of an absurd look for an otter. It mostly ended up looking cute. Vex had no idea how to process any of this.

"We're wasting our time here, guys," Sev said, sighing dramatically. "Let's go. We'll find an inn or something and investigate this by ourselves. I'm sure having one of the *best wizards in Elyra* on our team will help."

"Sev!" Vex complained. Then he paused. "Actually, no, you can keep going."

The cleric just snickered at him, choosing not to go on any further; Derivan spoke up instead. "Sev is correct," he said. "I am sure this will only take us a day or two—"

"A day or two!" the otter exploded. "It took us weeks just to narrow down the possibilities, and we still have almost nothing to show for it! You're not going to do it in a day or two!"

Sev grinned.

The otter face-palmed.

"Fuck," he said.

CHAPTER 16

AN OTTERLY FASCINATING HISTORY LESSON

"This is everything we know," the being that was apparently both an otter and a mage said.

His name was Noram, because of course it was. Vex had exchanged worried glances with the rest of his friends when the mage finally introduced himself, but none of them had said anything. They needed a better picture of what was happening first.

Otter-Noram led them up to the second floor of the tower, where two other mages were seated around a glyph painted on the floor. Mana swirled around both of them, coalescing into an orb at the center that glowed and shifted; a dozen dark branches spiraled off that orb, each one fading into nothing. Among them was a single dark-blue branch—a remarkably familiar shade of blue, actually. That branch, and only that branch, was connected to a small, tight spiral of white.

"It's a visualization of the Roads," the otter explained. He looked at them, his gaze flicking somewhat furtively over the darkened branches, like he was worried. "Those are the dead Roads. Nothing we've tried has brought them back. The one remaining Road, the one you came from—it looks like it's dying. The white node over there is your town and everything surrounding it. Fendal."

For a moment, the five of them stared in silence at the map of the Roads. The other two mages didn't say a word. They were each deep in concentration, though Vex could make out very little else about them; everything else was obscured by their robes.

"I'm still not sure I get what exactly the Roads are," Misa said with a frown. "They don't just teleport people, right? We noticed spatial compression magic, so I thought maybe this whole place was just *really* far underground.

But we've been told something about the Roads also . . . 'translating' people? Whatever that means."

Noram grimaced slightly. "Yes. Well. The Roads don't just reach through space," he said. "I suppose it's a bit of an open secret. That spatial compression is a subcomponent of a deeper magic at work. But explaining all of that is . . . a deeper lesson on the history of our world than I want to get into."

"We have time." Misa crossed her arms. "We were also told time runs differently here."

Noram sighed.

"I'll give you a quick summary," he said. He gestured to the map of the Roads again. "Or as quick as I can make it. Mana is, quite literally, the life force of this world; it empowers nearly everything we do. It might not be the same where you're from—but a couple hundred years ago, it started acting erratically. Almost dangerously.

"Some places in the world got completely blocked off from us. It was slow, at first—so slow, we barely even realized what was happening. Maybe there was some small corner of the kitchen you wouldn't be able to teleport into, or your cabinet might be smaller than it was supposed to be. Nothing big. Nothing insidious. Not enough for people to talk about, to realize it was a pattern. Most of us thought it was just a problem with our magic or some small mistake we made when casting.

"Then the spells we used to travel far and wide stopped working properly. Those broken spaces got larger. The mana began to physically herd us into groups, away from our old cities and capitals; every time we tried to teleport or use any movement-based spell, it moved us somewhere else instead. Anyone who didn't use those spells it forced out, through some application of forced teleportation or flight, and then it sealed those places off completely so we couldn't go back.

"We didn't know what to do. But we noticed that anyone living underground didn't seem as affected, so we eventually decided to *dig*; we built underground cities and moved there as best we could. The mana didn't stop us—if anything, it seemed stronger there. It *wanted* us underground, although we didn't know why."

Otter-Noram frowned, as if trying to find the right words. "We tried to remember what the world was like. We told stories of it: what the sun looked like, what the seasons looked like. We had spells to keep those memories perfectly preserved. We told stories of the seasons and the weather . . .

"And then we just . . . forgot." The otter shook his head and clenched his tiny fists. "After a hundred years. Don't know why it happened. Don't know how. Half the spells we had banked to remember were just fucking *gone*, just like that. So we tried to leave again and see if we could get back what we lost, and we found that we could access the surface again.

"But nothing was the same.

"We're not *sure*, because of how much we lost. But the places we could go back to didn't feel right. Some of them were outright hostile. The rules didn't make sense anymore. You needed magic just to stay attached to the ground in some places. In others, the wind scoured your fur, or the grass would try to climb into your limbs, or the very air would fracture and detonate within your lungs.

"It was a disaster. Safer to stay isolated within our cities, we decided. Whatever had happened to the surface, it wasn't worth it.

"And then the mana gifted us the Roads." Here, Noram hesitated. "They're something we call deep magic. A magic we don't fully understand, because it works based off none of the rules we know, and simply off the will of the mana. When we go through the Roads, we don't need extra magic just to keep ourselves alive. If possible, we're adapted to fit. Or we just . . . become mana-ghosts. Able to survive and return, though it's hard to interact with the world unless we're *very* experienced.

"The destinations of the Roads always change. Sometimes they bring us to new places, and sometimes they bring us to other cities like our own, underground cities or kingdoms built in the aftermath of whatever the mana did to the surface.

"And then, a few weeks ago, our Roads all simultaneously just . . . died. And the mana is acting strangely, even here."

Otter-Noram sighed. He seemed suddenly exhausted just from telling the story, or perhaps from reliving that history; he seated himself on a small chair that had been hiding in a corner of the room, slumped backward on it, and stared at the four adventurers.

"That's my part of the bargain," he said. "That's almost everything I know. We've had some disappearances in our local supplies—mana slivers keep going missing, and we keep a store of that for emergency ritual magics we need to perform. We don't have any leads on that. We keep an eye on those, and they just disappear. Right in front of our eyes. So if you have *any* idea what's going on, I'd really love to know, because so far none of our magic has come up with anything."

Vex had so many things he wanted to say. So many questions, even. But he bit his tongue—now wasn't the right time for those questions, and he wasn't sure if there *was* a right time for those questions. This version of Noram seemed to have lived for a very, very long time, and Vex had so many questions about that point alone, yet...

He seemed so *tired*.

Sev and Misa looked like they were trying to figure out what to say too, slowly soaking in what Noram had explained to them. Derivan was watching him carefully. From what Vex could tell, he was on the verge of saying something, and was trying to decide whether or not he should.

He chose to speak. "If I may ask," the armor said slowly. "When you told us your story, your gaze was more frequently directed at Vex and me. Why is that?"

"What?" the otter mage frowned, evidently not expecting that question. "...I don't know. You two felt more familiar, I guess."

A small piece of the puzzle. Vex's heart beat hard; this place was connected to Fendal in more ways than just through the Roads, if that hadn't been obvious already. This was just the only evidence they had that the connection was *active*. That it was continuing, even now.

"I think," Sev said slowly. He'd evidently come to the same conclusion. "That we're going to need some time to discuss everything we've just learned."

The otter scoffed. "That was a lot, was it?" he said, his words holding a small bite of bitter sarcasm.

"I wasn't saying I wouldn't share," Sev said with a sigh. "It's just that what you told us is—it's a *lot*? And I don't want to give you the wrong information based on just guesses. We need to talk and figure out what we *know* and what's just a guess.

"But I will tell you what we do know for certain," Sev added when Noram opened his mouth to protest, and the otter clamped his mouth shut again. He watched Sev in a mixture of suspicion and anticipation. "We know that Fendal's been experiencing what they call goblin raids, and that those words do not accurately reflect what is happening in Fendal. We know that they've had raids on their mana crystal stores, which parallels what's been happening to your mana slivers. We know that a dungeon is involved."

"What's a dungeon?" Noram frowned. "I know about two kinds of dungeons, and I'm pretty sure you're not talking about either of them."

Sev coughed. "No," he said. "It's—complicated."

And that, of course, led to a long conversation about the nature of the system, of dungeons, and how they affected the world—or the slice of reality that the Road connected to. By the end of it, Otter-Noram was looking about as confused and lost as Vex was sure he had looked at the end of the little history lesson the otter had given.

"It doesn't sound like our Road is just connected to a small slice anymore," Noram said, looking troubled. "Maybe that's why all the other Roads are dead? And I don't understand how this is related to *us*."

I don't think that's why your Roads are dead, Vex wanted to say, but he kept his mouth shut and glanced at the others instead—Sev caught his look and shook his head just slightly. It was one of the things he wanted to discuss.

"I'm assuming you four need a room here?" the otter suddenly asked them, and Vex blinked at him. "There's an inn nearby. The Rising."

"The...Rising?" Sev sounded confused; Vex was busy thinking about how this was a strange parallel to what happened with Gensen. Noram shrugged his little shoulders and hopped off his chair.

"I didn't name it," he said. "I'll get you some slivers so you can pay for a room there. I don't know how long you'll be staying, but if you want to stay any longer than a night, I suggest you find some odd jobs. The local alchemists are always needing test subjects. And there are sometimes monsters on the outskirts, if combat is more your thing."

"Oh, good," Sev said faintly. "For a moment I thought you were going to give us a key to a room at the inn."

"Why would I have keys to the inn here?" Noram stared at Sev. "Do things work that differently in Fendal?"

"Believe me," Sev muttered, "I wish I knew."

—⚏—

This time, the inn wasn't completely empty when they arrived—though it wasn't bustling and full, either. Vex looked around fascinated at all the little trinkets used to decorate while Sev spoke briefly to the innkeeper, who was a being of ethereal flame that sounded like a tired old man. *His* name, apparently, was Nesnub.

If nothing else, not everyone they were meeting was someone they had already met in Fendal.

A quick exchange and five slivers netted them a room, one that was much smaller than the one they had in Fendal, admittedly. But going back and forth through the Road seemed like too much of a hassle and was risky besides, so Sev had figured they would have to settle.

"I mean," Sev said, looking around the room. "It's *kinda* fancier than I was expecting."

Vex looked around as well. For all that it was a small room, it was rather exceptionally cozy; small glyphs decorated the walls, radiating both light and a sort of comforting warmth. Even the room seemed to be arranged like two wings spreading out: two beds in the corners, and one in a little alcove in the middle.

"I want that one," Vex said, pointing to the alcove. "Please?"

"Sure," Sev said with a chuckle.

"I don't mind." Misa shrugged.

"I do not need a bed," Derivan said. Vex grinned happily at getting his own little alcove but was quickly distracted by Sev clapping once.

"But first," Sev said, "let's talk about what's going on."

CHAPTER 17

THEORYCRAFTING

"There was a lot there to digest," Vex said with a slight frown. He'd been thinking about what the otter version of Noram had told them, and he was churning with ideas. He just hadn't put them all together yet.

"The names are one thing, but I think what stood out to me is *when* he said all of that started. He didn't give us an exact timeframe ... but a few hundred years is about as long as we know the System existed." Vex's brows furrowed in consideration. "That's about as far as Elyra's historical knowledge extends, too. Anything further back is ... vague."

"Infolocked," Sev supplied, and Vex nodded.

"Probably," he agreed. "But it all lines up too well. Which means there's gotta be something we can figure out about what's happening based on what's *different* about our two histories."

"If we assume that there's a relationship at all between their world and ours," Misa said. "We don't know that for sure. The coincidence might be a dungeonfuck; maybe it can only create history as far back as the system exists."

"A ... what?" Vex stared at her. Misa shrugged.

"I figured we need a term for when dungeons do the thing," she said. "Planeshifters have *mindfuck*, right? Dungeonfuck. Same thing."

"I do not feel like that is the same thing," Derivan commented.

"Well, *I'm* using it." Misa grinned, seemingly satisfied with herself. Sev rolled his eyes but smiled.

"The bonus rooms all seem to hide clues, though," the cleric said after a moment. "The way Onyx talked about it, and the [**Look Up**] skill ... We don't even know what red means in the context of the system. But it looks like Onyx—and maybe some other gods—manipulated that dungeon into forming, somehow."

"If they did, then some warning would've been nice," Misa said, crossing her arms and leaning back in her chair. "But that might explain the red. System can't figure out what it is because it's not within the scope of the system."

"Or it's been purged from the system," Sev said. "Though if that was it, then the anchor would be red, too, so . . . yeah, maybe it's that. Red is outside the system."

"We do not know much about the Administrators yet," Derivan commented. "Nor of the foe that struck at the orb and almost killed the delve team, back in the dungeon. But perhaps red is an artifact of Administrator access, or what happens when someone that is not an Administrator attempts to modify the system."

"Multiple groups trying to modify the system would explain all the errors," Sev grumbled.

"I'm worried about where that arrow-fucker went," Misa said with a scowl. "But we've had no news on that so far. Nothing from Elyra or Anderstahl."

"What did he look like?" Vex asked suddenly, a memory flashing into his mind—the man he'd seen in the door-based dungeon inside the copy of their room, *holding a crossbow*, disappearing into the wall exactly like Misa had said. "I— Shit, I can't make illusions here. Um. I think I saw him. When I was investigating the door dungeon with Derivan."

"What?" the question came from both Misa and Derivan simultaneously.

"I did not see him," Derivan said, frowning.

"Why didn't you tell us?" Misa asked.

"I didn't know! And he disappeared so fast, I thought it was my imagination . . ." Vex wilted a bit. "I saw him for a second inside that copy of our room in the dungeon, Deri. Then he vanished."

"Talk about fucking ominous," Misa said, tapping her fingers on her chair. "You think he's been messing with us?"

"Almost certainly," Derivan said. The armor's eyes glowed with a sort of subdued caution and worry, and Vex realized that Derivan was feeling guilty about *him*—about not spotting the danger when he did.

"But I don't think he's related . . . *directly* . . . to this," Vex added. The image came to his mind again, sharply focused and fully detailed. "He looked— I dunno; he looked more like he wanted to remind us he was there. Like this is a game to him. Or like he wanted to mess with us specifically."

"The fuck's that guy's problem?" Misa grumbled.

"We can't assume he's not related, but we also can't do anything about it if he's here," Sev said. The cleric glanced around the room once, as if paranoid, and then coughed and cast a [**Holy Ward**]. ". . . I'll do that just in case.

But we need to get back to talking about the differences between this city and Fendal.

"Let's assume the two places are related. The people in Fendal were behaving strangely, and that's probably related to the bonus room, but we're missing a connection somewhere. The people I met while interviewing felt . . . one-note?" Sev frowned a bit. "They kept me held up in their conversations, but they didn't share any personal history, exactly. I don't know."

"It was convenient for Gensen to have the key ready for us," Derivan commented. "And the mana was behaving strangely there, too."

"There's a connection between the mana and how people are behaving," Vex muttered to himself. "We know that the Roads 'translate' people when they go through it, so we know it's a possibility that some people went through the Roads and ended up being . . . what, ghosts in the mana?"

"That was how it was described," Derivan said. "Though it seems vague."

"It doesn't mean much, because we don't know what mana-ghosts can do," Vex said, shaking his head.

"Let's put that aside for now," Sev said. "What do we *know*?"

"We know that the histories of the two worlds diverged around the time the system came into the picture," Misa said. "Or, well, we don't know that for sure, but that's what we're assuming for now. If we take that at face value, then the mana is acting to solve some problem, the same way the system is presumably here to solve some problem for us."

"That's a good start," Sev nodded. "We can assume that the mana and the system are both acting to solve a problem. I'm also going to assume that problem is what resulted in the stars going missing."

"Right," Vex said. "Which is . . . a little terrifying. But okay, both worlds have survived for a few hundred years; everything probably isn't going to collapse in the next few months."

"But we do know that the system is decaying," Derivan pointed out. "The system is more unstable today than it was before. And Misa's reality anchor is decaying, too; that means that the other reality anchors are probably decaying, even if the dungeons they are in are stabilizing them in some way."

Misa sat up straight. "Do you think that's what dungeons are doing?" she asked. "Stabilizing the anchors?"

"I assumed the anchors were the ones stabilizing and influencing the dungeon," Sev said with a frown. "But if you're right, and the dungeons are the ones stabilizing the anchors . . ."

"Oh," Derivan said. He blinked once, looked around a little helplessly, and then did the most awkward shrug Vex had ever seen the armor attempt. "Perhaps I should have shared that thought earlier?"

Sev groaned. "Derivan . . ." he started, and then he shook his head and sighed. "You're right, though. It fits with what we know. Dungeon breaks occur if the dungeons are not delved frequently enough and reality anchors decay over time."

"This flips things around," Vex agreed. "If the dungeons are supporting the anchors and not the other way around, then the anchors must have another function. It . . . I wanna say it feels like magic did something similar here? But it's almost the inverse. Dungeons are hostile to us, and the rest of the world is safe; here, their cities are *like* dungeons, even if they're huge, and the rest of the world is hostile." Vex frowned, leaning forward to stare at the hardwood floor as if he could divine something from the patterns within. "There's a connection I'm missing."

"If dungeons require people to delve them to maintain whatever they are doing," Derivan said, "what does the mana require here, to open up new Roads?"

"Slivers," Vex said, snapping his fingers. "I mean, this is all just speculation. But these mana slivers seem to occupy the same space as mana crystals do in the system. We have crystals being stolen from Fendal, and slivers disappearing here . . ."

He picked up a sliver, examining it critically. "It doesn't really look like a mana crystal, though."

"Different methods to solve the same problem, I guess?" Sev said, peering over at the sliver Vex was holding.

"Except it doesn't quite solve the problem, whatever the problem is," Vex said. He tucked the mana sliver back into his tailpouch. "And neither does the system."

"Fuuuuuck," Misa commented. She thought about this for a moment while Vex stared at her, wondering if her only comment was going to be a long, drawn-out *fuck*. She nodded to herself, as if satisfied, then repeated herself. "Fuck," she said, eloquently.

"Something you want to tell us, Misa?" Sev asked, raising an eyebrow and hiding the laughter in his voice.

"I need a drink if we're going to have this conversation," Misa declared. "I feel like I'm getting hung over already, and if I'm going to have a headache I might as well feel *good* about it."

"Fair enough. You *could* probably get one downstairs." Sev said, glancing in the direction of the door. Vex followed his gaze, briefly worried they'd see yet another parallel to Fendal and that all the inn's residents would just suddenly disappear.

They did not. The noise and laughter from below continued.

"Anyone else want one?" Misa asked, raising a brow at the rest of the group. Most of them didn't really drink. Vex shook his head, and Sev shrugged before he indicated that he'd take *one* glass of whatever they had available. Misa nodded and disappeared down the stairs a moment later.

"You do not want a drink?" Derivan asked, glancing at Vex. Vex made a face.

"No. Alcohol tastes like shit," he said, sticking his tongue out petulantly. Derivan's gaze focused briefly on his tongue, and Vex drew it back into his mouth, embarrassed.

"You licked me, you know," Derivan said. "The last time you were drunk."

"I did *what*?" Vex half-yelled, nearly tipping over backward in his chair; halfway through, the yell turned into a squeak, and the only reason he didn't tumble was because Derivan caught him. Sev, sitting opposite the both of them, started laughing hysterically.

Derivan ignored Sev and gave Vex an alarmingly serious nod.

"You licked me," the armor said. "And then you accused me of being the one to do it, because my armor happened to be where your tongue was."

"Oh by the gods." Vex buried his face in his hands.

"Are you—are you saying you want Vex to get drunk again?" Sev asked, still chortling and barely holding back the mirth in his voice. "And Vex, I cannot believe you licked him without even taking him out on a date!"

"What is a date?" Derivan asked.

"I am never getting drunk again," Vex said, his voice muffled by his hands. "I swear off alcohol. Forever."

"I would not want him to get drunk if he did not want to," Derivan said seriously. There was not a hint of mirth in his voice, but Vex thought he saw the slightest glimpse of fond amusement in his eyes. "But it was a good memory, to see you relaxed. I cherish it."

Sev grinned at his friend. "You hear that, Vex?"

"What I'm hearing is that I need to develop a [Sink into Floor] spell," Vex grumbled.

The three of them lapsed into a comfortable silence for a little while, though Vex felt the many unspoken words still floating about the room. He remembered the little promise he'd made to himself to talk to Derivan...

Sev was watching the both of them too, a small smile on his face. Vex wondered if the cleric would mind if he went to him for advice. Probably not?

Maybe he would do that first, talk to Sev and see what he thought, and then go to Derivan and just ... tell him.

That might work.

Really, he just needed a way to deal with all his nerves.

Misa swung the door while Vex was musing, carrying—of all things—a *barrel* on a shoulder, and two empty tankards. "I got the good stuff!" she said, and then she blinked at Sev. "Why are you smiling like an idiot?"

"It's just those two again," Sev said, gesturing at Vex and Derivan. Derivan tilted his head curiously, and Misa groaned.

"I just went down to get some beer," she said. "You're telling me I fuckin' missed it?"

"You didn't miss anything," Sev said, to Vex's relief—though that relief was immediately cut short when he continued. "Derivan was just telling us about how Vex licked him when he was drunk."

"You *what*?" Misa rounded on Vex, looking delighted. "You didn't tell us about this."

"I didn't *remember*," Vex protested. "And Derivan only told me about it just now!"

"I cherish the memory," Derivan repeated, looking rather pleased with himself, and Misa snorted a laugh before slamming the barrel down onto the table and slumping back into her seat.

"I leave for *five minutes*," she said with a grin and a shake of her head.

Vex, from his position with his face buried in his hands and his snout pressing against the table, let out a muffled "Let's please change the topic back to what we were talking about before."

Sev and Misa exchanged glances and to Vex's relief apparently unanimously decided to stop teasing him.

"All right, well—we only know an overview of their history here," Misa said, getting right to business, though she filled her tankard from the barrel as she spoke. Sev did the same, but he only filled it halfway, and made a bit of a face as he drank. "I don't think that's enough to make any assumptions about what the mana did or is doing for them. I think we can make a reasonably educated guess that the mana and the system are both working to solve "A Problem." Capital letters. We just don't know what that problem is."

"We know a little bit about it," Vex said. "We know it's probably linked to the stars disappearing and getting conceptually erased on top of that."

"It is worrying," Derivan said. "If there are other things being erased, and we do not yet know..."

"There are," Sev said. "The gods, for example."

"We need to know how much time we have," Misa said with a sigh.

"Let's start with what's happening here," Sev said. "How do we think the bonus room is affecting Fendal? The obvious conclusion is that there are some pranksters that were mistranslated by the Roads and are using the opportunity to steal mana crystals."

"But that doesn't fit," he added after a moment, shaking his head. "It doesn't explain the slivers going missing *here*. Or the way Gensen and the villagers were acting."

"The way the villagers act reminds me of the stories I heard of other adventurers going into 'bonus rooms' that were essentially historical reenactments," Vex said thoughtfully. He glanced at Misa. "It's the reason what you did with your family hasn't been done before. I think I mentioned it then. When 'people' are generated by a bonus room, they don't act . . . complete? They feel like they're following scripts."

"Noram did not feel like he was following a script," Derivan said.

"He didn't," Vex agreed. "That's not a complete theory either. And everyone *here* has felt pretty real, from Anyati-the-shopkeeper to Noram-the-otter . . ."

"Which is worrying," Misa said. "Because if we take that at face value, then everyone *here* is real and the bonus room is Fendal."

Vex froze. Sev stopped drinking mid-sip and put his tankard down slowly. Derivan stared.

"Oh," Misa said, realizing what she'd just said, and then she narrowed her eyes. "But that's not . . . Oh, *shit*."

CHAPTER 18

PLAN OF ACTION

Vex stared up at Misa as she paced, vaguely worried that she was going to wear a hole in the floor or that their neighbors would send them a noise complaint.

"This makes too much sense," Misa said. "I mean, it's not complete, obviously, but... Anyati's inn not having anyone in it until we were there? Gensen just conveniently having keys for us in the town hall, of all things? The goblin raids sound exactly like the sort of challenge you'd get if you were in a bonus room, and it explains why everyone saw it differently. It explains why my mom said Fendal wasn't all there! Nothing in Fendal was *real*."

"It's not a perfect theory," Vex countered, mostly because he felt obligated to try to make a defense against the somewhat-terrifying idea that Fendal had somehow switched places with the dungeon-generated bonus room, at least conceptually. "And if it *were*, it would mean that the system recognizes Fendal as the bonus room and this place as the real-world equivalent. But we still don't know why that is."

"But if *this* place is real..." Misa muttered, then finally flopped back onto her seat, to Vex's relief. Watching her pace around had been making him nervous.

Kind of like how your brother paces around, a small, traitorous voice whispered to him; a brief flash of a memory hit him, the sensation of being bound—

"What if it is not the place that is real, but the people?" Derivan asked, interrupting Vex's thoughts, much to the lizardkin's relief. "Or what if realness, as it were, is a property that can be transferred?"

"That's fucking terrifying to think about," Misa said.

"But it might be true," Vex said, latching on to the idea. "It's not just what you said. Food didn't fill Noram until we were around. A lot of the species hanging around in Fendal just don't *exist* in Obreve in that kind of abundance. There were kobolds there—that should have been a sign."

"The kobolds were cute, though," Sev said.

"Okay, yes, they were cute." Vex paused, slightly thrown off his train of thought. "The problem is just . . . we don't have a real way to test any of this. We've come up with a few theories that explain what's happening, but that doesn't give us a solution."

"Okay," Sev said. "We need a way to test our theories, then."

"My mom's still back in Fendal with the two guards I summoned," Misa said. "We could ask them to keep track of things there while we investigate what's going on here. Noram's there too, so he can confirm if he knows anything about this . . . other version of Noram."

"About the food," Derivan said. "Why did food only fill him when we were around? We do not possess some quality that makes things more real."

"We do," Sev said. Vex blinked and stared at him, and then it clicked in his head.

"The reality anchor?" he asked. Sev nodded at him, then glanced at Misa.

"That's . . . true," Misa said slowly. "You think the reality anchor is affecting things right now?"

"You can check," Sev said. "How's the integrity on it?"

Misa frowned and seemed to gaze into the air for a moment. Then she froze slightly, mouthing some words to herself; she shook her head.

". . . Five months, three days left." Misa wasn't angry, exactly, or she didn't seem that way to Vex—but part of her seemed to deflate. "The degradation rate still says *medium*, but it's definitely lost a couple days more than it should have, and there's another warning about additional stress being put on the anchor. Fuck. I should've checked this earlier."

"Is it possible it's just because your mom's still summoned?" Vex asked. "When did you last check it?"

"I've checked the anchor notification before, during a summon, and there wasn't any notice about an extra drain," Misa said, shaking her head. She scowled a bit. "And I looked at it before we got into Fendal. Wish the damn thing would give me more notifications."

"We know now, at least," Derivan said, angling his tone toward comfort. "Though we do not know if this began in Fendal or . . . here."

"It's a start," Sev said, and then he frowned. "We never asked what this place is called, huh? We'll have to ask next time we head out."

"No need," Misa said dryly. "I asked while I was downstairs. This whole place is called Teque; it's a dedication to the guy who led them down here, or something."

Vex grabbed one of his notebooks and scribbled a note; when Derivan peered over at him, he promptly hid the notebook from his friend. "Nope!" he reprimanded. "*Secret notebook*. I will explode you."

He wasn't even kidding. Derivan could take an explosion. He'd only come out hotter for it. Literally.

... Vex tried to pretend his brain hadn't just thought that.

Sev, meanwhile, had no idea what was going through Vex's head. "Huh."

"It's not *that* surprising that I asked questions about this place." Misa scowled, folding her arms across her chest.

"I didn't say anything," Sev protested. Misa held the scowl for a moment more before grinning at him, and the cleric relaxed with a sigh; even Vex could tell, though, that her heart wasn't quite in the banter. Her gaze kept flicking off a little to the right, like she was still looking at the reality anchor's item screen. Not even seeing Vex tease Derivan about getting exploded had really helped her, and that almost always did.

There was a small silence for a while.

"Anyway," Misa said, clearly noticing that everyone was trying to find the words to talk to her. She forced herself to smile a bit. "Don't worry. I'm not ... I mean, okay, fuck, I *am* blaming myself a little bit. But there's no point dwelling on it."

"Better that we learn this can happen now," Vex offered, a little meekly. "With minimal damage to the anchor. You know to keep an eye on it now."

"That's ... a good way of looking at it." Misa hesitated, looking for a moment like she wanted to say something more, and then she shook her head and gave Vex a smaller but more genuine smile. "Thanks."

"We still need a plan of action," Derivan said. His tone was soft, like he was trying to acknowledge the conversation that just happened while guiding it gently back to its original purpose. "We have some ideas about what is happening but no ideas for a solution."

"Bonus rooms typically have an objective." Vex's brows furrowed as he thought. "We don't know what the objective here is. The dungeon in Fendal, such as it is, tried to copy the bonus room in Elyra's primary dungeon and failed; that failure still leaked out, because something went wrong, but we don't know how to patch a hole in the system like this."

"And we do not know what will happen if we do," Derivan said. The others all grimaced slightly when he spoke, and for a while, the table went silent again.

Vex sighed.

"I think we just have to investigate the slivers and mana crystals going missing," he said after a moment. "That's the only obvious correlation between Fendal and..."

Vex paused, then checked his notebook.

"Teque," he said. "Between Fendal and Teque. So if we figure out why the slivers are going missing here, and the crystals in Fendal, we might have a better idea of how to stop the 'raids.' Although at this point I'm not sure who we're stopping the raids *for*."

"So you're saying we do a stakeout," Sev said.

"I feel like they've probably tried doing a stakeout," Misa mused.

"We have something they don't," Vex said. His gaze slid to Derivan, then promptly slid away when the armor took the opportunity to watch him back. "Uh. Deri, you have Shift, right? If there's something here that's stealing things that mages can't detect, Shift might be able to find it."

"I had not considered that," Derivan said, his voice thoughtful. "Yes. Perhaps we can investigate..."

"What about Noram?" Sev asked. "Do we tell him... everything? The bonus room stuff is going to sound unbelievable at best."

"I doubt he's going to let us near the slivers if we don't at least explain that," Vex said with a sigh. "So let's go find him again and talk to him, convince him to let us keep an eye on the slivers, and... hopefully that'll fill in the rest of the gaps in our knowledge."

That was the hope, anyway. The plan still felt like a shaky one, and Vex saw that uncertainty reflected not only in himself but in the others around him; Derivan was the only one who didn't appear particularly troubled. He seemed contemplative instead.

Focusing on the future, perhaps.

Vex discussed a few more potential plans with his friends, but they had nothing else solid—the ideas they had were difficult to investigate. They felt they had the broad strokes right, and they could use any further information they found to refine those ideas, at least; that was the closest they would get for now.

"We'll have to consider the possibility of a fight," Sev said at last. "Worst-case scenario, if we do find something where Noram and his mages haven't been able to, we might get attacked. If that crossbow guy is related to this, it'll be even worse. We need to be careful, and we need to be ready. Everyone on board?"

Vex nodded, and the others nodded with him.

Before they retired for the night, Misa managed to get an update from her mother, as slow as it was with the time difference between the Fendal and

Teque. According to her, in all the time they'd been down in Teque, only a few minutes had passed in Fendal. That was another data point to add—if crystals were being stolen every few days in Fendal, then much, much more time passed in Teque between each robbery.

That was... well, it was a data point. It didn't tell them much. Hopefully, they wouldn't have to wait too long before the next set of slivers went missing; it had, after all, already been a few days since the last raid.

—⚘—

"Hey, Sev?" Vex asked.

They'd pretty much all gotten ready for the night—Derivan was off by himself near the center of the room, apparently experimenting with small-scale attempts at magic without going through the system, or something like that. Vex was excited about doing that himself with his newly acquired, beautiful magelight, but he had more important things to do first. Misa was far away at the opposite side of the room, and Vex had approached Sev while he was sitting at the side of his bed, apparently engaged in his nightly commune.

From what he understood, Sev treated it more like a divine pen pal sort of situation, for all that he no longer got replies from Onyx.

"What's up?" Sev smiled at him. "Need something?"

"Kind of," Vex admitted. He took a breath—he felt nervous, and he didn't even know *why*. It wasn't like he was actually talking to Derivan about this! But he felt like he needed to talk to *someone*, and Sev felt like the right person to approach. "I just wanted to talk. Um. Ask for some advice, as it were."

"I'm all ears," Sev said, putting his focus to the side and looking attentively at Vex; he folded his arms across his lap and waited. He didn't even crack a joke. Instead, he patted his bed in invitation, and Vex sighed as he sat himself down next to Sev.

How to handle this...

"I really like Derivan," the lizardkin blurted in a whisper, then immediately cursed himself for discarding all subtlety. He glanced quickly to the side to see if the armor in question had heard him, but Derivan was still seated in the center of the room, mana carefully dancing between his fingertips. Vex looked away after a moment and tried to calm his heart; he'd only started getting used to talking about his feelings recently, and this was the first time...

...well, it was the first time *he* was reaching out about it. Sev and Misa had both made it pretty clear they knew, and Derivan was probably oblivious. He seemed oblivious, anyway.

"I know that," Sev said, his voice tinged with a faint touch of teasing amusement. "And you know I know that. You know Misa knows that, too."

"I— That's beside the point." Vex buried his face in his hands. "It's just— What do I *do* about it?"

"Talk to him about it?" Sev suggested mildly.

"I was going to," Vex said, because not all that long ago, he *was*, and now he found he was doubting himself again. The lizardkin sighed and drew his legs up into his chest. "But I dunno. I'm worried about messing things up. We're a good team."

"We're not going to be less of a good team if you two get together," Sev said, and then paused, making a face as he reconsidered the statement. "Maybe if you fight. The Guild doesn't really encourage this for that reason. But fighting together, facing dangers together... It's pretty inevitable that it happens from time to time."

"Has it happened to you?" Vex asked.

Sev laughed. "No," he said. "Honestly, I've never really liked anyone that way, and I don't think I ever will."

"Really?"

"Yep." Sev shrugged, shifting slightly on the bed; Vex caught a contented smile on the cleric's face, to his surprise. "But I'm pretty happy. Really happy, actually. I have you guys, and... I think that's all I need? I just want to hang out with you guys, help people, figure out what's going on with the system, and not deal with weird evolutionary branches like mimics that pretend to be trees except sometimes they get up, walk off, and pretend to be a different tree."

Sev made a face at the end of his sentence, and Vex snickered. He was feeling a little better about talking to Derivan, at least. "Are you *still* thinking about that?" he teased.

"It's a *weird* fucking tree," Sev complained. "It'd be weirder if I wasn't. But don't change the subject. Are you going to tell Deri, or am I?"

"... You wouldn't."

"I would not," Sev said, and grinned, poking Vex in the snout. "But you should've seen your face."

Vex sighed, but he found he was smiling, just a bit. "I will," he said. "I want to wait for the right time, but... yeah, I will."

"Don't wait too long. Or do, and then I get to win the bet that Derivan confesses first."

"You bet—" Vex started, and then sighed, as though entirely unsurprised. "Before we reach Elyra," he promised instead.

CHAPTER 19

OPPOSING ELEMENTS

Derivan hummed in consideration. Mana played in front of him between his fingers, delicate threads of colored light hovering between the dark metal of his gauntlets. He needed to understand more about this new magic.

Vex was on the case, of course, and Derivan had no doubt that the lizardkin would succeed—but for now, if a fight broke out tomorrow, Vex would be defenseless.

Besides his dagger. And he *could* technically use his failed spells to make explosions.

But Vex was busy talking to Sev, and whatever they were talking about, Derivan felt it was important. So Derivan decided to do his part, and focused his own attempts on understanding this new, glyph-based magic.

He'd spoken with Vex on their suspicion that the magic performed by the system was artificial, after a fashion—there was something in the way he'd cast that one barrier spell without the assistance of the system. Vex had tried, on a few occasions, to copy what he'd done—to guide the magic into the spell instead of forcing it—and had never quite succeeded; the closest he'd gotten was that their time together that first night, when Vex had painted an imitation of his [**Starry Night**] skill and they'd guided the mana into it together.

Proper magic, then, needed a base. An anchor.

He'd seen that before, even, in Vex's version of [**Starry Night**]—when the skill had something to anchor on, it had been far stronger than his system-assisted version of the skill.

So . . . [**Mana Manipulation**] was a bridge. It helped, in a world where the mana didn't trust anything related to the system; maybe it was willing to help him as long as it wasn't *forced* the way the system did it, or maybe he was missing a particular connection in his own ability with magic, as explained by Anyati-the-shopkeeper.

Or it was the Magic stat. He felt his connection with that stat even more keenly than before, now, and he felt he was close to some kind of revelation on it; every time he turned it over in his mind, though, his thoughts simply went to Vex and the lizardkin's love for magic.

Regardless, in this place, where the mana presumably didn't know what the system *was*, it wasn't as useful. It wasn't that [**Mana Manipulation**] didn't *work*; the mana still did as he asked, dancing around his fingertips with a certain exhilaration he'd never seen before the moment he prodded it into doing so—but if he gripped any more strongly with the skill, he suspected, he'd face the same backlash Vex had suffered when he tried to cast a spell.

Mana here was more powerful than the system was. And Derivan wasn't quite sure how that thought made him feel.

"You are a curiosity," he murmured, watching as the light-green display of magic played across his senses. The mana wriggled between his fingers, as if in response to his words, though he thought it couldn't possibly have heard him. "What makes you different from the mana in our world?"

It didn't answer him, of course. Very gently, Derivan fed his [**Intermediate Mana Manipulation**] skill with a thread of willpower and guided the mana into forming the basic barrier spell once again; he'd done it enough times now that it was instinct, even though the spell that formed was never large or fast enough that it would be useful in combat.

A perfect, polished barrier formed in front of him, tinted a faint green, and Derivan felt the mana reacting the same way it had before—that same moment of realization, followed by the barrier beginning to flex and break in response. This time, he didn't fight it, and when the spell broke, the mana spun free, scattering about in the air like it was confused.

"So it was not just Vex's presence that made the spell fail," Derivan muttered softly, but the back of his mind was focused on the odd twinge he'd felt from within the moment the spell broke.

That odd feeling, as he understood it, was the influence of his Magic stat.

He remembered the first moment he'd gained that stat. It had happened in connection with Vex, when the lizardkin had begun feeding mana into him in order to test the growth of his Slime stat. He hadn't felt anything particularly special about it then, but as the stat grew he'd become more and more in tune with a nebulous *something* that he'd never quite been able to quantify.

Anyati-the-shopkeeper had mentioned that magic was always a little personalized to the caster; the broad strokes were the same, but the details would change. Derivan wasn't sure that he could do the same thing the casters in Teque did, nor did he think he could approach the same heights of magic that he was sure Vex would someday reach.

But he *did* have something that was uniquely his.

Derivan hummed once again, and this time he guided the mana into his gauntlet. He was operating on an instinct that wasn't quite his own—and he recognized that now, because he'd gotten more in tune with the feeling that working with the Magic stat gave him.

It was the same warmth he felt whenever he looked at Vex. It was the way he found his gaze always drifting to the lizardkin no matter what he was doing, ever interested in whatever puzzle the lizardkin had decided to solve that day. It was the sensation of Vex's scaled hand clasped within his own. It was the way the lizardkin's kindness shone through, no matter how scared or anxious he was.

It was the part of him that enjoyed listening to whatever the lizardkin had to say, even if he didn't quite understand what it was Vex was saying all the time.

He did that same thing now with the mana, trying to listen to whatever it had to say. Just the gentlest nudge from [**Intermediate Mana Manipulation**], to let it know he was there.

Derivan watched in quiet wonder as the mana soaked into the metal of his body and began to trace out the faint, almost invisible engravings. The designs in his armor didn't *mean* anything, as far as he knew. He hadn't exactly been created with a purpose in mind—the decorative elements of his armor were just that—but it still made him shine, and when the magic was sufficiently suffused into his armor, he reached out and allowed the stat to guide him.

A faint trail of magic followed his fingers when he moved, like his own personal magelight. Without thinking, he began to draw a vague mimicry of the style of the light glyphs he'd seen before—but while he drew in flowing lines and swoops, his mind settled back on his connection with the Magic stat. It hummed through him, feeling like it was stronger than before somehow, and when he was done . . .

Derivan glanced at the glyph he'd drawn. It looked like a shield, almost, except it was really more of the *suggestion* of a shield; the lines intersected with one another in a way that looked more like a dance, and the colors were all various shades of green. He wondered if there was significance to that, and he felt his gaze slide to where Vex was in some deep conversation with Sev—

The spell formed, and Derivan's attention snapped once more to the spell he was casting.

It was... *like* his barrier spell, but he could feel that this one was different from the one before. It didn't threaten to snap and break, like the one he'd cast without a proper foundation. This one held steady, a translucent barricade against anything that might cause him harm.

It was also shaped like a book, oddly enough. He wondered if that had something to do with how he'd been thinking about Vex when the spell formed.

He liked it, though. It was like a small reminder of his connection with Vex and the bond he had with the lizardkin.

The spell itself was... not unlike Misa's ability to block. Derivan felt almost instinctively that this spell, whatever it was, was stronger than any [**Barrier**] he would be able to conjure up with the system. He'd have to test it to be sure, of course, but even now there was a link he had with this book-shield that he simply didn't have with [**Barrier**]s; he could move it at will, open and close it, and there was almost certainly more he would be able to do with it in time, so long as he iterated on that opening glyph. There was even a sense of an extra, additional function to the spell that would directly assist Vex rather than benefiting himself, though he had no idea what it did—he just knew it was *there*, because he could feel the link it shared with Vex.

This was a small victory, in the grand scheme of things. A single spell. But it gave him a stronger ability to *protect* than he'd ever had before, and if things went badly tomorrow...

He would have just the slightest bit more of an edge in making sure Vex wouldn't be hurt, even without his magic.

Part of Derivan was excited about this development, and yet for whatever reason, Derivan found that he was looking forward to sharing this new discovery with Vex more.

And the rest of his team members, of course.

Derivan stood up, and a small, gleaming pile of mana slivers scattered onto the floor.

"You figured out a spell?" Vex was looking at Derivan with wide eyes. "You got *mana slivers*?"

Derivan nodded. "I believe I understand the Magic statistic a little better as well," he said. "It has increased to 21."

"Does anything feel... different?" Vex asked, curious, and Derivan shook his head.

"Only in my understanding," Derivan said. "I believe, more than anything else, it is a guide—though I am uncertain where that guidance comes from. It feels very much like you, Vex."

"Does it?" Vex stiffened a little bit, a darker color flushing across his scales. "Um. I hope that's a good thing."

"I enjoy listening to you," Derivan said. Physical Empathy told him Vex was embarrassed, but what he had to be embarrassed about, Derivan really wasn't sure.

"You'll have to show me the spell later," Vex said. "I was gonna experiment a bit with the magelight and glyph, but I was a little tired last night. And I had other things on my mind."

"Gladly," Derivan said.

The four of them were hiding just outside where Teque's version of Noram said the city kept its main store of mana slivers. Vex had tried to ask after a little more information on the slivers—in fact, he'd tried to ask for clarification on a whole host of things, and had in fact prepared a *list* of questions—but Noram had waved him off tiredly. The poor otter seemed like he was on the verge of outright falling asleep. There was the question of what had kept him so busy, but Noram wasn't awake enough to answer even that question properly.

Something about the Roads, he'd said. Something about odd screens showing up, and haywire magic. That had been enough for Sev and Misa to exchange worried glances, and for Derivan and Vex to start asking questions—but the otter was already gone, apparently getting himself ready to keep fighting off whatever crisis this was.

They'd discussed canceling their stakeout plans to go pursue this new problem instead, but eventually they talked themselves down from it. They understood the system the most, certainly, and could provide guidance—but from what it sounded like, the system notifications that popped up were random and sporadic, never tied to any specific person. More importantly, no one here had access to mana crystals to bind themselves to the system with.

They'd need to get a copy of what one of those notifications looked like as soon as they were done with this. But since the stolen slivers seemed like it was likely to be linked to the mana crystal raids in Fendal, this seemed to be their best lead.

The warehouse was nothing like they expected. It was a plain building that didn't look any different from the others—security through obscurity, or something like that. Inside was a plain expanse of gray rock and a few crates of slivers. Not a *lot* of them, either; if this was their main supply, then they either didn't have a lot to begin with, or they'd lost quite a number of mana slivers over the course of the raids.

Now to wait.

CHAPTER 20

SYSTEM SHIFT

Derivan spent a little more time trying to understand his stats, in the week they had spent waiting and then traveling toward Elyra. He'd been trying to understand how it was that he acquired new stats and why he hadn't gained any since gathering Shift; there was the chance that he'd simply hit his limit, but that didn't seem likely.

Yet there was so little in common in how he'd gained each of them. The only thing he could really say was a common factor was that he was involved, which wasn't helpful. In four out of five cases, someone else had been involved in the acquisition of a stat; the problem there was that Physical Empathy was an outlier. He'd gained *that* one seemingly at random, when he'd been trying to interpret the feelings of his friends.

He'd always had trouble understanding the breadth of the emotional reactions the others had, and he'd simply wanted to try to *understand*, and then . . . new stat.

But the actual mechanism almost certainly wasn't that simple. He'd made attempts at gaining other stats since then, but he'd gained nothing beyond the five he already had so far.

Slime. Magic. Physical Empathy. Golden Geas. Shift.

An odd array of stats, to be sure, and a difficult one to create . . . a "build" around. Slime was still growing, and he suspected there was no upper limit to the stat; moreover, he had discovered that there was an ability to absorb ambient mana attached to it, just as Vex had described. That ability got better as the stat grew, but the amount of mana he needed to draw in to overcharge his mana pool increased too.

He'd talked the math out with Vex, who had plotted out a graph, and they had both eventually concluded that it was probably not a good use of his time to sit for centuries in a field, absorbing ambient mana just to grow his Slime stat. (Vex had certainly seemed inspired, though, and started talking about how slimes had "cores" that grew over time, and how having a core to study as it grew might revolutionize slime farming, at which point Derivan had to remind the wizard that they were not, in fact, out to farm slimes.)

The lecture had been amusing and enthralling to listen to, though, even if Derivan hadn't understood most of it. He *had* understood he would probably gain and grow this "slime core" himself, if he kept growing the stat, but had no interest in doing so to that extent. If it happened over time, so be it.

Magic... was a stat he was still learning about, and here and now it seemed especially relevant. It gave him an insight into the whims of mana, perhaps? It guided him, allowing him to work with mana in a way that didn't belong to the system—which was odd, given the stat was provided by the system to begin with. But it was his best guess, and the stat was hardly part of the system's normal functions.

Physical Empathy was *his* stat and the one he used the most. It bridged the gap that made it difficult for him to understand others. It had been invaluable and had only continued to grow as he used it; the number sat at a comfortable fifty-one now.

He'd more or less resolved not to use Golden Geas as much as possible, not liking the autonomy it took away from others.

Shift... had something to do with... disparate wavelengths of reality, as best as he understood it. He suspected that it brought him more in tune with those disparate wavelengths, and grew the more he interacted with reality outside its baseline. It was growing now, he could feel, albeit only by decimal points; this entire place was Shifted, very slightly, as a result of the bonus room's contents spilling into the world.

And that—that right there—was something he should have paid attention to. Not that the place was Shifted, no, but all the *times* he had encountered Shifted reality. He'd never really thought about it.

But now that he did? Except for the planeshifted, every instance of Shifted reality they had encountered had been imposed by the system.

Dungeon boundaries existed because the dungeons themselves existed in a Shifted space, one or two wavelengths above the baseline; that was the reason he had needed Shift to break in, and how he had aided Misa in blocking the attack on the delvers within the dungeon, albeit inadvertently. The bonus room that Misa's village had once been in had been several wavelengths above that. The Serpent of the Night Sky, the Overseer in which Aurum had been trapped—that had been many wavelengths away, but the boundaries had weakened when they had injured it, and he had been able to rip his way through the rest of those layers of reality until they found themselves within.

Even the gods weren't above the system, as they had learned not so long ago, and so the fact that they had their own planes . . . there was something there. Perhaps it wasn't that the gods had their own planes of power, like many religious scholars assumed. Perhaps they were simply trapped in their own planes. Histre had implied as much, even, when the angel had mentioned a "cost" that Aurum had had to pay to send them down.

The reality anchor they owned, the one hidden within Misa's skills—that was Shifted away, too, which was the reason he'd needed to shift the mana input into visibility for them to see it.

These "wavelengths of reality," or layers, or whatever they truly were—they seemed to be a tool mainly used by the system. Something it used to keep some things apart and other things together; Derivan was concerned, just slightly, about the extent to which that was true. He would learn more as the stat grew, he suspected.

But that meant, first of all, that the stat was far more important than he assumed, and he needed to find a way to train it that wasn't simply spending more time in shifted reality.

Second of all—and perhaps more importantly—in hindsight, he *really* should have known what those intruders likely were *before* he Shifted them into visibility. He'd just sensed something moving nearby and *reacted*, and now . . .

<L/E#V#L #3.$7 S/YS TEM P/A#TCHE/R>

The words floated in the air, the only boxes they saw here besides their own. They flickered like they weren't supposed to exist. The text warped and changed every half-second, broken letters barely spelling out a name.

"What the fuck," Sev said. His hand was gripped tight on his staff, and he was tense. Vex's tail was stiff, and he had retreated slightly, automatically keeping enough distance to throw a [**Fireball**] even if he couldn't use one here. Misa stepped in front of him, and her aura flickered black with [**Guard Stance**].

Derivan could only grip his sword and gently pull Vex to his side. He'd learned new spells, but no new skills had been offered to him by the system, and magic here was unreliable unless he used the new glyphic spell he had found—and that took him *time*. He prepared himself to use them anyway, just in case he could, and just in case they needed it; he would find a way to buy them time.

There was a feeling of wrongness blanketing the air.

Something is wrong.

It wasn't a thought of his own. It wasn't an instinct imposed upon him by the system, a feeling he remembered from what felt like a lifetime ago. It wasn't a guess.

It was a feeling from the mana. Fear, anxiety, anger. A hint of resonance with a memory from a world that never existed.

Derivan could see that Vex had felt the same thing too; the lizardkin stiffened and his eyes narrowed, and now the worry in his face became something more real.

Yet... there was a fierce protectiveness in his expression that hadn't been there before.

Derivan felt a surge of some foreign emotion he didn't understand; admiration, perhaps, for Vex's love for magic. Even without being able to use it—even with the mana angry at *him* due to his connection to the system—Vex loved magic and fought to protect it.

And then the System Patchers spotted them.

The names were legible after a moment or two, the garbled and changing text slowing down just enough to make them visible. What was less easy to handle was what they looked like. Perhaps that was one of the reasons they were Shifted away at all instead of working out in the open; their appearances were so foreign that they would instantly draw attention even in a city full of strange, magical creatures.

They were vaguely insectoid, in the sense that they had a carapace. But that carapace was the strange system-blue of the boxes that recorded their stats and levels, and that was where any similarity to any living creature quickly ended. Every one of the Patchers were an amalgam of chitinous *limbs*. And every one of them was different, too—some had five thin, sticklike arms, waving out in an array that mocked the general concept of anatomy, and others had three bulky ones that would not have seemed out of place flexing for attention in a tavern.

Others had more. Five, nine, eleven; always odd and asymmetrical. There were five of these System Patchers in total, and Derivan had pulled all five of them out of reality like a fool; part of him wondered if he could shove them *back*, but already he could feel resistance pooling in that part of his soul.

Shift was a stat, which made it a part of him. But it was what Derivan imagined a muscle was like, for organic species; he had pulled it too hard, and now it would take time to recover before he could push that hard once again.

"I cannot send them back yet," Derivan informed, his voice tense. "I apologize."

"We needed to see what we're dealing with, anyway," Sev said grimly. "Pulling them all is better than getting ambushed."

"I've been waiting for a fuckin' *challenge*," Misa grinned, baring her teeth.

"I . . . can't help," Vex said, and there was a slight tremble in his voice that made a part of Derivan tighten in turn. He shifted so that he, too, was slightly in front of Vex, positioned to guard him. But Vex spoke up again, stepping to stand beside him. "But I'm going to try."

Vex held his dagger in one hand and his magelight in the other. Derivan wasn't sure he even knew how to use the magelight yet, but he was clearly willing to try.

And then they waited.

The air was tense and charged with electricity; no one else was around, because the mana slivers were kept in a derelict-looking warehouse guarded by dozens of security spells right at the edge of the city.

The System Patchers regarded them curiously at first. Derivan could only read that emotional context because of Physical Empathy; the stat helped him skip all the steps he would have needed to learn how to read a new people, a new species. They weren't necessarily enemies.

And yet all his instincts screamed at him to be *careful*, that there was *danger*. And the others clearly felt the same way.

Which was a good thing, too, because the Patchers rushed at them all at once—though strangely, even then, they didn't seem hostile. They simply . . .

"They think we are a problem to fix," Derivan said. His words echoed strangely in all the extra empty space in the warehouse, and the Patchers kept moving.

They weren't fast. They moved with a strange, loping gait, bodies twisting and contorting so the hands and limbs could make contact with the ground.

And then, when they were closer, they *screamed*.

All at the same time, a keening, chittering sound emerged from them, one ripple bouncing into the next and joining together until it turned into a solid wave that resonated not only with the air but with the baseline wavelengths of reality.

That air around them shifted impossibly. Stone and dirt changed at random where the wave connected, turning to grass, then fire, then sea, and then something dark and *wrong*—

Misa flinched first, seeing what the skill did. And then her face set, and she *blocked*.

It took all her branched timelines to do it, too. It was visible, just as much as the strain on her was; she looked like she was laid over on top of herself, differing versions all straining against the same attack, each offering a different guard, a different counter. She *struggled,* and Derivan was forced to reach out and strain himself with a smaller use of Shift, compressing that attack down onto a single wavelength, and the block resolved with Misa looking only a little worse for wear.

But only because he'd acted. If he hadn't . . . He wasn't sure what would have happened.

An unfamiliar spike of fear rose within him, followed by resolve.

The attack snapped back onto the Patchers, that outward ripple collapsing inward into five separate impacts that knocked them back. Misa didn't seem to care.

"These aren't fucking level thirty-seven," she growled instead. Her face was paler than usual.

"They're attacking using the system's mechanisms," Vex said, his scales paler than usual. His eyes flashed with the traditional color of his [**Mana Sight**], though Derivan had no idea what his friend was doing. This didn't seem to be a matter of mana. "We can't—we can't fight with system skills. Bad idea."

"That block was taking something out of me," Misa agreed. There was a certain anxiety set into her shoulders now. "I think Derivan stopped it. But that was—"

She shook her head and cut herself off.

Derivan stepped forward, because now seemed like the time, and Misa had *bought* him the time; whatever had happened with the block and Shift, the Patchers seemed disoriented, rolling on the floor in a disjointed jumble of limbs.

Mana flowed into his gauntlet just like it had before. He drew the same glyph he had before. The one that coalesced all his thoughts of magic and of Vex into a single, shining barrier.

If the system wasn't an option . . .

Maybe magic could be.

CHAPTER 21

PATCHING PAIN

The glyph completed.

Just like before, mana rushed into the glyph, completing it in a way that was not unlike how runic inscriptions were charged with mana—and yet there was something *more*. The glyph came to life, the outer edges of the shield collapsing down into the vague form of a book, outlined in shimmering green.

It happened just in time, too. The five Patchers skittered upright, twisting and rotating unnaturally before letting out yet another rippling screech; the air rippled again, struck the barrier of Derivan's spell—

—something strange happened.

The effect was connected to him, first of all, anchored to him much like a real shield would be. When the ripple struck the barrier, Derivan could feel himself being pushed back, and he had to dig his feet into the ground to avoid being forced back by the sheer metaphysical *weight* behind the attack. There might be something he could do to detach the spell, prevent it from anchoring to him in such a way, but if there was then he didn't know how.

Second was a strange feeling in the mana that he sensed almost as soon as the ripple hit the barrier. Vex sensed it, too, judging by the way the lizardkin perked up and narrowed his eyes again; Derivan couldn't quite spare the attention to check on him, though, because the Patchers were beginning to push forward against the barrier. Two of them scattered to the side, trying to go around it while the others pushed dumbly against the magic, and Derivan tried to react—

—Vex reached out and touched his shoulder, the lizardkin's eyes determined. Derivan felt Vex's mana trickle into him the way it did when they were testing his stats, but this time, it did something different. Instead of entering and merging with his mana pool, it now tangled with the part of his soul that was currently interacting with the spell; Derivan almost shivered, finding the sensation strange.

Not unpleasant, though.

The barrier Derivan was holding on to flexed and expanded into a semicircle around them. The two Patchers that had shifted beat their too-long limbs uselessly against the barrier. These weren't *intelligent* enemies, Derivan realized. They were machines. Programs that were set to do a job.

"Sev," Vex said, his voice a little tense. "Please get some help."

"Me?" the cleric asked. He opened his mouth, as if to protest—Derivan saw the way he gripped his staff and glanced nervously at them, as though worried they would be hurt and die without him—but then he snapped his mouth shut into a grim, determined line, spun on his heel, and ran.

"You have a plan?" Misa asked. Her voice was terse, and she was watching the Patchers with wariness; Derivan sensed the same thing she did. The barrier wouldn't last forever. Every strike against it drained some of his mana.

"We need magic to fight them," Vex said. There was an oddness in the way his eyes shimmered, and he blinked and shook his head, like he was trying to get rid of something in his eyes. Derivan was starting to get the feeling that Vex had somehow understood a lot more than he had from that strangeness in the mana. "I dunno how to explain. The mana here doesn't... It doesn't *know* the system. Not really. But it understands reality. It spent a *really long time* trying to understand reality."

"You know something?" Misa glanced sharply at Vex. Not accusatory, but with urgency. "How?"

"I just do." Vex hesitated, then pointed at the barrier—at the small, fluttering books that made up its expanded semicircle. They weren't actual books, of course, just impressions in the magic—but the pages flipped and turned with every strike against the barrier. Derivan remembered the feeling the spell had given him the first time he'd cast it—the feeling that it was connected to Vex in more ways than one.

This was the connection. Whatever the barrier was doing, it was feeding Vex information about the Patchers.

As if to confirm his thoughts, Vex tensed. "They're going to try something else," he said. "We need to hold them off—"

There was a flutter in reality. A slight change.

A small Shift.

But small as it was, it was one that cascaded, bouncing between the five Patchers and accumulating in strength. Derivan felt it this time, as the mana tried to compensate and stop them—the mana in Teque did *not* like the system—but they Shifted further and faster, and as much as he tried, Derivan found he couldn't stop what they were doing.

An instant later, they had stepped through the barrier like it was nothing.

Yet something was different. The system-blue of their chitin was slightly burnt and chipped. They'd hurt themselves, doing whatever that was, not that they seemed to care. They screamed again, but the echoes of that rippling Shift didn't reach quite as far as before. It was weak enough that neither Derivan nor Misa had to try to block it before it dissipated.

It still left the stone behind it broken and warped.

"I'll take three!" Misa called loudly, before either Vex or Derivan could make any sort of tactical call, and she sprinted forward—it didn't take her that many steps. Three large bounds and she smashed her mace into one of them, the *crunch* of carapace and limbs loud enough to echo in the building; she spun on her feet almost immediately, launching herself past the scream of a second one to kick and snap one of its lower limbs. Black lightning crackled around her in the form of a [**Paralyzing Bash**]—

"Misa!" Vex called out, ever so slightly paler beneath his scales. Derivan winced. Vex had said not to use system-given skills, and [**Paralyzing Bash**] *used mana* on top of that.

But there was no runic inscription. It wasn't a spell. Instead, mana briefly enveloped Misa before abruptly beginning to Shift to the black lightning that was typical in all paralysis skills.

And then Derivan saw why Vex had warned them.

Before Misa's mace could strike the third Patcher—before the Shift into black lightning had even completed, with only half of the mana completing the Shift—the Patcher somehow seized something in the skill mechanism. Derivan couldn't sense precisely what happened. He felt the Shift her skill was using forced to change, and the skill never completed.

Instead, black lightning turned into fire, and Misa *screamed*.

To her credit, she didn't let it stop her. The scream transformed into something halfway between a growl and a snarl, a sound caught between determination and pain. She completed her blow, smashing her mace into the center of the Patcher that had done this to her and throwing it a good five feet back.

The skill snapped off, and the fire vanished. Misa breathed.

She looked *pissed*.

And that was all Derivan had the time to see before the two remaining Patchers were among them. Almost instinctively, Derivan tried to step in front of Vex again, but the lizardkin was insistent on not letting Derivan fight alone; he had a dagger in his hand, and he danced backward with surprising finesse when a Patcher tried to swipe at him, and a second time when it screeched.

...Perhaps Derivan was worrying a little too much about his friend. Even without his magic, Vex was quite capable and nimble, and it was apparently something he'd focused on improving with the levels he'd been recently gaining. He saw Vex trying to use the magelight every now and then, but all he managed were loose swipes of mana in the air before he was forced to defend himself again.

As much as he would've liked to keep watching, the armor diverted his attention to the Patcher that was coming for him. There was a hint of an idea percolating in his mind, related to his recent thoughts on his stats.

Save for Physical Empathy, each one of them had been gained through the action of another on or around him.

He'd seen what that Patcher had done to Misa.

Derivan dodged once as the Patcher swiped at him; the second time, he grabbed the limb that was coming for him. This was the Patcher with the thin, sticklike arms, and for a moment he tried to bend them against their joints, to snap them—but it was stronger than he'd expected, and he had to retreat as another screech made the air and ground ripple around it.

Well. He still had his sword.

The next attack skittered off the edge of his sword as Derivan stepped past the Patcher, and the sticklike limb dug into the stone of the floor instead. The armor took a split second to realize exactly how dangerous the limbs were—the moment it stabbed into the floor, the stone around the boxes began to dissolve, fizzing and bubbling—before he stepped out of the way of the next strike.

Safe enough to strike, safe enough to block. Not safe enough to get hit by. Derivan wasn't sure his armor would hold up, and he didn't want to test it. He needed to try his plan. He needed to use a skill—

"Vex!" Misa called out, derailing Derivan's thoughts. Her voice was strained. "Don't get hit by them! Health doesn't shield you!"

Health didn't—

Derivan spared a glance to Misa, and he felt a surge of worry and trepidation. The burn marks on her skin had stayed after the spell, and there were nasty cuts and bruises on her olive-green skin. She'd clearly used her skill to block more than once, and there were fragments of her potential selves still shifting around her, like the skill hadn't entirely resolved; some of them were more injured than she was.

Vex hissed in pain. Derivan glanced back to see a long gash down one of the lizardkin's arms, and a second attack rearing back to hit him—

—Misa appeared, clearly triggering that block once more, and staggered backward as the Patchers seemed to try to twist the skill; it struggled, though, the Patcher's own abilities catching on something before failing, and Misa kicked it back. Vex whispered a thanks—

—Derivan needed to deal with his Patcher. They were being spread too thin. Part of him understood why Vex had sent Sev for help; healing was something they needed, but far more crucial was the ability to block an attack that would otherwise be deadly. Something about prevention being better than the cure, he imagined the lizardkin saying...

...It didn't stop him from worrying.

He needed to focus. He kept getting distracted by his worry for Vex, and he didn't know *why*; nothing about this was that much more dangerous than the worst fights they'd been in.

There was something he could gain here if he was right about how he gained stats. He frowned at the Patcher and cast a [**Barrier**] through the system.

Mana began to trickle through the runic inscription that the system created, but before the spell could complete, Derivan engaged the Patcher again; he allowed the spiderlike limbs to crash against his sword, and he felt the Patcher reach into him, trying to twist his cast. Whatever mechanism the system used to create runic inscriptions was manipulated, and he felt one skill transforming into another.

But in the corner of his vision, where he had called up his status to see if he was right, two things had changed.

The text for [**Barrier**] had glitched, shifting into a different spell called [**Void Shards**]; he cancelled that spell quickly before he could find out what it would do.

And second, perhaps more important, was the new stat.

Patch: 1

CHAPTER 22

A SONG OF CHANGE

Derivan didn't particularly have the time to figure out what the new spell or the new stat could do. It was easy enough to guess that the spell wouldn't be anything good, with the way the Patchers had twisted Misa's [**Paralyzing Slash**]; mid-combat was *not* the time to try to understand it. As for the stat...

He had a rough idea. But this wasn't the time to try it out—he had *one point* in it, and was in the middle of active combat besides—

A half-formed insectoid arm whiffed past his helmet, so close he could hear the whistle it made through the air; Derivan jerked his head away from the near miss, glaring at the Patcher attacking him. One part of him kept a close eye on what was happening with Vex, who was still dancing away from the strikes of his own Patcher, and Misa, who was handling all three of the ones she was fighting remarkably well but was clearly taking hits.

He needed to take one of them off of her. Sev would be back soon, no doubt, once he was able to find help. They needed to survive until then, or Shift needed to recover enough for him to push all of them back away from this plane of reality, or *something*—

—Derivan blocked the next attempted strike with the edge of his sword, using a sharp, twisting motion to crack open one of the Patcher's joints; he transitioned smoothly into a kick, heavy metal smashing into the center of the Patcher and sending it sprawling back. Before it could recover, he took three quick, large steps—

"Misa!" he called, and she seemed to understand exactly what he wanted. She shot him a grin.

"Kept me waiting," she shouted back.

Two Patchers attacked her at once; the last was still dizzy from whatever strike she had used against it, and swaying on its feet. She stepped past one of them, letting the momentum of that strike send the Patcher directly into her mace.

The crunch of false chitin shattering sounded in the air.

The second attack Misa dodged—but she used her one free arm to grab the limb the Patcher used in the attack, and then moved *with* the Patcher, turning the attempted charge into a throw. It sailed through the air directly at Derivan, and the armor hefted his sword, cutting deep into the center, where all the limbs were joined together.

Up until now, the Patchers screamed when they attacked, sending out a wave of energy that somehow Shifted the air around them. This time, the one he'd cut into *wailed*, making a sound that was somehow painful and threatening all at once. This one didn't have the accompanying deadly wave, and yet...

In that sound was a song he didn't expect. A song he expected he wouldn't have been able to hear at all, if not for his new stat. Derivan would have frowned if he could have; as it was, his eyes darkened into concern and worry.

His understanding wasn't perfect. But the Patcher seemed like it was trying to finish something—to do whatever it had come here to do to begin with.

Vex seemed to realize the same thing. "Careful!" the lizardkin yelled, and there was a flare of panic in his voice that hadn't been there before. He sounded just a little bit out of breath, but Derivan was more concerned in that moment with getting the Patcher he was fighting to *stop wailing*.

He could see what it was doing. Not a Shift, exactly, but small-scale attempts to change the mechanics of the system; for one thing, it was weakening their connection to it, and for another, it was trying to change the effect of their stats—

—but it was getting confused. Because his stats were different, and it didn't understand.

Derivan pushed his sword the rest of the way into the center of the Patcher. There was a *crack* as something fundamental within it shattered, and whatever was holding those disparate insectoid limbs together abruptly fell apart; four limbs scattered to the ground, suddenly lifeless.

That left four Patchers.

Derivan took another two steps even as the one he'd been fighting before caught up to him, and stabbed his sword into the joint of one Patcher just as it tried to hit Misa. It screeched at him, clearly angry.

"I am taking two of them," Derivan informed Misa, because he saw how hurt she already was. Before she could protest, Derivan hopped several steps backward, flicking his gaze to Vex as he did so—thankfully, as far as he could tell, Vex was *fine*. The lizardkin was practicing avoidant combat rather than actively trying to hurt the Patcher; his dagger didn't seem to be able to do much against it, anyway.

Derivan still worried. But that worry wasn't productive, and he pushed that feeling aside for later examination.

Fighting two Patchers at once, Derivan quickly found, was harder than Misa had made it seem—they were quick, and they didn't move like organics usually did. They moved and attacked with the same limbs, which made it easy for them to turn an attack into a sidestep and a dodge into an attack. One of them, he could handle.

Two he could *also* handle, but like Misa, he couldn't do it without taking a few hits.

Derivan—for the first time in quite a while—hissed in displeasure as one of the Patchers finally managed to score a hit on him. He'd been trying to dodge one and block the other, but hadn't quite been able to move fast enough; he no longer had the benefit of Agility, after all. One Patcher turned its attack into a slight shift to the side, and then followed it up with a stab toward him in a move that was so smooth he almost didn't see it.

Derivan's armor was tough. He'd been built as a set of armor, after all, and he was a set of armor in a high-level dungeon to boot; Vex had asked him what his armor was made of before, and Derivan had honestly not been able to answer. None of his spells had been able to identify whatever type of metal Derivan was made out of, either. All they knew was that it was very durable and conducted magic very well.

All of which was to say that the single limb with no sharp edges encountered only a bare amount of resistance before it cut through his armor anyway.

It happened the same way it had when he'd seen a failed attack strike the ground. The rock had simply parted ways, fizzing slightly with the aftereffect of whatever it was the Patcher had done; it was the same thing here. He felt a moment of pressure as the natural protective magics in his armor held back the attacking limb, and then that pressure turned into a sharp, unfamiliar bite of pain—

—Derivan leapt backward on instinct, then felt the wall of the storage building pressing against his back. He glanced at his friends. Misa was getting tired, he could see, and so was Vex; the half-orc was in a slightly worse state than Vex, but neither of them were doing well.

He wasn't going to count on either of them interfering.

It was odd, though, that the Patchers' attacks could bite through the ground and even his armor, but blocking them with his sword didn't cause it to break in the same way. Derivan ignored the aching pain coming from the hole in his torso-piece and considered what he could do.

The Patchers, unfortunately, did not grant him the courtesy of time. One of them screeched again, the air rippling with that odd Shift that made the air pause and the stone flicker; the other was the same one that had hurt him the first time, and it had clearly seen that its methods worked, because it was just trying to stab him again.

Derivan used an application of Shift to force the air and ground back into stability. His sword redirected the stab, sending chitinous arms into the wall behind him instead of into his armor yet again. The wall hissed behind him, whatever enchantments built in to protect the mana slivers not giving so much as a peep of a reaction.

Derivan went on the offensive.

He kicked off against the wall, using the boost it gave him to blindside the Patchers with a burst of speed. They could be hurt; he knew that much. His sword could cut them, and Misa's mace could crush them, and yet even as he burst out past the two Patchers, his sword aimed directly for the center of one of them—

—there was no shatter. No break. Whatever purchase his blade had caught with the first Patcher failed to manifest here, and his sword bounced uselessly off the system-box chitin instead. He had to duck under the follow-up attack, only the barest glimpse of a moving limb in the edges of his awareness warning him that it was coming.

He'd have to rethink his strategy.

Already, he was channeling mana into his gauntlet again, but drawing that glyph was complicated when two of the Patchers were fighting him—he had to abort several times when they launched themselves at him and he had to duck out of the way. A few times he slammed his sword into the Patchers, breaking off bits and pieces of system-blue chitin but never quite finding the same weak spot he had with the first one. Maybe Misa had weakened it in some way?

Derivan didn't quite get the chance to find out.

There was a brief flicker—a jump in what he could sense with his Shift stat, followed by a flash of light from somewhere behind him. Derivan didn't have to turn around to guess what had happened, and in fact kept his focus on the Patchers in front of him; they suddenly seemed confused, their arms waving in the direction of the newcomers like they wanted to head for them instead.

Derivan *did* turn around, then, to see that three mages and one cleric had arrived. Sev looked out of breath and was even now panting heavily; the other three mages, Derivan didn't recognize. Noram wasn't among them.

A Patcher staggered toward Derivan, intent on moving past him and toward the mages, but the mages apparently had no intention of wasting time. Streaks of light burst out from strange-looking foci, piercing each Patcher several times over even as Derivan watched. Small pieces of the beams deflected off that protective chitin, but by and large . . .

Wait. No.

Derivan had assumed they'd solved the problem by cutting through the Patchers—but while the magic had clearly done a lot of damage, the Patchers were somehow still *alive*.

This was going to be more complicated than he'd hoped.

CHAPTER 23

FIXING PROBLEMS

If nothing else, Derivan reflected, the tides of the battle had definitely turned. That was . . . about all he could say for the situation they were in.

Unlike their own weapons, magic—"proper" magic, as it were—was apparently able to punch through the bodies of the Patchers with little to no trouble. The problem was that the Patchers simply *didn't die*. Whatever had allowed them to kill one of the Patchers wasn't something they could replicate, for all that Derivan tried to strike at the same point on the other Patchers; any damage they dealt simply healed over slowly.

Not quite like health, where the damage was reversed after it was done and became nothing but a number on a sheet. Not quite like they didn't have health, either, or Derivan would have been able to deal with them himself; his sword still did *damage*, even if it did so slower than the magic did. It simply didn't kill the Patchers.

Even when he struck at what seemed like their weak spot.

"It's like they patched it out," Sev said, irritation lacing his tone. Derivan glanced at him just in time to catch the way he narrowed his eyes, then let out an exasperated sigh. ". . . That's exactly what they fucking did, isn't it."

"I am unsure what you mean," Derivan offered.

"They *fixed it*," Sev said. "That's what they do, right? They're *Patchers*. They fix things. I don't know exactly what they're here to fix, but obviously they can fix things about themselves, too, or they wouldn't be healing back like this."

"Whatever it is they do," one of the mages said—he was a large, chitinous fellow, with a slightly rounded shape that reminded Derivan of the little beetles that would sometimes land near or on him, thinking he was another part of the scenery—"you need to find a way to stop them. We cannot keep this up for much longer."

He was telling the truth, too. Each of the mages fought either by using their foci or by tossing out little emblems with glyphs pre-painted onto them, firing a variety of spells through—lances of light, bolts of fire, and twisting, shifting shadow, among other effects—and yet none of them permanently disabled the Patchers. Even the more-esoteric spells didn't seem to do much. The equivalent of [**Sleep**] had simply failed against them, and they'd broken out of any of the cages that the mages created in short order; in that sense, it was a miracle that Derivan's barrier had lasted as long as it did.

Although he supposed that this *was* an opportunity to draw up his barrier again.

The mages fought in a way that was quite unlike any other adventurer they'd encountered, though. Derivan wondered if they would be nearly as effective without the massive stream of mana flowing above them. As far as he could tell, there was no form of [**Mana Manipulation**] happening here; if there was a variant of that at play, then he couldn't sense it.

Instead, small streams of visible mana fell from above, connecting to the mages like they were puppets on a string, though the imagery was far more striking. That mana flowed through them and into the glyph-painted emblems, and the emblems would flare with the color of the spell.

It was a mesmerizing sight, and a display of skill, too. Derivan saw the way they moved, the way they breathed. There was a gracefulness to it—almost like the dance they were performing was another way of calling the mana. He remembered what the shopkeeper version of Anyati had said about the personalization of mana, and how it could be a little different in expression for everyone...

He wondered.

But now wasn't the time.

It *was* an opportunity for him to draw up his barrier again, but a barrier wasn't what would save them here. He could wait to recover and try to Shift the Patchers back through all the layers he'd pulled them through; whatever muscle he used for Shifting seemed almost recovered. That was an option.

Until that was an option, though...

Sev had said that they were Patchers, and they were fixing themselves; patching their own problems, as it were. They had a weakness, and they had removed it—but now he had access to what was presumably the same mechanism they used. If he could just reach out with Patch—

It was a new stat. He didn't understand all that it could do, yet; he could barely find where it was located in his soul. If he focused, he could sense an oddity in the air in front of him, right where the Patchers were. If he focused even more, he could sense strange complexities from the Patchers, like interlocking gears he couldn't quite make heads or tails of.

It was a lot easier to break something than to fix it, though. If it was a complex mechanism...

He reached out without quite understanding what he was doing just yet, using the same sense he'd used to notice this phenomenon at all. The delicate touch of his stat might as well have been a hammer, or a war axe—he had not nearly the stat he needed to make a *gentle* change.

So those metaphorical gears, ticking away invisibly, following some invisible script—they were smashed to pieces.

The Patcher shuddered, slowing down; the next barrage of spells from the mages, another set of luminous beams, tore through those insectoid arms and left gaping holes and bleeding chitin, except this time, those holes did not heal.

Derivan, though, simply stared. He wasn't sure exactly what he'd done there—but he had the feeling that the Patcher had been dead before those spells had hit it. He'd torn apart something vital in a creature that fundamentally relied on the system to exist, and the stat—or the part of him that was that stat—didn't like that. It was supposed to patch. To *fix*—

He suppressed that spiral before it could begin, but Derivan felt uncomfortable. That stat was strange. He'd have to learn to work with its compulsions. This was the first time he felt like he'd *lost* points in a stat, though it wasn't visible in the system interface.

He hadn't even known it was possible to lose points in a stat, and yet the feeling of it was smaller within him.

The new sense, though, hadn't diminished with the slight reduction in Patch—and now that Derivan was paying attention, he could feel how every one of the Patchers showed up on it, complicated pieces of machinery that seemed entirely driven by the System. His friends showed up on it too, though their machinery was more opaque to him—the intricacies of how the system tied in to them and their skills were obfuscated, somehow, or shifted many layers away.

The mages were blank—they had never been tied in to the system. And Derivan himself...

His system was in shambles.

It reminded him of the way the mages were tied to the great mana flow above, streams of mana trickling down to them to feed their spells. Long strings of system-stuff trailed out of that obfuscated box that he saw over each of his friends, like a dozen strings tied to him had been cut, and those strings vanished into the distance, fading entirely out of the new sense.

Derivan wasn't sure how to feel about any of that. But he *did* know now that Patch could kill the Patchers, even if it came at a consequence.

"I will send them back," he said. There were three Patchers left—no doubt he could use Patch to take out at least one more, but he wasn't sure where that would leave his stat, and the feeling of forcing it troubled him. He wanted to understand a bit more about the nature of the stat and the consequences for pushing against it.

"Did you *summon* them here?" one of the mages asked incredulously, staring at him. She was a thin, wasplike figure, though most of her was shrouded in her cloak; he wouldn't have even known she was staring at him if she hadn't rather pointedly made sure he could see her eyes. "Summonings are not legal without the approval of—"

"Oh, come off it, Helg," her companion rolled her eyes; this one had the pattern of a ladybug, and she was taller than either of her two companions. "They came here to help; are ye really going to shove the rules up their collective arse?"

"We should wait for more information," the first mage—the beetle one—said. The next emblem he drew sprayed cloudy, sticky-looking spots of light into the air; they hung there for a moment, ethereal and impossible, and then promptly dove toward one of the three remaining Patchers.

And then they began to *spin*, tearing off the limbs of the Patcher one by one.

... Some of this magic was brutal.

"I did not summon them," Derivan answered, trying to focus on the question at hand, though Patch proved to be a distracting itch. "They were already here; I simply... pulled them closer so we could interact with them. They are likely what has been stealing your mana slivers."

"And you want to send them *back* so they can continue?" Helg asked, her voice acerbic.

"I want to send them back because we cannot fight them as we are now," Derivan said, and then he made the decision for them, before they could convince themselves they could fight anyway. "We will find another way. We now know the cause, and that is progress. Please stand back."

He didn't wait for a response from the mages. Instead, he pushed forward with Shift, feeling now more than ever the way the layers of reality pulled back from him, even when he wasn't actively using the skill. He felt it brush against each of the three remaining Patchers, forcing them forward—

—felt the Patchers slide through several layers of reality, tumbling from the raw force of the Shift—

—and sent them back. The Patchers vanished, fading from sight, and he felt the walls of reality solidify; they would not be able to Shift back for a while.

There was a short silence.

". . . How the hell did you do that?" Helg asked after a moment. She squinted at him, suddenly radiating suspicion. "I didn't sense you using any mana."

"It is a long story," Derivan sighed.

CHAPTER 24

GLYPHS AND SIGNS

Whatever they'd done to engage with the Patchers seemed to have thrown off their plans, if they were capable of having plans at all. As far as Derivan could tell, they didn't return to whatever they were planning to do with the mana slivers; instead, the Shifted presence he felt fled, roughly in the direction of the road back to Fendal.

Which he *was* concerned about, admittedly, but the time variance between Fendal and Teque gave them enough leeway to talk and figure out exactly what was going on.

"I'm waiting," Helg said, folding her arms. The wasp woman didn't seem like she was going to just let them go. Her companions seemed frustrated by her brusqueness but didn't argue with her.

"It is our job to know," the beetle-man told them, sounding somewhat apologetic.

"Why don't we go find Noram first?" Sev suggested smoothly, stepping between Derivan and the holes Helg seemed to be trying to glare into his helmet. Derivan wasn't sure exactly what issue she'd taken with him, but she certainly seemed offended by him in some way. Perhaps it was the fact that he'd apparently been able to do magic without using mana.

... In fact, he could sense a spark of aggression even in her companions, though they seemed much more amiable. They were suspicious when they looked upon him.

"Why should we do that?" Helg asked. She lowered her hood and raised a metaphorical eyebrow at him, one antenna twitching above the other. "He's a busy man. Otter. We don't need to bother him."

"Because if we don't do that, we're going to need to explain this more than once," Sev said with a sigh. He glanced around at the rest of his party, and they all nodded in agreement—Helg stared at them suspiciously, then finally gave an assenting nod.

"Don't try anything," she said sharply.

"You know we've already met Noram, right?" Misa asked, folding her arms. "We met him while he was taking a nap. If we wanted to do anything—"

"You would've been cut down by the spells he puts around himself when he's asleep," Helg interrupted. Vex opened his mouth to protest, then seemed to think better of it, snapping it shut and looking away instead; the waspish lady flicked her gaze to him anyway, sharp eyes drilling into the lizardkin. "Got something to say, lizard?"

"His name is Vex," Derivan said, sounding a touch more aggressive than he had intended.

"I don't care," Helg said.

"He didn't have any defenses up," Vex said quietly. "I would've seen them. Just a basic alarm trigger connected to the stairs."

Helg stared at him for a moment—long enough that the weight of her gaze became uncomfortable for the lizardkin, and he took a slight step backward. She seemed to soften just slightly at that, though there was still a distinct sort of aggression set into her body.

"Then he's an idiot and needs to be taught a lesson again," she said shortly. "But we'll see, won't we?"

Without another word, Helg began marching back toward the center of the city, presumably toward wherever Noram had decided to hole up for his nap. Her ladybug companion started hurrying after her, casting an apologetic glance back at them, and the beetle moved last of all.

"I am sorry about her," he said. "She is connected deeply to the mana. It is ... uncomfortable, at times. It tunes her to its emotions."

"Is the mana ... angry?" Vex asked quietly. The question seemed important to him.

"It is agitated," the beetle-mage replied after a slight pause. "Which is another part of what has been plaguing our city of late, though you will not hear many speak of it. The mana is celebrated here, a force that supports the thriving of our peoples. Few here will admit to anything being wrong with it."

"But you will?" Misa challenged.

"I say things as I see them," the beetle-mage replied. He bowed slightly toward her. "My name is Anton. The other mage is named Unea. We have not introduced ourselves, I realize; I hope this does not cause offense."

"I mean ... no?" Misa answered, glancing around awkwardly when she realized he was talking specifically to her. "I'm not the leader here or anything, y'know."

"Ah," Anton said. "I apologize. You are quite beautiful, you see. I had simply assumed."

"Oh my god," Sev said, muffling a laugh. Misa looked . . . mostly unimpressed, though she glanced over Anton as though judging how capable he would be in a physical fight.

"Hurry up already!" Helg called back after them, and Anton gestured for them to follow him.

"He wasn't kidding about being direct," Sev muttered as he followed. Derivan fell into step beside Vex, even as Misa shook her head.

"Weird timing for a compliment," she grumbled.

It didn't take long for them to find Noram.

What *did* take much longer than it should have was waking the otter up. The first time, he'd woken up as soon as they'd begun to climb up the stairs of the tower, presumably triggering some automatic detection he'd rigged. This time, he'd done the opposite—he was sleeping on a glyph that he'd painted onto the floor. In a very, *very* abstract way, Derivan thought the glyph looked rather like it was shaped like an otter sleeping on a bed.

Which was, to be fair, exactly what the otter was doing. A glowing bed made of blue magic rested beneath him, and he was curled up in it, as comfortable as could be; a dome surrounded him, a perfect shield through which Helg was apparently attempting to break with a death stare, judging by the intensity of it.

"He's got his personal Sign up," the ladybug-mage—Unea, Derivan remembered—said.

"I can *see* that," Helg growled. She stalked over and kicked the dome. "Wake up!"

"He cannot hear you," Anton told her.

"*I know that*," Helg hissed.

"Um," Vex ventured, and all three of the mages looked at him. "What do you mean, *personal Sign*?"

Helg stared for a moment, then threw her hands up. "I'm leaving," she said. "You two can handle this. Call me when Noram wakes up."

Sev opened his mouth, like he was about to say something snarky—Derivan could practically see the sass forming in his throat—but he seemed to reconsider at the last moment. "Is she all right?" he asked instead. He glanced at Anton. "You said something about her connection with the mana agitating her. That can't be pleasant."

"It is not," Anton acknowledged. "But there is little that can be done. Given time, she can work her way past it, but it has been . . . difficult, here, for the past few months." Now Anton seemed uncertain. "It is odd how different this place has been in that time."

"What do you mean?" Sev asked.

"I remember this place being much more alive," Anton said. "But when the Roads deactivated, many people seemed to lose a spark. For weeks, people did not speak at all, simply following a routine; I was among them, and I did not think it strange at the time, though I do now."

"That changed when the first set of mana slivers was stolen," Vex said, and Anton glanced at him. The beetle-mage's mandibles folded together in a sort of frown.

". . . That is correct." Anton looked over the lizardkin carefully. "Do you know something about this?"

"No," Vex shook his head, and then he hesitated. "Maybe. I don't . . . I don't know, exactly. That's why I want to know what a personal Sign is."

"You forgot about his question, ya dingus," Unea finally spoke up. "Was wonderin' when you'd notice."

"Ah," Anton said. He had the courtesy to sound contrite. "My apologies."

"Each an' every one of us gets at least one personal Sign," Unea said. "Issa personal thing. You grow your relationship with mana, learn somethin' about yerself, and bam! You find a Sign. Somethin' that represents *you*. You gotta learn more about it and grow it, and it becomes stronger over time."

"And Noram's is . . . for sleeping?" Sev asked, glancing at the otter, still snoring peacefully in his dome.

"He's one of them lucky motherfuckers that got more than one personal Sign." Unea snorted. "I'm thinkin' he got that one after he became Archmage an' all. Needed more sleep. He deserves it, the poor fella."

"I can't believe he got one just for sleeping," Sev muttered, staring at the dome.

"Can personal Signs be used by others?" Derivan asked. Unea blanched a little bit at the question, and Anton used the opportunity to respond.

"Once they are discovered, then yes, although most guard their Signs jealously," Anton said. "It is an expression of who they are. But it is in the nature of art to want to be shared and looked upon, so in truth, it is not difficult to copy such Signs. It is simply that it is considered taboo to do so."

"Can Signs be combined?" Vex asked, almost too soft to hear.

"They can, but combinin' them is about as hard as breakin' glitterstone," Unea said, apparently glad to have something to talk about other than the idea of using someone else's personal Sign. "Easy-peasy with glyphs. Signs? Ye gotta really work for it."

"And breaking glitterstone is . . . hard?" Vex tried.

"Very," Unea said, nodding seriously. "Glitterstone is about as hard as yilrite, it is."

"I see," Vex said. Derivan had no idea what yilrite was, and he doubted Vex did either, but the lizardkin only glanced at him contemplatively. He looked like wanted to say something but was second-guessing himself.

After a second, though, resolve hardened in his eyes. "I think you might have . . . figured out my Sign for me, Deri."

"I did?" Derivan asked, surprised.

"When you cast your spell," Vex said softly. "The barrier was yours, but the book . . . that was mine, I think. When the Patchers were attacking it, it felt like the spell was trying to understand what they were doing. Logging them, studying them the way I would, feeding the information back to me."

"That should not be possible," Anton commented with a frown. "If your friend was able to cast such a spell, he should have received that information, not you. And there is no precedent for being able to discover someone else's personal Sign for them."

Vex didn't look convinced. "It's what happened," he said.

"Maybe you were imaginin' things, hon?" Unea tried. "It does happen sometimes—"

"If he says that is what happened," Derivan interrupted, "then I am inclined to give him the benefit of the doubt."

Vex shot him a grateful look, and there was something else in his eyes; a little bit of his usual anxiety, certainly, but also a strange bit of sureness. "I don't know how, but I think he did figure out the combined Sign," he said.

"We'd have to see it in action," Unea finally said.

"I'd like to see it in action too," Noram said, and they all startled, turning to look at the wizard. The little otter let out a yawn, stretching and pulling tiny fists above his head. "That was a good nap. Didn't think I'd wake up to see you all here, though."

"I'll go get Helg," Anton said with a sigh.

"Go on," Noram said, nodding at Derivan. The armor hesitated for a moment but eventually called on the mana again, guiding it to his gauntlet; once again, he drew the book-shield glyph he'd come upon just the previous night. Noram stared at it contemplatively, even when the shield formed in front of Derivan.

Then, without warning—and without Noram really moving at all—mana darted in front of him, flowing rapidly into a glyph that looked to be a terrible combination of open maw and sharp fang; what rushed forward from it wasn't so much a physical spell as it was the impression of something gnashing. Yet Derivan felt with certainty that anything in front of that psychic impression would be shredded to pieces—

—It struck his shield and shattered, psychic teeth flying everywhere. At the same time, Vex grimaced slightly, and then his mouth opened and he blinked, staring at Noram.

"If you're right about what that spell does," Noram said, "then you're probably right about whatever else you figured out from that spell. "

Vex nodded, and Derivan watched as a calm confidence came over him, his nerves settling. "I'll tell you what I know."

CHAPTER 25

A HINT OF THE PAST

Vex took a moment to concentrate.

The system always presented information about skills and spells in a neat, orderly sort of way. His glyph did the opposite, in the sense that it fed the information directly into his skull and didn't seem to bother to filter it, meaning he got a whole lot of irrelevant information on top of the actually useful stuff.

Not unlike the way he tended to take research notes, actually. So on that front, there was a possibility that this was slightly his fault.

Just a bit.

It took him a second to sort through and organize the most important information in his mind.

Sign of Renewal
The result of a merge between the personal Sign of the great Archmage ###a#, merged with the Sign of the Great Wyrm during their confrontation many eons ago. The original Sign of Devouring is a unique-class Sign that takes on the form of a set of metaphysical teeth, consuming everything in its path. Tempered with ###a#'s unique Sign of Birth, the result is a spell that consumes the essence of an object and turns it into a seed, to be grown anew.

There was a *lot* of information that Vex had to discard to put even that together. Part of it was a scrambled list of things the Sign had previously been used on and the resultant seed that had been created; Noram—or this version of Noram—had evidently used it on a number of plants that Vex recognized as the same ones along the streets of Teque.

Derivan's spell was, interestingly, not on that list.

Then there was a mess of information about the emotional state of the caster, the names of everyone that knew the spell—useless information that Vex had to sort and discard before it crowded out the more-useful stuff. He did learn *why* the plants had been Renewed, though; apparently, many of them were plants on the surface that they'd lost access to after the mana had closed it off. The Sign didn't keep everything the same, but it was close enough.

It was a small reminder of the breadth of the world they'd once had.

"Renewal," Vex finally said, looking at Noram; the otter's eyes widened slightly, but he didn't say anything. "It consumes something on a metaphysical level and then rebirths it, a little different than before. You use it to preserve some legacies from the surface that don't last down here in Teque."

"An information-gathering personal Sign, then," Noram said thoughtfully. The otter hopped to his feet and glanced at the door, where Anton was bringing a grumpy-looking Helg into the building—not that Helg ever looked *not*-grumpy, as far as Vex could tell. "Those are . . . rare. And not often as potent as yours."

"We don't know that it's mine," Vex said, embarrassed.

"The fact that it's feeding that information back to you and not your friend is good enough evidence for me," Noram said with a shrug. "Though how your friend discovered your Sign for you and managed to integrate it with his own is another question entirely."

"It is because I was thinking about Vex, I believe," Derivan supplied. "He is the reason I am close to magic at all."

"I'm—" Vex started, and then promptly buried his snout in his hands. He *wanted* to hide behind Derivan, because that was what he always did, but this time Derivan was the source of his embarrassment, so he couldn't hide behind *him*—

Noram, watching the two of them, snorted and grinned. "Yeah, okay, never mind, I figured it out."

"Doesn't take long, does it?" Sev commented.

"If you tease him any more, he might explode," Misa said. "Can't have him exploding. It's bad for wizards."

"Have experience with that, do you?" Noram asked, raising a single ottery brow.

"*So much*," Misa sighed. She pulled Vex close to give him a presence to anchor to, and he gratefully hugged into her. She'd always had the most understanding of his anxiety besides Derivan, and Derivan at the moment seemed to be too busy trying to figure out what everyone was talking about . . .

"He'll figure it out," Misa whispered to him. "I think he just did, actually. Fuckin' finally."

Vex decided he really needed to figure out that sink-into-floor spell. If only his friends would let him *try*. It had only blown up twice before! It absolutely wasn't the big deal everyone seemed to think it was—

"Can we get back on topic, please?" Helg finally spoke up, looking disgruntled and vaguely annoyed. Her arms were crossed, and her antennae twitched slightly in irritation. "In case you forgot, we have rogue elements loose in the city, and the Guard can't deal with them because *apparently* they don't hide using spells."

"You said your spell gave you some information on them," Noram said. "What kind of information was that, exactly?"

"It's incomplete," Vex said, grimacing a little as he spoke. Maybe he'd played it up too much—all he knew was that the Patchers gave him a very bad feeling, along with an assorted set of impressions. Every time they struck Derivan's shield, it was like he could feel something being drained away, but it was much harder for him to learn what the Patchers were doing compared to what Noram's spell was doing...

Though that made sense, he supposed. The Patchers were part of the system, and his Sign or glyph was part of the magic here in Teque, or whatever they called their greater world. They opposed each other, in a way.

"It's a lot fuzzier than trying to read the spell," Vex elaborated when he saw the others looking at him; he tried not to fidget, and he felt Derivan stepping up to stand next to him. The large armor's presence calmed him, and he sighed, trying to sort through his thoughts. "I can start with the obvious, I guess—the Patchers work the same way the system does, since they're its agents. They can edit aspects of the system, grant themselves skills, and to a limited extent, they can cause minor shifts in reality."

"The thing is, the ones here are trying to do something *specific*, and that's what I'm struggling with." Vex hesitated, searching his mind for the words. "It's not... Whatever it is they're doing, it's not *good*. But I need more. It's just..."

The Patchers were gone were the words left unsaid.

Helg frowned. She pulled out an arm—quite literally, in fact; Vex felt the shift in mana as she dragged the literal arm of one of the Patchers out of some dimensional space—and held it forward. "Can you use this?"

"Um," Vex said, and then glanced helplessly at Noram. "Probably?"

"You might want to try Signing it yourself," the otter told him, as gently as he could. "It may open new aspects of your spell that aren't available in the combined Sign. Also—no offense—but your current combined Sign is amateurish at best." He glanced at Derivan.

Derivan simply shrugged. "It was my first attempt," he said. "I am not surprised. But I am eager to learn what it could do, if properly combined."

"One might call that a rather intimate act, combining two personal Signs," Noram said, his tone just a bit teasing, and Vex tried to ignore the way Derivan glanced contemplatively at him.

"Anyway!" he said, trying to ignore the way his voice pitched a little higher than usual. "How do I— Um. Right. I have this." He rummaged around in his tailpouch, eventually pulling out his magelight; the inscriptions on it glinted in the light. Noram watched him with something that looked like a spark of recognition but didn't say anything.

Vex used [**Splash of Mana**], feeling it feed into the magelight and fill the chamber within, and then . . . hesitated.

This was, already, different from anything that the people of Teque did when casting their magics. He'd never seen any of them use their own mana to cast; they worked *with* the mana that streamed through Teque. Their glyphs were all preprepared, with the only exception he'd seen being Noram's use of the Sign of Renewal just now.

"What did you just do?" Helg muttered, staring at him, and Noram shook his head and shushed her. Vex decided to ignore them both for now.

He needed something that represented *him*. And he had some idea of what his Sign might look like, thanks to Derivan; it would be something like a book . . .

He still hesitated after letting some of the light-green mana he'd generated soak into the brush of the magelight. The bristles gleamed, and he *knew*, with an instinct he hadn't known he had, that he could now use it to cast—but the thought of what he should draw left him entirely. His Sign was a book, certainly, but what kind of book? Was it open or closed? What were the details—

Derivan placed a hand on his shoulder. "You are overthinking," the armor said quietly. "Clear your mind. Draw what comes to you."

Vex . . . breathed. And then he began to paint. He began to draw like he always had for most of his life.

In his darkest moments, art gave him comfort. It had since he was a child. It had while he had endured years of channel burning while his father and his siblings ignored his protests.

It would now, too.

He could sense, somehow, that Derivan was guiding him—that the armor himself wasn't exactly sure what he was doing, only that he was helping. He felt himself being guided, slowly, toward a clearer image. His hand was moving on its own now; the brush strokes were familiar, like he'd been drawing and painting all his life, and when he was done...

"Oh," he said softly.

The glyph represented his first empty notebook.

There were a few glittering shards beside it—no doubt mana slivers. Vex remembered what shopkeeper-Anyati had said, that the mana would award an act of true creation with some slivers; he wondered if there was significance in the number or the size. Derivan had gained the same thing.

Judging by the look Noram was giving him...

But he didn't care about that right now. More important was the surge of emotion the glyph brought with it.

For all that his family had a focus on studying and researching magic, not all of them enjoyed it; some of his brothers and sisters, he knew, found greater joy in understanding the combat applications of magic, or how illusions could be twisted toward beauty. He was the only one among his brothers that had taken to studying and documenting everything, and the memory of his first notebook was something...

He didn't treasure the memory. Not exactly. But it *was* his first gift. The first thing he could truly call his own, gifted to him after his parents had seen how he spent all his time analyzing and studying every piece of magic he came across; it was a small thing, loose papers held together by a copper binder that spiraled through the pages, but it was *his*.

And that was the form the glyph had taken.

Vex swallowed the well of complicated emotion that rose up inside him. He watched instead, silent, as the mana around him began to move—flowing from the great river of mana up above and drifting slowly, carefully toward his glyph at first; then faster and faster, charging it to a brighter potency with every passing second. Noram's eyes widened slightly. Helg reached out, as if about to say something—

"Give me the arm," Vex said, as a small piece of the puzzle unraveled for him and he understood how to use the glyph a little bit more.

The wasp-lady handed it over without another word, her eyes lingering on the mana slivers he had created or been awarded. Vex took the arm, a small part of him disturbed by the fact that he was essentially holding on to a part of a corpse, but the rest automatically following the instinctive instructions that came along with the casting of the spell. He placed it in front of his glyph, and thin tendrils of magic burst from the notebook, latching on to it—

Vex felt the information flow in, and his face paled quickly, even beneath his scales.

CHAPTER 26

ON THE NATURE OF BEING

Vex had known it was bad.

He'd known it was something that scared him; there had been enough spillover, enough intrinsic understanding from the Patcher's attacks that he could grasp that bare essence of it.

But this?

This... *he didn't know how to fix this*. He didn't know if they *could*! He didn't even know how to begin—

"Vex," Derivan said gently, and Vex heard the note of worry in the armor's voice. Derivan's presence helped, and he tried to calm himself.

The purpose and intent of the Patchers lay bare in front of him, resonating in his mind.

They were here to fix a problem. That problem was the fact that the bonus room hadn't activated properly, all the way back when Noram had activated it; the partial activation meant the system had created a shallow, not-quite-there shadow of the real Teque, if there was a real Teque. Vex still wasn't exactly sure what the system drew from. And the system was still trying to fix that error—only, "fixing" the problem meant, in this case, that the bonus room had to be fully activated.

And the resources it had to do so were limited.

There was another reason, too, he sensed, but his mind was more occupied with an understanding that left him feeling slightly sick.

"Misa," Vex said. He tried to control the anxious dread creeping through him. "You know how we talked about how Fendal might be the bonus room?"

"Yes," Misa said cautiously, but her expression was dark and worried. She knew she wasn't going to like whatever Vex was about to tell her.

"Most bonus rooms aren't like your village," Vex said. "I've read about how adventurers have tried to talk to the people in bonus rooms, and they give ... canned responses. They're shadows of the real thing, a simulation by the system. But our bonus rooms are different."

"Right."

"The people in our bonus rooms are ... well, they're people." Vex hesitated. He was stating the obvious, avoiding the truth. "But a lot of people in Fendal were kind of like the shadows I'm talking about. You noticed how the guards reacted to us, right? And the way Gensen behaved?"

"Noram felt real," Derivan pointed out. "Anyati ... Well. We did not interact much with her. But she did not feel as Gensen did."

"Yeah," Vex said. He tried to steady himself, felt the panic creeping into his voice again as he spoke, and looked to Derivan for comfort. One hand found the armor's own, and Derivan squeezed his hand gently, as if to reassure him. Vex wasn't even sure it was a good idea to say what he was about to say out loud, but ...

It didn't seem right to keep it a secret, either.

"You were kinda right," Vex said to Misa; his gaze flickered to Noram and Helg and Anton and Unea, and he felt that unease in his heart growing. "But it's ... not that simple. Fendal is *becoming* a bonus room—the regular kind, the one where the people just have to follow a script—while Teque is becoming more like J'rokksur was, where everyone here is real and whole. The system doesn't have enough juice or whatever it uses to make things *real*, and it's stealing it from Fendal and putting it *here*, and the Patchers are what's doing it, and I don't—I don't know—"

Vex's voice cracked a little. He felt Derivan pulling him into his arms, and he leaned in to that touch, unable to find the words to complete his thought.

The implications terrified him. Because he *understood* what was happening now, and it was worse than he found himself able to express. He understood what the raids were exactly—the idea that there were mistranslated residents of Teque harassing the people of Fendal had been horribly wrong.

There were residents of Teque in Fendal. That explained the greater population of magical species there. Teque was much larger than Fendal in population, and so the system had diverted some of them toward the small town—those deemed not necessary for the bonus room's objectives were effectively piloted into Fendal so they could be harvested like the rest.

And the raids, then, weren't raids at all.

They were *perceived* as such, because Fendal was a town that was near-constantly paranoid of the monsters swarming near them, and whatever the

Patchers were taking from them required a weakness to exploit. A crack in the psyche of those it stole from. It manifested in their memories as a small point of irritation against something they held close: too much noise outside an inn, or precious flowers being chewed on. Guard patrols being disrupted by goblins, ruining the clockwork order in the city.

Every "raid" was a Patcher, stealing something precious and copying it for Teque. Anyati-the-shopkeeper and Noram-the-otter—those were almost certainly not their original names, maybe not even their original selves. How long had the otter version of Noram here been named Noram? Had his name been something else before the Patchers had come along?

And how could they *fix* this? Destroying the Patchers wasn't enough; the system might send more, or if it didn't, then half of Fendal and half of Teque would be stuck halfway between complete and incomplete. Unacceptable. As was sacrificing the people of either town to allow the other to function, complete and whole. He couldn't help but search for a solution, trying to find something that would *fix* this, a way to let both the people of Teque and Fendal live fully—

"Vex."

Vex startled at the sound of his name; he glanced up and realized that Misa was staring at him, a worried look on her face. Derivan was still holding him gently, but even the armor seemed worried; the glow in his eyes was dim, and he held Vex like he was scared he would break.

He'd never seen Derivan frightened before.

"I'm okay," he said, even though he wasn't.

"No, you're fucking not," Misa said. Something like anger passed over her face, but it was gone as quickly as it appeared; it didn't seem to be anger at *him*, in any case. It was replaced quickly by sorrow and then a pained sort of acceptance. "And that's fine. You're allowed to be not okay."

Vex didn't want to talk about it. He looked around instead. Noram and Helg had vanished; only Anton and Unea stood around still, somewhat awkwardly. "Where . . ."

"You were muttering to yourself the whole time," Derivan told him gently. "They went to talk to the other mages. To try to find a fix."

"I don't think they can find one," Vex said quietly, numbly. "I don't . . . I'm not sure there are any good answers here."

"Maybe not." Sev finally spoke up. He'd been quiet for a while, contemplating. There was a shadow over his face, too—no one here was happy, really. "But we'll decide after we know everything. We still don't know why the Patchers were raiding for mana crystals and slivers; those actually went missing, in both Fendal and Teque. We checked. Do you know why they're gone?"

Vex was silent for a moment. The information was *there*. He'd forgotten about it in the flood of everything else, and now he took a breath, trying to steady himself, in case what he found was even worse. "I think so," he said.

Derivan hummed a comforting tune next to him, squeezing his hand, and Vex gave him a grateful smile before turning his mind to the task.

Mana crystals and mana slivers. What did the Patchers want with them?

The information on what mana crystals and mana slivers actually *were* was locked away from him—too far away from what the Patchers were doing. He'd have to run the spell on one of the slivers himself, and he had the feeling that his glyph wouldn't be nearly as effective at deciphering what they did; he needed to spend some time understanding the real limitations of the spell.

But it was still enough for him to understand *why* the Patchers were stealing the crystals and the slivers. The crystals were easy: they needed more crystals. The usual mechanism of having them be spent on maintaining a connection to the system wasn't enough, especially now that those in Fendal were cut off from it. *Why* the system needed those crystals, when it was the one that awarded them to begin with . . . that was a little more up in the air.

The mana slivers, on the other hand, were complicated. As far as Vex could tell, the Patchers thought that the slivers could be *useful*; they had a protocol they had to follow for anything that might help the system perform its tasks. They would have stolen more at a time, even, but for whatever reason, it was difficult for them to transport the slivers. That was the other reason this bonus room had priority over Fendal: the system recognized something *useful* in it.

"It needs the crystals for something," Vex said. "The system, I mean. And it thinks it can use the slivers somehow. But I don't think that . . . helps us."

Sev looked down; Misa clenched her fists, then unclenched them when she saw that Vex was watching her. Derivan simply stayed close, and Vex found that he was grateful for it; he just wished . . .

Now wasn't the time.

"Can you tell us a little more?" Anton asked; he sounded worried, as he had every right to be. He sounded like he'd been holding back that question for a while and was only speaking now that it was silent and he couldn't stand that silence any longer. "Helg and Noram believed you. But I do not understand. What do you mean, *make things real*? Why would there be anything we need to fuel us to be real?"

"I wish we could answer that question." Sev spoke when Vex just curled up on himself a little more, and the lizardkin was grateful for it. He stared at the glyph he'd drawn as it slowly dissipated into motes of light green in the air. "You know what the system is?"

"It is some sort of globe-spanning spell network, as I understand it," Anton said. "One that grants power and the ability to cast spells within it."

"Not a spell," Sev said, shaking his head. "But close enough. It's been there as long as we can remember."

"Which is only a couple hundred years," Vex added, though his words were mumbled. Anton caught on anyway, and his eyes narrowed, making the same connection they had.

"About since the mana began shepherding us underground," Anton said.

"That's what we think," Sev said with a sigh. "The system's been known to . . . I dunno; it's going to sound ridiculous. It handles many of the basic facets of reality."

"The skills it gives us let us do things that mana wouldn't let us do," Vex offered quietly.

"The two forces are opposed?" Anton suggested.

"Mana doesn't seem to like it when we use spells through the system," Vex said with a sigh; he looked down at the ground, at the stone patterning on the floor. "I can imagine why, after seeing the magic here. It's all so much more . . . alive. There's so much *meaning* when you cast spells."

"Your spells aren't like that," Anton said, and Vex shook his head.

"No," he said. "They're empty. They . . . I don't think it *kills* the mana, exactly, but it takes something out of the mana. Makes it something lesser."

Anton nodded, looking troubled; Unea, beside him, remained silent. She still hadn't said a word about all this.

"Your explanation makes sense," Anton finally said. "I do not want to believe it, but . . . it explains all those months of me seeing everyone act so strangely. Like I was in a dream."

"Why're *you* able to remember that?" Unea asked suddenly. She looked at him, stepping back for a moment. "I don't. I don't remember nothin'. I remember the Roads dying off a week ago, not months."

Anton frowned. He paused for a moment, like he hadn't really thought about it until now, and Vex watched him; there was a nagging feeling in the back of his mind, like maybe the answer to this question was important.

". . . Now that you mention it," Anton said, and then he looked at the table, where the mana slivers Vex had been rewarded were still glowing, "I believe it may be because of those."

CHAPTER 27

BETWEEN A ROCK AND A HARD PLACE

Vex listened as Anton spoke.

He had, it quickly came out, happened to be carrying a large load of mana slivers when the Roads had shut down—presumably the exact moment the bonus room had been created and this little pocket of reality had become "real." Or more real, at any rate. Anton explained there was a blip in his memory there; he'd been overwhelmed by a harrowing sensation of deep *nothingness* before his thoughts had flowed back to him, and when he came back to himself, he was lying collapsed on the ground, the mana slivers scattered all over.

He hadn't managed to come fully into being immediately. What Anton remembered—and had never really questioned until now, when the memory was directly called to his attention—was that he'd simply carried those slivers around and gone about his daily routine. It'd been what he was *doing* at the time, after all, and so he kept going on autopilot.

Anton's face couldn't go ashen. But Vex watched as he slowed his words mid-explanation, as though he was finally thinking about the *state* he'd been in, and he just . . . stopped talking. He sat there for a moment, not saying a word, and Unea shot him a concerned look a moment before he shook off whatever fugue had briefly taken him.

". . . At some point," Anton eventually continued, "I suppose I remembered enough of myself to divert from the path. I finished delivering the slivers I was carrying, and then I wandered."

"You just wandered?" Misa asked.

"I do not think I was fully awake, even then," Anton said. He reached out for one of the slivers on the nearby table, and Vex didn't stop him from taking one to gently roll between his fingers. "I did not think anything was *wrong,* explicitly; I remember only the vague thought that the closure of the Roads made everyone subdued."

"The important thing here," Sev said, "is that the slivers can fix this."

"I think so," Anton agreed, but he looked hesitant. "But it still took a *long time*, and it took a lot of them. When I finished delivering them, I think about half the original load was gone. I assumed I lost them while carrying them around, but . . ."

"It's possible you absorbed them somehow." Vex glanced at the slivers he'd inadvertently created while trying to understand his own personal glyph; they shone there, oddly tempting, shimmering with a prismatic light. Now that he was actually paying attention to them . . .

They weren't like mana crystals at all. He didn't sense mana in them the same way he did with mana crystals.

"Why are they called *mana slivers*, anyway?" he asked. "Do you know what they are?"

"The mana only started rewarding them after we got stuck down here," Anton said. He shook his head. "They help us cast. Extend the effects of some spells, or let other spells do things they should not be able to do. They are valuable. That is why Teque keeps a store of them—we do not store it for citizens but so that we can cast citywide magics if we need to."

"Have you ever needed to?" It was Misa that asked the question. It wasn't sharp and pointed, exactly, but there was a certain tenseness in her words.

". . . Once." Anton frowned, and Unea looked at him; the ladybug-woman seemed like she wanted to speak up. When Anton didn't continue, she did.

"It was hard for him," Unea said. "He had ta make the call to use it. Parasites got in here through the Roads—nasty little fellas. Latched on to mana signatures and ate away at people, then puppeted them with their own personal mana. And in case you're wonderin', no, that ain't happening now. They're shit at pretending, and we checked."

"It was one of the first things I looked into," Anton muttered softly. Unea shot him a sympathetic glance.

"He lost his family in that spell," she said. "Though I s'pose they were lost before that spell was ever cast. A lot of us lost someone. We have magic, but we ain't got any glyphs or Signs to fix anything like that."

They were silent, at that. What was there to say?

"I'm sorry," Vex offered quietly, and Anton tilted his head slightly in acknowledgement.

"The important thing," he said, changing the subject, "is that the slivers might be able to reverse the effect you speak of, somehow. Or if not reverse it . . . then perhaps replace whatever it is that your system takes away from us. Took away from us, when it brought us here."

"We need to understand more about these slivers," Sev said with a frown. "I thought they were just a currency, but it's obviously a lot more than that."

"We have tried," Anton said. "It was—and still is—a focus of study for many of our mages. But the slivers are mostly opaque to our magic, and we have not discovered any Signs that can manipulate them. Perhaps yours will be able to identify something we have not?"

Anton gave Vex a significant glance, then, and the lizardkin blanched slightly under the weight of the beetle-man's gaze. "I . . . Maybe," he said, his words hesitant. "But I don't think it's going to be that easy."

He didn't say the words he wanted to say—that the use of his Sign wasn't exactly comfortable for him. The memory of his first notebook was certainly a large part of who he was, but it was also a reminder of many things he didn't want to remember.

Derivan saw, of course. A metallic hand came up to rest on his shoulder, and for once, Vex didn't feel that much better. It still helped, but . . .

He shook his head and drew on the mana once more; the magelight brush danced beneath his fingers with a practiced ease he shouldn't have had, and the glyph he drew shone brightly.

And yet, when those tendrils reached out for the sliver, they seemed to slip straight through.

"Nope," Vex said. His heart was heavy. "Whatever it is, it doesn't really seem like mana can act on it. It can act on mana, though."

"And we are no closer to understanding them than when they first began to appear," Anton muttered. "I am not sure this is a solution. It brought me back into myself, but it was a process that took time, and even then it did not fully restore my person. Even if it worked completely over a longer period of time . . ."

"There are more people in Fendal and Teque than you have the slivers for," Vex said with a sigh. He'd seen what they had stored up in the so-called warehouse, and considering the number of people in Teque, let alone the population of Teque and Fendal combined—

"Acts of creation great enough to be rewarded with mana slivers are . . . not rare, as such, but perhaps uncommon," Anton said, confirming Vex's worries. "And while we try to use them sparingly, there are still dangers here we use the slivers to combat. Though . . . not as much now, I suppose. Not since the Roads were closed."

"Trying to restore people using slivers is going to be a long and slow process," Sev said with a sigh. "I guess we could take advantage of the time distortion? Bring people into Teque, give them some time with some slivers..."

"Or," Helg said, "we let your system keep doing what it's doing."

Her interruption was met with silence. Helg stood at the top of the stairs of the tower, looking down at them with something that looked like a cross between a frown and a look of sympathetic pity—yet there was a hardness in her gaze, too, of a sort that made Vex flinch and recoil from her.

He was familiar with that look. That was the "hard decisions" look; the kind of look someone gave before they said they were making a decision that was hard but necessary. It was the look his father had given him, the look his brothers had given him, the look his sisters had given him.

Except sometimes—many times—those necessary decisions weren't necessary at all.

Misa bristled at her words almost immediately, and she took a step forward, her fists clenched. "You can't sacrifice a whole other town—"

"Misa," Sev said quietly, and the woman stopped, putting visible effort into restraining herself. Her fists clenched and unclenched, and Helg watched her, impassive to her fit of rage. "Helg, we're coming up with a solution. You don't have to go that far."

"You don't know that your solution will work," Helg said. "And I don't trust that you won't interfere with what your system is doing. Especially since *our individuality is at stake*. Even if I trusted you, I'm not sure I'd be willing to bet on something like that."

"We won't," Sev said. "We want to find a way to fix this, not—"

"The slivers you want to use are crucial to our security," Helg said. "Let's say I do trust you and we go ahead with this plan of yours. Do you think the people of Fendal that we save are going to be grateful? Or are they going to look at their friends and family, half-alive, and decide that we're the ones causing it? Because we *are*, whether we choose to do that or not, and there's one *very obvious solution to that*: kill every single one of us so that your system doesn't have to choose. Meanwhile, we throw away one of the tools that make us as effective as we are."

"Fendal isn't equipped for fighting," Sev argued.

"Neither are we," Helg snapped. "We have mages that can fight, but the majority of our population isn't built for fighting. Their glyphs and Signs are for learning and studying the nature of the world, not combat. *I am not risking our people*, and *you* are mistaking this for a discussion. It is not.

"I am telling you to leave both Fendal and Teque. Your presence here is no longer welcome. You have two hours to grab your things and leave, after which we will use force."

Sev clenched his fists now, angry. Vex wanted to speak up, but he saw the burning in Helg's eyes, and his words caught in his throat; what could he say here that could help?

He should have seen this coming. Should have kept what was happening a secret, so they could figure out a fix before—

"You're just completely fine with letting others suffer for your sake?" Misa asked. She was angry too, but she kept her voice controlled, like a tightly wound spring. "Noram? Even you?"

Vex hadn't even seen the otter. But now that otter version of Noram— or perhaps he wasn't Noram at all, and simply someone that had taken on Noram's name in the exchange of whatever reality-stuff it took to make a person—stepped forward, a little ways down the stairs. He'd been hidden in Helg's shadow before.

And he looked *awful*.

Not physically, exactly. But there was a sense of defeat in his shoulders, and the spark he normally had was gone; he stared blankly at the four of them like he didn't know what to say.

"Well?" Misa demanded.

Noram looked down and then away; that alone spoke volumes. Vex couldn't help but wonder exactly what Helg had said to the archmage to get him to look so downtrodden.

"This is wrong." It was, surprisingly, Anton that spoke up in their defense. The beetle-man stared straight up at Helg. "We should at least look into helping them—"

"Maybe years from now, if we have enough slivers and we're confident that we can take on Fendal," Helg said. "But you gave up your right to make these decisions because you couldn't take it. You gave this position to me. And I am using that authority."

Helg stared down at the four of them. "Two hours," she said. "And then you leave. Whether you want to or not."

CHAPTER 28

NO GOOD ANSWERS

Two hours.

It wasn't a lot of time. It was barely any time at all, Vex thought, and maybe that was exactly why Helg had chosen it. It was just long enough to seem kind but not long enough for them to actually *do* anything with it.

Not that she had seemed kind at all, if that was her goal. Vex glanced around the room—Sev was gearing up to argue with her, and Misa was stepping forward with her fists clenched, ready for a fight. Derivan was the only one that was standing back, observing what was happening, and Vex saw the armor's gaze flicker to him occasionally, as if trying to see how he was doing.

Vex wasn't sure. There was a panic roiling in him, still, but he was in crisis mode; he would have the time to panic properly later.

Anton and Unea stood out, among the six of them. Anton's countenance was indignant and fiercely protective; Unea was standing a little ways back, as if not really wanting to involve herself, but from the way she leaned toward Anton, Vex suspected she agreed with him.

"It's not up for debate." With her hood off, Helg seemed much fiercer than she had before—and it revealed that she wasn't entirely like a wasp, either. Her sharp, angular face was slightly more flesh than chitin, though her mandibles were still plated and shone with polish.

More interesting were the glyphs tattooed onto her face. One was a sharp, angry-looking spiral, which Vex didn't recognize but understood to be aggressive, likely something for combat; the other was strangely symmetrical and perfect, orderly.

"Helg," Sev tried, and it was obvious he was doing his best to be reasonable. Vex had seen him do this before, usually negotiating with other adventurers. "Some of the people in Fendal are your own people. I've seen them.

You can't let the system take away everything that makes them *them* just so you and a handful of others in Teque can carry on like nothing's happened."

The wasp-woman stiffened and glowered, in a strange twist of her mandibles. "You're acting like I'm the villain here," she said. "If there's a villain here, it's *your* system. Your world. All I'm doing is making sure what's left of us stay that way."

"At the cost of everyone else," Misa said. "That sounds like cowardice to me."

"Your solutions are not *better*." Helg glared. "You have empty promises and the beginnings of a solution you don't know will work. I am protecting what's left of us. It is not an *easy* decision."

"I—" Sev began, but before he could continue, Helg cut him off with a sharp shake of her head and a *buzz* of foreign magic that cut off all sound.

Except for hers, apparently. Her voice was cold and detached. "We aren't going to agree on this. I'm leaving. Like I said, you have two hours. If you figure something out in that time, you're welcome to find me. Otherwise, settle whatever affairs you have left here and *leave*."

Before any of them could respond, Helg withdrew a staff from her cloak. Where she'd been hiding it, Vex had no idea, though the swirl of mana made him suspect it was the same sort of magic that she'd used to store the Patcher's arm. She tapped it once on the ground, and Vex caught a rapid shift of mana moving like lightning—striking from the stone at the tip of the staff to a little glyph she kept on her waist. The glyph flared with magic—

—and then she was gone.

Noram too, Vex noticed belatedly. The otter had gone with her. Vex had wanted to ask him why he'd agreed to her plan in the first place; she'd clearly had to convince him, and that was the reason she'd dragged him with her upstairs to begin with. She didn't want them there while she spoke with Noram. Which meant she knew they'd be able to change his mind.

But... there was nothing to be done about that now, short of finding them again. There was no trace of mana in the air he could use to find out where they'd gone.

"Anton," Sev said, clearly thinking the same thing. "Do you know where she went?"

"I do not." The beetle-mage looked frustrated. "We can go pretty much anywhere in the city with that teleport. It's good for emergencies, but we don't have a way to track each other when we do it."

"Shit." Sev scowled, the expression uncharacteristically fierce on the normally calm cleric.

"Doesn't that apply to her, too?" Misa frowned. "She's not going to be able to know where we are. How exactly is she going to *make* us leave?"

"I don't know." Sev glanced at Anton, who shook his head.

"I suspect that is why she took Noram with her," he said. "There are some magics she could use, probably, but nothing us combat mages would know."

Vex could feel a headache growing. "I shouldn't have said anything," he said quietly. "I'm sorry. If I kept quiet about it, maybe we could've figured out how to fix it ourselves."

Sev's face softened. "No use worrying about that now," he said. "Keeping a secret like that would demolish any trust they have in us."

"They already don't trust us," Vex said.

"They trust us enough that this didn't immediately come to blows." Sev paused for a moment, trying to find the words. "If we'd tried to keep that a secret and it came out that we were hiding this . . . that might have been an immediate fight. Two hours isn't much, but it's time for us to figure some things out. It gave us time to talk to Anton and find out that mana slivers can help with the problem."

"Speaking of which," Anton said. He picked up the slivers that appeared earlier, when Vex cast his spell, and gently pressed them into the lizardkin's hands. "You should keep these."

"Don't you need the slivers?" Vex asked, looking up at Anton.

"We have enough," Anton answered mildly. "It will be easier for you to do your research the more of them you have, and you earned this gift from the mana. I only ask that you keep us apprised of anything you discover. I . . . we will continue searching for a solution here."

Somewhat belatedly, he glanced up at Unea, who nodded; her normally jovial expression was dark, but she'd apparently settled on a decision sometime in the middle of the conversation.

Vex thought she looked rather frighteningly pissed, actually.

"Right. We don't have to give up even if Helg *does* make us leave." Misa frowned for a moment, staring into the air as she presumably brought up her system interface. ". . . You don't have access to the system yet, though. We can't communicate that way."

"There are communication glyphs," Anton said. "I will find one to pair with you, and we can stay in touch."

"I think . . ." Derivan spoke up for the first time in a while, and Vex glanced up at him, almost hopeful that the armor had landed upon some miracle solution. That hope was quickly dashed when Derivan continued. "I think that perhaps leaving may be for the best, as much as I disagree with Helg."

"But . . . if we can figure out what's happening here . . ." Vex protested.

"Yes," Derivan agreed. He crouched, leaning low so he could speak face-to-face with Vex. Vex felt himself freezing up in response, and yet . . . he couldn't deny that small bit of comfort he took from the gentle kindness of the armor's voice. "But this place . . . it is a copy of another. Perhaps the answers we seek are not *here*; perhaps we can learn more about mana slivers and their true nature *there*, in the full bonus room in the depths of the Prime Dungeon in Elyra."

. . . Maybe Derivan had a point.

Or maybe Vex just really wanted to believe him.

"I guess it is there," Misa frowned. "Considering the door and all."

"If we're going to be leaving," Vex said, "I want to go back to Fendal. I want . . . I want to talk to the other Noram."

Noram reminded him of himself, and he'd promised to share the runes he'd discovered in those ancient ruins, in that little story he told the younger lizardkin. Besides that, the least he could do—the least all of them could do, really—was to warn everyone in Fendal that still had their selves intact to leave. That way, the worst that could happen with Helg's plan was that everything here would stay the same . . .

. . . which was more or less what she wanted, anyway.

It was with a subdued air that they left. Anton got them the communication glyph he'd mentioned in short order, pairing the carved rock with one of his own, and this time—while they were making their way back through toward the Roads—Vex paid attention to the people of Teque.

Not just the magic like he did before, though that was still awe-inspiring. The river of mana still flowed above, an agitated turbulence that felt like it directly reflected the turmoil he felt in his heart. He wondered how much of this had impacted Helg's decision in the end. Anton had said that she was more sensitive than most to the mana, that her emotions were directly impacted by it . . .

The only thing *he* could see was that the mana was still angry, still frightened, and it was only getting worse as the influence of the system trickled into Teque.

But mana aside, it was the people now that fascinated him. Teque was different from any city or village Vex had ever been to. Very few of the people they ran into were of the same species, unless they were together as a group; many of those species would be designated as "monster" under the system, a condition they still didn't fully understand. There was a set of kobolds laughing and talking amongst themselves, for example, running down the street;

there was an ogre managing a stall; there was a butterfly-looking person, flitting about between the lamp-glyphs, filling in any parts that had eroded with a flutter of their wings and a touch of glitter on the ground.

. . . Then they passed that same group of kobolds once more, as they circled around the building, and Vex realized how much of the city was an illusion—a construct of the system, used to make it feel alive. For all that the system was draining from Fendal and feeding it to Teque, Teque itself still needed these so-called "minor characters," to prevent the people from realizing that something was wrong, that their city was much smaller than it should have been, and the people much lesser.

A little bit of perception manipulation kept the illusion just real enough. And people like Helg, the ones that were willing to accept things as they were, because it was safe . . . they would be able to make themselves believe that illusion, even if they knew otherwise.

Because it was easier.

Because taking something at face value was easier than peering into the flaws within and correcting it, and risking the pain it might cause.

Vex's fists tightened, though he didn't realize it, and didn't loosen until he felt Derivan's hand rest gently on his shoulder; without thinking, he reached up to put his hand in the armor's instead, a split second before he realized what he was doing—

—and then he relaxed.

It was comforting. It felt right.

He'd worry about the specifics later, when he wasn't worried about the very nature of their existence, and how to save the people of Teque.

It was enough, at least, to set his mind turning over the puzzle of the mana slivers.

The end of the Road brought Vex and the others back into Fendal, albeit in a much more somber mood. They went straight back toward the Sleeping Bird to gather their things, brushing past this version of Anyati and the rest of the people of the town; it occurred to Vex that everything they learned explained why they'd appeared out of nowhere, too, like the system had only bothered to bring them in when it was necessary.

Noram, Charise, and the two trackers—Volaro and Juni—sat in a small table in the corner of the inn. Their expressions made Vex do a double take and put the lizardkin almost instantly on edge—and he wasn't the only one, either. "Mom?" Misa asked, concern heavy in her voice. "What's up?"

Charise looked up to meet Misa's eyes, and then nodded toward Noram.

"Hey!" Noram said, waving; his words were bright, but his eyes were not. Vex felt his heart sink. "Good to see you. I wanted to ask: do you think you can teach me anything about magic? I'll pay you."

CHAPTER 29

SENTIMENTALITY

Vex felt something catch in his throat, and a small piece of his heart broke. He'd spoken to Noram not long before. It had been a little over a day in Teque, and with the time differential between the two places ... it couldn't have been more than an hour in Fendal.

Noram couldn't have changed this much in that time, surely? If things happened this quickly, it would have been too obvious. Fendal would've sent for help from the Guild sooner. The Patchers didn't even move this fast! And they'd been *beaten*. Shoved back.

As far as you know, a treacherous voice whispered, and Vex tried his hardest to shut that voice up.

"We already talked about teaching you magic," Vex said, his words coming out stumbling and awkward, his heart beating heavily in his chest. Some small part of him felt like an observer, like he was just watching himself speak from some distance away, and for a single absurd moment, he wondered if this was what it was like for all those who had their personhood stripped away by the system. He wondered if they were forced to watch themselves follow some unseen script, designed to create an illusion of life.

He knew that wasn't true, of course. Probably.

"We did?" Noram frowned, cocking his head; he seemed to give the idea barely a moment of thought before smiling enthusiastically. "Did you agree? I'd love to learn some magic! I want to become an adventurer."

"He's been like this for a while," Charise said. There was a certain heaviness in her voice that brought home exactly how she felt about all this. "We just brought him back here. He seems ... more comfortable." She hesitated before saying the last words, as if holding back something else she wanted to say.

"It's where I'm supposed to be," Noram said, oblivious to the tone of the conversation, and smiled blithely in a way that made Vex's heart drop further.

"This is pretty fucked-up," Volaro said. He wore a scowl half-buried in his graying beard, and his fists were clenched, though hidden in the way he crossed his arms over his chest. Vex saw the faint lines of tension in his shoulders. He was angry more than he was scared—angry at the system, angry at what it was doing...

Vex wondered if Volaro knew that this could have happened to him and the rest of J'rokksur, too, had they not stolen a reality anchor for themselves.

"We haven't gotten much in the way of updates. You know what's going on here?"

Vex glanced at Sev. He wasn't sure he could explain it—not again—but fortunately, the others took over. They explained everything, though a little haltingly and mostly without Vex's help. The lizardkin tried once or twice, but his gaze kept sliding back to Noram and the way the younger wizard didn't say a word to even acknowledge the conversation they were having, and that was...

That *stung*. He remembered how bright and curious Noram was. It reminded him of his brother. He'd been so eager to help. He'd never gotten the chance to give Noram the runic circles he was interested in, never gotten the chance to help him get the spell scrolls he needed to learn to be a proper mage—

Vex pulled back from his thoughts, curling in on himself a little.

The explanation helped, but only a little. Charise nodded as if she had been expecting something like this to be the case all along, but both Volaro and Juni grew more tense. They looked around like they were expecting to be attacked by the Patchers at any moment. It took a rap on the table from Charise to calm them both down, and even then it was clear that Volaro was pissed, and Juni was scared.

"We're safe," Charise said. "We're not really here. Everyone else, though..."

Charise glanced rather significantly at Misa and then at the rest of the party. Derivan shook his head and stepped in.

"I will sense the Patchers should they arrive," he said. "It should not be a significant risk... though given the difficulty we had fighting them, I do not know if we want to engage in a second fight before we understand more."

"How fast did it happen?" Vex asked quietly. He glanced again at Noram and watched as the lizardkin just smiled back at him. Part of him hadn't completely accepted what had happened yet. He didn't know Noram *well*, but he'd resonated with him; they were alike in so many ways...

It was eerie, too, how easy it would have been to pretend that there was nothing wrong. He wondered how many people in Fendal were doing exactly that—maybe some of them had *noticed* and simply chose not to acknowledge it. He wondered if that was Helg's plan, to ignore what was obviously wrong in favor of security and safety.

No; he knew that was her plan. She was well aware of the problems within her own city. She knew her solution would only save a fraction of Teque's own civilians.

"It happened fast." Charise glanced over at Noram and sighed. "I thought something was wrong, but I couldn't figure out what, and we didn't have anything that could stop it. I think the feeling lasted about five minutes, and then he was just . . ."

Her voice trailed off; she didn't know how to continue. Vex fidgeted slightly in the ensuing silence and then made a decision.

"Hey, Noram?" he said. The other lizardkin looked up at him, offering a bright smile, and Vex tried not to let his voice shake. A part of him—a *small* part, he told himself—kept thinking about his little brother, and it made everything about this worse.

Vex took a breath.

Out of his tailpouch, he gathered a few things: his stash of mana slivers, the first gift the mana had given him. The magelight he'd gotten from the moth shopkeeper Anyati. The notebook that had his notes on runic circles as well as a plethora of other notes on various forms of runic circuitry, and several dozens of the little sketches he'd been worried about anyone else seeing before.

That worry seemed so far away now.

He hesitated for a moment with the last two. The notebook held some of his first memories with Derivan and with this party of friends. The magelight he hadn't held for long, but it was precious to him; it was a beautiful gift, and it was a mark of a whole new system of magic he'd been eager to explore.

. . . But it wasn't like he couldn't use glyphs without the magelight. He'd find a way.

He kept one sliver for himself—a promise, a reminder, and something he could do research on. The rest he placed on top of the notebook, put it together with the magelight, and then stared at it for a moment.

Anton had said something about mana slivers helping him recover his sense of self over time. He didn't know how many slivers that took, or how *long* that process took, but . . . maybe this would be enough.

And if it wasn't? It wasn't like they were giving up.

"Here," Vex said, and gently pushed the small stack of items over to Noram. "You wanted to learn magic, right? Here are the notes I promised, and . . . something that should help you here, when you no longer have the system's help to cast."

"You promised me notes?" Noram blinked once at Vex, barely registering everything else Vex had said. "Well, sure! Thank you. Let me get you a reward—"

"—Please don't," Vex interrupted, shaking his head. The last thing he wanted was a reward for this.

"But I gotta," Noram told him, and something about the way he said it made Vex look up cautiously.

He wasn't awake. Not exactly. But there was a faint spark of rebellion in his eyes; something in him was *trying*.

Charise picked up on it as well. The woman frowned, her eyebrows furrowing, and she gave Vex a quick, furtive nod. *Take it.*

". . . Okay, then," Vex said, still a little reluctant but recognizing that something about this was significant. Noram reached into his pocket and withdrew . . . something he definitely should not have had.

This was a quest reward. Not the kind of quest reward that was obtained from the Guild when a quest there was completed; it was the kind of quest reward that was obtained from completing sub-objectives in a bonus room.

Not an item. An Item, graded and described, recognized by the system.

Part of him was almost *angry* that the system had deemed a small act of kindness to be *transactional*. He didn't need a reward for this. So much of this could be seen as *his fault*.

The other part of him paid attention to exactly what it was he was being given, and *that* pushed him over into genuine anger. Not at Noram, and maybe not even at the system, but at the cruelty of turning something like this into a quest reward.

[Spelldisk] [Grade: Rare]
A sentimental item that belonged to a young would-be adventurer. He crafted this in the dead of the night, where his parents would not be able to see, each day pressing a new rune into the circuit along the edges.
On the surface, it casts a simple Light spell. But Light exists to cast away Shadow, and in the same way, the Spelldisk may bring a secret to light.

"Are you sure you want to give me this?" Vex asked Noram. He knew what the answer would be, but it felt wrong not to ask.

"Of course!" Noram said, as Vex knew he would, but then he leaned forward and nodded as well.

How much of Noram was still in there, exactly?

Maybe there was something here that could help.

". . . Okay," Vex said, and took the [**Spelldisk**] from Noram. "Thank you."

"Thank *you*," Noram told him; he smiled yet again, taking the slivers and the notebook and the magelight and vanishing them into his pocket. Vex didn't know what to say, so he only swallowed and nodded, and glanced back to the others for support.

Each of them had equally grim expressions on their faces.

"I don't like the idea of leaving like this," Misa said. Her fist was curled tightly around the mace at her side, and she gave the weapon an almost-absentminded twirl that made several of the other patrons of the bar flinch. "If we *know* what we need to find is in Elyra, that's one thing. This feels too much like just abandoning them to this shit."

"I'm not okay with leaving like this either," Sev said, shaking his head. "We've got Anton to help out on the inside . . . What about Charise, Volaro, and Juni?"

"We can stay, but it'll mean that Misa can't summon us again in Elyra if we're needed. We'll need to be dismissed here before that can happen." Charise considered this for a moment. "As long as this isn't a permanent cost in some way, I think we should stay. We can help coordinate things if you end up being forced to leave."

"Good fucking luck forcing us to leave," Misa muttered, but Vex noticed that she looked worried. He agreed. Maybe there was nothing left here to find and the true answer would be in the dungeon's bonus room. Maybe he needed to trust Anton and Charise and everyone else who was on their side and hope they would be able to find an answer themselves to this mess.

And yet it seemed wrong to leave . . .

Before Vex could follow that train of thought any further, there was a flare of *magic*.

Vex startled. Derivan did too, the prickle of intensity making him look up toward the Road where Teque lay; even Noram, with most of his self stripped away, glanced in the direction of Teque almost instinctively.

A massive barrier of pure mana rose up from the underground city, traveling through the Road at speed; it did nothing as it touched Fendal, passing through the buildings and people that lived there like it wasn't even *there*. But there was no reason to cast a magic like this save for one—

"Misa," Vex said quickly. She was already on it; her mace glowed in front of her, but the glow flickered and died, and she shook her head in frustration.

"It's not an attack," she said.

Not an attack. That meant it wouldn't damage them, wouldn't violate their selves or personhood in some inextricable way. But it was still a wave of solid mana that was approaching them at speed—it certainly *looked* like an attack, and Vex worked fast to try to interpret exactly what the magic *did*.

But there was no runic circle for him to decode, no glyph for him to interpret. All his understanding emerged from the baseline knowledge that magic required an anchor.

"It is Shifting everything," Derivan said, to Vex's surprise; he glanced at the armor and saw Derivan's eyes glowing deeply as he concentrated. "Not a lot. But just slightly, to be out of tune with everything else. I do not think—"

And they were out of time, and the barrier struck them.

Like Misa said, it wasn't an attack. It took none of their health, did no damage to them, did nothing to rip away anything important and personal. It didn't try to violate their minds.

It pushed Vex and the others backward, though.

Them and everything they owned. The expanding mana barrier *filtered them out*, like they were foreign, unwanted objects. Even without Shift, Vex could feel the way he was altered to be just slightly out of tune; a wave of nausea overcame him as he was pushed through the walls of the inn and the various objects in Fendal like they weren't even there. He was intangible to them, and they were intangible to him.

He tried to fight it. He grabbed his dagger and tried to cut a rune into that bright wall of mana, tried to force a spell out through the system, tried to do *anything*. He had an immense amount of mana to bring to bear himself—

But it all happened too quickly.

There was a moment of vertigo, and they were all dumped unceremoniously outside of Fendal.

Misa looked quite understandably pissed. "That *fucker*," she cursed.

CHAPTER 30

VELYKOS-FRIENDSHIP AND GUIDANCE

Meanwhile, Velykos was not entirely sure how he had ended up in this situation.

Intellectually, he supposed, he understood exactly how he'd ended up like this; the strides he could take as a large, towering stone elemental were much larger than the strides of any of his skeletal companions, and as a result, he could move much faster with less effort than the other five. This was fine and expected, and he had intentionally slowed down so they could move at the same pace. He did not need to get anywhere in a rush.

They did not particularly seem to agree, though, once they noticed. It hadn't taken too long after that for Iliss-the-lizardkin-lady to suggest that they simply sit on his shoulders, and Velykos hadn't really had any reason to object; they were all relatively light, and it took no great effort for him to carry any of them.

It was just that, well . . . they didn't all fit on his shoulders.

Which was how he'd ended up walking along the desert with two skeletons on each shoulder, and the captain perched on his head.

Velykos *almost* sighed but didn't; the act would have disrupted Harold's balance, and the poor man had already fallen off once.

Besides . . . he didn't hate this. He'd grown fond of his companions over time, and as awkward as this was, it was one way they would leave a permanent mark on his history—anything they did would be permanently etched into his stone, even if it was only by the smallest amount. Every tiny chip and small bit of rock that eroded away because of them was another memory of the people he'd come to consider friends.

Normally, he'd say that it was a way for mortals to leave a permanent mark on him, even after they were gone—but he supposed that this particular group of companions weren't necessarily mortal anymore. Maybe now he could have smaller friends that would stick around for a long time...

He rather liked that thought, he found. It had been a long time since he could consider having friends that would last. There was a reason he had decided to devote himself to his chosen god instead, keeping most of his interactions with mortals to something short.

But kind, of course. Always kind.

"What're ya thinking about, big guy?" Harold asked him from atop his head. "You're makin' them thinking sounds again."

"I do not make thinking sounds," Velykos rumbled, amusement clear in the rolling pebbles of his voice—or at least, *he* thought his amusement was clear.

"Ya do. I can hear 'em. Sounds like sand tricklin' down." Harold nodded, and Velykos felt the movement through the tiny vibrations in his stone. "... Not that I'm sayin' your brain is like sand or anything. But there's a sound, I'm tellin' ya!"

"You've been going on about this *sound* for days," Iliss grumbled from his left shoulder. "He doesn't make thinking sounds! I can't hear anything!"

"Just 'cause *you* don't hear any sounds don't mean he don't make any! Ya just ain't got any ears."

"Neither do you, *Captain*," Iliss pointed out, folding her arms obstinately. Ixiss—who *was* in fact her brother, Velykos had learned, and was sitting next to her—groaned.

"Oh by the *gods* you two have been arguing about this for days," he said. "Who cares! It's just a noise!"

"It's a noise that doesn't exist!" Iliss protested. "Our captain is hearing things!"

"I can *hear you*," Harold said, glaring at her.

"See! He's *hearing things*."

"When did ya get this sassy, I swear," Harold grumbled.

Velykos, who was quite content to simply wait them out while they bantered, let out a chuckle when they were done. He didn't address the conversation at all—he didn't think he made any noises, though Harold did have an uncanny ability to notice when he was lost in thought, so perhaps there was in fact something the captain was picking up on. Instead, he changed the subject. "We are close to the next marker. We can take a break there, I think."

"By *we* you mostly just mean you," Iliss snarked. "Wait, do you even need to rest?"

"He's got no muscles," Ixiss complained, punching his sister in the shoulder and making her bones clack uncomfortably; she glared at him. "Why would he need to rest?"

"I don't know; maybe his magic gets tired?" Iliss shrugged. "I don't know how stone elementals work. Do *you*?"

"I do not need rest, necessarily," Velykos interrupted before the argument could go any further; as much as he found the banter between the two siblings amusing, he found it could get to be a bit much rather quickly. "But I find it is good to have structure. It is easy to lose track of time and self if you simply wander with no regard for what surrounds you."

"You speak from experience?"

It was Olag, that time, who spoke. The orc sat on his right shoulder, with his human friend half-curled up beside him; Nathan was still having trouble actually participating in the conversation.

"I do, yes," Velykos answered. "There was a time when I did little but wander. It is . . . easy to lose time when you do this. And I suppose I was grieving, in my own way."

The others fell silent. He'd spoken of his story to them before, of the priest that had guided him through so much of his early life and then simply vanished; his mortal friends didn't seem to know quite how to react.

"Sometimes, we need a little time to get used to our circumstances," Velykos added gently. The words were directed toward Nathan, and the man in question twitched slightly but didn't say anything.

He'd tried, over the last couple of days, to see if he could reach out and connect with him—but it was difficult. Depression was the barest beginning of what he was going through; he was half-catatonic most of the time, staring at the missing flesh on his hands.

Velykos understood. He'd even tried to help, in his own way; tried to find a healing spell that would reverse their condition.

But there was nothing. Not even when he spoke to Nillea; she had no clue of a solution, either. Their state wasn't a *status effect*, was the problem. The system didn't recognize it. It was simply something that *was*, due to an odd circumstance that would almost certainly never be replicated again. He'd heard a little bit about that from them, and what Misa had managed to pull off was certainly an impressive feat.

Everyone was grateful, even if not necessarily happy with the circumstance they were now stuck in—all of them except for Nathan, who simply curled tighter in on himself.

So all he could provide for Nathan were companionship and hope that the young man would find a way to grow comfortable with his body in time. Or perhaps they would find a new solution for him! A way to move his soul into another body?

It was a thought, at least.

"I can hear ya thinkin' again," Harold told him, and Velykos... well, he didn't particularly understand the mortal habit of sighing, but he was very much starting to.

The desert they were in was the one where he had originally spawned; it was a breeding ground for stone-aligned mana, although Velykos couldn't help but notice that the concentration of it seemed rather lesser these days. Little makeshift quarries of stone were scattered across the desert, a small stone tower in the center of each acting like a little beacon to draw in more mana. That mana would slowly seep into the stone and rock around them and, over a long period of time, create a new stone elemental.

The quarry he was looking for was the one he had spawned in. The one he'd met that priest in, so long ago. But it was far, deep in the depths of the desert, and so for the time being—

"Oh, fer cryin' out loud," Harold muttered.

—they would have to take refuge from the heat in yet another quarry.

Not that there was any real need to do such a thing, since none of them needed protection from the heat, exactly. They all just agreed it was uncomfortable, and there was always a little bit of history they could learn from each. Like it or not, his tiny friends were all learning a little bit about stone elemental culture.

...Which was mostly just a lot about stone elemental babies. Though that wasn't *quite* the right word for it.

"Are we ever going to rest somewhere different?" Ixiss muttered.

"What is wrong with the quarries?" Velykos asked, framing his question as though it were an innocent one, and he felt perhaps the smallest amount of satisfaction in the way Iliss simply folded her arms and sighed.

"I just don't want to get almost crushed by a newborn elemental again!" the lizardkin-skeleton complained. Velykos shrugged—making all four of the soldiers on his shoulders yelp in response, grabbing on to steady themselves—and then lowered them all down to the floor of that quarry.

"It is a learning experience," he told them sternly.

"We already learned that lesson!"

"It is a learning experience *for the stone elementals*," Velykos clarified with what amounted to a grin, flecks of dirt and smaller stone falling from him. Ixiss groaned in response.

"Dammit."

There was a small ritual Velykos had taken to doing now, at every one of these quarries they stopped at; they didn't stop all that often, after all. So every time they did, he knelt down by the stone tower in the center, and he prayed to Nillea.

Not all that long ago, it would have been a simple prayer for protection before he moved on. Now, he tried to do a little bit of what he'd learned from Sev—that the relationship between gods and mortals perhaps did not have to be so blindly transactional, with favors rewarded in return for faith and obedience. That whole thing was merely a construct. Instead, he could begin his prayers with a single question:

How are you?

Nillea never answered directly—but something about the bond he had with his chosen god pulsed, and he felt his connection to the earth deepen in response; she was, after all, the goddess of the earth. And the earth right now felt to him like it was something shallow and desperate; the soil here was that of a desert, so it was all loose sand, and yet there was something else to it—

Ah. The desert was *empty*. That was what the connection rang with: a response to his question, an emptiness and a loneliness.

It was true that there were a lot fewer stone elemental children around than there should have been, on top of the strangeness of the mana. Velykos wondered how much of that was Nillea specifically, and how much of that might have been the rest of this problem of missing gods; could they really know how much was missing in their knowledge?

"Hey," he said out loud, surprising even himself; when his companions looked up at him, he tried to smile in response, though he'd been told that his attempts at smiles were largely terrifying. "Would you like to try something together?"

"... And what is that, exactly?" Iliss asked.

"I would like to sculpt an offering to Nillea," Velykos said. He had been mulling over the thought for a while, the idea of creating something as a dedication to both the old and the new. Perhaps it was an activity his new friends would enjoy. "A small token to commemorate a moment I hope will become important."

Velykos hesitated before he shared his next thoughts; saying the words felt like it would make them more real. Iliss stared at him curiously, but it was Nathan looking up slightly that spurred him to speak.

"... And perhaps," he said slowly. "It will also be a small dedication to the god I may have once had."

CHAPTER 31

PAST TRAUMAS

Vex sat with his tail curled, feeling the solid barrier of mana press into his back.

"*Fuck*," Misa said again.

The good news was that their caravan had been pushed out too. Whatever spell that was, Helg had at least been considerate enough to include everything that belonged to them—that, or she'd known somehow that forcibly taking their property might have constituted an *attack* by the confines of Misa's skill. Charise and Volaro and Juni all stayed within Fendal, presumably because they were a product of Misa's skill instead of being anything "real."

The bad news was that this barrier was solid and impossible to break. The Shift embedded into the spell allowed it to force them out without harm, and now it was layered within the mana in a way that was so obscured, neither Vex nor Derivan could make heads or tails of it. And that was ignoring the fact that it was a solid chunk of pure mana with no flaws Vex could see, even with his advanced version of [**Mana Sight**].

An hour had passed since Vex and the others had been forced outside of Fendal, and they still hadn't been able to make their way back in. They'd tried everything they could think of to break the barrier, to no success—no amount of magic broke through it, and there was a weight to it that Derivan couldn't simply Shift through. They'd tried to dig underneath, but the barrier extended beneath the ground and up into the sky in a perfect sphere.

And it was *visible*. That was the worst part, Vex thought; it could call in people to see what was happening rather easily, and he wasn't sure he wanted to know how Helg would deal with new adventurers knocking at their door.

"We're going to have to leave, aren't we?" Misa scowled. "She got what she wanted. Fucker."

"I mean, I don't think we should stay," Sev said, sighing. He stared at the barrier, then beyond it, into Fendal; most of the people in the town hadn't even reacted to their being forced back. Charise, Volaro, and Juni had all rushed out after them, of course, and stood on the other side of the barrier—but they couldn't do anything to break through it either.

Misa's connection to them via her skill was weakened too. She couldn't dismiss them even if she wanted, which presented . . . a whole host of new problems, really.

"We don't have any way to get in," Sev elaborated when no one else spoke up. He was trying to justify it to himself too. "We might be able to find another way in from somewhere else. But not if we stay here."

"I need to understand glyphs more," Vex said quietly. "I don't mind if we finish traveling to Elyra and deliver the food. I . . . I need to know how Helg was able to do this. This spell is nothing like any barrier spell I've seen before."

Because no spell he'd seen before had interacted with a fundamental facet of reality the way Shift did. And yet, there the barrier was, doing exactly that—and doing it to such an extent that even Derivan couldn't break through it.

It meant there was something to learn. Something he could take and make his own.

And once he made it his own, he could break it.

Probably. Those were the words he told himself, but he could feel a sick nausea infecting him, and he tried his best to calm his panicking heart.

This is not your fault.

"I should've expected Helg to do this." Sev exhaled, his fists clenching and unclenching; he paced around in the grass, and Vex watched as the greenery sprang back to life beneath his feet. He let himself get lost in that minor, repetitive sight: weeds and flowers and grass sprouting from the dirt as Sev paced. Was this a new skill? Or was this just divine energy leaking out from Sev, driven by his anger?

Those were easier questions to ponder. He tried to distract himself with them.

"I *did* expect Helg to do this." Unlike Sev, Misa was leaning back against their caravan—Vex could tell from the tension in her arms that she was just as angry, though. Her anger was just held in like a tightly wound spring. "I just thought we'd be able to fucking *do* something about it. What the fuck even is this?"

Misa had always been strong. Physically, yes, but mentally, too; Vex could always count on her to lean on. But she was tense, and angry, and she hadn't yet even glanced in his direction, too busy staring at the bright wall of mana keeping them separated from Fendal.

"A Shifted barrier," Derivan said. He didn't have nearly the same body language as the others, but Vex recognized the uncharacteristic stillness in him. Derivan usually made some attempt at mimicking the movement and life that organic life typically had.

Now all that life and movement was gone, and if not for the glow in his eyes, he might as well have been an empty suit of armor set on display.

Vex shuddered at the thought, and a coldness pooled deep in his gut.

"I know *that*," Misa said, scowling—but the heat in her voice wasn't directed at Derivan. "Did you manage to figure out anything else?"

"Only that the mana is just Shifted enough to make it near-impossible to impact with any variant of [**Mana Manipulation**]," Derivan said. "And the sheer quantity of it... I cannot Shift enough of it to make an impact."

Vex curled up a little more, hunching down, making himself as small and unseen as possible. He didn't want his friends to see him like this.

"I just want to know what the hells she was thinking." Sev kicked at a clump of dirt before collapsing dejectedly to the ground.

"... Vex? Are you all right?"

Derivan had noticed. Of course he had. Kind, wonderful Derivan, who had done nothing but be supportive of him, who was now worried about him *again*.

There was a part of Vex that understood he was panicking. There was a part of him that knew this was just the events and emotions of the past few days all catching up to him and hitting him all at once. He curled his tail around himself so he could hug it close and tried to calm his rapidly accelerating breathing. He couldn't answer Derivan. If he spoke now, they'd all know.

He didn't need to break down. He *couldn't* break down. He couldn't. So much of this was riding on him—so much of this had been *caused* by him, caused by the stupid door with the stupid symbol of his stupid family. So much of this *reminded him of his family—*

"She doesn't even realize what she's doing." The words spilled out of Vex before he could stop himself; he hugged his tail close, gripping it tight enough that it almost began to hurt. "She doesn't—she doesn't know. The system makes it *so easy* for you to trick yourself if you want to. It makes it so easy for you to believe your own lies, to pretend everything is fine, to pretend that bad things are *good*."

"Vex—" Misa began, but the words had already begun to spill, and Vex found he couldn't stop himself. He did see her concern from the edges of his vision, the way her anger spilled away into raw concern, and it only made him feel worse.

"*You don't understand.*" Vex spoke the words with more force than he intended. "I've seen all this—all this *shit* before. My whole family, pretending nothing's wrong, pretending that channel burning is fine, telling me that I'd come out *more powerful*—"

He had to stop talking there. Vex's breathing was shallower than he wanted it to be, and he was briefly aware that he was hyperventilating, sucking in air and not quite getting enough. He told himself to calm, but—

—he remembered those moments strapped into the chair, mana flooding into his body in a way that made every nerve scream with protest, the mana bar in his status slowly ticking *up*, and his parents whispering sweet, encouraging nothings to him to try to help him through the pain—

He wasn't fucking *calm*. He couldn't be.

What he'd seen in Helg's eyes was the same thing he saw in the eyes of his older brothers and sisters. They had been through the same thing, and wasn't it normal, to grow up like this? Every noble family in Elyra had to make some kind of sacrifice; the specifics were up in the air, because each one kept their own secrets, their own Principle. But it was very rare that the secret they kept was something pleasant.

Elyra rewarded results, after all. It didn't particularly care how you got there. He'd never known there could be something *better* than what his parents and siblings told him was normal, not until he was allowed out into the streets. That was long after he had gained stats in the excess of thousands of mana even at a measly level of one, and he'd seen some children playing together in the streets.

Playing. Not studying! Not learning magic, or any of the deeper secrets of the world. One of them fell over and started to cry, the scrape on his knees calling the attention of his mother, who fussed over him and gently bandaged the wound.

Vex had scraped his knee before. He hadn't even flinched. That amount of pain was nothing to him.

But he understood something that day, though he hadn't quite been able to put it into words at the time: he understood how easy it could be to force someone to make a choice without ever using force at all, simply by not letting them know there was another option out there.

His parents had never forced him into that chair. He hated it, of course, and he whined and begged to not have to do it, but they would nod at him sternly, and he would sag and sit in the chair anyway. It was what he was supposed to do. Every sibling he spoke to would say they felt the same way—that they had hated the process, but it had been necessary to make their family strong, to keep them within the noble class. And how they had celebrated that strength! Every point of mana was awarded with a new dessert, or a new toy, or more often a new book about magic he could study. His love for magic was genuine, and he could always spare a few more seconds in that chair if it meant he could get another book.

All of these were, technically, choices he had made. His parents had spent those few years telling him how brave he was, how special he was, how he would do great things. He believed them. How could he do otherwise? They were his *parents*. He'd grown up with those stories of believing in great heroes with massive mana pools. He'd seen his siblings go through the same thing.

He'd never understood that it wasn't something he *had* to do. He never considered the possibility that there was any other choice at all. And now he saw the same thing, reflected in so many others: people making choices they didn't really have to, because they felt they were forced into it by their circumstances.

People making *hard decisions*. Vex felt a cold resentment sweeping through him at the idea. Hard decisions were real, certainly; they were a required part of adventuring—but all too often, it was just an excuse for not looking harder, for not finding a better way.

"She thinks she's making the hard choice," Vex spat. "But she's not. She's making the easy one. The one where she doesn't have to trust anyone else, the one where she doesn't have to make her or her people *vulnerable*. She has no way of knowing things are going to stay the same. She can't know that the system will keep finding Teque *useful*. Once it's done with the mana slivers . . ."

"Her logic is sound," Derivan said quietly, and Vex opened his mouth to protest; it shut again when he saw the light of Derivan's eyes.

It *burned*. It burned with a quiet fury that matched his own, almost bright enough to sweep his own fear and panic and anger away. Derivan's voice was tightly controlled when he spoke again. "But sound logic does not excuse cowardice."

Somehow, seeing his friend this angry snapped him partially out of the panic threatening to overtake him.

"I just— I don't want this to be *my fault*." Vex's voice was small. "This is my bonus room. I feel like—I feel like I did this. And I feel like I need to do something. I can't just leave and let this all continue. I *can't*. But . . ."

". . . Look." Misa said. Vex looked at her, and he saw her visibly packing away her anger and tension. Her voice was gentle when she spoke, though it was clearly difficult for her. "Blaming yourself for something the system assigned to you isn't going to get us anywhere. You weren't involved in any of this—not the creation of the room, not whatever made this room get copied. We *know* that the arrow fucker is involved, remember? You saw him in our room."

Hearing the words . . . helped. A little. It helped less than he thought it might, but maybe that was because they would be heading back to Elyra again, and the dread for that was clouding his mind. Or maybe it was just the thought of Noram, stripped away of whatever element it was that had made him alive and real.

But though it made him feel a little guilty, having someone else to blame helped.

There *had* been interference here. Interference by the same entity that had nearly killed the entire delve team, including Misa. He remembered the smirk on his—on its face.

He doubted it was human.

"We can't do anything else here," Sev told him quietly, and Vex saw that the cleric had approached him too, crouching so he could speak at Vex's level. "We have people on the inside. We'll keep getting updates as we go. I'll send the Guild an update, too, and see if anyone they've got can break in through the barrier. We don't have to do this *alone*, and we need to have faith that the people we left in there can help. *And* we might be able to find out more in Elyra."

Vex heaved out a sigh.

Right. Elyra. Home.

Sev's look was sympathetic. "Not looking forward to it?"

"No," Vex admitted. He closed his eyes for a moment—he'd nearly had a breakdown. He *had* had a breakdown. And Derivan and the others had brought him back, but . . . he couldn't keep hiding this. He couldn't keep ignoring it. "And I think I should explain why. Just . . . it's going to be a long story. Let's—let's talk about it once we get back in the caravan."

He still wasn't *better*. His heart still hammered in his chest, and it was hard for him to look anyone in the eye, but . . . for now, he had the strength to pretend.

"Sure," Sev said. He looked like he wanted to say something else, too, but backed off after a moment, glancing back at the barrier instead and then sighing. ". . . Fuck. This feels a bit like losing, doesn't it."

"Feels a lot like losing," Misa said. "I don't like it."

"We have gained new tools," Derivan said. "I gained a new stat, too, in the fight against the Patchers, but it is . . . different from the others. It feels more dangerous to use. I would like to take the time to explore it."

"And . . . I need to learn more about glyphs." Vex hesitated; he wanted to contribute, but it felt a little empty at the moment. He took a second to watch the patterns of mana in the air. Outside of Fendal and Teque, it all seemed a lot more lifeless. He wasn't even sure if glyphs would still *work* out there . . . He reached for his magelight again, only to remember that it was missing. He'd given it to Noram.

He'd just need to make a new one.

"I would like to help," Derivan said quietly, watching him. "There are many glyphs we do not know of, I am sure. We could learn some from Anton, but perhaps more crucially, we should learn how they discover or create them in the first place."

"Right," Vex said. "I . . . That'd be useful, yeah. I'd love your help. Um, especially if you can quantify how you were able to figure out our Signs and combine them. I need to make some notes and sketch them both out, and then maybe we can get Sev and Misa to figure out their own too . . ."

Vex trailed off a bit. He didn't know how genuine he sounded. This *was* interesting to him, but there was a fog hanging over his heart.

"Let's go," he said instead.

Misa exchanged a quick goodbye with her mom, though Vex didn't miss the worried glances they shared with each other. Sev went to prepare to leave. There was one more stop they had to make before Elyra, but that quest was not a dangerous quest at all.

A small part of him knew it would be a good break, a way to rest and reset. But the larger part of Vex wanted to rush to Elyra and demand access to the dungeon, in the hopes they would find something to solve all this.

He sighed.

Or maybe, he thought, he needed to trust the people they were leaving in Fendal instead.

Now he just needed to gather the courage to talk about his family and the reason he wanted so badly to get his brother *out*.

CHAPTER 32

CATHARSIS

Vex and the others were back in the caravan, with Derivan and Vex seated across from Sev and Misa as it chugged along the road. No more wasting time at the barrier. They knew what they had to do, and Anton and Charise were working at the Teque and Fendal sides of the crisis, respectively; there was nothing else to be done.

Not before Anton had sent them an update through the glyph, though: *Time dilation has been failing. Fendal and Teque now operate at a 1:2 dilation.*

Which was, in some ways, a relief; if things went poorly, the people in Teque wouldn't suffer for months or years.

Then Anton closed the connection, and the caravan became silent.

Which meant it was Vex's turn to talk now. The others were all looking at him expectantly.

Vex took a deep breath.

It took him a few minutes to get haltingly through the explanation of what had happened to him when he was only six: the forcing of energy into his mana channels just to increase the stat, and all the trappings that followed. How his love for magic had been used against him; how he'd been shut away from others, so he couldn't know how different other childhoods were. How he'd never known things could be different.

How pain didn't register to him on the same scale as anyone else now.

There was a heavy silence after Vex was done. He hung his head slightly, feeling oddly ashamed—not that he thought any of what his parents did was his *fault*, necessarily. He'd long since gotten out of that mindset. And yet... the shame was still there. Maybe he *did* blame himself, if only subconsciously.

Sev was mostly quiet, though his apparent calm hid a certain amount of anger; Vex saw the way his fists were clenched.

Derivan's expression was more unreadable than it usually was, but the armor's hand was still gently clasped over his own. He had noticed Vex starting to tremble while telling his story, and slipped a hand into his in response. This time, there was no blush, no rush of anxiety and instinctive worry to accompany the warmth he felt. Vex had seen it for what it was—a small comfort that his friend felt he could provide. He had squeezed that hand back appreciatively, not knowing if Derivan could even really feel the pressure of his touch but hoping that he could, and then continued.

Misa's reaction was perhaps the most overt. She took a moment to gather her thoughts, still, but she was the first to speak after Vex was done. "I'm going to kill them," she said simply.

Vex felt a certain horror at the utter certainty in her words.

"Misa," Sev said quietly.

"*What*," Misa snapped once, rounding on the cleric, and then stopped when she saw the stricken expression on Vex's face; she sagged abruptly. "Fuck."

"This is why you mentioned kidnapping your brother," Derivan said; it wasn't a question, but Vex nodded anyway.

"He was three when I left," Vex said softly. He let himself get lost in the gentle reverberations of the caravan; it helped, the sensation of something smooth and rhythmic, pulling his mind away from the memories. "They start the process when you're six. I tried to get them to stop, to at least wait for him to grow older, or something, but . . ."

He trailed off and let the gentle hum of the caravan take over. Misa was the first one to speak.

"Elyra just *allows* this?" she asked. "There's . . . no fuckin' way they just allow this."

But the anger in her face said otherwise; she didn't believe what she was saying. She remembered just as well as Vex did what had happened with the scientists back at the dungeon—what had happened to Kestel simply because he had tried to delay reporting back, worried about what would happen to the soldiers.

He still needed mana crystals to be cured. They hadn't had the chance to gather any, not yet. The hope was that they would get some while in Elyra's Prime Dungeon, preferably enough to heal Kestel and more.

"Noble houses can do whatever they want," Vex said, shaking his head. Misa snorted, but she seemed like she had more or less expected his response. "It's . . . That's the core thing Elyra is founded on, or at least what they tell us. Anyone can become nobility if they discover something important enough;

nobility is awarded on merit, not blood. At least not entirely blood. And they don't ask that you share your secrets, only that the results of those secrets are used to benefit the Kingdom."

"That's..." Sev frowned, like he wanted to say something more, but eventually he sighed and shook his head; maybe he'd decided it wasn't worth saying. Instead he gave Vex a small, pained sort of smile—the kind of smile that wasn't really a smile at all, but was the best comfort he could offer. "Thank you for telling us, Vex," he said softly, his words genuine.

"Where do you want to bring your brother?" Derivan asked him softly. Vex wasn't sure when it had happened, but he found his one hand clasped between two of Derivan's; they held his gently, as if afraid he would break.

"I... don't know," Vex answered honestly, looking away. "I haven't thought about it that much. I just... Anywhere that's not *here*. Maybe not in Elyra at all. I want to bring him with us, but..."

"Adventuring is just a bit dangerous for a child," Sev agreed. The cleric hesitated for a moment, as if debating whether he wanted to say his next words or not, but then he closed his eyes and exhaled, and said them anyway. "Do you... If you want to take care of him, we wouldn't blame you."

Vex felt Derivan's hands tighten over his own, though the armor didn't say anything. He didn't need to. Vex felt the same way; the thought of *leaving*, even to take care of his brother, made him blanch.

"I can't just abandon you guys," Vex said, and then he paused, trying to find the words. "I didn't—I don't think you understand what you did for me. I was just going to try to figure everything out on my own, you know? I was going to try to discover something big, big enough to be recognized in my family, another secret for us so Riss won't have to suffer. I was alone for a *year*, just looking for something, ignoring everything that wasn't magic.

"It's so easy to get lost, even when you're doing something you love." Vex fidgeted slightly as he spoke, his claws digging into the wooden floor of the caravan. "I didn't think it would happen to me. But it *did*. I had idea after idea, but nothing *worked*, and I..."

"I forgot why I loved magic," he said, the words coming out in almost a whisper; the thought was almost sacrilegious to him now. He bowed his head, ashamed.

His memory of that time was a blur, in truth. He had little notes and research papers filled with theories, a desperate search for a secret he didn't know was there. He remembered night after night of checking off his ideas, one failure after another, each one feeling like his only chance at giving his brother a better life was slipping away.

Slowly forgetting why he cared about magic at all. Vex shook a bit, feeling his eyes fill with tears, and the worst part was that he didn't even know *why*; this was over and done with!

"You guys insisting on coming with me on that quest was *dumb*," he said, the words coming out fiercer than he intended; it was what he had felt at the time, irritation and exhaustion. The idea of needing to adventure with other people felt like it was something that would slow him down. But...

"But I was dumber for wanting to go on that quest at all," he admitted. It wasn't something he could have done alone. "But you came with me, and you kept asking me questions, and you were so *kind*, but you never asked for anything in return the way my parents did—"

Vex's voice cracked then, and he curled up into himself a little; he didn't know why he felt so emotional, only that he *did*. These were the first true friends that he'd had, and he'd met them at the age of twenty. Before that, he had his family and no one else, really, and now...

"You're my family now," he said, almost too soft to hear. "I can't just leave."

"Vex," Misa said quietly, and before the lizardkin knew what was happening, she had pulled him into her arms, tugging Sev along with her. Derivan followed by not letting go of Vex, and in a short instant they were in an awkward pile on the floor of the caravan, hugging his still slightly trembling form, and he *did* cry then.

Because he knew he wouldn't be judged; because he knew nothing more would be asked of him. Because he knew they were grateful he had shared, and just wanted to show him that they *cared*.

And he'd never put it into words before, how much he genuinely loved them, what they had done for him, just by virtue of being there, even when he hadn't known he needed it.

"Thank you," he said eventually, because he didn't know how to put everything he felt into words, and those two words seemed to encompass everything he felt; the caravan hummed quietly beneath them, a gentle white noise to make the silence a little more comfortable.

"You're welcome," Misa said, and then just to cut into the mood a little, she gave Vex a playful sort of smirk. "We love you no matter how many times you blow up our cauldron."

"I had reagents I wanted to test!"

"You also blew up your room."

"I was testing out a spell!"

"And that one poor innkeeper."

"He was a *fire elemental*! He was fine! He ate the explosion!"

Vex was protesting, but he felt a certain gentle warmth circulating in his chest, and he could tell his friends felt a little better too. He'd been so afraid of telling them all this for so long. Not because he thought they would judge him, or because he was worried about what they would do. He just... hadn't wanted to revisit those memories.

But revisit those memories he had, and in the warm hues of the caravan's light and with the company of his friends, it hadn't been nearly as bad as he had feared.

A few minutes later, the four of them untangled themselves to go back to their seats; as nice as the moment was, the wooden floor of the caravan just wasn't a pleasant place to be spending their time. It jostled and jerked with every movement in a way that the seats didn't, mostly because the seats were magically anchored and stabilized against the walls.

"Now you know why I'm nervous about going back to Elyra," Vex said, trying to smile. It was a brittle attempt, but it was real.

"If your parents try anything, I'll beat their skulls in," Misa said bluntly. "I have a mace for a reason."

"Please don't," Sev sighed. Then paused. "Not unless Vex gives you permission."

"Thanks," Vex said, a little wryly. He appreciated the thought, at least. It was just... He had a hard time divorcing himself from the idea that his parents were kind, even now. He resented them for what they had done to him in his childhood and would do to his brother, and yet...

There was that small voice in his head, telling him it could have been worse.

It could have been, certainly. They could have been crueler, withheld even a single drop of kindness, forced it to go longer. He could go as far as to call his father a victim of the very same treatment from his own parents, the secret of their nobility passed down through the ages.

But no. The choices they were making now were their own.

Vex leaned back in his seat and sighed.

The situation in Fendal wasn't gone from his mind, even with all of this; far from it. There was an air that hung around all four of them. There was a little bit of tension that didn't quite go away, even in moments like these, because for all that they weren't done, for all that they planned on finding a way back in, and on finding a solution—

It still felt like they'd lost.

Because they *had*.

But losing didn't mean that things were over. Vex had learned that from this group of friends, too, the same way he'd learned how to care about his magic again. There was always something new to do, always another path to take.

And they were never, never alone. Anton and Charise's respective groups proved that. Even if the answer for Fendal wasn't in Elyra, he had to trust in the teams they'd left behind to handle it.

Now he just had his own problems to deal with, and a promise to uphold.

"Hey, Derivan," Vex said, glancing at the armor. He tried to keep his voice casual; he didn't know why he felt so nervous. "Let's train a bit tomorrow? I want to see if glyphs still work out here. And maybe we can figure out how your new stat works, too."

"Of course," Derivan agreed easily, with that signature tilt of his head and shift in his eyes that signified a smile. "I look forward to it."

CHAPTER 33

A NEW MAGIC

That night, once again, Derivan cast [**Starry Night**]. They took a break on the side of the road for it, though they could have let the caravan keep running through the night; this was important to them, and they needed to use some crystals to refresh their connection to the system besides. So they gathered in a small circle, and Derivan allowed the magic of the skill to flow.

As always, he paid attention to the way the mana flowed.

Derivan had cast this spell a number of times, since the first time he had tested it back in the forest with Vex; each time, he told himself to pay attention to the mana, and each time, he found that he couldn't quite keep his attention on it, like something was obscuring part of the process. Vex found he had the same problem. There was a point where the mana seemed to vanish, obfuscated by something that wasn't quite an infolock or a Shift.

This time, he looked at it with the new sense he had gained—with Patch—and he realized *why*.

[**Starry Night**] wasn't a spell. Maybe it had been, at one point—Derivan saw the way the mana flashed into shapes that looked remarkably similar to glyphs, even while it was being absorbed by the system—but this was a system skill, and the mana was simply being pulled into the system, used to turn some metaphysical gears and call the effect of the skill into existence.

He wondered why. What made this a skill and most other similar effects a spell?

The last of the mana finished running into the system. A few hundred points in total, something like a puddle's worth of the liquid energy he felt in his soul; he felt something click in the gears of the system, and...

... something in the nearest reality anchor responded. The one Misa was holding on to, that was being held inside her interface, somehow.

Once more, those balls of fire manifested in the sky, this time smaller and brighter than before. Once more, a cool mist flooded out among the stars in striated shades of blue, creating what looked just for a moment like a living painting. Gently, he pulled on those mechanisms in the skill, watching with Patch as the reality anchor resonated, and the stars shrank and multiplied accordingly, until it was as close as he remembered to how the Serpent of the Night Sky they fought had looked.

That, presumably, was what the night sky had looked like. They still didn't know *when* the stars had vanished, only that it had most likely been recent.

"Looking at it always makes me feel a little sad," Vex said into the silence, staring up at the sky.

"Because we know it's supposed to mean something to us," Sev said quietly. "But it doesn't."

"We'll give it new meaning." Misa folded her arms. "It's what we've always done, right? We're the ones giving meaning to things, anyway. So if some shit takes it away, we'll invent something new, and we'll hold it even closer than before. See if these fucks can take it away then."

"Misa." Sev chuckled a bit, the word more affectionate than anything else. Derivan noticed, though, that there was something about the cleric that was just a little bit tense—the topic had touched on something personal for him. "Not everything is a fight, you know."

"I think they made it one when they took the stars away from us," Misa said with a shrug. "I'm not an expert on sentimentality, but the sky is one of the things that stays mostly the same no matter where you are. If I had to guess, they were one of the things different cultures had in common, something related to the stars. I bet there were skills and classes centered around them, even."

"We *know* there are skills centered around them," Derivan said, even as [**Starry Night**] slowly faded from his control. "And that means there were classes. I wonder what happened to them."

"Knowing the system? Nothing good," Misa said with a sigh. She picked out the four mana crystals she'd brought out from the caravan, tossing one to each of them. "Time to use the crystals?"

"I will keep an eye on what they do," Derivan said, because he thought perhaps he could observe something about how this usage of the crystals functioned. A tap on the system's interface brought up the appropriate window.

THE NATURE OF MAGIC

> **Fill this week's mana crystal quota? Your System link will degrade if you do not.**
> **0/1 crystals required**
> **ACCEPT**

For a moment, Derivan thought about how absurd it was that the system box didn't have an option to "reject," even if he could back out of the screen if he wanted. Then he reached out to tap the button anyway. They'd agreed to do this one by one, in case there was anything Derivan needed to focus on in the process, and so he had the time to figure out if there was anything different for each of them. He would go first, then Vex, then Misa, and finally Sev.

In the dark of the night, with nothing but the moon to light up the grass and the road around them, Derivan felt Patch resonate. He almost flinched as he felt the heavy machinery of the reality anchor suddenly expand around him, descending upon him; he saw Vex give him a worried look and realized he probably *had* flinched.

He couldn't help it. The machinery was enormous. Was this happening everywhere, every time a crystal was "donated" to the system?

Metaphorical pincers reached down to grab the crystal he was holding on to, and he saw with his eyes as it began to dissolve; in his mind's eye, with the combination of [**Intermediate Mana Manipulation**] and Patch, he saw what was actually happening. The mana was being drawn up into the system, and then *something* happened to it. Whatever that something was, the mana that fell out afterward seemed dim and lifeless. What was left of the crystal—the "shell"—disintegrated into blue dust, and that blue dust was fed back into that complicated core at the center of his soul, where he was attached to the system—

—except for *him*, that dust simply fell to the floor, his particular link to the system too broken to utilize it. Derivan frowned.

"Vex," the armor prompted gently, and the lizardkin nodded, and tapped his own system interface.

Once again, the same thing happened. This time, that dust took root somewhere in Vex's connection with the system, reinforcing it; he saw the line of power the system used shimmer as that blue poured into it.

It was the same with Sev and Misa, too.

"I do not think I need to use a crystal to stay connected with the system," Derivan said slowly.

"What?" Sev blinked.

"Are you sure?" That was Misa.

"That's— That could help so many people, if we can figure out how to break other people's systems like that," Vex said; his tail curled around again, a little nervous tic, and for a distracted moment, Derivan thought about how endearing such a small thing was. He shook it off after a moment, not certain why his mind had gone in that direction. There was that thought he'd had a while back, a single moment where Physical Empathy had inspired a moment of understanding back in Teque...

But even then, he didn't truly understand yet.

More importantly, Vex was right.

"I am unsure if we *can* break other systems the way mine is broken," he said carefully. "But if we can, then perhaps we should. It is best we first make sure I am right, in any case."

"We'll skip this for you next week?" Misa proposed, and the four nodded in agreement. A quick dinner again, this time with some prepared, preserved food rather than cooking any large meal, and they were back on the caravan; Derivan's mind, however, was still spinning with thoughts about what he had seen.

Because he had just the faintest nagging feeling that he had seen that machinery *before*.

Vex was poring over his notes.

It would be another day before they arrived at the place where the next request was situated—they debated rushing ahead to Elyra and ignoring the quest, but it seemed to be a short and relatively harmless one, and they didn't expect it to take more than a couple hours of time.

For now, they had most of the day to themselves, even if that time would be spent in the somewhat cramped interior of the caravan.

"I don't get how you can look at your notes," Sev grumbled; he looked a little green, and Derivan blinked curiously.

"I have never seen a human look like this before," he said. "Are you all right?"

"Just a little nauseous," Sev answered, waving a hand a little dismissively. "Shouldn't have tried to read."

"Can't heal yourself?" Misa raised an eyebrow.

"I can only heal these kinds of status effects by absorbing them, remember?" Sev grimaced slightly. "Can't exactly absorb my own pain. Don't worry about it; I'll be fine."

"Now you know how I felt on the way to Fendal," Misa said, her tone half-smug.

Vex snickered a little bit as he listened to their banter, but he continued going through his notes anyway—the ones about what had happened in Teque were a little sparse and evidently not as filled out as he would've liked them to be. The lizardkin sighed after a moment. "Hard to look through these notes without thinking about what happened back there," he said. "Maybe if I understood those glyphs a little better..."

"That is what we are trying to do now, is it not?" Derivan prompted.

"Yeah." Vex glanced outside the caravan, staring at the passing trees. "...Do you think those Patchers are going to become a problem again? They didn't seem to be able to fight off glyph spells very well. I don't know how they'd fare against system spells."

"They'll definitely become a problem again," Misa said, her tone grim. "I've been thinking about that too. I don't like how useless I was against them."

"You fought three of them at the same time," Vex pointed out.

"And I didn't kill a single fuckin' one." Misa glared out of the window as if she could shatter it with her gaze. Vex flinched away from it a little bit. "Holding them off isn't good enough, and considering what they're *doing*, I just... We need to figure out something more. If we'd killed all of them back there—"

"The system might have just sent more," Sev said. "Let's... try not to dwell too hard on the what-ifs. Stick to what we need to focus on—which is that we need a way to deal with Patchers that isn't just shoving them back where they came from."

"You managed to kill two of the fuckers, right?" Misa slumped back into her seat. "How'd you do it?"

"I shattered the core of one of them," Derivan said. "And they... fixed it, after that. When I gained the new stat, I used it to shatter a second one, but the stat resonated strangely, and I thought it unwise to push without understanding what was happening."

"Resonated?" Vex asked, perking up a little bit. He'd started to look worried and withdrawn again, but this seemed to give him something to focus on.

"Like the stat was decreasing, if only slightly." Derivan did his impression of a frown. "I am not worried about losing it... but I had the feeling that something worse than just a stat decrease might have happened if I had pushed it more. I am uncertain."

"The stat is for patching, but you were using it to break?" Vex guessed.

"That is my suspicion," Derivan said. "I will have to test it carefully when I get the chance. It is difficult to do so now, since all of us are attached to our systems and my tools are still limited; I suspect working with any complicated mechanism is likely to break it entirely. For now, you wanted to focus on glyphs, did you not?"

"I did," Vex said, and glanced over his notebook again with a frown. He sighed, closing it after a moment. "But I don't really know where to *start*. It's a whole new magic system..."

"You have the perfect way to start," Misa pointed out. "Your Sign lets you learn about things. So... use it on itself. And the concept of glyphs."

Vex paused. "I feel like that shouldn't work," he said, uncertain. "And I don't have my magelight. I don't know if I *can*. I can try?"

"Try," Sev said, smiling. "We're long overdue for some new exploits."

"I don't think I'd call it an *exploit*," Vex said, but he grinned, the familiar conversation easing his heart. "I don't even know if glyphs will *work* now that we're back under the system..."

So he tried, a little nervous. It took him much longer without the magelight; he had to alternate [**Splash of Mana**] and [**Delineate**] to slowly create the shape of the glyph. Derivan gave him an encouraging little smile when the lizardkin looked over at him, and it settled what remained of his nerves.

Mana flowed. It hesitated, arriving at the glyph in the air—but then something seemed to *change*.

And for the first time in a long time, in a world dominated by the system, magic happened.

CHAPTER 34

THE BASICS OF MAGIC

It wasn't until Vex was back within the confines of the system that he could feel how *different* this form of magic was, strangely enough. It had been overwhelming and wonderful in Teque, but there, something had been dampened in his senses. Perhaps it was the nature of Teque itself as a half-realized space, or perhaps he'd simply been preoccupied by what was happening to the city. Perhaps it was the tension of knowing they were going back to Elyra, hovering at the back of his mind, the knowledge that he had to tell his friends, explain what had happened to him . . .

. . . Well, he hadn't *had* to. But he'd wanted to, and he had, and things had turned out all the better for it, and now there was a weight on his heart that wasn't gone but lessened. He'd never noticed it before.

Either way, the magic blossomed in front of him, vibrant and *alive*, and he understood that he understood nothing at all. That glyphs and Signs only began to scratch the surface of what real magic could do, if given the opportunity.

It had just . . . never been given the opportunity. Not here.

His Sign floated in the air in front of him, that same outline of his old notebook, a little bit blockier and more haphazard than normal without a magelight to carry his mana. But it was enough for the magic to activate, for those same small tendrils of light to emerge from his notebook, and now here was a difference: He could almost feel what the magic was doing.

It was *remembering*.

Not learning about what he was looking at, necessarily; not going through the motions of what he would have done, the research he would have had to pore through, although the information that poured into his head was certainly organized like he'd personally sorted it. It was like there was something within the mana itself that was unfolding, and it was picking information out of a massive fractal of knowledge—

—though as soon as he glimpsed it, that fractal vanished. He was left with the knowledge he had acquired, which felt surprisingly small in the wake of what he'd seen, and he scrambled to pen it all down in his notebook before it left his mind.

Sign of Research
The result of a young wizard making his first foray into True Magic, the Sign of Research represents not only a scholar eager to learn but one that is willing to *discover*. Years of research and love for that research have compressed that process into a Sign that represents all of that work. Make no mistake, however: knowledge rarely comes for free.

... The last part was a small note tucked away in the corner of his mind as he cast it; Vex recognized, albeit somewhat distantly, that the system was helping him sort this information out. He certainly wouldn't have described himself in the third person like that. It seemed the system couldn't interfere in the magic itself, but its presence and connection with him gave it access to the information he was discovering.

He wasn't sure he liked that.

But it *had* given him information and knowledge that he would have missed on his own. He had the feeling that if he leaned on that, he could push all that information into a system box, to organize and share it ... but he didn't. Not yet.

Derivan was leaning forward too, watching him intently; he wasn't sure why, and he felt slightly embarrassed to be under the armor's keen gaze. Still, he kept at it, pushing the spell a little further—trying, like Misa had suggested, to focus the spell on the *concept of Signs* and not on his Sign in particular.

And—to his surprise—it worked. Not *well*, not nearly as in-depth as he wanted it to. But it gave him what he needed to know. He sorted that information again in his head.

Once again, he wrote a little section in his notes, not sorting it beyond what was being fed to him.

Glyphs and Signs
Glyphs form the foundation of True Magic—an odd paradox, given that the greatest feats of magic involve no glyphs at all. A glyph is foundationally a tribute that is paid by the mana toward a great work of art,

simplified down into a form that can be easily painted and recognized; almost every glyph created has a basis in some great work that was created and remembered by many, with the main exceptions being personal Signs.

Notes:
Glyph is the term used to describe these great works—art that has passed into history and now forms the foundation of magic. Many of the basic mana elements have glyphs to represent them, and more complex glyphs are often combinations of these smaller, basic glyphs.

Sign is the term used to describe something meaningful not to the world at large but to the person using the magic. Such magic is inherently far less effective when used by someone who the Sign does not belong to, and though personal Signs can also be combined with one another, both individuals must feel a true connection for that combined Sign to operate. Such Signs can change in effect as the nature of the relationship between those individuals change.

Note that although many glyphs and Signs are visual constructions in nature, not all works of art are visual. Some magics are invoked by song, and still others by the sensation of rhythm; there are mages who express themselves entirely through their food, or by arranging a perfect bouquet of flowers, such that their aromas form something unique. Anything that has creative value can create magic.

"Well?" Misa asked, raising an eyebrow at him.

"It sort of worked," Vex admitted; he couldn't keep the disbelief entirely out of his voice, and Misa laughed at him, folding her arms and leaning back in the caravan like she'd won.

"I knew it," she said, smug.

"What did you learn?" Derivan asked him curiously.

"Not as much as Misa was probably hoping," Vex said, giving her the most petulant look he could manage, which wasn't actually very petulant at all. "But still, important basics. We kind of already had the idea from what the people in Teque said, but glyphs are created from works of art, and Signs are representative of the person who creates them."

"Signs, huh?" Sev said, and Vex's eyes went wide.

"Oh gods, I can call it Signing," he said, sounding entirely too smug about it. Sev groaned, and Vex's grin only grew wider. "Everyone has a signature! It makes sense!"

"I never said it didn't," Sev grumbled. "It making too much sense is the *problem*."

"Spoilsport," Vex said dismissively, but his grin hadn't faded; the byplay was just a normal part of a good pun.

Derivan hummed in consideration, letting the banter pass by him. "We need a way to know what the general glyphs are, then," he said thoughtfully. "We have two Signs, and we know the glyph for light."

"I made a note of it when we went to inspect some of those lights in Teque," Vex said with a nod. He flipped through his notebook to find the glyph in question, and cast the Sign of Research once more.

Glyph of Light
A simplification of the sun, worshiped by many in old times. Though the first representation of this was a mere circle in the sand, it was a means by which many found meaning.

This glyph is capable of producing minor amounts of light.

"Not a lot of information," Vex said, but a part of him was bubbling with excitement. His magic wasn't just telling him what the magic did—it was giving him a *story*. Pieces of history! There was every chance that he would be able to stumble upon something from before the system this way, if only he could find the right glyphs, the right piece of art—

—though his excitement was quickly dampened as he realized there was every possibility that the mana was giving him information from Teque's history and not his own.

But that . . . didn't make sense. Right? Teque was a product of a bonus room—the mana he was using, the mana he was interacting with now, this was the mana *of this world*. There was no reason it would know anything about Teque or about the alternate history that happened in that version of the world.

Yet the mana was *remembering*, and that memory came from something he'd managed to glimpse. He wondered if there was a way for him to access that archive beyond the limitations of his spell. If he could see the entirety of what the mana remembered, what would he discover?

"Vex?" Misa prompted, raising an eyebrow at him, and Vex jumped; he realized that everyone was looking at him.

"Uh, sorry," he said awkwardly. He'd been focusing on the magic and the potential paths he'd be able to take; maybe if he could find a glyph that focused on memory, or something that focused on accessing spaces . . . "Did someone ask me a question?"

"He's still distracted," Misa muttered to Sev, though she was half-grinning, teasing him; Vex huffed a little bit.

"I can focus!" he said. "It's just new magic; I get to be a little excited about it."

"I think it is cute," Derivan said, and *that* made Vex shrink into his chair a bit, covering his face. Derivan's tone gained a touch of worry. "... Did I say something wrong?"

"No, buddy," Sev said, giving him a sympathetic smile. "It's just—"

"Magic!" Vex interrupted, flailing his arms to try to get their attention. He wanted to talk to Derivan about this, but he wanted to do it *in private* and not in the caravan, where everyone could listen in on him. He'd *planned* to do it today, but he hadn't thought they'd end up doing this inside the caravan! "Um. I still don't know what you asked. If anything. But the glyph for light basically just lets me produce light. Nothing special."

"But special enough to get you lost in thought for five minutes?" Misa smirked.

"It's not that part that got me." Vex struggled for a moment to try to find words for his fascination with what the mana was doing, how it was delivering this information to him. "It's what the magic is doing. It's not just telling me what the glyph can do—it's telling me how it was discovered, what it was based on..."

"You're telling me you get *lore*?" Sev asked. He sounded oddly scandalized.

"Yes! I could put it into a system box, too, I think, but that's ..." Vex frowned. "I don't know how I feel about that yet. That feels like I'm letting the system have access to what I discover. But I think... it already does? It's not *doing* anything with the information I have. Just kind of organizing it for me. As far as I can tell."

"I did notice an oddity in the way the system was acting, with Patch," Derivan commented. *That* had been why the armor was staring so closely at him, then. Vex wasn't sure if he was relieved or disappointed. "I was uncertain what it was doing, but strangely, it seemed to be acting from Misa's reality anchor."

Misa straightened, at that, her half-grin slipping away and turning into something serious; her eyes steeled, and a hand fell upon her mace. Vex blinked at her, unsure why she'd gotten so serious suddenly. "What was it doing?"

"I do not know." Derivan shook his head. "I only know that it was the source of the system's actions."

"Did it do the same thing when we were using the mana crystals?" Misa asked.

Derivan hesitated. "I did not think to observe in that direction," he said slowly. "When the apparatus for handling the crystals descends, it is . . . large. It is difficult to see past it to a source. But I will try to pay attention should a new notification pop up, or should we notice any new oddities."

"Please," Misa said, and she sighed, leaning back against the wall of the caravan once again; she stared into the air, a telltale sign of her looking at a system screen. Vex could guess what she was looking at.

"Did the integrity go down by a lot?" There was a thin tremor of nervousness in his voice; Vex wasn't sure he wanted to know the answer.

"No." Misa hesitated. "It went . . . It went *up*."

CHAPTER 35

COMBINATORICS

"That's a good thing, right?" Vex wasn't sure how to phrase his question, exactly, but Misa looked more tense than he would have expected for such a revelation.

"It's not that it going up is a *problem*," Misa said, but she looked frustrated anyway, her brows furrowing as she spoke. "It's that I don't know what's causing it to go up and down like this, and my—my *family* relies on this. My whole village. It's linked directly to me, and I don't even get a notification when it happens."

"That means something happened to raise it, though," Vex said. "We know that now. It's more than we knew before. We can figure out what we did . . . It's probably related to the magic, right?"

"Maybe," Misa grunted. She didn't look too much happier. "We'd have to keep testing. I don't know *when* this happened, so it could have been from something back in Teque."

"I may be able to fix the notification problem," Derivan said. Misa blinked once, turning her gaze to him and staring, and even Vex looked at Derivan askance; the armor tilted his head slightly, as if he was confused by the stares being directed at him. "That is the purpose of Patch, is it not? Or it appears to be. Patch allows me to fix issues with the system. I do not know how to use it yet, but with enough practice . . ."

"Are you *sure* you can do that?" Misa asked.

"Not sure," Derivan admitted. "But it should be possible."

"We'd be able to change so much if Patch is able to do what you think," Sev muttered out loud. He shook his head, looking contemplative. "It can't be that easy."

"It likely will not be. But I am willing to try."

"We should work on figuring out what Patch can do," Sev decided. "I mean, we were going to do that anyway, I guess, but we can put together some ideas. Figure out a way for you to train the stat. Maybe smaller problems you can fix?"

"At the moment, the stat appears to let me sense aspects of the system and influence them in some small way," Derivan said. "But it is rather like wielding a hammer when a smaller tool would do a better job—imprecise and difficult to handle."

"So, we need a small problem for you to handle?" Misa frowned. "We know the system has a dozen little errors in it, but..."

"Rather," Derivan said, "we need a problem that does not require an intricate solution, something I can hammer back into place, so to speak."

"I can't think of anything at the moment." Misa glanced around to everyone else. "You guys got anything?"

"We don't have a reference point for errors," Vex said. "The best we can do is wait for the next time an error shows up and see what it looks like for Derivan."

"The good news is that at the rate we encounter errors, that shouldn't take long at all," Sev said, and a light scattering of chuckles broke the tension in the caravan.

"Any chance we'll encounter any with the next quest?" Misa asked. "You said it was a short one that we should do before we go to Elyra proper, right? Remind me what the details are?"

"It should be a diversion of a couple of hours at most." Sev glanced at the paper he held in his hands, wincing a little bit. "It's another one of those quests a lot of adventurers don't pick up because it's too easy. Need to help someone pick some of her vegetables."

"And... Why do we need to help someone pick their vegetables, again?" Misa gave Sev a bemused stare. Sev shrugged.

"They're magic," he said. "Apparently, they're kind of hard to harvest."

"You could've just said she needed help harvesting alchemical reagents."

"I did the first time." Sev grinned. "Calling them vegetables to fuck with you was funnier."

"He's got you there," Vex said, grinning a little bit.

Misa rolled her eyes and turned away to hide her smile. "Of the four of us," she grumbled to Vex, "I would've expected you to care most about being accurate with terminology."

"I do!" Vex protested. Misa smirked, and the caravan lapsed into another small silence.

"Do you have a plan for discovering more glyphs?" Derivan asked after a moment had passed. Vex looked over at him.

"I'm not sure," the lizardkin answered honestly. "I was thinking I would ask Anton for some of the basic ones through the glyph, the next time he . . . Wait. That's right. *We have another glyph.*" Vex's eyes gleamed, though inwardly he felt a little guilty for being so excited about this; the circumstances by which they had been given this glyph were, after all, far from ideal.

He took the glyph they were using to communicate out of his bag a little reverently. It was the only line of contact they had with Anton; Charise was still within the barrier, and Misa could chat with her mother through the system, though Charise informed her that the version of her within the barrier was quickly losing access to both the system itself and the skills offered by the system. It was only because she was in two places at once that she was unaffected—the version of her in the new J'rokksur was still fully connected.

Charise was not, however, in contact with Anton—and from what they'd been informed from both sides, Fendal and Teque had been sealed off from one another. Anton was trying to find a way to work through that inner barrier even now; he claimed that it would be an easier task than working through the outer one, for the nature of the barriers were different, though when pushed, he wouldn't explain exactly why or how they were different.

All of which Vex was worried about.

But! Communication glyph! What could he find out from this?

"Is it costing you any mana to cast these new spells?" Sev asked curiously, and Vex blinked; he hadn't even *thought* about it.

"It does," he answered after a moment. The feeling of mana drain was all the same, even if the process was slightly different; in this case, he used [**Splash of Mana**], which drew mana out of him and into the glyph—and then, as the spell was cast, there was a link formed between him and the spell that continued to consume his mana.

If he tried to paint or draw the glyph himself with something other than mana, it didn't activate—and they didn't have a way to directly activate the rune Anton had given them, either. They'd tried, and he'd dismissed it as something he would learn with time; simply pouring mana into the rock didn't seem to work.

. . . Though, come to think of it, that was a rather distinct difference between how he used glyphs and how the residents of Teque evidently used them. They almost exclusively drew their glyphs onto surfaces and then channeled into them.

But there was another rather crucial difference, wasn't there? Each time someone in Teque used a spell, they had a massive river of living mana above them to fuel it; the magic would flow down toward them as if called. Vex didn't have anything like that; if he drew a glyph without magic, the ambient mana simply didn't react.

Vex wondered what made this *different*, even as he Signed his own Sign of Research and noted down the information as it poured into his head.

Glyph of Communication
A coalesced wish, born from a woman whose husband left for war; every day, she would write letters, yet no couriers came to her house to fetch them. When he came home, he read them all and cried.

This glyph allows the communication of thoughts and ideas across vast distances, after pairing with another glyph.

Another little snippet of history. Vex wondered what it was like for that woman, that her letters were considered a great work of art, to be remembered and preserved by the mana. He wondered if he would ever do something like that of his own someday.

"Are you doing okay?" Misa asked him. A note of worry entered her voice. "That *is* a communication glyph, right?"

"It is," Vex answered, realizing how his silence must have looked. "Don't worry. I was just distracted."

"Learned something interesting?" Sev cocked a brow at him.

"Just that this glyph came from some letters someone wrote." Vex stared at the rock in his hands for a moment. The communication glyph appeared to be a series of curling letters, though closer inspection would reveal that those letters were not real letters at all, just a looping cursive made to imitate. It was nothing nearly so complex as a series of letters one might send their love. He wondered how the mana decided, exactly, what a glyph looked like. Or *when* a given work of art transformed into a glyph.

But there was something else that was a little more exciting.

Vex knew two glyphs now. General glyphs that could be combined with one another, if he understood what he'd learned from his Sign correctly, and it wouldn't even be all that complicated to combine these two—the glyph for light was a relatively simple circle, surrounded on four points by a series of simple flames, and all Vex had to do was write the false script of the glyph for communication along the inner circle.

He wasn't sure *how* he knew that was the way to combine the glyphs, only that it made the most sense that way; the looping letters of Communication fit perfectly on the inside of the circle for Light, and Vex barely even realized that he was painting this with mana, not merely scribbling it in his notes.

His tongue stuck out the side of his mouth in concentration as he finished the last looping letter—

—Mana flared. A yellow-green light erupted from the glyph, throwing the caravan's cabin into stark contrast and bathing all four of them in light; Vex flinched at first, and Misa reached out for her mace like she was expecting to have to block an explosion, but nothing further happened, and Misa slowly lowered her mace, although she still stared suspiciously at the rune.

"What was that?" she asked.

"I, uh . . . don't know." It had been, it occurred to Vex, a little reckless of him to cast that spell in an enclosed space. Especially since he didn't know what it did. There was no reason to expect that anything *bad* would happen— *light* and *communication* hardly spelled an explosion—but still.

"*Vex*," Misa said, a touch of fond exasperation in her tone, and Vex squeaked.

"I'll be more careful next time!" he said. "I got excited."

And he was *still* excited, because he had another confirmed spell he could look at with his Sign, and he did, taking down his notes as he did so.

Glyph of Letterlight
A combination of the Glyphs of Light and Communication, the Glyph of Letterlight represents the desire to share meaning through the visual mediums of art.

This glyph is capable of one-way transmission of thoughts, concepts, and ideas to any being that comes in contact with the light emitted from it.

Ah. That made sense.

Vex hadn't been particularly prepared for the spell, and so the only thought he'd put into it while the spell was casting was that he hoped it worked; the thought had been easy enough to dismiss, though each of the three others did admit they felt something along those lines when Vex had cast his spell.

"Lotta applications for that spell," Misa said with a low whistle when Vex described what it did. "As long as you can direct that light."

"It may be worth experimenting with," Derivan agreed.

"No slivers for that combination, though," Vex noted, looking a little bit worried. "What if I can't get any more?"

"You didn't give all your slivers to Noram, did you?" Misa asked.

"No," Vex said; he rummaged around in his tailpouch, trying to find the one sliver he'd kept for himself. "But I was hoping we'd be able to get more now that we know how magic works..."

He paused.

His fingers had brushed against the sliver in his tailpouch, and the system had responded.

> [**Unknown Shard**] [**Grade: Unknown**]
> \<ERROR>
> *Item description still processing.*

"... The system recognizes the slivers now," Vex said slowly, staring at the box. He didn't know how he felt about it. For some reason, he felt a strange, creeping dread.

"Does it tell you what it is?" Derivan asked.

"No. It says it's still processing." Vex fidgeted. "But this *does* mean that the system is actively studying the slivers ... I'm worried about what will happen when it's done."

"Next time Anton contacts us," Misa suggested, "you should ask about glyphs for making this trip faster. Just in case."

"Was there any change in integrity?" Vex asked. The half-orc glanced at her status and sighed.

"Too small for now, if there was anything," she said. "But let me know the next time you work on this magic, and I'll keep an eye on it."

Vex nodded. "I need to know what other base glyphs there are," he said, his tone contemplative. He was always excited about new magic, of course, but this was something new, and he was just starting to get a glimpse at it...

He wanted to learn *more*.

And it would help him with his family in Elyra, too, he hoped.

CHAPTER 36

UPDATE

Anton's call came not long after Vex was done with his first series of glyph-tests. As before, the glyph they held began to glow with mana, which was interesting; without having mana sight, it wouldn't be possible to notice that the glyph was "receiving" anything. There wasn't even a thread of mana linking the two glyphs, which made Vex wonder how exactly the mechanics of the spell worked—but that came secondary to what Anton had to say.

The beetle-mage was focused on trying to give them an update about the situation in Teque. Apparently, the time dilation had dropped to almost nothing, which was at least one worry dealt with.

On the other hand, Helg was apparently calling for the citizens of Teque to gather so they could determine who the system was feeding and who the system was not. It was for everyone's safety, she claimed—but Anton's words were tense, and he sounded worried.

"I do not think we should be categorizing our people," Anton said through the mana-link; a projection of him floated above the glyph so all four of them could hear him, though how Anton had unlocked that particular functionality, Vex had no idea. "I am worried what that might lead to. But I have not had much luck in getting Helg to change her mind."

"Have you had a chance to speak to Noram about all this?" Vex asked. "I still don't understand why he just . . . agreed to this."

"He has been locking himself away in that sleep bubble of his." Anton frowned. "I am worried about him. I was never very close to him, but I cannot imagine what Helg said to him to make him like this."

Vex sighed. "Keep us updated," he said, casting a significant glance to Misa; she'd been keeping in contact with her mother. Charise and her two guards were the only people in Fendal left that possessed their own faculties, it seemed, and they'd been trying to keep an eye on everyone they cared about—Noram in particular.

So far, no change in behavior. Vex had hoped the slivers would do something... but maybe it took more time than this.

"Anything else before I cut the connection?" Anton asked.

"Do you know why I can't use this glyph myself?" Vex asked. "I've tried pushing mana into it, but that doesn't work. And I'd like to know a few more basic glyphs, if you don't mind sharing them."

Anton made a bit of a face. "Magic lessons, huh?" he said, but the question was rhetorical. "I am not the best teacher of those, but... I suppose with how differently the magic in your world works..."

"I'm hoping I can understand more," Vex said. "Then we won't be caught so off guard by magics like this."

"Helg burned part of our mana sliver supply to make that barrier as strong as she did," Anton said bluntly. "You will most likely not have to face magic like that."

"We're going to be visiting other parts of your world," Sev supplied, from his corner of the caravan. "Anything you give us will help. It might help us find a way through."

"I am aware." Anton fidgeted slightly, glancing away as if he was worried someone would walk in on him; Vex was abruptly reminded of his plans to learn obfuscation magics, and wondered briefly if he would be able to find something along those lines in this new system of magic that he could teach Anton. Assuming the mage didn't know them already. "I'll share a few of the basic glyphs I know. But just knowing the shape of the sign isn't everything—"

"I know," Vex said. "My sign can handle the rest."

"Right," Anton said, and then grumbled slightly. "Knowledge Signs."

"Do you know how they work?" Vex asked.

"Mana has memory," Anton recited, almost automatically. "And memory shapes the world. Knowledge taps in to that, but I could not tell you how or where it holds that memory, exactly. Our scholars are still trying to figure that out."

Anton glanced away again and then frowned. "I will send a basic package of elemental glyphs, so you have somewhere to get started. Many glyphs build up from those basic elements. I am sure you will figure the rest out. I must get going."

Anton's projection disappeared almost as soon as he said the words; at the same time, Vex blinked, a package of six glyphs suddenly appearing in his mind in a way that was ... arguably a little intrusive. He didn't complain, though, shaking his head slightly at the small headache it had introduced instead.

Derivan still noticed, of course. "Are you all right?" the armor asked.

"Fine," Vex said with a small smile. "Just not used to the communication glyph. Don't worry about it."

"He sent you what you needed?" Misa asked, and Vex nodded.

"It was kind of him," Vex said quietly. "He didn't have to. I don't know if he was ... annoyed, at the end there? He's trying to set things right in Fendal, and here we are, just ..."

"Stop," Misa said firmly, shaking her head. "That line of thought won't help us."

Vex was silent for a moment, then eventually nodded; what else was he supposed to do? Misa was right. She exchanged a look with Sev that was basically unreadable to him, and he decided instead to focus his energies on deciphering the elemental glyphs that Anton had given him.

It was a pretty simple set of elements, in the end. It didn't even include the more obscure types of aspects he'd seen. Just fire, water, earth, air, light, and dark; light was redundant, too, given he already knew the rune for that.

But even with just that set—plus the glyph for communication and their own personal Signs—there was so much he could do. Experiment with.

"Do you think that Magic stat of yours can help you find new glyphs, Deri?" Vex asked, angling his gaze toward the armor, who tilted his head in consideration.

"... Perhaps," Derivan eventually answered. "The last time I tried, I ended up creating a combination of our Signs instead."

Vex blinked. Derivan sounded almost *embarrassed*. He hadn't really thought about it, but everyone from Teque had mentioned that combining Signatures like that was an intimate thing, hadn't they? And that had been corroborated by the information he'd been fed from his own glyph when he'd tried to query what glyphs and Signs were in general.

His mind wandered, briefly, into what that meant for what Derivan thought about the two of them, and a pleasant warmth filled him at the thought. He looked down and away, not quite meeting Derivan's eyes, and from the corner of his sight he thought he saw the armor look down, too.

Neither Sev nor Misa said anything. They seemed to sense that the moment was private, however small it was. And after a moment, Vex gathered himself and managed to speak with more confidence than he felt.

"I'm looking forward to exploring magic together," he said honestly, and Derivan did that almost-smile he always did, reaching out for him; Vex reached *back*, taking his hand, and that was that.

A moment of quiet affection, held in two hands.

The conversation ended there, drifting into a comfortable silence. Part of him wanted to spend the rest of his time experimenting, but his previous experiments and the conversation with Anton had drained more mana than he anticipated, and they were due to arrive at the site of their second request soon; he'd need his mana for what they were going to do there.

Which, yes, was just harvesting magical reagents. But the Guildmaster had picked out that quest for them for a reason: magical reagents or not, many of the plants the questgiver had were still *crops*. Food.

And since she was versed in magic herself, there was a chance she would have some insight into the food and crop shortages plaguing Elyra.

Vex knew about this woman, though he'd done a poor job of explaining who she was to Sev and the others. Talking about Elyra still made him nervous, and eventually, Sev had simply asked if he was ready to talk about it; when Vex shook his head no, Sev had hugged him and told him it didn't matter unless it was the sort of thing that would affect their quest. And it wouldn't! It was just that this woman was semi-famous within Elyra's walls, and, well, she was personally funded for the benefit she was able to provide to Elyra.

Technically, in fact, she even counted as nobility. She would be a full Lady if she chose to move into Elyra's walls at any point, but she seemed content out here, and as far as Vex was concerned that was a point in her favor.

Okay, it was probably best he mention that fact before they actually arrived. He could already see her hut in the distance, and the massive fields that she apparently maintained alone.

"So, uh, Lady—well. Emily is Elyran nobility, technically," Vex said, breaking the silence in the caravan; Sev glanced at him but didn't seem particularly surprised, and Misa just blinked several times at him askance. Derivan barely even had a reaction, which made sense, given he understood little about the nuances of nobility.

"Does that... matter?" Misa eventually asked.

"Not really." Vex shrugged. "I just felt like I should mention it. Just in case."

Misa laughed a little bit, and Sev smiled; Derivan reached over to ruffle the frill-spikes on the back of his head, and Vex felt himself relax.

It was the first time he'd been able to talk about Elyra without the surge of tension and fear that came along with remembering everything that happened there, without the constant worry that he wouldn't be able to save his brother from what had happened to him.

It was nice.

—⚡︎—

"Hi!"

Emily was very, very pretty. Vex noticed this in an abstract sort of way, the way one might notice a beautiful painting and comment on how technically brilliant it was; her skin was dark and flawless, and she sported tightly braided hair that hung down to her shoulders. She wore a perfectly tailored sunset-yellow dress, too, right down to a flowing skirt that Vex couldn't help but think was a nightmare to work in the fields with.

But no, actually; there was a faint shimmer of magic around it. That made sense.

"Hello," Sev greeted with a small but polite smile. "We're from the Adventurers' Guild."

"Here to help with the harvest, right?" Emily smiled brightly. "Thank god. I was worried I was going to have to ask someone from Elyra to come."

"You don't like working with Elyra?" Vex couldn't help but ask, perking up slightly.

"*God* no. Have you worked with Elyra? Half the time, they send these pretentious little mages that can't tell the difference between magic and makeup." Emily mimicked a false shudder, her lips quirking in momentary disgust. Vex couldn't help but snicker.

"I've worked with a few Elyran mages in my time," he agreed, and then, in a fit of bravery, continued. "Um . . . I was one. Technically. But I left."

"Good!" Emily said, and then turned to open the door to her cottage and wave the four of them inside. "Come in. You're going to need some gloves if you want to help me with the harvest. We'll need to split into teams, and . . . You know some magic, right? The lizard. I should have gotten your names, sorry."

"I'm Sev," Sev said, and gestured to the other three. "Misa. Derivan. The lizardkin is Vex."

"I'm going to mix up those names a bunch, I'm warning you now," Emily said immediately.

"We're used to it," Sev said with a shrug, and she grinned and led them in.

CHAPTER 37

MEETING

Emily's home was unremarkable, for all that she was apparently a witch of sufficient prowess to warrant the coveted position of nobility in Elyra.

Derivan thought it was *cozy*, certainly; there was clearly a lot of care and effort put into every detail of the house. The place was spotless. The walls were painted a bright white and had paintings of a multitude of exotic plants hanging on them, nothing Derivan had ever seen before. One of them even looked like it had a mouth. Which was . . . a choice, certainly.

Handwoven baskets hung from the ceiling, with flowering vines drooping from them, dangling low enough to touch even Vex's head. Derivan almost didn't have the space to walk around. Even the baskets were about the same height as his helmet, forcing him to duck and weave between them to get to a seat on Emily's couch.

Before long, however, they were all seated, and Emily was preparing some tea for all of them, despite their protests. Derivan in particular had no idea what he was meant to do with his tea and was vaguely tempted to pour it into the slits in his helmet that were meant for his eyes.

That would probably be stranger than just not drinking the tea, though. Plus, having the tea slosh around inside him wasn't a particularly pleasant thought.

"I have to thank you again for helping me out with this," Emily said. "I was a little worried no one was going to pick up the request."

"You said you would've asked Elyra for help if that happened, right?" Vex asked.

"Yeah, but like I also said, I don't want to." Emily made a face.

"I was more wondering if you knew anything about the food and crop issues they've been having." Vex glanced outside at the fields; as far as he could tell, all of Emily's plants were healthy.

"Ah." Emily seemed to sober up a little; Derivan noticed a small spark of reluctance, like she didn't entirely want to talk about this. "I've noticed that it's taking a lot more mana to push my crops to grow," she said. "Do *not* tell Elyra that, though. I don't want them to come over here to 'investigate' again."

"Had issues with that before?" It was Misa that asked the question, an eyebrow rising slightly at their host.

"Mostly because I keep refusing to live inside the main Kingdom and benefit from being a noble or whatever, yeah. They want to know how I make my reagents." Emily shrugged and smiled. "I'm not telling them, though. And they're not going to get me to live in Elyra so I can be one of their spoiled little nobles."

Vex coughed at that, trying to cover up his snicker. Sev cocked his head. "I mean, shouldn't you be worried that *we're* from Elyra?" he asked. "We haven't shown you a Guild badge or anything..."

"You also haven't tried to pry any secrets from me or climb into my fields without my permission." Emily grinned a slight grin. "I would've known if you were from Elyra; trust me. You're adventurers. Though now that you mention it, yes, I would like to see your badge."

Sev handed them over, and she whistled. "*Gold?* I didn't think they'd be sending *Gold*-ranked adventurers."

"Silver, by leveling standards," Sev said, sounding a little embarrassed. "It's not that impressive."

"If you're Silver by the normal standard and the guild gave you Gold badges anyway, I think I'm even more impressed." Emily handed the badges back with a shake of her head. "Now I'm worried that I'm keeping you from doing more important things. Don't you have ancient dungeons to delve? Deep secrets to uncover? Maybe a town to save?"

Derivan didn't react—but Sev, Misa, and Vex all grimaced a little bit at that.

Emily noticed, of course. The smile faded from her face, and she frowned a small frown. "*Am* I actually keeping you from a town to save?"

"Not exactly," Sev hedged. "Think of it as... we can't do anything about it right now. There are people working on it that aren't us. We're going to see if we can't find a way to help."

"Not giving up." Emily nodded to herself, pouring herself a second cup of tea. She'd apparently already finished the first. "You're classic adventurers, I see. The heroic types."

"I don't know if *heroic* is the right word." Vex fidgeted. "We're just trying to do the right thing?"

"... What do you think heroism is?"

Vex deflated a little. "I just don't think it should be all that special," he said quietly.

There was a small silence at that. Emily watched Vex for a moment, sipping her tea, then sighed and placed it delicately back on the saucer in front of her; when she spoke again, her voice had lost a lot of its levity and the weight of her gaze on them had grown. "It shouldn't be," she said. "But it is."

Derivan felt those words resonate with him. He felt Emily reach for a skill, closing her eyes and searching...

"Fendal," she said. "It's... blocked off. Can anyone get in?"

"They've made a couple of attempts, but it hasn't worked," Sev said. Not even Max's [**Right Place, Right Time**] had been able to break through the barrier. "It's not... It's probably not correct to say that it isn't urgent. But it's reversible, hopefully, and no one is dying."

Yet was the unspoken word that all three of the other adventurers heard. Derivan cast a glance to Emily to see how she would react, and saw that she seemed... contemplative.

"Good to know," she finally said. "Hm. Do you want to talk about it? I'm not a therapist or anything, but I've had a few people use this place to air out their worries."

"Well, it's not why we're here," Sev said, glancing around to make sure that no one else seemed to want to take her up on her offer; no one did. "Thank you for the offer, though. We're just here to help you with the harvest. We've, uh, had our moment of catharsis."

"Speaking of," Vex said, changing the subject. "That thing about it taking more mana to grow your crops is really weird. It's not a mana-shortage problem, right? If that were it, Elyra would definitely have a means of getting enough mana."

"Right. The Ashion House." Vex flinched a little bit when Emily said the name, but a lot less than he usually did. Derivan watched as Misa gave him an encouraging thumbs-up. "Keep in mind you're still not in Elyra proper. The effect is a lot stronger closer to the Elyran agricultural fields, I've heard. To the point where all the mana put into those spells get instantly sucked up."

"Oh. That's... worrying." Vex frowned.

"Yup." Emily shrugged, took a final sip from her tea, and lifted both cup and saucer up into the air. Derivan stared as vines reached down from the ceiling baskets and whisked both away toward the kitchen. "Nothing to be done about it, though. At least the Guild is kind enough to send assistance

". . . Anyway! The harvest. How many of you are versed in magical-reagent collection?"

Derivan stayed silent. Of the four of them, Vex was the only one that raised his hand. Emily watched them for a while, pursing her lips, and then nodded to herself.

"Yeah, I can work with that," she said. "One is better than nothing. So!

"First thing to know: magical plants are very sensitive to mana usage! That's not to say you can't use mana at all, but if you use it, you better know what you're doing. A stray [**Mana Manipulation**] can ruin a whole plant and all the ones next to it. *Any skill that uses mana* shouldn't be used, whether it's a spell or not. That's worse than [**Mana Manipulation**]."

Derivan paused in thought, drumming his fingertips on the wood of the table in consideration; he wondered if that had something to do with the way the system interacted with mana. They'd seen the difference in mana now between Teque and the rest of the world, and Vex had talked about how the usage of system skills could chase ambient mana away. From what he could see, Emily's fields had the same carefree mana they usually observed in forests and plains, away from people.

"Second! I have gloves for you. They're gloves that are specifically enchanted to provide some mana insulation and also protect you from the harmful side effects some of these reagents have on contact. Keep them on at all times. Do not ever, *ever* touch your eyes with those gloves. Actually, just don't touch any body part with the gloves. Unless you want to experience an unnecessary amount of pain."

". . . Concerning," Sev commented, picking up a pair of gloves and staring at it with what was probably an undue amount of suspicion. Misa did too. Vex just put his on, looking a little bit silly with how the too-big gloves fit onto his hands; the sleeves fit all the way up to his biceps and made bending his arms awkward. He seemed used to it, though.

Derivan stared blankly at the set of gloves that Emily was offering him, and then glanced around at his party helplessly. They did not look like they would remotely fit on his armor.

"Is that amenable to a size enchantment?" Vex asked, evidently deciding to help him. Emily blinked, glanced at Derivan, and then glanced back at the pair of gloves she was holding.

"Can you not just take off the gauntlets or something?" she asked. "A size enchantment would probably break the magics on this thing."

"I am afraid they are quite stuck," Derivan said. "As is the rest of my armor, unfortunately."

Emily glanced at him, then at the necklace he still wore; he'd almost forgotten about it after the Guildmaster had gifted it to him. "I won't ask," she said, without questioning it any further. "I'm honestly not sure if I can replicate the enchantment on your armor. Do you know if it protects you from magical effects?"

"What sort of magical effects?" Derivan asked.

"Just the usual ones," Emily said, and when Derivan looked at her blankly, she elaborated. "Heat is probably the one you need to worry about most; there are some ice effects, and some more-esoteric ones that might warp flesh if in direct contact—"

Sev choked a little on his tea as she said those words, and she ignored him. "—But nothing that should affect metal, as far as I know. As long as your armor itself isn't too magical, it shouldn't be a problem."

"I am . . . unsure how magical my armor is," Derivan said, glancing at Vex for help. He essentially *was* just magic armor.

"His armor's pretty magical, but the effect is mostly focused inwards," Vex said. "It shouldn't affect your plants—it hasn't affected any of my magic."

"I'm going to tentatively trust you on that," Emily said with a slight frown. "I'll want you working with him, to make sure that doesn't affect the plants, and I'm going to be present for the first few harvests before I go help out the other two. Just in case."

"We're splitting into teams, then?" Sev asked.

"Sev and Derivan on one team, Misa and Vex on the other," Emily said with a nod, and then paused. "Wait, which one is the lizard again?"

"I'm Vex," Vex said.

". . . *Vex* and Derivan on one team, Misa and Sev on the other." Emily gave them a playful scowl. "Your names are way too similar."

"Believe me," Sev said with a weary sigh, although he sounded amused, "it's not the first time we've gotten that."

CHAPTER 38

FINALLY

Derivan had to admit to himself that he felt a little lost. Of all the things that he'd had practice doing ever since leaving the dungeon that had spawned him, harvesting magical crops wasn't one of them—never mind the intricacies that apparently went into harvesting these particular magical crops. It wasn't that it was overwhelming, exactly; he just didn't understand why there were so many *steps*.

"The leaves of the *Heuna maloris* need to be plucked one by one," Emily instructed. Apparently, even Vex didn't know about some of these plants; the lizardkin was watching Emily in fascination, his eyes glowing with his version of [**Mana Sight**]. Derivan wasn't sure what he saw; his own skill wasn't advanced enough to show him the way mana was moving within the plants. "Only pluck the leaves that have turned green, and keep in mind the leaves might change color once you start plucking them."

"Fascinating," Vex murmured. "The mana's moving around every time you pluck a leaf. The green ones are the ones with the most mana?"

"You can see that?" Emily raised an eyebrow, impressed. "Yeah, that's basically what's happening."

"Is that a defense mechanism or something?" Vex asked.

"It's hard to say." Emily shrugged. She plucked another leaf carefully, and Derivan watched as the entire plant shifted hues; some green leaves turned a deep red, and red leaves shifted into a vibrant yellow. It would have been startling if he hadn't seen it a few times already. "It's not a very good defense mechanism, if that's what it is. It might be able to confuse some insects and pests that prey on high-mana leaves, and make them waste energy moving around, but it's not going to stop other animals from just eating the whole plant."

Vex was frowning, tapping a finger on his chin. "But it's pretty good against those specific pests," he said, more to himself than to Emily, and she nodded.

"A lot of these plants are only magical because I worked on them, though," she said. "So it's not like there's evolutionary pressure to force it to be a certain way. Maybe magic guides it to behave in ways to protect itself? But I'm mostly interested in growing the plants better and not the *why* of the magic."

"That's where I come in," Vex said cheerfully, and Emily laughed a little.

"Sure, if that's what you want," she said. "You're welcome to try to understand, and if you figure it out, let me know. I'm not telling you how I make them, though."

"Don't, don't." Vex waved her off. "I want to figure it out myself!"

Derivan hummed, pleased, watching the two of them interact. He didn't feel a need to step in, nor did he have much to contribute to the conversation. Emily led them through a few more of the plants that Vex wasn't familiar with harvesting, and each time had Derivan try harvesting the plant at least once while they both observed to make sure his armor didn't mess with any of the intrinsic magic of the plants; fortunately, it didn't.

There was a flower that needed to be watered right before being picked, or else it would explode into flames. There was a strange, *long* flower embedded with red beads that Emily said was her attempt at recreating "corn," though if plucked too violently, each bead would puff up and release a cloud of water-aspect mana, drenching the harvester. There was a root vegetable that needed all its aboveground leaves to be pulled together, or else the leaves would detach and it would jet all the collected mana straight up into the air.

Very, very strange plants, all in all. Derivan could practically hear Sev complaining.

"Aw, man," Emily muttered, looking a little bit put out once she was done. "I just realized I should've kept you four together explaining those. Now I'm going to need to explain these to your friends all over again."

"Good luck," Vex said sympathetically, hiding a grin.

". . . Why *good luck*?" Emily squinted suspiciously at Vex. "Am I going to have *problems*?"

"Oh, no reason." Vex kept his expression as straight and innocent as possible. Emily stared at him for a moment, narrowing her eyes.

"Right," she said, and then straightened. "Well, I'm going to go teach them how to harvest plants, then. And you better be half-done with your section by the time I'm done!"

There were quite a lot of plants in their section. Derivan was about to protest, and then Vex just shrugged and said that was fine, and that made

Emily narrow her eyes all the more . . . but she turned and left anyway, and Vex almost immediately burst into giggles once she was out of earshot.

"Sev is not going to like this," Derivan said, sharing in Vex's amusement.

"And Misa's going to want to try *so many things*." Vex grinned. "I mean, I have questions too, but I want to try to figure this out myself first. There's so much that's new to me here! And I still have the glyphs to figure out—I dunno, maybe I can find some place where magical plants intersect with glyphs; natural mana seems to interact with the environment in mostly the same way when the system isn't involved—and now that I think about it, we don't actually know how mages in Teque figure out the glyphs at all. I mean, what counts as 'a great artwork'? How do they know when the mana decides something is worthy of being remembered? How do they figure out what the glyph to represent that art piece is?"

"There are many questions to answer," Derivan agreed. They were good questions, though he found himself instead watching Vex carefully. The lizardkin was buzzing with the questions he always had when he found something new, but this time without the pressure of a mystery on his back, and for just an instant he let go of everything he was worried about: Elyra, his brother, his parents, Teque and Fendal . . .

It wasn't intentional, exactly. It was just Vex getting excited over something like he always did. But the moment felt significant to Derivan, and he wasn't sure why until he searched his own emotions and realized the answer.

He wanted Vex to live in a world where he could just do *this*. Where he could ask a million questions about anything that intrigued him and pour all that excited love and energy into whatever new project came of it. He wanted Vex to be able to do this without the stress and worry that came with others being in danger, or blaming himself for whatever new thing was going wrong, or having his heart broken by a stray cruelty from a stranger.

He wanted to protect him.

And what a strange thought that was! He wanted to protect all of his friends, of course; Vex was not special in that regard, and yet his feelings felt different when it came to the lizardkin.

"Deri?" Vex said, looking up at him, and Derivan blinked, suddenly realizing that Vex was standing on his tiptoes and trying to wave his hands in front of his face—though he could barely reach, even with the tiptoes.

"I was distracted," Derivan said by way of explanation, and smiled kindly down at his friend. "I apologize. Shall we get on with the harvest?"

"Oh, yeah, definitely," Vex nodded. Sev's voice echoed across the field to them, a dismayed cry of "But what's the *point* of exploding if it's harvested wrong?!" followed by Misa laughing boisterously. "We only have like two hours before those two are done, probably."

Derivan chuckled. "I feel you may be underestimating them."

"Three hours, then?"

"That is not what I meant." But Derivan smiled, and Vex grinned back at him; the lizardkin suddenly ran forward and gave him a hug for no reason at all and then went straight back to looking at the plants.

"I'm going to start in this row, okay?" he said. "And you can start in the one next to me, and let me know if you forget how to harvest anything, or if you get to a plant Emily didn't cover."

"Yes," Derivan agreed.

And so they got to work.

They worked in a companionable silence for a while; there were words to be spoken, but neither of them knew what to say, so they distracted themselves with the harvest instead. They'd been supplied with handwoven baskets that were not unlike the ones Emily used for decoration in her home. Vex kept a whole half-dozen of those baskets floating behind them, using some odd spell he refused to name, citing embarrassment because it was "too specific."

Derivan was careful to sort his pickings into those baskets. It was repetitive work, but it drew him into a peaceful lull, enough so that he was surprised when Vex broke the silence. "Hey, Deri?"

Derivan looked up to find the lizardkin watching him with an inscrutable expression. Well, inscrutable to most. Physical Empathy told him the lizardkin was nervous, determined, and a little bit scared, all at once. "Yes?" he asked, not knowing what else to say.

Vex took a breath. "I've been meaning to talk to you about this for a while, but it never felt like it was a good time," he said. "And now is... maybe the best time we're going to have in a long time. So I wanted to say it now."

"Say what?" Derivan asked. He'd gotten an inkling before, back down in Teque, but he'd dismissed it as something he didn't understand; even now, he only *thought* he understood.

"I like you a lot, Deri," Vex said, and he hesitated a little bit, as if searching for the right words to explain himself. He'd stopped with harvesting the plants and instead stepped up close to the armor; Derivan noted with some amount of surprise that—for the first time in a while—Vex wasn't being *shy*. He was nervous, certainly, but there was a determined sort of look in his eyes.

He'd been thinking about saying this for a while, it occurred to Derivan. It was on his mind while they were harvesting, and it had been on his mind even before that. He recognized this countenance, the look in the lizardkin's eyes, even if he didn't have the words for it.

"I want to try to be more than we are," Vex said quietly. He looked up at Derivan, his gaze earnest. "If you're okay with that, I mean."

Derivan was silent, and Vex waited. Oddly, he didn't seem nervous anymore. It was like all of his nerves had gone with finally saying the words that he'd been wanting to say, and now he was simply waiting for a response.

So Derivan finally found the words to speak.

"A few moments ago," Derivan said, "I was thinking about how I feel differently for you than I do for Sev, or Misa, or any of the other individuals in our lives. It is . . . difficult to put to words. I care for all of you, and I wish to build a future with all of you, strange as that may seem.

"Sev and Misa are—the closest analogue is 'family,' I believe. They are family to me. And yet you are the one that comes to mind when I think of who I wish to protect. You are the one I wish to comfort and hold, the one I do not wish to see hurt, and . . . I do not know more than that. These feelings are unfamiliar to me. But I do know that you are important. And so I would like to try, so long as you know that I have much to learn."

Derivan gazed at Vex for a while after he finished speaking. The lizardkin had started to fidget as Derivan spoke, and now he avoided the armor's gaze entirely; whatever confidence he'd gained in his confession had slowly slipped away as Derivan spoke, and now he seemed shy again.

It was cute.

Derivan reached out to take one of Vex's hands and made a small, surprised sort of hum.

"You are very warm," he said.

"Yeah, well," Vex muttered, still not meeting his eyes but managing a barely held-back smile. "That's what happens when you say romantic things to me."

"Was that romantic?"

"It was to me." Vex tugged on Derivan's hand, and the armor knelt down obligingly; he leaned forward to press his forehead against Derivan's helmet. It was a small moment of intimacy. They had shared similar ones, too, before—and yet this one somehow felt closer than all the other times they had shared those small touches and quiet moments.

"Thank you," the lizardkin said to him, softly. And it was only now, stripped away of all the nervousness and fear and awkward shyness, that Derivan felt Physical Empathy ping with the emotion underlying it all: not love, for it was still too early for that, but hope. A simple joy in sharing in his company.

And in *that*, at least, he knew he felt the same.

CHAPTER 39

MECHANISMS OF MAGIC

Derivan found that the harvest went rapidly after Vex's impromptu confession. That had, apparently, been the only thing holding the lizardkin back from putting all his efforts into the harvest—and, more importantly, into trying to identify the problem with growth spells that had apparently affected Elyra.

"I was afraid I wouldn't get the chance to talk to you about it if I didn't do it then," Vex admitted, when Derivan asked. "We're going to go to Elyra after this... And we need to figure out what's going on with the crops, we need to get into the Elyran dungeon, we need to find a way to backdoor into Teque, if we can. Maybe just learn enough of their magic to break the barrier. And I doubt we're going to be doing any of that without having to deal with the nobility, and with my family in particular."

"You are not looking forward to that," Derivan noted with sympathy, and Vex just shrugged.

"I have you guys," he said. "It's... more than I had before. And I feel good about what I can do with your help."

Vex offered him a small smile then, before turning his attention back to the magic he was casting. Derivan watched curiously—they'd long since finished their section of the field, and a full dozen baskets were sitting beside them, each filled with a variety of magical plants that had been... well, not *perfectly* harvested, but very close to perfect. Vex had examined them and declared them "good enough," and Derivan knew Vex well enough to know that if he thought it was good enough, it was likely to be perfect to anyone else.

Now the lizardkin sat beside a small plant that he'd acquired permission from Emily to experiment with. A half-dozen runes floated around the plant, circling it almost lazily.

"There's nothing wrong with the mana circulation or absorption as far as I can tell . . ." Vex muttered. "But the growth spell is still taking more mana to take effect. I don't understand."

"Which one is the growth spell?" Derivan asked.

"This one." Vex flicked his dagger at a runic circle that was glowing a ruddy green; Derivan watched the mana flowing into the circle and frowned slightly. There was a fraction of mana that seemed to just . . . vanish as it moved into the circle. "The other spells are stabilizing and reversing any output from the growth spell. I'm trying to avoid too many mutations in the plant."

"Mutations?" Derivan felt a little lost in this conversation, admittedly.

"Science from the planeshifted," Vex explained, a little distracted. "The more times you try to grow the same plant, the more likely it is to gain deformities. It's fine if you just do it once in regular crop-harvesting, but quite a lot more dangerous if you're constantly growing and, uh . . . un-growing a plant, for lack of a better word. Hence the stability spell."

"I see," Derivan said. Strange! He was learning new things about the world every day with Vex. This wasn't something he could help with, though, and so he focused his attention on the disappearing mana instead.

He'd seen pretty much that exact thing before, after all, many times over. Mana disappeared when it was being consumed by the system, and the system freely Shifted it around to obfuscate that fact . . .

. . . except that didn't seem to be happening here.

"It does not appear to be Shift-related," Derivan remarked, surprised, and Vex blinked at him.

"I was about to ask you to check that next," he said with a sigh. "The mana can't just be disappearing. Mana doesn't just . . . disappear. It changes, or it turns into energy, but it doesn't vanish."

"Perhaps it is something the runic circle itself is doing," Derivan suggested. Patch didn't reveal anything strange happening with the system either.

"I . . . don't think it's *absorbing* the mana." Vex hesitated slightly, bringing both runic circles closer to him, so he could examine them; the circles for **[Plant Growth]** and **[Genetic Stability]** hovered in front of him. "They generate the same amount of waste heat, so it's not that. The circle itself doesn't seem to be any stronger. But **[Plant Growth]** is taking almost five times more mana than it usually does."

Derivan considered the issue for a moment. "Perhaps we could try casting it like it was a glyph?"

"Drawing it out?" Vex frowned. "They're kind of similar in how they work, but runic circles work more like circuitry, and glyphs are an imprint that the mana acts on. And runic circles are usually too complicated to draw without system assistance."

"The broad strokes, then," Derivan said; he was already doing it as he spoke, painting purple lines into the air. The runic circle for [**Plant Growth**] was complex, with dozens of tiny, branching lines that were completely incomprehensible to him—but he could see the general shape and direction of those branching lines...

His Magic stat was at work, he realized belatedly. Vex was watching him with undisguised interest.

"*Are* circles and glyphs related?" Vex muttered to himself. "I didn't think they were, since they operate in ways that are so different—but if runic circles are just the system trying to replicate what mana can already do... Maybe the system uses the glyphs as a *base* and then turns it into a circuit to replicate the effect..."

"I believe it does not need to," Derivan said. "But I suspect that it does, because it needs a base to work off of. It is only a guess, however."

The glyph completed. Mana sang, dancing into the shape he'd created; it *worked*—

—but that mana vanished too. Only the smallest remnant of the effect followed, a slight jolt in the plant he'd been trying to enchant; [**Plant Growth Reversal**] quickly pushed it back into place.

Derivan and Vex both paused and frowned. Vex's eyes widened as a realization hit him. "It's not system-related."

"I do not know what else it could be," Derivan said, but he scoured his mind, and a small memory tugged at him, a strange behavior they'd experienced before, when it came to mana. Something *familiar*. "But... I believe we may have seen this before?"

"I think so, too," Vex said.

"Let us ask the others," Derivan suggested. "Perhaps they will remember."

Almost entirely on impulse, Derivan held his hand out to Vex. Vex glanced at it and, as though suddenly remembering what they'd had a conversation about not too long before, promptly colored.

He still took Derivan's hand, though.

The plan to check with the others was, unfortunately, somewhat stalled by Sev and what he'd managed to do the one time Misa had her back turned. To be fair, Derivan thought, this was close to the end of the harvest—a good six hours into picking magical reagents and following a host of rules. Vex and Derivan had only gotten done so quickly by virtue of Vex's Agility stat and his experience with these things.

Still, though, for *Sev* of all of them to trigger a reaction from the plants! He was normally the most careful of them all. He looked fully disgruntled, too, and halfway torn between amusement and annoyance.

"You need to sit still," Emily said, a bit of amusement in her voice. Vex, Derivan, and Misa had all gathered back in her home and sat scattered around the house while Sev grumbled, sitting on what Emily had jokingly called "the throne of shame."

It wasn't much of a throne, really. Just a magically enchanted stool designed to slowly strip away any remaining magical effects on a person, while allowing Emily to cast repair spells so that all the tears and burns in Sev's robes could be fixed. It was a rather impressive construction, from what Derivan could see, though he would need to ask Vex for the details...

"I can't believe you have this," Misa said, amused. Emily chuckled.

"This kind of work is complicated at the best of times," she explained, not looking up from her task. Sev sat as still as he could in the light of her magic, pouting only slightly. "I always expect at least one accident when I get help. I didn't expect Sev to set off a *chain reaction*, but it's good to know that kind of thing can happen."

"I have many questions about the kind of operation you're running here," Sev muttered, mostly to himself.

"I have many answers!" Emily said cheerfully. "But just so you know, most of them will start with 'that's proprietary' or 'it's just a private farm.'"

"What did you *do*, anyway?" Vex asked, apparently finally unable to hold the question back.

"I plucked a leaf too early," Sev said, not looking him in the eye. "Which would have been fine, because it just administers a light shock, but I was stepping on the root of a plant that reacts to electricity, and *that* plant *apparently* summons wind blades if you shock it."

"To be fair," Emily said. "That part was kind of my fault. I probably should've kept those farther apart."

"*Why would you make a plant that summons wind blades when shocked?*"

"I don't know." Emily shrugged. "It seemed interesting at the time? I wanted, specifically, to see how magical plants deal with mana aspect conversion, because they do it very quickly compared to spells and mana manipulation."

"Why *wind blades*, then?" Sev asked, exasperated.

"Magical plant development is an art, not a science," Emily said severely. "I don't control the effects that come out; I just rapidly iterate and nudge them in different directions. It's just in its wind-blade phase. It'll grow out of it."

Sev paused and stared at her. "I can't tell if you're joking or not."

"It's part of how I manage to keep my secrets so well." Emily grinned at him. "Seriously, though, thank you all for your help. This was going to take days if I did it all myself."

"Why *did* you need our help, anyway?" Misa asked. "I know it'd take longer, but you'd still have gotten it done before we managed to get here, I'm pretty sure. And you wouldn't have to wait for Elyra to send people to help you."

"Proprietary."

"So she probably has to harvest all the plants in a small time frame, for whatever reason," Vex concluded.

"I will neither confirm nor deny that."

"It doesn't matter," Sev said, as the finishing touches on the repairs to his robes were done; he stood up, brushing himself off gingerly. "We're not going to try to figure out her secrets; she already told us she wants to keep them, and we're going to Elyra right after this, so it's better we don't know."

Emily beamed. "Thank you! I knew I made the right choice."

"The right ... choice?" Sev blinked at her.

"The right choice of chair."

Sev stared, then shook his head. "I'm not going to ask."

"Good choice!"

Derivan chuckled at the byplay, enjoying the lighthearted conversation, even as his mind continued to ruminate on the problem of mana and what was happening with Growth spells in particular.

They exchanged a few more friendly words before they left—Emily insisted on leaving them with a rather large package of reagents, which Vex had seemed excited about, and a small batch of seeds that Vex had seemed awed and honored by. Sev and Misa clearly didn't quite get it but could tell from Vex's reaction that it was valuable, and so were appropriately grateful anyway; Derivan just offered a small bow.

And then they were back on the road. They'd let the caravan keep going through the night, this time, Sev said; they were only twelve or so hours away from Elyra, and that would mean they would arrive in the morning, which gave them plenty of time to get settled and start looking for access into the dungeon.

Next, to Elyra; to the dungeon it held and the bonus room that was likely there; to Vex's family and all that dealing with them would entail. And, hopefully, to solving the food shortage.

"Hey," Misa said after a moment, breaking the low hum of their caravan with her words. "Isn't it weird that those plants damaged Sev's clothes? Usually health stops that."

"The plants weren't really a system hazard," Vex said. "They're probably just not part of the system. Non-health damage and all."

". . . So what you're telling me is that since Derivan also does non-health damage, his attacks can strip off people's clothes?"

"What?!" Vex spluttered. "No, wait—"

"If he doesn't have health, he can just use any kind of fireball, and it'll destroy most armor! We can just use *shame* to win fights!"

"Do I get a choice in this?" Derivan asked, amused.

"It's all just hypothetical—"

"I told Derivan I liked him," Vex interrupted, desperately trying to change the subject.

There was complete silence for a moment.

Then the caravan erupted in questions, and Derivan chuckled faintly to himself, allowing most of it to pass over him, except when Vex wanted his input on something.

At least they were going to be entering Elyra on a good note.

CHAPTER 40

THE GATES OF ELYRA

Elyra's walls loomed over the horizon.

Vex's stomach turned a bit as he stared at them—he never thought he'd see them again so soon. He knew, *objectively*, that it had been more than a year since he'd left; it still felt like he was returning too early. He'd expected to have three years before being forced to return.

It had only been one and a half.

Only a few weeks before, Vex would have said he wasn't ready, even with all the progress he'd made with the Guild and with his friends. Now?

He still didn't feel like he was ready; he wasn't sure he ever would. But at least he felt like he could do it, even if he wasn't ready. He could face down his parents and demand they give up his little brother, and convince all his siblings to turn against them . . .

. . . well, no, that second goal was a little more farfetched. Vex knew most of them bought in to what his parents had told them. Even his sister Lyssa, who sympathized with him the most, believed it was simply a necessity to maintain their noble status.

And they weren't even *wrong*, was the thing. He couldn't dispute that it was the truth. It was the fact of what they were doing that rubbed him the wrong way—starting at the age of six, too young for them to really understand what they were accepting, what they were giving up—

"Are you okay?" Derivan's voice interrupted his thoughts. He spoke in his usual calm baritone. The lizardkin paused, brought back to reality, and gave Derivan a small smile.

"I will be," he said, turning to stare back up at the walls.

"You have us, whatever you need," Misa said. "Although if I get my hands on your *fucking* parents . . ."

"Misa," Sev warned quietly. Vex could tell his heart wasn't in it, though; it was more an automatic response than anything else.

"I *know*," Misa said, looking down and gritting her teeth. "I know. Just . . . why aren't *you* angry?" she blurted, directing the words to Derivan. "Even *Sev* is mad, no matter how good he is at hiding it, and you're *not*? I don't get it."

Derivan was silent, and for a moment, so was the cabin; Misa was opening her mouth to apologize, looking awkward, when Derivan finally responded.

"No matter how much I wish to be like all of you," he said, "I am different, I think. My thoughts do not turn toward anger. I do not understand revenge, except perhaps in a very abstract sense. When those that are close to me are hurt, I think only about protecting them, not about harming those that caused it. Perhaps this is a blessing, or perhaps it is a failing. I do not know. I do know that I have little control over it.

"Perhaps I will feel differently when we meet them. But . . . I find my thoughts veer more toward the direction of keeping his brother safe." Derivan paused. "I am sorry if that answer is disappointing."

Misa just sighed. "No, I'm sorry," she said. "I shouldn't have put that on you. It just . . . It feels fuckin' weird that *I'm* the one most angry about all of this."

"Is it that weird?" Sev glanced at her, offering a small smile, though it was a little tentative. "Aren't you always?"

"Kind of." Misa frowned a bit. "I dunno. This feels different, you know?"

"Let's not talk about this?" Vex gave them all a strained smile. He appreciated them all, but he didn't know how to handle this; having people angry on his behalf—or wanting to protect him, in Derivan's case—was somewhat foreign to him still. "Come on. We're almost at the walls."

And they were.

The gates were well guarded, built several lengths high with spellcraft-shaped redstone; the mana traces were a telltale giveaway, and they created lovely little striations in the rock, too, for anyone with mana sight.

Near the too-ornate gate was a troop of about ten guards: two stationed on either side of the gate, two at the center, and the remaining six lining the walls on top—equipped with ranged weaponry, if the shadows of their staffs and bows were anything to go by. For a fraction of a second, Vex thought he saw a man holding a crossbow, distinct from all the others—

—but no, it was just a normal guard like the rest of them, now that he looked more closely. He breathed, trying to calm his hammering heart. Were they still being watched? He'd almost forgotten, with their time with Emily being so peaceful . . .

He cast out his [**Advanced Mana Sight**], just in case they *were* being watched by the man with the crossbow. If he was present, Vex would be able to detect him through the small bits of wood mana trapped within the crossbow, or the metallic mana threaded through the bolts.

His sight did turn up several people skulking around invisible to the naked eye, and he had no doubt there were a few more that even his sight wouldn't catch, but...

No men with crossbows.

Good.

The number of guards and invisible men here was more theater than it was anything else. When was the last time any force had tried to invade or sneak into Elyra? If anything, people were more likely to try to sneak *out*. But maybe that was his bias speaking.

"State your business," one of the guards spoke to them, his voice gruff.

"We're adventurers on a diplomatic mission," Sev answered, flashing their adventurers' badges at the guard and gesturing toward the back of the caravan. Vex stayed well behind, closer to Derivan. "Delivering supplies to Elyra. The Guild here should be expecting us."

"We haven't received word of this," the guard said with a frown.

"You haven't?" Sev's brow furrowed. "We should have been expected since a week ago—"

"The badges are legitimate, either way," one of the other guards said. "Adventurers are allowed in the city. We might as well let them in."

"Corelius." The first guard scowled, something in his expression turning ugly. Vex wasn't surprised. It wasn't the first time he'd seen this kind of corruption among the guards. "What have I told you about speaking up without being prompted?"

"... To not do it, sir," Corelius said. The man stepped back and bowed his head slightly, though Vex saw his lips twist slightly, as though in disgust.

"The entrance fee is ten gold," the first guard said bluntly. "You can't come in if you don't pay."

"What? Ten gold is *exorbitant*." Sev frowned. "Give me a moment to send a message to the Guildmaster—"

"Twelve gold," the guard said.

"—Oh. This isn't a rule at all; you just want a bribe." Sev's brows furrowed, and Vex felt his fists clench. "I'm not inclined to bribe you. We're here to help Elyra; we'll be donating to your food supplies regardless."

"Food, eh?" The guard's eyes immediately lit up with greed. "Shit, you should've told me; I thought your supplies were just wood and junk. If you're giving us food, then all you need to do is give me ten percent, and I'll let you in."

"What? No! Do you have any idea—" Sev clamped his mouth shut as he spoke, took a breath, and switched tactics. "We will *not* be doing that."

"You will let us in," Vex said quietly. Sev blinked and turned to look at him in surprise, and Vex gave him a small nod; he could handle this. He needed to handle this.

"Who the hell are you?" the guard sneered at him. "Don't interrupt when the big boys are talking."

"Who the hell calls themselves 'the big boys'?" Misa muttered in the back, to Vex's amusement; he'd flinched a little bit when the guard spoke to him, but that remark made a smirk tug at the corner of his snout.

He straightened his back and strode forward.

"I am Vex of the Ashion House," the lizardkin said, glaring at the man with his haughtiest look. "You will let us in."

". . . No you're fucking not," the guard said, but his face was considerably paler.

"Richard," one of the other guards warned; this one hadn't spoken before, but he clearly recognized Vex, because his face was much paler than the man who was presumably named Richard. "Do the test, or you're going to get us all in trouble."

Richard gritted his teeth. "*If* you're a noble," he said. "And I'm not saying that you are. Then share a drop of your blood, and we will validate your bloodline."

The last words were recited and well practiced; Vex still frowned, then held out his hand anyway. He was used to this. The guard stared at him for a moment and then promptly used a small black box threaded with a gold needle to pierce Vex's scales. Blue blood oozed out for a second, and the guardsman allowed the blood to flow into the well of a second, smaller device.

For a moment, nothing happened, and a satisfied grin began to spread across Richard's face—

—until the whole thing lit up with a buzzing green, and Richard flinched, almost dropping the box. "Shit," he said, and frantically waved at the men atop the gate to start opening it. "I'm so sorry for the inconvenience, sir. Please don't report me."

"I won't," Vex said, not meaning a word of it. The guard looked relieved anyway, apparently trusting the lizardkin to keep to that promise; he wondered how many nobles the man had met before, to think that he could gain their favor just by catering to their every whim.

Probably too many.

He hated this, though. This was another part of the reason he'd left Elyra in the first place—too much worship and attachment that came with his name. No one treated him like a person.

But he *did* have people who treated him like a person now, so he wasn't above using his status to let them get into the city faster.

"There's something wrong with the Guild here," Sev muttered to himself, already busy with his system and apparently rapidly scanning through a message, if the way his eyes flickered was any indication. "They haven't responded properly to Guild communications in days."

"They went dark?" Misa asked.

"No." Sev shook his head. "They're responding. Just disregarding all the communications protocols. The Guildmaster says she tries to rotate people here to make sure corruption doesn't take root, and the last shift was pretty recent, so I can't imagine . . ."

"I guess we better visit the Guild branch here first thing, then," Vex said quietly. "It's this way."

He knew the way by heart, and he quietly adjusted the caravan's magic to account for the new route. He'd been planning his journey for so long, after all—he knew that the Guild was his one shot at getting out of Elyra and having a chance at earning something close to prestige. There were, technically, more opportunities by his parents' sides, but . . .

Those opportunities felt tainted, somehow. Becoming an adventurer was, at least, his own choice.

The roads of Elyra, unlike many of the towns they had been in prior, were built for caravans to make their way through—and so they had no issue navigating the surprisingly crowded streets. There were other caravans on the street, too, doubtless owned by nobles, for how big and ostentatious they were; the streets were only built as wide as they were so they could accommodate the absurdly overbearing vehicles.

And yet, besides the prominence of moving caravans as a mode of transport, the place felt surprisingly quiet. It was almost chillingly reminiscent of Fendal, though Vex knew that was just his imagination. There were no strange strings of dancing mana here. Any mana that could conceivably be called alive avoided Elyra for miles around, even.

Part of the quiet emptiness was doubtless the food shortage. Vex's heart sank to see how different it was from what he was used to—he was not a fan of Elyra at the best of times, but often there were people in the streets that were *happy*, at least; now there was an empty listlessness with which they walked the streets, and too many people seemed too thin for their clothes.

Hunger was a very real ailment, despite the system. Health wouldn't prevent death by hunger; it would simply appear as a [**Malnourished**] status effect that got steadily worse, cutting off more and more maximum health.

Sev let out a sharp breath at this point, and Vex looked up, alarmed.

"Is the Guild building supposed to be that... you know..." Sev gestured, staring up at the Guild branch.

And he really did have to stare *up*.

The building definitely had not looked like that when Vex had left.

When he had left, the Guild had certainly been a well-maintained building, with ample space for its adventurers to room and sleep in, as all the Guild branches did. It had *not* been a *massive cathedral*, which was the best word Vex could think of to explain the vast change in architecture that had occurred. He was pretty sure at least two adjacent buildings had been demolished just to make room for the damn thing.

"Uh... no?" Vex managed. "No. It definitely didn't look like that before."

"Something's up?" Misa said.

"Something's definitely up," Sev agreed.

"I have a number of concerns," Derivan said, and cocked his head forward slightly. "One of which is related to the fact that that building is connected to the system."

"It— *What?*" Vex jerked in his seat. "A *building*? That's—"

"It appears to be connected to the system in the way that monsters are, yes," Derivan said. "If it is any consolation... there are many smaller signals within as well. So the Guild branch here is not dead, at the very least."

"Gods forbid we have to deal with a building-sized mimic," Sev muttered. "This better just be some stupid experiment. Okay, come on. Let's go."

CHAPTER 41

ENTRENCHED SYSTEMS

There was at least one good thing that might come out of whatever was going on with the Guild building, Derivan thought, once they found a spot within the Guild's grounds where they could leave the caravan. A small magical barrier flickered into place, automatically activated by their badges once they left.

He'd been needing a target to test Patch on for a while now. He couldn't use it on himself or any of his friends without risking breaking all the complex mechanisms that went into maintaining it, and they hadn't encountered any monsters along the way to Elyra for him to practice on.

As such, he hadn't really been able to work on training the new stat at all. He could use it to *observe* things, certainly, but that evidently didn't count as training it, considering it remained at a steady *1*.

But now there was something clearly happening with the Elyran branch of the Guild, and whatever that something was, it was related to the system in some way. Derivan had not forgotten what Xothok and the others had said. They had said that they had tried to get help here and been rejected.

Internal corruption had seemed like a likely possibility at the time, despite the Guildmaster's attempts to circumvent it. The presence of the strange system-structure over the entire building...

Well. Derivan did not know if it made it more or less likely that the Guild was corrupted, but neither likelihood was good, he thought.

The Guild cathedral towered over all of them, spires of gold and white rising into the sky. Without Patch and without Vex to tell them it had changed, Derivan wasn't sure he would have noticed anything wrong with it at all. But the claw of the system hovering above it had been clear the moment he had *looked*.

He had never seen anything so complex.

"Any ideas, yet?" Sev asked beside him, and Derivan shook his head.

"It is connected to the system, as I said," he said. "But I do not yet have the ability to examine its interface. Perhaps if we knew someone who could [**Identify**] it..."

"You'd think someone would've done that already." Misa stared up at the building. "You can't tell me this fucking thing popped up overnight and no one tried to check it out."

"It would be unusual to try to [**Identify**] a building," Derivan noted.

"And maybe someone did," Vex said quietly. He shook his head after a moment—followed closely by a full-body shake, like a wiggle to force himself to focus. "We won't know more until we go in. Derivan, can you make sure nothing happens to us with the system? I'll keep an eye out on the magic side."

"I'm still here, you know," Misa grumbled. "I can block these things."

"Please stay prepared for anything we can't see, Misa." Vex's eyes were still locked on the front doors of the building. For whatever reason, the lizardkin seemed to have decided to take charge here. Derivan wondered why that was, when Vex was so frequently allergic to leadership. Perhaps it was because Elyra was so close to him?

Or perhaps because this was where Vex first joined the Guild at all, and the place that had given him the opportunity to leave.

Whatever the case, Derivan thought that Vex wore his confidence well.

Derivan, Sev, and Misa all stood behind Vex in silent support of that decision, and the lizardkin pushed open the doors.

There was no *reaction* from the building, as far as Derivan could tell. The system still hovered there, far too present for Derivan's liking—and here, from the inside, he could see the problem was worse than he had realized.

For most people, the system was simply something that attached itself to them, stemming from the closest reality anchor and creating a complex metaphysical cage that interacted with their souls and substance. It was capable of modifying them, implanting traits and skills within them.

In *here*, it looked like that cage had... metastasized. Derivan might not have understood precisely how the system worked, as yet, but the mishmash of broken gears reminded him of the mess that his own connection to the system was, yet somehow worse. The sight made him feel distinctly uncomfortable.

"Hello!" someone from the front desk called—a broad orcish man that was just a hair taller than Misa, just enough that it looked like he fit rather uncomfortably in the small space behind the desk. The wall behind him was covered in scratches, strangely enough. Derivan wondered if that was a normal sort of decoration in Elyra. The receptionist also had a bewilderingly large, double-bladed sword strapped to his back, so Derivan could believe that their customs here were strange. "Shit, is that you, Vex?"

"Rekka?" Vex blinked at him. "I thought receptionist duty was punishment duty. You're still here?"

"I decided I liked being a receptionist," Rekka said, puffing his chest out proudly, a statement that struck Derivan as very at odds with the weapon on his back. "What're you doing back here, man? I thought you were gonna go out and... You know, you didn't tell me what you were gonna do. But you said it'd take a while! Years!"

"It's been a year and a half," Vex pointed out.

"But not two years, man!" Rekka leaned forward and flashed Vex a bright smile. "You look a lot better than you did before. And you found a team! I was worried you weren't going to look for one."

Derivan found himself suddenly fighting the urge to step in front of Vex. Strange.

"I didn't," Vex admitted. "They sort of found me."

"Vex is the team mascot," Sev quipped.

"Hey!"

"We did sort of adopt him." Misa grinned in the back, her stance relaxed—but Derivan saw the way she kept her hand close to her mace. She was staying prepared to fight.

"You gonna introduce me to your friends?" Rekka said, oblivious. Vex huffed, folding his arms together obstinately for all of two seconds before giving in.

"Fine," the lizardkin said. He gestured to the rest of the team. "This is Sev; he's the party leader. Uh, most of the time. I guess I'm acting party leader now? And this is Misa. The ho—" Vex coughed abruptly. "The big scary armor guy is Derivan."

"Hello," Derivan said, wondering what Vex had been about to say. Misa just waved, still keeping a hand near her mace.

"Pleasure to meet you all!" Rekka said, boisterous as ever. "I'm guessing you're here for a room? Registering... What are you all doing in Elyra, anyway?"

"We're the diplomatic envoy that the Guildmaster sent," Vex said, a slight frown entering his expression. "You didn't get word?"

"I'm... not sure." A flicker of uncertainty—and something *else*, dancing across Rekka's face almost too quick for Derivan to catch. The armor traced both the lines of magic in the air and the system structures he could feel with Patch as carefully as he could, to watch for anything strange.

There was nothing that he could see. But the resolution of his vision wasn't perfect as yet, and he stayed cautious.

"But let me check my records," Rekka added cheerfully, and started flipping through a number of binders he kept behind his desk. Vex watched him, and Sev glanced carefully at Derivan—the cleric seemed like he was worried, too. Misa just kept up her act, and Derivan saw just the faintest flicker of [**Guard Stance**] enveloping her body.

Everyone was still cautious, and no one was letting their guard down. Good.

Nothing happened, fortunately. Rekka simply looked up from his books with a small frown. "Found it," he said. "I'm not sure how I missed this. It says we're supposed to send out a message to the guards to let you in, too, but I don't think we ever did that. Did you get any trouble?"

"A little," Vex said. "Nothing I couldn't handle."

"Ah, nobility." Rekka wrinkled his nose a bit, though in disgust or jealousy Derivan couldn't be sure. Then he leaned in, and Derivan saw the system structure of the Guild... pulse. Almost nauseatingly.

The look on Rekka's face was definitely jealousy now. Rekka continued, lowering his voice into a faux whisper, "We might get that chance too, you know. Shh. It's a secret."

"What do you mean?" Vex blinked at him, but Rekka had already straightened and was pretending he hadn't said anything at all. "Rekka?"

"I didn't tell you anything," Rekka said with a wink. "I've got a room for you guys, and if you've parked your caravan outside, I can get people to start unloading and delivering the food to the nobles so they can distribute it."

"Um," Vex said. He glanced at the others for a moment, then visibly steeled himself and shook his head. "Don't do that yet, please."

"No?" Rekka frowned at him. "Why not?"

"We want to deliver it ourselves," he lied.

Rekka stared at him for a moment, then shrugged. "I mean, hey, suit yourself," he said. "Want me to get the documentation ready for dungeon entry? I see the Guildmaster sent some correspondence about that. High-priority dungeon entry... It might still take a couple weeks to get everything in order."

"You *had* a couple of weeks," Sev objected, his brows furrowing.

"We sent in the request as soon as we could." Rekka shrugged. "There's a long queue. Sorry, man."

"It's pretty important," Vex said. "Please? We need to get in there. People might... People might be hurt if we don't do it fast."

Rekka glanced down at Vex, and he softened slightly. "Aw, you know I can't say no to you, buddy," he said. "I can try, but there really is a long queue. It might help if I can use your name to speed things along."

"Go ahead," Vex said. "If you need to. Please."

"Really?" Rekka looked surprised. "You didn't want to leverage being a noble before... All right, if you say so."

"I still don't," Vex said. "But this is important, and I don't know if it can wait."

"I getcha," Rekka said. He plucked four keys deftly from the drawer and then tossed them to Vex, who caught them all without flinching; Derivan saw Rekka's eyes widen slightly, impressed. "Whew. Wasn't expecting you to catch 'em all. Got your Agility up?"

"We're all Silver now," Vex said, and Derivan thought he saw a small hint of true pride in the accomplishment.

"Whoa," Rekka said. "Fast! Shit, I thought you could only level that quick with noble support or something. The Guild help you out with that? 'Cause if they have programs like that, I'm going to have *some words*, lemme tell you."

"No, we just, uh... got into some dangerous situations," Vex said, shifting a bit uncomfortably. "Nothing you'd want to get involved with; trust me."

"If you say so," Rekka said, crossing his arms and looking just a little bit disbelieving. His expression relaxed a bit in a second, though. "Glad you're doing all right, little man. Anything else I can help you with?"

"No?" Vex said, sounding out the word as a question. He glanced around at the relatively empty Guild hall, and Derivan watched as nervous uncertainty resolved into determination. "Rekka, I thought you didn't care about being a noble. Do you want to be one now?"

"Oh, come on now; that's a bit of a personal question to ask in front of your friends," the orc grumbled. Derivan saw the system attached to the Guild pulse again, shaking and shuddering in an almost-nauseating roll.

"It's important," Vex said. "I can ask them to go away if you want."

"Nah, nah, it's whatever," Rekka said, waving a hand. He leaned back, the overwhelmingly large sword on his back scratching into the wall with a *thunk*, and Derivan realized exactly why the wall behind him had so many scratches. "I dunno. I've been rotated in and out of Elyra a few times, right? And it's just annoying getting in without being a noble. So it'd be cool if I *was*? Then I wouldn't have to deal with all that bureaucracy."

"Isn't nobility supposed to be a status applied to families?" Sev asked.

"Yup!" Rekka said. "That's the big deal about all this. They're thinking about granting the status to the Guild as a whole, but it's very hush-hush. I'm not actually supposed to tell anyone anything, but Vex is cool, and his friends are cool by proxy, so."

Misa and Sev exchanged glances, and Derivan frowned slightly, the lights in his eyes shifting visibly. Vex seemed uncomfortable.

"But you've seen what the nobility here does," Vex said.

"We can do better."

"But you *didn't*." Vex stepped forward, and Derivan saw a fire light up in his eyes. "We fought off some bandits when we were on our way here, and if it was almost anyone *besides us* that fought them, either the bandits would be dead or their victims would be. They told us they tried to join the Guild before resorting to banditry. You're supposed to accept anyone that applies as long as they don't fail a basic standard—"

Vex trembled, then took a breath; he turned his eyes to Rekka, who suddenly looked uncomfortable. "*Did* they fail some standard?" he asked, almost pleadingly. "Were they terrible people? I only know their side of the story, so maybe I'm missing something. What *happened*?"

"... if the Guild is to gain noble status ..." Rekka began, and then he lapsed into silence. He sounded a little sullen, and then suddenly angry. The Guild's system roiled angrily along with him, and Derivan saw something in Rekka try to pull away. "FUCK. I didn't think— I was at the meeting when we discussed accepting them. I didn't vote. But you can't blame—"

He cut himself off before continuing that sentence, half-growling under his breath. Vex waited, and Rekka calmed himself down slowly.

Derivan watched the mechanism of the system tick both around him and behind him.

Rekka's system was normal. The lump of system stuff attached to the Guild was not, and something about Rekka's anger seemed to affect it. Derivan stared at the thin, organic strings that stuck Rekka together with the metastasized system stuff attached to the Guild, and his eyes narrowed as he saw Rekka's part of the system *shudder*, as if trying to pull away.

One string fell. Through Patch, Derivan could feel this mutated system reaching out to try to fix it, to reattach it—

No.

Derivan flexed the destructive aspect of Patch, grabbing those stringlike tendrils and tearing them apart; it tore a small piece of system stuff off the system, too, and he felt the massive system shudder angrily.

But there was no retaliation, no diminishing of Patch. If anything, Patch had grown stronger.

"... I'm making excuses, aren't I," Rekka said, slumping just a bit. Derivan watched him carefully; Physical Empathy was pinging his emotions as far more stable now.

"Their actions aren't your direct responsibility," Vex said. "But the Guild chose to take responsibility—this is what we *do*. We're supposed to give people a path. You did it for me."

"You were nobility," Rekka said. "Are. You would have been accepted anyway."

"My parents didn't want me to be, and you could have denied me for that reason." Vex tried to soften his voice, but the lizardkin was wound up.

Rekka was silent for a solid minute that felt like it stretched for too long.

"It didn't seem like much at the time," he muttered to himself, and then he shook his head; when he looked up again, his eyes were bright. "I'm going to talk to the Guildmaster. We've been in talks for ages. I'm seeing— Shit, I'm seeing what they might be doing now. I'm not sure. It looked harmless, but they didn't want us telling the Guildmaster, and maybe that should've *made* it fucking obvious—"

Rekka interrupted himself with a half-snarl. "I'm gonna find out," he said. "It shouldn't have taken you guys coming in to make that obvious. Something happened there and I don't fucking like it."

"We'll help," Vex said.

"You gotta focus on getting into the dungeon, right?" Rekka said. "And I bet you wanna know what's up with the crops, too. We have some documentation on that. I'll hand it off to you."

"Thank you," Vex said, blinking.

"I need some time to think," Rekka said. "You guys go up—I'll talk to you again later. We need some eyes on this that aren't us. Fucking ... fuck. Okay. Sorry. Just ... give me some time."

"Of course." Vex's voice softened a little, seeing the orc's clear anger. "We'll, uh, come back down later. Or when you call us."

"I'll call you later," Rekka confirmed, and pulled out what was probably the largest binder Derivan had ever seen; it slammed onto the desk, and he began flipping through it fervently.

Then he stopped and looked up at Vex. "Thanks for coming back, little lizard," he said. "If you didn't call me the fuck out..."

"Just doing my job," Vex said, embarrassed.

As they left to go up to their room, Derivan surreptitiously used Patch to pick up the little shard he'd seen break off from the system, holding it in metaphorical hands.

"This better not be another mystery to solve," Misa grumbled. "I'm tired of not knowing shit. Rekka didn't even tell us *why* they were going to get noble status."

"No mystery," Derivan said with a shake of his head. "I believe he will tell us when he is less angry at himself. But also . . . I believe I understand the gist of it."

Using Patch, he picked up the little shard he had observed, invisible to everyone else.

It was a small fraction of a system window.

CHAPTER 42

AVOIDING THE MYSTERY ARC (THIS TIME)

> **[CONNECTION BROKEN]**
> Reconnecting...

There was some text above that, but it had been cut off; all Derivan could see were scattered letter-fragments that didn't mean anything to him. It was strange that the window looked like this to him at all—no matter what errors the system had encountered before, he'd never seen the system windows themselves break. They weren't a physical thing to begin with.

But then he was observing this with Patch, and not with his conventional senses, so... perhaps that made sense. There was an impulse in him, even, if he paid attention—an impulse to *fix*.

Mildly concerning. Derivan tucked that fact away to be reexamined later.

More important was the fact that that wasn't *all* he could see with Patch.

It took him a moment to see it, and he had to dig deeper; like with his other stats, there was an intuitive understanding of how to use them, but he had to find the lever to pull first. Derivan was barely aware of Patch slowly ticking upward. He noticed it when he paid attention, like a faint humming in his soul, but the rest of him was consumed by that process—the process of pulling apart the details, trying to find what was wrong.

There was a problem here that needed to be fixed. For a problem to be fixed, he needed to understand it. And the facts unfolded in front of him, through the little fragment he held and in the raw, twisted machinery of the system that oozed through the building. The extent of what he could see grew as Patch did, until he could feel the pulsing force of the entire building's system.

He still couldn't see its interface, exactly, but with this shard to lens Patch through, to see how the "connection" was interpreted—

"It is not a mimic. The building itself is able to grow in levels and acquire skills," Derivan said out loud, though he was only dimly aware of his own voice; the majority of his senses were still focused on what the Patch stat was feeding him. "That explains its change in appearance."

"... That *sounds* like something Elyra would award nobility for," Vex said slowly. "You think it's connected?"

"It is," Derivan said. His Patch vision swam a little, and for a moment, he worried that it was the system shifting to attack them—but no, it was his own sight, unable to keep steady. Sev was watching him with slightly narrowed eyes, like he'd sensed that he might need to act.

"At the very least, the building is artificially connected to the system; many of the problems are caused directly by this. The larger system is unable to recognize the nature of this connection. This has created several side effects—one, the system does not know how to connect to it fully, and so many of its normal mechanisms are simply growing out of control; two, in its attempts to fix itself without any Patchers, it is simply linking itself to and piggybacking off of working systems. It was connected to your friend until I broke the connection."

Vex shifted uncomfortably, his grip on his dagger tightening. "Is it going to connect to us?"

"No," Derivan said, and then observed for a moment more, trying to ignore the growing headache he was developing. What a strange sensation that was; he'd never had to contend with discomfort in any real capacity. "I am unsure why. Or... No. I believe I know."

He had to push both Patch *and* Shift to be able to see it. None of their systems were attached to the Elyran dungeon like the system in the Guild building was; he could almost sense the trail that led off to where the dungeon presumably was, deep, deep underground. "Our systems are not connected to the local dungeon," he said. "I do not think the building knows we are here."

"Is it *alive*?" It was Misa that asked the question; she was tense, glancing around the room as if she expected it to attack her.

"There are two levels the system uses to fix errors, I believe," Derivan said. "There are automatic protocols that activate to try to resolve problems, and if those problems cannot be solved, they are elevated to either Patchers or an Administrator, depending on the nature of the issue."

"But the Patchers are occupied with Teque and Fendal," Misa said out loud, her brows creasing with worry. "Are they sending *every* Patcher there? That's..."

"Those shards you hold are important, although it is difficult to articulate why." Derivan nodded toward Vex. He'd given his own stash of slivers to Vex a while back.

"I have some guesses," Vex said, one hand going to the pouch; the lizardkin's tail shifted nervously behind him.

"So why not summon an Administrator?" Sev asked. "Not that I want them to do that, obviously; it's basically been a disaster every time we've fought one. The first one we beat by *literal* deus ex machina, and the second one we could only defeat because there was a reality-stripping barrier around the village the system was trying to defeat. If one appeared in the middle of Elyra—"

"Elyra's own Platinums would be able to handle it," Vex said.

"Would they?" Sev asked, frowning slightly. "I'm not so sure about that. Look at what Misa had to do just to be able to block that [**Meteor Storm**]."

"I . . . Maybe," Vex admitted, losing a little bit of his surety. "I haven't worked with most of them. But I know they're powerful."

"It is not a situation we want to risk, but it is also likely irrelevant," Derivan said. "This falls strictly into the Patcher territory; there is no need for someone to make a decision or to coerce us into changing our paths. Those are the only times Administrators are called upon."

"And you're *sure* about this?" Sev frowned slightly, looking at Derivan. The armor stared back impassively, though the floor felt like it was tilting slightly . . .

"Deri?" Vex said, suddenly sounding worried.

"*Derivan*," Sev suddenly snapped out, his eyes sharpening. "Stop focusing on Patch. Now."

The command came through more sluggishly than it should have—but Derivan obeyed nonetheless. When Sev spoke *like that*, most of the team reacted automatically; it had saved their lives more times than they could count.

And it was like a fog lifted from his head.

Derivan blinked several times, the lights in his helmet flickering, and he realized that he'd been swaying on his feet. The armor shook his head, straightening. "I . . . do not know what happened."

"Is Patch draining you somehow?" Sev asked. "You need to tell us."

"It is . . . I do not know. I do not think so," Derivan said. He glanced at his status, bringing it up briefly to check on the numbers, and was unsurprised to see that Patch had gone up by two points. If anything, he was surprised it hadn't been more. "It has grown to three. I suspect that because this stat is likely used by the Patchers themselves, it carries with it many of the instincts that the Patchers themselves carry."

"You think most of your stats are things that have fallen by the wayside in the system," Sev said slowly, "but this one is something the system is actively using."

"In essence," Derivan agreed. "It is more complete than the others."

"But you can turn it off, right?" Vex asked, a tinge of worry in his voice, and Derivan found it in himself to smile at the worried lizardkin, though there was a certain exhaustion that was now bleeding through his soul—from resisting the stat, most likely.

"I can," Derivan agreed. "As long as I am not focusing on it, it is not a problem."

"It's something we should keep an eye on, though, just in case," Misa said, folding her arms. "At least we know I can block bullshit system-instinct stuff. We've done it before. There's no reason we can't do it again."

"You are right, of course," Derivan said. "But the last time we did that, it broke the system—and if we were to do this, it would likely break the stat. It is something we should keep in mind but perhaps not the first option to jump to."

"If you say so." Misa grumbled lightly under her breath. "Anyway, if you know what's going on, then I think we're wasting time here. We just came here to discuss what's happening, right? We kinda know what's happening now. I say we find Rekka or whoever's in charge of this place and tell them to stop with the bullshit."

"The building's system piggybacking on all the systems within it is likely what has led to the change in behavior of the Guild's occupants," Derivan said, nodding. "The system is linked to our souls in some way, and a corruption of that link can lead to a corruption of the soul in turn . . . I suspect. We should not waste time."

Misa nodded. "Then let's go," she declared, kicking the door open.

Literally. Derivan thought that was perhaps a *little* unnecessary. This wasn't even her room. It was his.

"I'm *telling you* we gotta stop whatever the fuck you've been doing!" Rekka practically roared out the words; alarmingly, he had his weapon in his hands. Derivan still didn't know what it was, but he wielded it like it weighed nothing. How high level *was* Rekka, exactly?

"And you haven't given us a single good reason why!" the man that he was arguing with thundered right back, not the least bit intimidated. The man was a high-ranking adventurer of some sort, judging by the gold Adventurers' Guild pin on his cloak; he was an older man with a thick beard dotted with small, white hairs. The kind crinkle in the corners of his eyes contrasted sharply with the angry look he was giving Rekka.

"Excuse me," Sev said politely. They'd walked into the room mid-argument, using Derivan's ability to sense systems to find Rekka, though that use of Patch had strained him. Both Rekka and the other adventurer turned sharply to face them, lanced with irritation, but Rekka's expression quickly collapsed into surprise.

"I thought you were gonna settle in," he said, and then he grimaced slightly. "I didn't want you guys to see this, man, I'm sorry."

The other adventurer snorted. "They're the reason you came in here, yelling about nobility and the project?" he said, folding his arms. "You know better than to let new adventurers know about that, Rekka. We want to surprise the Guildmaster. And most of the time they react like *this*. I thought better of you."

"And I thought better of you," Rekka said steadily. "I thought better of *us*. What the fuck are we doing? This is exactly what the Guildmaster was trying to avoid—"

"What rank even are you?" the man said, ignoring Rekka and turning an imposing stare at the four adventurers. "You can't be more than Silver. What are your levels?"

"See!" Rekka latched on to that, glaring. "That's *exactly* what I fucking mean, Lendel! When did you give a flying fuck what people's ranks or levels were?"

Lendel leveled an exasperated stare at Rekka. "It's the chain of command, Rekka," he said. "I have to care. *You* have to care. It's how the Guild is organized."

"And yet we have to get approved before going up a rank." Rekka's anger had calmed now; Derivan was just watching. Their whole team was, really. This seemed... personal. "Why is that, Lendel?"

Lendel frowned. "... To ensure that those of the commensurate rank use their power appropriately."

"Exactly." Rekka's gaze sharpened. "And what the fuck is all *this*, Lendel?"

Lendel hesitated.

Derivan watched carefully and—with a little bit more care, now that he knew Patch affected him—began to watch what was happening through Patch.

And what he saw was... concerning.

Rekka's system hadn't been corrupted in any significant way; in some ways, it was almost pristine, though there were marks where the corrupted system had connected to it. That same system now seemed almost nervous, however, afraid to try to reconnect with him lest its connection be broken again.

Lendel's, on the other hand?

Most people had systems that acted like cages around themselves; Derivan could look at them and see the intricate mechanisms of the system hovering around them. He had no ability to perceive the souls of others, but he could use the shape of the system around them to identify where it probably was, even if he was only guessing. For all that he was concerned about the system, the individual systems he saw were beautiful, tightly woven constructs.

Lendel's system wasn't broken, but it certainly wasn't a beautiful, tightly woven construct. It had what could best be described as *masses*; where Rekka had a few small, exposed connectors to connect to the guild building, Lendel had more than ten. Each of them looked almost grotesque, like swollen tumors not unlike the nodes Derivan had seen in the building.

Where Rekka had organic strings loosely attached to him, Lendel had thick, weaving tendrils leading right back to the building's corrupted system.

It occurred to Derivan that the sense of repulsion he felt might have been part of the Patch stat, and he quickly shut off his connection to it. He'd seen enough. Rekka had been able to break off his connection fairly easily; Lendel's connections were twitching, like they were being stressed, but it certainly wasn't enough to break them.

He could break them, though. Patch was at three, and still didn't have nearly the kind of finesse he would have wanted before he was comfortable using it to actually fix and tweak his own system. He needed to level it further. And this?

This was the perfect opportunity. Some things needed to be broken to be fixed.

Lendel was still considering his response to Rekka.

Before he could finish, Derivan signaled to his party that a fight might break out; he saw all three of the others shift slightly in stance.

Then three things happened in quick succession.

One, Derivan reached forward and snapped every connection Lendel still had to the Guild building, wielding the force of his Patch stat and the full bluntness of its power against the tendrils.

Two, Lendel stumbled forward and *screamed,* loud enough to make Derivan flinch. A wave of energy rippled out from him, a skill Derivan thought the corrupted tendrils might have accidentally activated as they were shattered.

Three, two other people that Derivan didn't recognize rushed out of a side door he'd failed to notice—and judging by the red cloaks they wore, they were part of Lendel's team.

"Ah, shit," Misa muttered. Derivan couldn't help but agree.

CHAPTER 43

BATTLE OF THE GOLDS

There was, unfortunately, no time for a conversation. Derivan would come to regret being quite so impulsive with breaking Lendel's connections, in time, but he'd had no reason to believe that it would make the man fly into a rage; Rekka's connection had broken, and all that had happened was that the orc had learned exactly how he'd been acting all this time.

That was not at all what happened with Lendel.

The man's scream turned into an enraged yell—and his party members, running out of the side room, didn't spare a moment to *think*. In a way, Derivan admired how quickly they reacted; they'd worked together for a long time, if they knew to immediately jump to the defense of their teammate.

It still would have been nice if they'd *tried* to understand what was going on, though. But their weapons were already out. Lendel's teammates were a human wizard and an orcish cleric respectively, if their clothes were any indication. Considering the wizard proceeded to pull out a book and the cleric raised her holy symbol, he decided he was right.

"Derivan!" Misa snapped out—and then she *snapped out*, suddenly materializing in front of him right as Lendel's enraged face appeared in his field of view. Derivan took a step back, his hand reaching for his sword automatically even as odd, sickle-shaped weapons appeared in Misa's hands, to mirror the ones that Lendel was wielding.

"Flickerblades!" Vex called out, identifying them quickly. The lizardkin was already beginning to cut into the air with his daggers, but a flash of motion distracted him; the opposing team's wizard was casting, a runic circle appearing in the air for a split second and gathering an immense amount of fire mana—

Derivan didn't have the time to react, but Vex evidently did. The little wizard acted *fast*, leaping forward with a flicker of motion that made Derivan wonder exactly how many points he'd put into Agility. His dagger stabbed *up*, almost directly toward the enemy mage's face and missing only by a hair's breadth, and if Derivan hadn't thought to keep his [**Intermediate Mana Sight**] running, he wouldn't have seen the way the dagger nicked a cut into the opposing mage's circle.

He hadn't even known that was something that could be *done*.

The wizard clearly hadn't known that either. His gaze flashed up to his circle in a panic, and he let out a sharp curse, backpedaling desperately; Vex moved forward, uncompromising, and stepped deliberately on wizard robes as they dragged on the floor—

And the wizard tumbled backward with a yelp and a panicked scream, flailing. Vex didn't miss a beat. A second cut in the runic circle made it shatter, his version of [**Mana Manipulation**] apparently superseding whatever iteration the other wizard had. Then he lunged at the fallen wizard, and it was only the enemy healer tackling him out of the way that forced him on the defensive.

Sev was chanting, his eyes locked steadily on the battlefield; Derivan could feel the buffs slowly rising around them. The other healer was behind, forced to stop in order to protect their wizard from Vex, and Derivan . . .

Well, he was waiting for an opportunity.

"Stop fuckin' *fighting*!" Rekka yelled. "They're not here to fight— Dammit, Tibeus, Lorella, *Lendel started this!*"

"If Lendel started this, he had a good reason," Lorella said steadily; she was the healer of the team, and she was facing Vex with a wary look on her face. "He doesn't get angry for no reason."

"I'm tellin' you he *did*," Rekka said angrily.

And then Derivan didn't have time to pay attention to their conversation anymore.

Lendel had been held off by Misa for long enough, but he couldn't be held back for long; the Gold badge wasn't just for show. Derivan vaguely recalled what flickerblades were—Vex had talked about them at one point, and it was part of a briefing on esoteric weapons he insisted they all listen to, at some other point.

They were weapons that "could be in any position they had a reasonable chance of being in."

And now Derivan saw exactly what that meant.

In theory, they were deadly weapons that could readjust and skewer an enemy in a moment's notice; in practice, they were . . . well, they were still those things, but they looked rather ridiculous. Lendel's arms flickered quite literally into different positions, and Misa kept up the same, her block calling her own flickerblades into existence and countering every strike precisely.

But it could only last for so long. She disengaged after a moment, gritting her teeth and leaping backward, and Lendel almost immediately changed targets; once more, the angry man came barreling toward Derivan, and this time, he was prepared; his own sword leapt to hand and moved to block—

Except it was a feint, of course. He wore armor that could keep most weapons at bay; he wasn't that interested in the possibility of those blades hurting him. He was more interested in knocking Lendel out so they could discuss what had just happened. There was a blind rage in his eyes, but also something close to desperation. Physical Empathy was pinging at him, telling him there was something more there, something underlying his actions that was close to a physical need...

That would explain a lot about all of this, really.

Derivan feinted his own block and then shoved the entirety of his body weight into Lendel; Lendel stumbled backward and then snarled at him, but he was harder to knock off balance than Derivan had imagined. Misa came in again from the side, her own weapon back to its default form of a mace, and she swung the full weight of it toward Lendel's head.

Lendel ducked. One blade flickered into existence beside Misa's arm just as she completed the swing, and she had to abort the momentum entirely to avoid impaling her own arm on the sickle; she twisted her arm with a grimace, the point of the blade still drawing a line of red on her skin. Derivan came at him then, trying to distract him from Misa, and the second blade flickered into existence with the point nearly within his throat, in that gap in his armor that enemies who did not know his nature always seemed to target—

—except the thing was headed toward his *amulet*, and he twisted at the last second to avoid it; if he had a heart, it would have been hammering. The amulet wasn't a weak spot, exactly. All it did was prevent him from being identified. But it was important to him, and Lendel seemed to have pinpointed that even in his rage.

Golds.

The man used some sort of skill and vanished, reappearing in position just behind Misa; the half-orc didn't bother trying to turn in time. Instead, she closed her eyes and let her block skill take over, her body twisting unnaturally so she could meet the blade. A chunk of mana tore itself out of her and disappeared into nothing.

Derivan took that moment while Lendel was still engaged to charge. His blade was quickly caught, nearly wrenched out of his grip by the combination of two sickles creating a powerful twisting force; he fought that by letting go of his blade, just long enough to let the twist complete and not long enough that he couldn't grab ahold of it after.

In the corner of his vision, he could see Sev, Vex, and Rekka engaging Tibeus and Lorella together. To their credit, they were managing to put up a serious fight despite the poor class matchups; Tibeus wasn't letting Vex close anymore after seeing how easily his spell had been modified, and Lorella had managed to create some sort of barrier around them that couldn't easily be broken.

Rekka's attempts with his two-sided blade created rippling cracks of dark purple in the gemstone barrier, and Vex had some sort of drill construct chipping away at it, but both of them periodically had to stop to account for the [**Fireball**]s the wizard would pepper them with. They hung around him like small pellets, little shooting stars that darted out of the barrier and struck with unerring accuracy; it was mostly Sev's efforts that kept them at bay, his own light barriers deflecting or forcing them to implode early.

If only he had skills, too; his glyph-styled magic still wasn't nearly fast enough for him to use freely in a fight, and [**Barrier**] was too weak to reliably use in a battle—

—but he didn't just have his skills, did he?

He had stats. They were different, sure, but they functioned *like* skills, and the way the flickerblades worked reminded him of the way Misa's skill worked, reaching into different iterations of the same timeline. That was in effect just another application of Shift, the way that many system functions were.

It was subtle. But he saw it when he looked; the way the sickles spread out into a range of possibilities, disappearing outside the apparent range he could see through Shift. That didn't matter—he didn't need to see every single possibility for the sickles.

He just needed to be able to lock them to *one*.

But not yet.

It needed to be timed well. Misa charged at Lendel again, and Derivan followed up at nearly the same time, allowing himself to fall a half-beat out of step with Misa. It gave Lendel just one extra thing to think about, one extra thing he needed to time himself to match; small, for an experienced Gold adventurer, but nevertheless just enough that it would likely be a distraction—

There.

Lendel's blades locked with his own and with Misa's mace, nearly simultaneously; he saw from the way the man tensed that he was planning to flicker into another position at a moment's notice, both with his blade *and* with his body, and a split second before he could—in that fraction of a second between decision and action—Derivan reached out with all the force of Shift and hammered down on it.

Even with that—unexpected and unprepared as Lendel was—the man almost broke through his lock. But *almost* was not the same as succeeding, and instead a brief look of panic overtook Lendel as his skills failed him. Misa didn't hesitate or question what happened. She saw the change in his expression and knew it to be an opportunity; she shifted with her mace and slammed it into Lendel's stomach, the spiked ball denting armor and splitting flesh for just a second before his system health pushed it all back into place—

What happened next wasn't planned, and was born just from Derivan and Misa having fought together long enough that they could almost read each other's thoughts.

Misa let go of her mace.

Derivan grabbed it.

It was hard for him to inflict injury with his sword; anything he did with it would inflict either too much damage or too little, or be vaguely horrifying in its impact. Derivan wasn't particularly inclined to cut off a limb just to make Lendel listen, even if it was something that could be fixed. He had less qualms about repeating the mace-smash into Lendel's stomach a second time.

He didn't have the same Strength stat as Misa, of course; his strength was based nearly entirely on the magic moving through him. He was strong, certainly, but not as strong as someone reinforced by the system.

It was still enough to tear both metal and flesh, denting armor inward and into the wound.

Lendel screamed for a second time, and this time, it was a raw sound of pain. "What—what the fuck did you do," he said, his words caught somewhere between breathless and agonized. "What did you do to me! It was you, wasn't it—"

"Calm down," Derivan said, though he realized as he spoke that his choice of words was poor.

"I'm not going to fucking calm—"

"Shut your damn mouth and think for a second," Rekka snapped at him. "Why the hell did you get so angry?"

"*He did something to me.*" Lendel glared at Derivan, panting heavily, his hands clutching at his blades as though they could help him; instead of getting up to fight, though, he stayed sitting on the ground. The pain was throwing him off enough that he couldn't think clearly.

"Sev," Derivan said. "Heal him."

"Are you sure?" Sev asked. The other three had managed to take down the wizard and healer both, though they were slumped, unconscious; Derivan didn't know how they'd won, but the scorch marks around them suggested the process hadn't been pretty.

"He is . . . out of balance." Derivan hesitated. "It is hard to explain. I think you could help him. Would it harm you?"

Sev was silent for a moment, staring at Lendel. Derivan felt the flicker of a skill activating before the cleric answered. ". . . I think I can do it," he said slowly. "But healing anything that has a mental effect is . . . tricky. I'll need you to hold me down."

"Are you sure?" Misa's tone was sharp and worried. "We can find another way if we need to."

"We don't." Sev looked surer of himself now, leaning down over Lendel, who flinched away from him; for an old warrior, he wasn't used to *extended* pain if he still wasn't fighting.

Or . . . no. He was waiting to be healed so he could fight again; Physical Empathy pinged easily on that.

That was fine. The healing would remove the anger. Derivan saw it now, how the system attached to him throbbed in sympathetic rage.

He saw how to fix it.

"I will be helping," Derivan said. "It should minimize the effect it has on you."

He readied Patch; the stat was hardly a scalpel, but it was no longer a hammer. He could wield it with enough finesse, as long as someone else helped.

That was the hope, anyway.

CHAPTER 44

CRACKS IN THE SOUL

The trouble with Lendel was that his system was a mess.

Derivan knew that his own system was in a far worse state—but there was a difference in the way their systems were broken. His own system was something like a broken cage, the pieces scattered around him; it was still attached in only the most abstract of ways.

With Lendel, it was a different story.

Derivan did not have [Soul Sight], or whatever system skill would have allowed him to touch upon another's soul; he didn't know if such a thing was even possible in the context of the system. He'd always been able to sense his own soul—which, now that he thought about it, was perhaps an oddity—but he'd never been able to sense anyone else's.

But now there was something. It came from Patch, oddly enough; the stat had grown high enough that he could see more than he could before. It could sense the way Lendel's system had grown *into* him instead of breaking around him, and through that, Derivan saw something he hadn't noticed before.

Everyone had that, to a certain degree.

Rekka, Vex, Misa—even Sev, though there was something strange about what he saw there. Even *himself*, as broken as it was. The system dug itself into all of them in a way that had previously registered as their connection to the system, but the connection was so much more than that; it was the way the machinery of the system infused itself into them...

...and yet it made sense. Derivan hesitated to think the thought at all, but it fit with everything that happened in Teque and Fendal all too well.

The system was supporting them in some fundamental way. He'd seen it in Teque and Fendal, the way it seemed to be able to give and take away *realness*, like that was a transferable property. He wondered now if this was how it worked, beneath the surface.

The people of Fendal had lost access to the system and had begun to lose themselves; in turn, the people of Teque gained life, and system boxes had begun appearing for them. If he'd had Patch at a higher level—if he'd been able to level it up and use it to investigate the problems in Teque instead of being forced to leave—what would he have seen?

What was the system *for*?

Derivan was beginning to see an answer, and he wasn't sure he liked it.

"The system attaches itself to people and reinforces both substance and soul," Derivan said out loud, mostly to feel out the words; they felt strange to him, resonating with an odd familiarity.

"What?" Sev gave him a strange look.

"It is nothing." Derivan hesitated. His mind was spinning. If he was right, then the reason that was necessary at all... "I will talk about it later," he added softly, seeing that Sev was still giving him a strange look, and the cleric paused for a moment and nodded at him.

There was a chance he was wrong. He forced himself to focus his attention back on Lendel's system, on what had triggered this whole chain of thought to begin with: the way the system was growing *into* Lendel's soul and substance. He thought he could see where cracks had begun to form, and if he traced them back he almost thought he could see the causality of it all.

The system's growth hadn't exactly been intentionally malicious here. The cracks had formed first, and then the system had grown in, preventing them from healing. If he ripped out those pieces of the system, it might be able to heal on its own—

—but the cracks were deep enough that the system was now also the only thing holding Lendel together. If he simply ripped out those overgrown pieces, Lendel would fall apart, and the rather horrifying thought occurred to Derivan that he might fall apart in more ways than one. It would not just be his soul; it would be his *substance*, that thing that made him real.

"Sev," Derivan said. "Are you ready?"

"I've been ready." Sev paused for a moment, looking worriedly over Lendel. "He's... pretty badly damaged, on some fundamental level. I don't think this kind of damage is normal."

"It is a damage that goes beyond health," Derivan agreed. "You will need to heal him after I pull out the pieces of the system that have grown into him."

Sev jerked. "Is *that* what's happening?"

"Yes." Derivan paused to consider the certainty of his words and then nodded. "I think if you tried to heal him as he is now . . . I am unsure what would happen. But you would fight with the system on some level."

"Yeah, let's not . . . let's not do that." Sev grimaced a little bit at the thought, massaging his head like he could already feel the headache forming. Misa came up behind him, steadying him, and Sev took a breath. "This is going to hurt. Derivan?"

"Go." Even as he spoke the words, Derivan was reaching out with Patch; he grabbed at those intrusive tendrils of the system, the ones that *should not have been there*, and yanked them out with all the subtlety of a warrior—which is to say, with very little subtlety at all. Patch didn't yet have the precision it could afford him, if he worked on the stat.

He wasn't sure he wanted to.

Pulling out those overgrown system tendrils felt like a relief, though, a balm to his soul; he felt something inside him, probably Patch itself, uncoil and relax as he did so. At the same time, Sev gritted his teeth and let out a groan. A bright glow began to emerge from his fingers as he cast.

[**Divine Inhalation**], no doubt. Derivan could already see the cracks closing, which was good, because a moment longer and they would have begun to widen instead.

Even with the both of them working, it took time. Derivan had to be more careful with some of the system tendrils; he left the most-complicated ones for last so he could rely on any increase in Patch to afford him the precision he needed to pull them out. Some of them were entrenched deep within Lendel, coiled inside of him in a way that would have torn him apart if Derivan had simply ripped them out.

By the time he reached those, though, Patch had risen to 10, and that was *just* enough to give him what he needed to pull it out safely, to nudge all those individual pieces out of the cracks and wedges before he began to pull. Even as he did, Sev was healing—

—But Misa had to hold him back, too. There was a terrible, uncharacteristic anger in his eyes. The skill continued running, like Sev had intentionally left it on autopilot, but Misa was grimacing as she pinned the cleric's arms behind his back and he fought to get loose.

Rekka stared, eyes wide. Vex was muttering something under his breath, rapidly cutting a spell into the air with his dagger.

Sev was screaming, shouting something angry. Derivan focused, pulled out the last of the tendrils, felt the last of the cracks heal over—not completely but just enough—

"Stop," he said. "This is enough."

Sev panted heavily. There was a wildness in his eyes that wasn't there before. For a moment, Derivan was afraid the skill wouldn't cut out at all—

A runic circle formed in the air in front of Vex, and mana drifted forward, enveloping Sev; the cleric slumped over, and [**Divine Inhalation**] failed.

Derivan took a breath he didn't need.

"Thank you," he said.

Vex nodded. "I wasn't sure if I'd need it, but I was preparing, just in case," he said quietly.

Derivan could almost see the source of Sev's anger. He could almost feel those same cracks imposed over the cleric's psyche, this time with Physical Empathy instead of Patch; the damage wasn't the same. It wasn't to his soul—it was to his mind.

But in very small ways, he could see those same cracks beginning to form in Sev's soul, too. Not so large that they would be a problem, and likely the kind that could heal, but...

"We made a hell of a sacrifice for you," Misa said, glaring at Lendel. "Tell us what the *fuck* is going on here."

Lendel just stared.

Derivan saw what was going on with him, in a way. The man was off-balance—he had no context for what had just happened to him. He knew that he had been angry and that that anger had been unnatural, but he didn't know *why* yet; all he knew was that they had done something and his anger had vanished.

But Lendel had a few more points of context, too. He could see the way Rekka was glaring at him. He remembered the conversation, and Derivan saw him slowly putting the pieces together.

"Fuck," Lendel said after a moment. He stared at his still-unconscious companions and then at Misa's glare, which was, at this point, only growing in intensity. And then he slammed his fist into the ground, hard enough to crack the wood and make Rekka jump. "*Fuck.*"

"Hey, man, it got me too—" Rekka started, even though he didn't really know what "it" was.

"You don't know how this works," Lendel said, staring at Rekka and then shaking his head; he turned to look at Derivan, at Sev, at Vex and Misa. Sev was still collapsed in Misa's arms, and from what Derivan could tell, those small cracks were already beginning to heal...

...but it was going to be hard to tell until they got to speak to Sev directly.

"What are you talking about?" Rekka asked.

"I'm saying it didn't 'get' me. Or you, for that matter." Lendel took a breath. "That's not how it works. There's an *element* of that, but it doesn't make us believe anything we don't let ourselves believe first. I have some ideas about what happened, but this is ... Dammit.

"This project was supposed to help the Guild," Lendel said softly, looking toward Misa. "A lot of our smaller branches can't handle dungeon breaks if they happen; we've had one or two branches get run over. We thought if we could ..."

He lapsed into a brief silence.

"I know that," Rekka said. "That's why I was on board to begin with."

"But Elyra funded most of this." Lendel's gaze sharpened. "They're partially aware of how this works. Some of them were trying to take advantage."

"No fucking kidding," Misa said. She glanced at Lendel's two companions and then at Sev, still unconscious.

"We can wake them up," Lendel said. "They should be awake. We need to talk about this. Get you all set up for your dungeon visit, and plan around whatever the hell Elyra was trying to do here, or at least the noble families we were working with."

"I don't know if waking Sev up is safe," Vex objected softly.

"Your friend incurs a cost for healing," Lendel said; it wasn't a question. "You don't want to let him sleep through it, in most cases. The sooner he's awake, the sooner we'll know if anything's wrong and we need to get him a healer. We'll wake him back up, and then we'll talk. Rekka, can you get—"

"—I'm on it," Rekka said, and he began to walk out of the room—but as he stepped out, he glanced back. "You better have a damn good explanation, Lendel," he said shortly. "Something here is fucked, and frankly, I'm not sure these guys should have saved you at all."

Lendel's eyes hardened. "I know," he said.

CHAPTER 45

MALUS

Sev woke up gagging.

[**Smelling Salts**]. He recognized the smell of them; it wasn't the first time they'd been used to force him to consciousness, although he *really* hoped it would be the last.

"Enough," he said, waving them away; he saw his team staring at him cautiously, worried, and he blinked away the last of the [**Sleep**]. "I'm okay. Don't worry about me. You made the right call cutting that off when you did, Vex."

The lizardkin in question relaxed a little, looking relieved. Sev managed a small smile. He looked around the room—they were in the same room, it looked like, though some of the furniture had been destroyed in the fight. He hadn't even noticed. Lendel was standing off to the side, far enough away to not seem like a threat.

... The sight of the man made a smoldering anger slowly rise within Sev; he closed his eyes and took a breath, letting it cool again.

That anger wasn't his own.

It faded after a moment, back to a burning that was far in the back of his mind. He could *remember* being angry; that memory was nearly at the forefront. When he'd begun healing Lendel, the divine magic had transformed the nature of Lendel's injuries into memory, as it always did—and where those injuries had affected Lendel's mind, Sev had taken them on, feeling the same anger Lendel did. The fact that Misa had had to hold him back . . .

Sev wasn't sure how he felt about it. Ashamed, maybe; the thought came to him that he should have dealt with that anger better. What would he have done if he'd been able to pull himself free?

On the other side of it . . . he understood how Lendel had felt now, perhaps better than even Derivan could with Physical Empathy. The anger he'd felt was unnatural, a soul injury, an overwhelming sense of *violation* directed at the person that had caused it—and that knowledge had been instant and explicit.

Sev felt an echo of that, though thankfully undirected and loose. It would have been more difficult for him if he'd gained that anger whole, focused unilaterally on Derivan and those associated with him.

Thankfully, that wasn't the case.

"Give me a moment," he said to the others, and tried to settle himself.

He was used to this. It had been a long time since he'd *done it*, to heal something this significant; the injury was near the limit of what he could safely heal. Sev grimaced a bit, hoped his friends didn't see the expression on his face, and then brought up his status.

Sev, Level 49
Class: [Traces of the Lost]
Health: 980/980
Mana: 370/370
Stats:
Strength: 16
Intelligence: 37
Wisdom: 55
Agility: 21
Status Effects:
   [Memory Loss] [Malus]
Applied by [Sacrifice to the Lost]. Your maximum memory capacity is limited, and you must sacrifice memories to gain new ones. Current capacity: 501/500
   [Fatebroken] [Malus]
Applied by [Sacrifice to the Lost]. Modified by <ERROR>. Details of this malus are obfuscated. *You are not your own.*
   [#######] [Malus]
Applied by <ERROR>. Details of this malus are obfuscated. *You have chosen your path.*
   Skill List:
   Base Class Skills (Cleric): [Light Blast], [Triage], [Diagnose], [Heal], [Greater Heal], [Greater Buff], [Area Heal], [Purify Food and Water], [Holy Ward]

> **Divine Class Skills:** [Divine Barrier], [Divine Inhalation], [Channel Divinity]
> **Class-Specific Skills:** [Sacrifice to the Lost], [Traces]
> **<ERROR>:** [Look Up]

Sev hated looking at his status. He hated the *reminder* of all the debuffs he had that he didn't know anything about—there was so little he knew about himself, about what had happened to him when he'd first arrived on... Velus? Hestia?

What the fuck was *the name of the world*?

A terrible fear gripped him for a second, like he'd lost something else that was precious, yet another thing taken from him, despite all the measures he took to control his class and the maluses applied by his skills; [**Memory Loss**] was an obvious counter to the effects of [**Divine Inhalation**], which could convert status effects into memory, but...

There was usually still something lost in that process. It wasn't a perfect workaround. He could control what [**Memory Loss**] took, to an extent. It was a small mercy granted to him. But it wasn't enough; memories were associative, and every time the malus kicked in to steal pieces of his memory, small things were taken along with it.

Sev let out a breath.

It was fine. It was nothing he hadn't dealt with before.

[**Memory Loss**] said his memory was overextended; the number would tick down, and he would direct it to strip away the anger he now remembered. He tried not to look at the rest of his status, the parts that threw him off the most—the small messages built into his other two maluses.

You are not your own.

You have chosen your path.

The system didn't lie, generally, but he *felt* like he was his own person. What did it mean that he wasn't? What did it mean that *he'd chosen his path*? He didn't remember choosing anything.

Worst of all, he still couldn't tell his friends about those aspects of his status. He'd tried. There was a moment coming soon when he would be able to; [**Fatebroken**] ate at him every time he tried to tell them before it was the right moment, which told him a lot about what that effect probably was...

Derivan might be able to do something about it, he thought. As long as he noticed. The Patch stat gave Sev a better opportunity than ever to break free from the constraints he'd apparently put upon himself, though once more he was forced to confront the idea that he might not want to.

If he'd chosen this path, then surely he'd had a reason.

Something to think about later.

"I'm ready," he said, his voice sounding a little more distant to his own ears than he had wanted. [**Memory Loss**] was operating full-time. It never *entirely* stripped away the memory of the pain, like the system didn't want him abusing that combination in quite that manner, but it was good enough. "How is Lendel doing?"

"I'm fine," the adventurer grunted. "Not sure exactly what you did, but it reversed... everything. Left me with a hell of a headache. Still... thank you."

"You should be more careful when you're leveling a building next time." Sev tried for a joke, and cracked a slight smirk when Misa groaned.

"Oh by the gods," she muttered. "I was fuckin' *worried* about you, but nope. You're fine." She raised her voice. "He's fine, everyone. He's making puns."

"You have to be careful when you're leveling a building!" Sev objected. "I'm not wrong!"

Vex snickered a bit, and Derivan gave him a light if still slightly worried smile, conveyed the way he always did—with a tilt of his head, a slight dimming in the lights of his eyes in his helmet. They all still kept an eye on him, though, each of them still a little worried.

Not enough of a facade. He almost smiled proudly. They were all too clever by half.

"We need to talk about what we were doing here," Rekka said, pulling the topic back on track. He stared at Lendel, then at his two companions, both of whom were now awake and silent. "What exactly happened to us? You said it doesn't make us believe anything we don't already believe."

Lendel was silent for a moment. Then he sighed and began to explain.

"It took me a bit to connect the dots," he said. "But I think I get it. Sort of. This project began in secret several years ago, when some nobles came by and dropped off a *large* donation—enough to renovate the entire Guild if we felt like it."

"And you didn't report that to the Guildmaster?" Sev asked, incredulous.

"The donation was conditional on me not doing that," Lendel said, grimacing slightly. "They had ways to know. And I didn't... I figured I could do things to benefit the Guild, even without the Guildmaster knowing. It's part of being Gold—you make some decisions on your own. There is implicit trust."

"A system that failed here, clearly," Misa said, a little harshly. Lendel winced but didn't protest.

"I figured they were up to something. I didn't think they were maneuvering me into my own corner," he said. "I had a project I was already working on, along with Tibeus and Lorella there." He nodded to the wizard and healer he was working with; they shifted, looking distinctly uncomfortable.

"A while back, we thought about how mana crystals are used to maintain a connection to the system," Lendel said. "And we thought—we wondered if we could take that process and apply it to something else. Create weapons and shelters that could level alongside us.

"Back then, Tibeus had a [Create Familiar] skill. It's a skill that requires the sacrifice of a grade-one mana crystal, and it creates a small, low-level creature that bonds to you. We thought maybe the mechanism there was similar; it had the same cost as maintaining a connection to the system, and it created a new creature that was connected to the system.

"But [Create Familiar] doesn't work on objects, obviously. It creates something *new*; it doesn't try to attach the system to an existing object. For that, we had to do research, and for that research we needed gold."

"How exactly would you even begin to do research on that?" Vex asked, frowning. "How would gold help you?"

"By letting us pay people to reveal their skill details to us." Lendel's lip curled slightly in distaste. "People don't like sharing the particulars of their skills, so we needed to find people with uncommon or rarer classes, with a skill that allowed us to *retarget* an existing skill. That took a lot of people to get through. Can you believe that we eventually found it in a series of common classes? It was a bunch of old, niche skills no one talked about, too."

"Yes," Misa said, her tone as dry as a desert. Sev almost smiled at that; he remembered the image of her village fighting off a swarm of meteors. [Common] skills were easy to get, but they weren't *weak*. They just needed to be used in combination with one another.

It was stranger that it had taken so long for people to figure that out. But then, so much of their history was missing, or just gone entirely...

...maybe people *had* figured out similar things before. Maybe there was a reason it was hard for rare classes to gather.

"I'll spare you the details, but you can look it up, if you want. We kept all the research logs. We had to experiment with a few different variants—sometimes skills didn't work out quite the way we expected them to—but someone offered to help, and we eventually got it to work. And Tibeus was able to apply the skill to a candle."

"Someone?" Vex asked sharply. Lendel tensed, perhaps recognizing something in Vex's tone.

"We don't know who he was. He wasn't a noble or anything. He just looked like an ordinary soldier or maybe a delver," Lendel said. "But he had the perfect skill for us in the chain of skills we needed."

"Did he use a crossbow?" Sev asked. It wasn't exactly solid evidence, and it'd be strange if their mysterious man always held a crossbow, but if he *wanted* to be recognized…

"Yes," Lendel said, frowning. "How did you know?"

"Not important for now," Sev said, his voice tight. "Please continue."

Lendel glanced up at his wizard friend, who took it as his cue to step forward and continue the explanation.

"It caused the skill to change," Tibeus said. "I presume we fulfilled some previously hidden prerequisite, but [**Create Familiar**] became [**Bond Familiar**]. Red rarity. We're unsure what that means as yet."

Sev exchanged glances with Vex and the others. They'd seen red before; it rarely meant anything good. Their existing theory was that it was caused by someone forcing something into the system. And if the crossbow man was involved…

"So [**Bond Familiar**] could be used on objects," Sev prompted, putting his thoughts about that particular danger aside for now.

"Correct." Tibeus frowned a little, as if he didn't like being prompted, and Sev stopped himself from scoffing. There was a part of him that was still angry at them for causing all of this to begin with. "We used it on the Guild building, but it wouldn't take to the whole building. I had to use it in parts—bond pieces of the building at a time, until the whole building had a single status window. We created one single Familiar that way."

"That is not what you did," Derivan muttered, his voice low; he glanced around as he spoke, presumably looking through the room with Patch. Sev wondered exactly what it was that the animated armor saw.

Tibeus glanced at Derivan, but his gaze softened a bit, remembering exactly *why* he was explaining all of this. "… That's what we thought it was, anyway. The new Familiar came with a skill that it offered to us when we stepped and stayed in the building for long enough," Tibeus said. "It's part of the reason we had to be a lot more discerning with who we allowed to work with us—it's a powerful buff. If we let anyone get it—"

"—No excuses, Tibeus," Lendel said, sounding tired. "I know what our logic was at the time. You know it conflicts with the Guild's principles. If we really wanted to, we could have housed them elsewhere. We could have disabled the Guild's skills, like we do when we rotate out. We made a decision because it was easier for us."

Tibeus didn't respond for a moment, and when he did, it was slow, like he was still fighting the idea. "... Yes. I suppose that's what we did."

"The buff the Guild building gave us was [**Reinforcement**]," Lendel said, smiling a slightly bitter smile. He summoned a system box and sent it off to the four of them; Sev caught his copy, and then caught his breath.

> [**Reinforcement**] [**Buff**]
> Applied by [**Guild's Hope**]. Reinforces health, heart, and soul.
> When within [**Guild's Hope**], gain a <400%> increase to health.
> When outside [**Guild's Hope**], gain an additional <200%> increase to health and <1000%> increase to resistance against mental changes.
> Reinforcement increases with connection to [**Guild's Hope**].

The health increase alone was monumental; it explained why they'd had such a hard time defeating the cleric and wizard, even though neither class usually had much health. But a resistance to mental changes...

Not resistance against mental attacks. *Resistance to change.*

At a guess, the nobles they worked with applied targeted propaganda to make the various Guild members believe in their ideals. When they were rotated out, the extra effects kicked in and those ideals stuck, becoming more entrenched.

"Elyra knew about the buff, I take it?" Sev asked, but he already knew the answer.

"The noble families we worked with did," Lendel said. He hesitated. "They... improved it, in their words. Did something to add the second buff."

"And those noble families were...?" Sev's eyes flickered to Vex, who was leaning in.

"Wisfield," Lendel said, and Vex seemed to relax by a fraction—but only a fraction. And then Lendel continued. "And Ashion."

CHAPTER 46

A NOBLE INTENT

"Ah . . . shit." Sev winced a little at the words. He couldn't help but glance toward Vex, whose face was as impassive as he could make it—but he knew Vex well. He saw the way the lizardkin hunched over just a little bit more, the way his tail coiled around his leg; he saw the disappointment swim in his eyes.

He was familiar with it, even. Part of him thought he recognized that sort of disappointment. It was a hope that the people you cared about had changed for the better.

"You're familiar with them?" Lendel asked.

"You could say that," Sev said, doing his best to keep his voice neutral. "We met up with Wisfield before, when they were negotiating for control of the new dungeon up north."

"Ah," Lendel nodded. "You're the team that dealt with that. I remember. The researchers that came back . . ."

Lendel paused, trailing off; he winced slightly. Sev noticed.

He remembered how nervous the researchers had been. So many of them had fought Kestel on delaying the report back to Elyra—presumably, to the nobles they worked for. Kestel had been left broken and bedridden, and even now required more crystals than they had to spare to heal.

"Did anything happen to them?"

"I . . . don't know." Lendel sounded reluctant to say the words, and didn't meet Sev's eyes when he spoke. "I would have looked into it, normally."

"Shit," Sev muttered again. He glanced quickly to the others—Misa looked pissed, Vex looked worried, and Derivan was inscrutable as ever, though he'd moved to stand beside Vex. The lizardkin was leaning on Derivan ever so slightly, though, and some of his worry for his friend abated.

"We can find out," Vex said after a moment, straightening. "Wisfield handles most of the researchers, right?"

"They come from a few different noble houses," Lendel said. "But Wisfield coordinates."

"We'll need to talk to Wisfield anyway, if they were the ones that funded you, and if they knew all this was happening." Vex's tail lashed about behind him. "This kind of funding is standard practice, though."

"They're not supposed to try it with the Guild, but they got us in a moment of weakness." Lendel sighed.

"That would make sense." Vex's eyes hardened slightly. "I noticed they made a lot of progress with their Principle the last time we met up."

"Principle?" Derivan spoke up, his tone questioning.

"It's what I mentioned before. Every noble house is founded on something valuable they discover about magic, or about the system. Basically, anything that improves Elyra's security or military might. They call it their Principle."

"That's a little pretentious," Sev voiced, frowning, and Vex gave a little snort.

"It is," he agreed wryly. "I didn't come up with it."

"What's Wisfield's Principle?" Misa asked, folding her arms. "I remember what you did with them, but you never explained what happened."

Vex nodded. "It's usually considered taboo to discuss a Principle outside of the house," he said. "But I think I don't really care right now. Wisfield's whole thing is telepathy and mental skills—communication, not control, as far as I know. It's why they're in charge of most negotiations. I wasn't really sure Drunkard's Beard would do anything to them, but I had a theory that it worked by tapping into whatever the system does to facilitate mental skills."

"And you were right. That's how they all got fucked up when you threw the moss at them." Misa grinned. "That was great."

"I guessed they found a way to link up and make their mental skills more powerful." Vex nodded. "I... don't like that I was right. That has implications."

The mood soured again. "No kidding," Misa muttered.

Sev had been watching Lendel, Rekka, Tibeus, and Lorella as Vex spoke; the four other adventurers each had different expressions on their faces. Lendel looked frustrated, like he blamed himself for not being prepared for the possibility. Rekka seemed like he was inflamed with righteous anger more than anything. Tibeus struck Sev as almost looking *bored*, and Lorella seemed the same, though slightly more controlled.

"Hey, Derivan?" Sev said. Derivan glanced up at him. "Do those two still have [**Reinforcement**] up?"

Derivan paused, and then glanced at the wizard and cleric. Both of them winced. "Yes," he said. "It is . . . not as entrenched within them as it was with Lendel. But there will still be some damage if I break the connection to the Guild."

"I'd like to know how you can do that," Tibeus said. "It would be useful for the Guild—"

"Tibeus," Lendel said, giving the wizard a withering glance. "Turn off [**Bond Familiar**]."

Tibeus paused. ". . . I can't."

"This isn't the time for games—"

"No, I mean, I *can't*," Tibeus said, a note of genuine panic suddenly filtering into his voice; Sev almost automatically let a pulse of [**Diagnose**] touch the wizard, though all he got back was that he was experiencing an entirely normal panic attack. "I just tried. [**Guild's Hope**] stopped me."

"Did you really name the Guild that?" Misa muttered, and Sev snorted; he'd had the same thought.

"I thought you said you'd be able to turn it off." Lendel's tone was sharp. "You've *been* turning it off every time we rotated out, haven't you?"

"I have!" Tibeus raised his arms up. "I don't know why I can't now!"

"He is not lying," Derivan said, glowing eyes flickering a little as he stared at Tibeus. "He is trying."

"*How do you know that?!*" Tibeus demanded, turning some of that panic into an entitled sort of anger, stalking toward Derivan; Misa stepped in front of him, large and glowering and towering right over him, and he balked.

"You said you can break the connection?" Lendel turned his gaze to Derivan. "Do it."

Derivan nodded. Sev watched as the armor reached out invisibly; there was no physical movement or change save for a faint dimming of his eyes . . .

Tibeus shuddered and stumbled; Lorella winced a second later.

There was a moment of silence.

"You didn't have the authority to do that, Lendel," Tibeus said, his tone affronted. The wizard's cloak billowed around him as magic began to gather, and Vex reacted, though subtly; Sev only noticed because he was used to the lizardkin. One hand slipped to his dagger, and small movements carved out a tiny rune into the air.

"I am the leader of this team." Lendel frowned at his friend. "What's wrong with you?"

"This." Lorella spoke, for the first time in this entire conversation; now that Sev paid attention to her, he saw a faint flicker of divine magic as she tried—and failed—to do something to heal herself. She reached out and he *almost* flinched, but instead, a box appeared in front of him as she shared a status effect.

> [**Remnants**] [**Malus**]
> Leftovers of a change.

At the same time, Tibeus lashed out, a runic circle suddenly forming in the air in front of him; fire mana gathered, strong enough that Sev could feel the heat even without any form of [**Mana Sight**].

Yet as soon as it finished gathering, the mana dissipated harmlessly; Vex's own spell triggered, the wizard having cast it in preparation before Tibeus had even begun to cast. Sev almost whistled—he had to bite his lip to stop himself.

"Holy shit, Vex," Misa said, not nearly as concerned about polite self-control.

"What the hell did you do—" Tibeus began.

"*Tibeus.*" This time, when Lendel spoke, his words resonated like he'd used a skill; Sev flinched, and even Misa looked up at him, her hand automatically going to her mace. The effect on Tibeus was far more significant—the wizard's gaze automatically flew to Lendel and stuck there, like he couldn't look away. "Stand down."

Tibeus struggled with himself. Lorella didn't say a word, just watching her teammate struggle against the binding of whatever skill Lendel had used. She didn't seem inclined to involve herself.

Slowly—forcing himself to do it, and looking like he hated every moment of it—he seemed to relax. The wizard stood completely still, closing his eyes and cycling his breathing.

"I want to ask if you can heal this," Lendel said, glancing at Sev, his gaze speculative. "But that costs you something, doesn't it?"

"... It does," Sev said. He would have hesitated to admit it, but it didn't seem like there was much of a point; Lendel had already seen him collapse when he cast the spell. He *did* want to help Tibeus and Lorella if he could. "I can try—"

"No, Sev," Misa interrupted, her voice harsh. "I'm not sure we should've let you try to heal Lendel at all, if the cost was going to be that severe. We're going to talk about that when we get a chance, believe me."

Sev... let that go. Misa stared at him for a moment, as if she was expecting him to have a response, and she seemed to relax a fraction when he said nothing.

"Most of us need to rotate out," Lendel said, glancing at Lorella and Tibeus. "This... isn't going to work. Most of us are compromised. We're not even the only adventurers in this building. I'm surprised no one else came running."

"Sheer luck," Rekka said. "Most of them are out right now, running errands and stuff. And it helps that we made the Guild really big, so everyone that *is* here is pretty scattered."

"No kidding," Misa said, eyeing the ceiling. Sev glanced up—

—Yeah, now that he paid attention, that ceiling was really far away.

"We'll need to break the [**Reinforcement**] effect before you rotate anyone out," Sev said, ignoring the slight sense of vertigo the sight gave him. "Unless you can do that manually somehow."

Derivan shook his head before Tibeus could answer. "There is no central mechanism that can be disabled," he said. "The effect will have to be manually broken, and we will need to try to reverse what has been done to the Guild."

"Can't we leave it like this?" Lorella asked, frowning. "It's bigger. It's nice."

"It will continue to grant [**Reinforcement**] if its connection to the system is not broken." Derivan glanced around. "I do not know if breaking that connection will restore it to its original size. There is a chance it will not."

"That's the first thing we need to do, then," Sev decided. "We can't leave the Guild like this, not if it's just handing out the buff to anyone that stays here long enough. Who's to say Wisfield and Ashion aren't already sending in people to take advantage of it?"

"That's not..." Tibeus started to say, and then he frowned, stopping himself. "Shit."

"No kidding." Sev gave the wizard the most deadpan stare he could muster.

"I'll set up a meeting with Wisfield in the meantime," Rekka said.

"Just be careful." Lendel glanced at the four of them. "This meeting isn't going to go like the last one you had with them; you don't have the benefit of the Guild's skill-suppression enchantments. They're going to be able to read you completely."

Sev glanced at Vex, briefly worried—but the lizardkin surprised him by grinning slightly, stepping forward with Derivan. "There might be something we can do about that."

CHAPTER 47

CRAFTING A COUNTER

"Goddamn that took a while," Misa grumbled.

Vex had to agree, although he was too tired to actually say anything. He let out a small groan in response, leaning most of his weight onto Derivan—who accepted him with grace and put an arm around his shoulders, despite being the one that had actually done most of the work.

They'd had to spend the last several hours cleaning up the errant, overgrown system. Or, well, Derivan had to. They'd chosen to stick together while he did so, though, just in case anything *else* decided to happen, like it so often did around them. Vex had gathered some basic supplies from the Guild to try to build his own magelight; mostly just ordinary paintbrushes kept in some small corner of the room. He needed to carve mana channels into it to carry his mana, the way a standard magelight did.

The project had been remarkably easy, actually. Using mana to burn a mana channel into an object turned out to be a simple affair, in part because...

...well, because it had been done to him so many times, morbid as the thought was.

Vex had moved on, testing the new brush with a [**Splash of Mana**], then let out a relieved sigh as the bristles lit up with magic. Good. Everything was working as planned. The new glyph he had an idea for was likely to be intricate; he'd need his magelight, or he supposed in this case his paintbrush.

Then, for the rest of the time Derivan had needed to fully clean up the Guild, Vex worked on the anti-Wisfield glyph he'd had an idea for.

For the most part, he'd ended up nowhere. He'd wanted to talk to Derivan about it, but the armor was busy and looked... not exhausted, exactly, but Patch seemed to take a lot out of him.

Vex was pretty sure he had the right idea. The Glyph of Communication was a glyph that fundamentally represented the sharing of thoughts and ideas; it was enough to touch on the very same thing that Wisfield's mental skills operated on. The problem was that this was *magic*, and that didn't work the same way system skills did.

He still had his sample of Drunkard's Beard, and he used it periodically to test if his experiments were working. He didn't need to block the effect—he was planning to use Derivan's Sign for that, anyway—but he wanted to see if he could latch on to whatever signal it was releasing. For testing purposes, he would try to amplify that signal instead of blocking it, directing it toward a willing victim.

Which was Misa, in this case. The conversation had gone something along the lines of:

"Hey, Misa, can I test this glyph on you? I'm trying to amplify the effect of Drunkard's Beard."

"Is that the weird moss that makes people drunk?"

"Yes, but I'll make sure—"

"Fuck yeah do it."

It was good to have someone like Misa on the team, Vex reflected.

Unfortunately, it had been a disappointing failure to both him and Misa. Misa had hoped that being drunk would help relieve the boredom of following Derivan around, and the failure of the spell to do anything made her grumble. On the other hand, it had been a relief for Sev, who was concerned about having to heal yet another hangover, despite Vex's insistence that Drunkard's Beard would do no such thing.

Ultimately, he'd ended up spending mana he hadn't needed to, and his legs were sore from walking around the *unnecessarily large Guild* to tear out strips of the system.

But at the end of the day, Derivan's efforts paid off.

[**Guild's Hope**] was eventually stripped down to just the bare essentials of a working system, a skeleton that was attached to the spine of the building—according to Derivan, anyway, though Vex had no idea what exactly the "spine of the building" was supposed to be. The Patch stat had increased several times in the process, which . . . was a little worrying?

But Vex trusted Derivan to say something if the stat began affecting him too much.

With the system mostly repaired, Tibeus was able to disable the [**Bond Familiar**] skill; the structure around the Guild building didn't go away, but it dimmed a bit, according to Derivan. [**Reinforcement**] wouldn't be disabled, but the effect would slowly weaken and eventually fall off entirely, as long as the adventurers with it were rotated out.

Which was Lendel's responsibility. None of them wanted anything to do with the management of a bunch of egotistical adventurers that had been slowly guided to think they deserved better than everyone around them. Though part of Vex *did* feel guilty for using his status to get them past the guard; that was one of the issues Rekka had mentioned...

He sighed. Nothing was ever simple. Nobility would benefit the Guild, it was true, but the current "buff" would hurt them and ruin the Guildmaster's careful planning as far as maintaining the Guild's culture in foreign territory went.

They were all back in their room in the Guild, now; this one was just a single large room that was set up for all four of them. It was simple, but it worked well enough. There were curtains around every bed that ensured they could each have a small degree of privacy, small dressers to keep their things in, and the classic enchanted cupboard that came with every Guild room.

"This definitely took longer than I expected," Sev said with a sigh. "And now we have this Wisfield meeting to worry about. Vex, you said you wanted to distribute the food ourselves? I wanted to ask about that earlier, but..."

"If we let the noble houses take charge, they won't distribute it fairly." Vex grimaced slightly, remembering his conversation with Rekka. "If we're in charge, we can at least make sure it gets to the people that need it and not just to the people that the nobles like."

"Should've known," Sev muttered. "That's going to be a lot of work for four people, but... good call."

"I can get us some help," Misa suggested. "Summon a few people with Anchor. And that should give us the opportunity to learn a bit more about what Elyra is like away from nobles and the like."

"There are a few people we could get help from," Vex said. He smiled slightly; part of him was excited to meet his old... He wasn't sure he could call them friends, really. But there were a few people that had opted to help him when they didn't have to, way back when he was trying to leave Elyra to begin with. Rekka had been one of them, and then there were others, too: small merchants, like the one that had given him the materials for his dagger; a librarian that had helped sneak him spellbooks that his family deemed unnecessary; a cartographer that had given him a map and directions to the nearest Guild branch. "I think it's better we talk to the locals. It'll help us connect better than bringing in half your village. No offense."

THE NATURE OF MAGIC

"None taken." Misa grinned, apparently entertained by the thought. "I can always bring them in if we need them."

"Were you able to make any progress with the glyphs?" Derivan asked curiously. "If we are to meet with Wisfield..."

"Rekka did say he'd set up a meeting for some time tomorrow, didn't he." Sev winced slightly.

Vex nodded. "I haven't made as much progress as I'd hoped," he said. "I was pretty sure that Communication would be able to do something, but it's not really letting me amplify or work with Drunkard's Beard at all, and it's what I've been using to test my ideas. Mostly just slight modifications to the glyph."

"You are working with it the way you do with runic circles," Derivan noted. "Perhaps glyphs require a different method?"

"You're probably right," Vex admitted. "But the other glyphs I have access to are just for the basic elements; I don't have any ideas what a new one would look like for specifically targeting mental skills... I do have *one* last idea."

Vex rummaged through his tailpouch as he spoke, feeling his fingers eventually catch on the mana sliver. He pulled it out, staring at the way the light caught on the off-white fragment of *something*; at some angles, always right around the edges of the shard, it shimmered with prismatic fractals.

There was still the question of what it was. The system had been trying to identify it, earlier; maybe it had made some progress?

> [**Reality Shard**] [**Grade: Unknown**]
> <ERROR>
> Item description still processing. Data collection in progress. Data collection at 30%.

Vex blinked.

That was... rather more information than before. They'd already known the system was studying the shards, but now it was quantifying the amount of progress it had made.

More importantly, it had a *name*.

"It's called a [**Reality Shard**]." Vex stared at it critically, holding it a little bit farther away. "Not a mana sliver? And not unknown anymore."

"System's figured something out, I guess." Misa eyed it, too, clearly thinking about something. "... My anchor integrity went up the last time you did this glyph magic. And your glyph magic produces [**Reality Shards**]."

"Reality anchors, [**Reality Shards**], magic," Vex muttered. "And [**Reality Shards**] have been used to amplify magic—we saw that. None of us could get past the Teque barrier."

"It was Shifted very deeply across all the wavelengths of reality I could reach," Derivan agreed.

"Which is something that Helg accomplished by using [**Reality Shards**]." Vex breathed out. "Magic doesn't work the same way as the system. The system manipulates . . . the fabric of reality directly. Magic is the manipulation of mana within reality? But the system can do magic, kind of; it uses runic circles, which I want to investigate further, because they look like an iteration on glyphs."

"And magic can manipulate the fabric of reality, with the help of [**Reality Shards**]," Misa said. "Something like that?"

"That's what I'm thinking." Vex frowned; something was tugging at his brain. "There are a lot of parallels here. Maybe just a couple of pieces we're missing, like where divinities fit into all of it, or 'monsters,' as the system deems them."

"Aurum still hasn't said much. And I have nothing new from Onyx." Sev fingered the holy symbol he used, tracing over the rough sculpt with his thumb; his brows were drawn together. "I'm a little worried."

"I'm sure we would have heard from Jerome if something happened to Aurum," Misa said, though she sounded sympathetic.

"Probably." Sev sighed, dropping his hand. "You think you can use the [**Reality Shard**] to do something?"

"I think so," Vex said, staring at it; an idea was sparking in his mind, and along with it came a touch of confidence he wasn't used to—a touch of confidence that he was finding came to him more easily these days. ". . . Yes. I believe I can."

This was the element he was missing. Something inside him resonated.

"Derivan," Vex said. "Can you help me out?"

"You only have to ask."

"I think the Magic stat will help with this," Vex said. "I need you to hold on to the shard and channel mana through it, the way you would if you were going to cast a glyph. And the glyph you need to draw is . . ." Vex paused, but only for a moment; he'd already been thinking about this, the whole time they'd been walking through the guild, trying to fix the system. He had a good idea of what they needed.

The communication glyph was a series of loops that pretended to be letters; he knew he needed to lay them on the inside of Derivan's shield-Sign, but it occurred to him as he began to draw that he didn't actually know what that Sign looked like. All he knew was what it looked like when it was combined with his own.

But then, Derivan had done much the same thing, hadn't he? He'd created a combined Sign without ever knowing what their individual Signs looked like. Vex felt a small warmth within him at the reminder, and closed his eyes, trying to touch upon what he thought the armor's Sign might look like.

Derivan was a source of comfort and warmth. More importantly, around him, Vex had always felt safe—and that feeling had only grown the more time they spent together. In Derivan he found someone that was always willing to listen to what he had to say, that always took an interest, someone who never shot down his ideas or told him to focus on something else that was more important.

Derivan was interested because Vex was interested; it was that simple to him.

In battle, Derivan often took on a secondary tank role, using what Vex now understood to be high-level tricks to defend against blows that would have devastated any of the rest of them, except perhaps Misa, who had to be aware of the blow first to block it. The shield made sense—it was protective.

But Derivan was more than a protector. Misa was their protector; she would stand in the way of any blow and in defiance of any fate that would befall them. Derivan protected them in ways both visible and invisible, acting like a buffer against any blow that missed their shield . . .

Vex almost laughed. Of course. He was their armor.

His Sign, then, was not a simple shield; it *looked* like a shield, but it was a series of interlocking plates. It gave them protection without restricting them and sought to keep them safe so they could grow. His role in the team was a little different now—he was more a strange, esoteric sword than a form of armor—but his personality hadn't changed. He sought to keep them safe, even now, in his own way.

Vex laid down the Glyph of Communication in looping lines around the edges of that armored shield, humming happily to himself—and then as a final detail, he drew that [**Reality Shard**] in the center, like it was empowering the armor-shield, little threads of power sliding into those interlocking plates.

Something inside him was humming. Something within his soul, perhaps, though Vex was only distantly aware of it.

"There," Vex said. "I think this will work. I'm not *sure*, but . . ."

"I rather think it will work," Derivan said quietly, and pointed. Vex blinked, and glanced back to the drawing.

Right where he'd drawn the shard, where it should have been placed—was another one of those [**Reality Shards**].

"Huh," Vex said. "I guess we *can* still get these outside of Teque."

It was less than it would have been within Teque, he suspected, but if it was possible for him to get them at all, it might change everything.

Now to make sure the new glyph worked the way he was hoping it would.

CHAPTER 48

PRIVATE COMMUNICATIONS

To say the glyph worked was an understatement.

They'd done two tests. The first of them was done with Vex's own Sign of Research, to make sure that the new glyph—or Sign; Vex hadn't really considered what to call these things that were a mix of the two—would do what they thought it did; there was a slight concern that casting it would *consume* a [**Reality Shard**], and those were in limited supply at the moment.

That concern was quickly addressed when the skill fed the information back to him. He was once again reminded that the Sign claimed there was a cost to using it . . . but he hadn't identified what that cost was yet. Something more than mana, almost certainly.

Private Relay—Glyph/Sign Combination
This combined glyph restricts all forms of communication to those whitelisted by the user, both outgoing and incoming. Any hostile form of information transfer will be blocked. This protection extends to written, verbal, and mental forms of communication, as well as any other means by which an idea might be communicated.
On casting, this glyph will create #### charms, which can be worn to render the wearer invulnerable to unwanted communication.
This glyph will cost one   [Reality Shard]. Charms produced will ##########, lasting ### as long as ####### # #### ######. ##########.

There was a moment while interpreting the glyph where a sudden static *burning* filled the connection Vex shared with whatever within the mana held all this information—it was enough to make the lizardkin wince, stumbling backward. Derivan caught him, and it took a moment or two before he could hear well enough to realize that the armor was asking him if he was all right; Vex had to swallow twice before he could answer.

"I'm—fine," he said, grimacing slightly at the strange hoarseness of his voice. Maybe this was the cost that had been implied. Maybe there were *gaps* in what the mana knew, and if he ran into them, it would hit him hard.

That was... concerning.

"What happened?" Derivan asked him, still worried, and Vex sighed.

"I'm not sure," he admitted. "I think if the information that my sign tries to retrieve is incomplete, there's some kind of backlash. That one wasn't too bad, but..."

There was the possibility that it would be worse in the future. He wondered if the system's errors were a way to filter through that kind of backlash; maybe there *was* a reason for him to redirect that information into system boxes for display.

But Vex dismissed that concern for now, directing his attention instead to the knowledge he'd gained. The fact that the glyph operated by creating charms was helpful; it meant that they could attempt the spell now, and those charms would likely still protect them by the time the Wisfield meeting came around.

On the other hand, there was the possibility that the charms could be stolen. There was the still-fuzzy information about the charms that implied they would only last a certain amount of time, or maybe only a certain number of uses.

"Well?" Misa raised an eyebrow. "Does it work?"

"Yes," Vex said, and then reconsidered and amended his statement. "It should. It'll make some charms that should do the trick, but we should still test it."

"Are you sure you do not want to do it yourself?" Derivan asked him, his voice low. "I feel you have earned this."

"Thank you." Vex gave Derivan an earnest sort of smile. "But I want to see you cast now."

"I see." Derivan sounded vaguely embarrassed, if that was possible; Vex had never heard that from the armor before. He stood up, his head threatening to scrape against the ceiling, and picked up the [**Reality Shard**] that Vex had left on the ground.

And then without wasting a moment more, he began to weave.

There was something about Derivan's movements that were different when he cast—the light in his helmet dimmed to almost nothing, like the magic that animated him was being supplanted by something else. His movements seemed to *flow* in a way his constituent metal really shouldn't have been able to.

There was something about it all that was akin to a dance.

Vex watched, enraptured, as Derivan went through the movements to draw the glyph he had created. The mana in the room gathered around Derivan, almost as if it was curious about what he was doing. It didn't run the way it always did when a system spell was cast. It didn't interfere with his spell, either.

Some of it even entered his gauntlet, voluntarily, joining him in creating.

In the midst of swirling mana, holding a glowing shard of reality, Derivan completed the last part of the glyph; as he had drawn, the shard had diminished, fragments dispersing into the glowing symbol like he was drawing with chalk. By the time he was done, the shard was but a single fragment.

And then that, too, dissipated.

The **Relay** symbol hung in the air for a moment, and the mana surrounding it rushed to meet it, like it was overjoyed to meet a new friend. There was a meeting between that ambient mana and the mana in the symbol.

In that meeting, those small fragments of reality stirred and made it something more real than before.

Vex didn't have the same senses that Derivan had. He *did* feel the oddness in the magic, the way it felt like it had suddenly gained substance to it; he felt his skills flicker in response, a few of them resonating curiously. There was something he could learn here—but almost as soon as it happened, almost as soon as he realized he could do anything at all, the feeling faded.

And so did the glyph.

In its place were nine—*nine* small objects shimmering with the same prismatic fractals as the original [**Reality Shard**]. They were shaped differently, each a circle with a closed spiral within. Convenient for stringing onto a piece of wire, perhaps, though Vex doubted that the magic had been considering *convenience* when it had been crafting them.

No. The charms followed the pattern of mana that had coalesced around Derivan as he drew. That was a decision the mana had made on its own.

Not for the first time, Vex wondered exactly how alive the mana was.

"That's... a lot of charms," Misa commented after a moment. She reached forward gingerly, as if worried the little spiral of stone would shock her—and when it didn't, she held it critically up to an eye. "Seriously. Maybe a little too many charms."

"It's better to have backups?" Sev phrased it like a question, eyeing the charms like they were going to explode.

Vex stared.

Something clicked.

"They're not going to blow up!" he complained, scowling.

"It's true," Misa said, nodding at Sev. "It was Derivan that cast the spell, not Vex."

"I mean, he still *made* the spell," Sev said, giving Vex a playful grin. "Maybe we should just make sure?"

"Oh by the gods," Vex muttered, burying his face into his hands.

"I am sure it will work," Derivan said, giving Vex a friendly, encouraging sort of nudge, though it mostly just made Vex curl up even more. "You only need Misa to wear the charm, right?"

"Yes." The words were muffled. "Then hold the Drunkard's Beard up to her. Have her eat a little bit of it, even."

"Eat it?" Misa said, her tone somehow haughty and affronted—a *weird* tone to hear coming from Misa, no matter that she was mocking the nobles. There was a faint *clink* as she strung the charm through, tying it around her neck. "I couldn't possibly dream of— Nope, fuck that, can't do it. Gimme it."

Vex rapidly pulled his face from his hands just in time to catch Misa tearing a—thankfully small—chunk of Drunkard's Beard off the sample he'd collected and swallow it. And then she made a face.

"Tastes kinda gross," she said.

"You're not *really* supposed to eat it," Vex muttered. Eating the moss actually diminished the effect; whatever allowed it to tap into the mechanisms the system used for mental skills—though that was an assumption on his part, he reminded himself—did not survive contact with the stomach acid of most species. "You just need to hold it close to your head. Or wherever your brain is."

"Then why did you tell me to eat it!" Misa made an indignant face, spluttering out the remnants of moss on her tongue.

"I didn't tell you to eat it," Vex protested. "I told Derivan to make you eat it. Not the same thing!"

Misa's eyes narrowed dangerously at him, and he swallowed. He was pretty sure this was just banter.

Mostly sure this was just banter.

To his relief, Misa grinned. "Whatever," she said. "Point is, the charm thing works. Didn't feel a thing." She held the rest of the moss up to her head, just to make sure. "Yeah, nope."

"Want to take off the charm?" Sev said. "You know, just to make sure that it's not the moss that's faulty."

"That's a *great* idea, Sev." Misa ripped off the charm, clearly about to say something else—the moss was still held up to her head, like it was an ice pack. Instead of continuing, though, she wobbled slightly instead. "Whoa." She looked delighted. "This is like . . . full buzz. Instant. Dang. How come you didn't . . . share this before?"

"I wouldn't dare damage the hallowed process of getting irresponsibly drunk by letting you skip steps," Vex said dryly, and then tried to hop up to grab the moss.

He failed, obviously. Misa was *so dang tall* compared to him. And also jumping to get it put his head dangerously close to the moss.

"Derivannn," he whined instead, and the armor chuckled. Reaching out, he plucked the moss away from Misa, much to her protests—though she didn't do much to stop him.

"Here you go," he said, gently depositing the sample back into Vex's tail-pouch. "I wonder where I would have to hold it, for it to affect me."

"Near your core, maybe?" Vex glanced over Derivan. It hadn't actually occurred to him before that Drunkard's Beard could likely affect even *Derivan* . . .

Actually. That seemed like a potential avenue of research. If he could figure out how to do whatever the moss did—a project that veered dangerously close to figuring out the Wisfield Principle for himself—then he could help Derivan taste food on his own terms.

That was something worth studying, right? Once there wasn't some sort of ongoing crisis . . . which might be never. So maybe just in his free time.

"Perhaps." Derivan hummed but didn't seem inclined to test it—and it was late enough in the day that Vex didn't feel like pressing the matter.

"Do we want to discuss strategies for dealing with Wisfield in tomorrow's meeting?" Sev glanced out the window. "It's getting pretty late. I figure we'll do that last, get some rest, and then hopefully Rekka will have scheduled the meeting bright and early so we can get it out of the way."

"Might as well," Misa agreed with a sigh. "Hey, if Wisfield is annoying, do you think I can block conversational attacks?"

Sev laughed, then looked worried. "Please don't try. I'm pretty sure the way you block an insult is by punching the person who said it in the face."

"I would never do that," Misa said, tossing her mace in her hand casually. "Never."

Vex eyed her and decided he was very glad she was on their side. So glad he went to give her a hug, which she seemed surprised by, but she smiled a genuine smile and hugged back.

So he probably wasn't going to get maced!

With that, the four of them settled in to talk. It was ... a drier conversation than even Vex would have liked, and he found himself drifting off, before long, leaning on Derivan's arm yet again.

CHAPTER 49

XOTHOK-WHO YOU COULD HAVE BEEN

Xothok was . . . antsy.

He hated using that word to describe himself. It was a stupid word, for small, stupid people. What use was anxiety? He'd never had to worry about it before, because before, his main concern had been about *getting food*. There was nothing to worry about besides that, and that was a pretty easy thing to worry about: either they had food, or they didn't.

But the Guild was giving them food, in the most baffling show of trust that Xothok had seen—along with the fact that, as far as he could tell, they weren't actually being kept at the Guild. They were given a place to sleep, and all they had to do to get food was head down to the mess hall; they didn't even have to fucking *pay*. They just had food given to them.

It wasn't *great* food, by any means. It was . . . palatable. What they needed to eat to survive. Hardly a luxury meal, or even a great comfort like the kind you could get at the more tavern-like section of the Guild, where they served big, meaty dishes, but he couldn't . . . complain?

Besides, the people in the mess hall sometimes sneaked them good meals, even. He could tell when they did it, because their own meals would be the gruel they were fed, and that meant they were feeding the bandits their own lunches, which was . . . what? Why?

He didn't fucking understand, and he hated it.

The worst part was probably the fact that he could have left. He was pretty sure any of them could have left. Max had stopped them from leaving when they tried to escape her, back when she was escorting them to the Guild—and by the gods was she terrifying when she was in battle, everywhere she needed to be and nowhere she wasn't, with not a single person being able to get past her guard—but when they'd actually *arrived* . . .

She arranged for them to have beds and told them they could have food whenever they wanted. If they wanted to join the Guild, they would have to apply, and they would have to start from Iron. Not even Bronze—Iron.

And then she left?

And *he* had to deal with the riot that ensued, with half the bandits under him demanding answers he didn't have, a quarter of them asking about joining the Guild, and the last quarter determined to leave. They'd even tried to leave, for a while, except they'd quickly gotten hungry and turned right back around, because the food was just... there.

So that little rebellion had ended as quickly as it had begun, and it was frustrating, because Xothok couldn't fucking decide what he was supposed to *do*. He didn't want to just bend over and become an adventurer—not only had the Elyran Guild fucked them over, but it felt like joining the Guild would be something like admitting defeat—yet more and more of the bandits wanted to join, and it was getting harder to find reasons not to.

If that wasn't enough, Byrrhon was still causing trouble—he was the only one that was, constantly picking fights with adventurers, even though each time Max handily shut him down—but it was starting to wear on the Guild, he saw. Byrrhon might single-handedly get them all kicked out.

And then there were the *dreams*.

He hadn't gotten the image of that stupid spell out of his head. The one that armored adventurer had cast that filled the air with frost and fire, the one that scattered lit fireballs into the atmosphere. It had sparked something inside him that he couldn't quite place, and now, every night, he would stare at the night sky and feel something inside him ache.

Xothok just couldn't place why. Part of him wanted to blame it on some sort of curse, but he already knew that wasn't true. All his men had seen the same damn spell, and most of them hadn't had the same reaction. *Two* had a similar reaction, but Two was... He wasn't sure what was going on with Two, actually. Sometimes the man seemed even more despondent about the sky than he was.

His dreams were related to this, he was pretty sure. He was still staring up at the sky in his dreams—but he could never remember clearly what the sky looked like. It was *different*, definitely. There was something about his dreams that was different from reality. What that difference was just refused to stay in his mind once he woke.

Except every so often, there would be a flicker of recognition. Usually during the night, if he happened to be awake, he would have a moment when he would *remember*...

But then he would forget again, and the moment would pass, and even though he'd made attempts to write it down—made attempts to speak to others—what he'd written remained meaningless to him. It was like the words he'd written simply passed through his head.

Which brought him back to now, tonight. The real reason he was feeling so antsy, and the reason he was sitting here, thinking about things, when normally he was the sort of person that would act. He'd have to try something different if writing it down didn't work. He needed to wait for the moment he remembered, and he needed to find any sort of way he could communicate this back to himself.

Because Xothok was starting to understand that there was a part of himself locked away from him.

He stared up at where the moon hung far above him, at the dark-blue sky beside it. The moon was a light-green disk in the air, a perfect, featureless circle. Something about that seemed strange, even though it had been that way for as long as he could remember. He felt that small ache in his heart again . . .

. . . and then something began to unravel.

Somewhere far away, someone cast [**Starry Night**], and a small part of Xothok *remembered*. It had taken time, and many casts, and he'd had to personally see the spell for it to even begin to awaken that part of him, but now that it had—now that he knew there was something he was missing, and was trying to remember—something broke.

Just for a second.

Stars.

Not just stars but his entire class—he'd been an [**Astral Navigator**] or something very similar. There was an error on his status sheet that he couldn't see—that his eyes kept glazing over every time he looked at it—

—there were marks on the walls, his various attempts at trying to remind himself of what he'd forgotten, a half-dozen messages written in code and implication that he just couldn't *see*—

There wasn't time to be overwhelmed. He'd been through this before, more than once. Every time, he wasted those precious minutes where he *remembered*, overwhelmed by the density of what he'd lost. Overwhelmed by the density of what they'd all lost, really.

He wasn't the only one.

Byrrhon had loved the stars. *Two had a name.* Something that was core to their selves, stripped away. Even now, with his memory of the stars returned, there were pieces and details that remained lost to him. He suspected they were lost forever. That this small piece had returned at all was a small miracle.

Writing didn't work. He'd written a message for himself last time, and his eyes glazed over the message the same way they glazed over the error in his status. He made a quick mark on his arm using the quill anyway—he couldn't remember *what* he'd forgotten, but this helped him remember that he'd forgotten *something*, and it had worked last time.

Then he scattered spilled ink onto the parchment he'd prepared, letting it spread and seep into the paper. He'd planned on writing another message to himself, but it was obvious that that route led nowhere; he'd tried enough times. Now he used the skills of his false class to his advantage, [**Steal**]ing away fragments of ink to make the appearance of those stars in the sky—and just so he wouldn't misunderstand the makeshift painting for something else, he stole away a large, circular section of ink, too, to represent the moon.

He wasn't sure this would work. There was every chance it would simply fail again, and he—

—he needed to ask for help.

That was the point of the Guild.

He'd seen it, in bits and pieces, in fragments of memories that were no longer his own. An Elyran house that focused on astronomy and navigating the stars—among the stars or beneath them, he didn't know and didn't remember—but they'd worked together with the Guild. He remembered something a clerk had told him.

We're just here to help. But sometimes, people don't know when to ask for help, you know? No one does everything alone, but in Elyra in particular, there's this sentiment that you should do things by yourself or just within your House. We end up with secrets layered upon secrets that hold us back, that hold back our progress. Seriously, if you ever need help, just . . . ask. We're always here.

He hadn't liked asking for help even when he'd been whole. That was even worse when he'd become a bandit, because *just asking* for food that was already scarce never worked out well, and the one time they'd asked to join the Guild, they'd been turned away. Xothok wondered for a moment if that was the real cause of the resentment he'd been harboring toward the Guild.

The fact that they'd offered to help, and they hadn't helped in the end.

But now they were here, and it was obvious that the Guild was more than what the Elyran branch had been. Now that he thought about it, there were other signs that the Elyran branch was unwell—details he hadn't noticed before—

He didn't have the time to think about this. He had to make a decision, before the clock ran out on whatever spell that stupid armored adventurer was using—

Fucking fine.

He slammed the door open.

It was simultaneously relieving and exasperating to find that Max was already there, right outside the door—relieving because he didn't know how much time he had left to remember, and exasperating because he still didn't know how she managed to be where she needed to be. She wasn't wearing her usual confident grin, though. Her brows were furrowed, and she stared past Xothok into the room, trying to see if anything was going on with the rest of the bandits.

"They're fine," he snapped, not even sure if he was right.

Max frowned at him. "Are they?"

"They're not the problem right now." Xothok was vaguely aware that he sounded ridiculous. "I need—"

The lizardkin stopped, his words catching in his throat. Why was it *so fucking hard* to ask for help? He gritted his teeth. "I need *help.*"

Max's eyes sharpened. To his relief, she didn't poke fun at him the way he'd half-expected her to. "What's happening?"

"I keep—*forgetting.*" Xothok fought the fog that was starting to creep in. Picturing the night sky somehow helped keep it clear, filled with those specks of light—filled with *stars.* "Need to remember."

"Ah, shit," Max muttered. She glanced into the air, presumably at an invisible system window. "Is this the same— It might be . . . Hold on. Guildmaster's on her way."

The Guildmaster was coming. The *Guildmaster* was coming? Why did this involve her? Part of him recoiled, not ready to talk to the person in charge of all of this. A woman came down the stairs then, at precisely the wrong moment, and he almost opened his mouth to lash out—

—but he recognized her.

Why did he recognize her?

The woman frowned at him, and then the Guildmaster spoke. "It's the same infolock," she said to Max. "I haven't made any progress against it. I think Gerard in the Anderstahl branch has made some steps getting around it, but his success has been pretty limited too."

"Sounds like we don't have a lot of options." Max glanced at Xothok, and her eyes turned sympathetic; he hated it.

"This infolock is tied . . . very deeply with you." The Guildmaster stared at him and hesitated. "This is an opportunity we would not normally have. There may be something I can do here, but it is not without cost."

"Just tell me what the fuck it is."

"A perception lock." The Guildmaster looked serious. "You're tied very closely to this infolock, and that's the only reason this is possible at all—but I can tie off this part of you, the part that remembers. Which means you're going to have this part of yourself severed from you, and it'll be like ... a voice on your shoulder. Someone you can talk to that remembers, but someone that's not *you*. And you'll be everything else—everything that remains."

Xothok paused.

"That's just what I am already, isn't it?" he asked. "I can remember some shit now, but not so much that I'm a different person. This part of myself is gonna remember more, isn't he? He's gonna be a totally different guy."

The Guildmaster remained silent, and that was answer enough.

"Do it," he said.

He wanted to see the person he could have been.

CHAPTER 50

REUNITED

Rekka had, fortunately, managed to schedule the meeting for early in the morning. He'd even tried to do them one better by asking the Guildmaster for permission to use the neutral meeting room, so Wisfield would at least be suppressed the way they had been in the first meeting—but that had been a dead end. It was in use, apparently, and Wisfield refused to use it besides.

Which meant they now had to meet up with whatever nobles Wisfield chose to talk to them with.

This was fine. They'd planned for this. They knew what Wisfield could do, even, an advantage that the people negotiating with them didn't always have—and they had a *counter*. That was something almost no one had.

Even with all of that, though, Vex didn't expect the people that walked in through the door, as they sat in their corner of their meeting room. He froze.

Two Wisfield representatives he didn't recognize, in the white-gold Wisfield colors. And then black-red, the colors of the Ashion House, wrapped around one adult lizardkin man, and the tiny, fragile shoulders of a four-and-a-half-year-old lizardkin child.

Vex's hands tightened into fists and didn't let up, even when Derivan's hand clasped lightly over his own.

Breathe.

They'd known this was a possibility. Not *this specific thing*, perhaps—Vex hadn't even begun to consider that they might bring his little brother to a diplomatic meaning; he was only *four*—but they'd known that Wisfield was going to do *something* to try to throw them off. That they'd chosen this method . . . sucked? It sucked. For a second it felt like all the progress he'd made was hollow, if this was all it took to undo him.

But only for a second. Because they'd known something like this was possible, even if they hadn't identified the exact means, and there was a very, *very* significant advantage they had identified when it came to the **Relay** charms.

All communication was restricted to what they chose to communicate. It didn't apply only to the mental skills and what Wisfield might be able to derive from them. It applied to anything they said. It applied to their body language. With those charms, they could speak freely, and Wisfield would hopefully be none the wiser.

Well, except for the part where they couldn't read them. Indeed, the Wisfield representatives seemed slightly nonplussed; if Vex had to guess, they'd tried to read them and failed. But they were *also* trained to react minimally to surprises, so as to not reveal what they had identified from their mind-reading, and he reminded himself that he might just be reading too much into their expressions.

"Holy shit," Misa said, her voice filtered under the effects of the charm. Neither Wisfield nor Ashion reacted; they were watching carefully, apparently trying to gauge the four of them for a reaction, and they saw nothing that they chose not to share. "Is that a fucking *child*? Is that—"

Misa cut herself off before she could continue, her own hands tightening into fists; her expression darkened like a storm, and yet there was not a flicker of reaction from Wisfield or Ashion.

So far, so good.

"Is that a child?" Rekka said, completely nonplussed and evidently not hearing Misa either. "He wasn't on the guest list."

"I just thought I'd bring my youngest along." The adult lizardkin—Karix, his father—spoke with a deep baritone, smiling a charming, kind smile. The same smile he wore while strapping Vex into that chair—

Breathe.

Vex stopped that train of thought before it could go any further. "He's my brother," Vex explained tersely, making sure the charm filtered his words; he didn't trust himself to speak yet. Not to *them*.

But he could only wait for so long before the silence itself became suspicious.

"They want you to ask why your brother is here," Derivan said. He was staring at the representatives of the two houses, his gaze flicking between Ashion and Wisfield; his eyes narrowed slightly on Karix. "... Wisfield wants to throw you off emotionally. They are ... anticipating. They are hoping you will stumble, and make your brother believe you do not want him here."

"That's fucking shitty." Misa kept her voice low, though she didn't need to. She *was* glaring harder at Wisfield, though, and clearly she wasn't trying to block *that*, because the Wisfield representatives were starting to look uncomfortable.

"Your father... he just wanted you to see your brother?" Derivan seemed unsure. "He is harder to read. I am sorry."

"It's fine," Vex said quietly.

Breathe.

The sensation of Derivan's hand on his own helped; the cool metal gave him something to focus on. Karix was still talking, saying something about how the Ashion family had all missed him, and how little Riss had missed him the most. Vex was fine with this. It gave him time to consider how he would react.

Slowly, calmly, he picked himself up from the table he was seated at and walked over to Riss. His little brother stared up at him with wide eyes, one hand still clutched in their father's; he seemed a little nervous to be there. If his childhood so far was anything like Vex's had been, then it had so far been kind and fulfilling.

One and a half years left until that was gone.

"Hey, Riss," Vex said; he heard his own voice crack slightly, but he held firm to the magic in the charm, only letting his gentle happiness at seeing his brother through. And there was a lot of it. The last time he'd seen Riss, he was so small, and in that small amount of time he'd grown so much—

Riss's eyes sparked with recognition, and his mouth fell open in the purest expression of joy; the kind only a child had. "It's ... it's my brother!" he exclaimed, tugging excitedly on Karix's hands. "Daddy! Look! It's my brother!"

Karix smiled down at him, letting go of his hand. "Do you want to go greet your brother, Riss?"

"Yes!" Riss bounced on his feet a bit and then ran forward the two steps he needed to reach Vex; he threw little arms around him, and Vex had to bend down quickly to catch his brother properly by the arms, lest the little guy end up hugging only his legs. "I missed you!"

"I'm surprised you remember me," Vex said with a laugh, doing his damnedest to keep the tears out of his voice; no matter that he knew the charm was hiding it, it was hard for him to talk properly. His throat felt like there was a rugfly lodged in it. "You were so much smaller the last time I saw you!"

"Of course I remember you!" Riss folded his hands indignantly. "You were big. And helpful!"

"*Big?*" Vex chuckled. "Where did you get the idea that I was big? I'm like the smallest of all our siblings."

"You're big *here*," Riss whispered, his tone almost conspiratorial. And then he pointed at Vex's head and then his heart.

Vex's laugh was genuine this time, though there was a small part of him that ached. "I missed you too," he said, reaching out to poke the tip of Riss's snout; the little lizard went cross-eyed trying to follow the movement, and wobbled on his feet. "Lemme introduce you to my friends, okay? They're really cool."

"I don't know . . ." Riss looked over Vex's shoulder doubtfully. "They look kinda scary. Except the human."

"They're very nice, I promise," Vex said, patting Riss on the head. "The big one lets me ride on his shoulders sometimes."

"*Really?*" Riss' eyes went wide. "He's so big!"

"Really!" Vex grinned, even though it had only happened once, and it had not been the most comfortable experience. "I can ask him for you later, if you want."

"Yes please!" Riss said, bouncing on his feet again, and Vex felt his heart go out to the lizardkin.

"He really has missed you," Karix said from above the two of them, rumbling in amusement. "For the first month after you left, he talked about you nearly every day. I hope you found something that was worth it."

". . . Maybe I did," Vex said, his words coming out a little bit more curt than he intended. "But we can talk about that later. After this meeting. What are you doing here, Dad?"

"Wisfield wanted us along with the meeting, and I thought it would be the perfect opportunity to see my long-lost son again," Karix said, smiling at him. "You look like you're doing well, Vex! Even a little bit taller. I'm proud of you."

". . . Thanks, Dad." Vex tried not to let his emotion show.

It would be *so much easier* if Karix was just pointlessly cruel. If he didn't have so many moments of genuine kindness. If he could dismiss Karix as just evil.

A storm of mixed emotions rolled over Vex as he stood to walk back to his seat. Riss didn't stop him; his little brother just waved happily at him, fully believing Vex would do as he promised and introduce them later. Meanwhile, the Ashion and Wisfield representatives sat on the other side of the meeting table.

"All right," one of the Wisfield representatives began—he was an old, grizzled-looking human that looked just ever so slightly bored, his gaze flicking over the clipboard he'd brought with him. "Let's get started. My name is

Henry, and my companion here is Wen. You already seem to know the Ashion House, so I won't bother introducing them. The stated reason of this meeting is that you want to gain access to the dungeon in Elyra, but there are two other agendas for this meeting. Is that correct?"

Wisfield couldn't read them, but they could still read the minds of Rekka and the others; no doubt they'd caught on to some of what this meeting was meant to address through that. The words were meant to throw them off. *Layers.* They couldn't read them, but were pretending they still could.

This was why Vex hated dealing with noble society. They *had* anticipated this, though.

"And what are those other reasons?" Sev raised an eyebrow at Henry.

Henry's brows furrowed, almost imperceptibly. "You wanted to address your entrance to the Elyran dungeon, air your grievances with Wisfield and Ashion for our indiscretions in funding the Guild for political favor, and identify what we have done with the researchers that came back from your little dungeon excursion."

"That's true." Sev let a flicker of admiration and respect flicker through the charm, from what Vex could tell. It seemed to help. The Wisfield representatives relaxed just a bit, though Karix didn't react at all. "The Guild isn't particularly happy with Elyra right now, Henry."

"I'd argue that everything we've done has been to the Guild's benefit." Henry folded his arms, and Vex let himself sigh.

This was going to be a *long* meeting.

Being able to sigh without the other party noticing was pretty cathartic, though. He fingered the charm around his neck briefly; it still seemed to be going strong, though the mana within it had dimmed slightly.

"You encouraged members of the Guild to pursue an avenue of research *without* the Guild's explicit oversight, and provided funding so that this could happen. There's no way you didn't notice the side effect of the [**Reinforcement**] buff, Henry; your House would have noticed it immediately. You just took the opportunity to try to cement the Guild as another noble power in the city."

"We *reward* nobility to those that have earned it."

"The Guildmaster doesn't *want* the Guild as a noble power here," Sev said, narrowing his eyes slightly. "We are a bridge between nobility and the average citizen. Noble status would affect our ability to recruit from the common folk. Image matters here. *And,* more to the point, the status of nobility would mean that the Guild would be beholden to Elyra for any military operations it wants to conduct."

"Hmm." Henry took a moment to absorb this, folding his hands across his lap. "Fine. We understand your reluctance, even though we disagree with it. We apologize."

Sev paused. "An apology is *not good enough* for the damage you have done to the Guild. It will take time for us to heal from the effects of [**Reinforcement**]."

"I would argue that the damage done by that buff is hardly our fault," Henry said, shrugging. "We just provided the money. We'll take responsibility for that. But the buff? That was all your people."

"You could have said something."

"We could have," Henry agreed easily. "But it hardly seems fair to blame me for what we *could* have done. Not taking an action is hardly a crime."

Vex gritted his teeth slightly—

"They are messing with us," Derivan said calmly from the side. Vex turned to look at him; the armor was leaning forward in his seat, eyeing the Wisfield representatives with a sort of detached curiosity. "They are frustrated at being unable to read us, and trying to provoke a response. They truly do not feel responsible for what has been wrought here . . . I believe that may be a difficult avenue to approach."

"Change tack, then?" Sev glanced to Derivan.

"For now." Derivan tapped his fingers on the table, punctuating his statement with the *clack* of metal on wood. "There is something else that they want."

"Fine," Sev said, both to Derivan and to the Wisfield representatives; Henry frowned at him, as if confused by how long he'd taken to respond. "We're not letting that go, but we're tabling that for now. I want to know when we can be allowed access to the dungeon."

"It may take some time," Henry said. "The recent changes have caused a resurgence of research applications, which, as you know, take priority. Perhaps a month?"

". . . A month." Sev almost didn't keep the disbelief out of his voice. "This is a high-priority request from the Guild."

"A month is a short amount of time for what you are requesting." Henry said; his words were patronizing. "Really, it's a privilege to be able to access the dungeon at all."

"There *is* a way around this." Henry's companion, Wen, finally spoke; she glanced contemplatively between the adventurers. "If you were nobles, you could submit a research application, and it would be approved. With some conditions, of course. But your friend there cannot submit one for you unless he returns to his family."

Vex froze. "Me?"

"Yes." Karix frowned at him, the older lizardkin finally speaking up. "Really, now, we've let you do this long enough. You need to come home. Riss misses you."

"I do!" Riss waved at Vex, completely oblivious to his father's machinations.

"You're not going to find a new magic all by yourself," Karix continued. "You've always been brilliant, but this is the kind of thing you need research teams for."

Ah.

There was the trap.

Nobility, or Vex rejoining the family.

Vex wasn't sure why this, of all things, he hadn't expected or planned for.

CHAPTER 51

THE BEGINNINGS OF A PLAN

Whether he'd expected this or not, though, Karix's words triggered something in Vex—a seed of an idea. He *had* already found new magic, and if he wanted to, he could show it off right now. He could make his father eat his words. He couldn't deny that it would be satisfying, even; the knowledge that he had a new magic in his hands was enough to give him leverage. Enough leverage to free his brother from the family's traditions, maybe.

He wasn't sure that was enough for him anymore.

There was something else he could do with that knowledge. Something that would mess with both Wisfield *and* Ashion even more.

And so despite himself, Vex grinned. "Sure," he said.

"Sure . . . as in *yes*?" Karix blinked, thrown off by Vex's sudden acceptance. "What?"

"Of course not," Vex scoffed. "Yes to your ultimatum. We'll become nobles. Why not?"

"Vex?" Misa blinked at him. She whispered his name, even though the charm rendered it unnecessary. Vex just smiled at her and signaled that things were fine.

He had a *plan*.

"I thought you didn't want the Guild involved with the nobility," Henry said, clearly suspicious.

"We don't," Vex said easily. "But let's not talk about that right now. The process is the same, right? A household—or the Guild, in our case—submits a request to the Voting Council, right? Along with proof of work?"

"The process has not changed," Henry acknowledged.

"Great," Vex said. He spoke with a surprising amount of confidence. "Now, moving on to the last item on our list. We want to know what happened to the researchers that came back here."

The rest of the meeting had been frustrating. Henry had been cagey and evasive, until they'd eventually convinced him to tell them what they'd done with those guards and researchers. The ones that had gone back to Elyra after interfering with their dungeon delve and nearly killing Kestel, their own head researcher.

Which was nothing.

The guards and researchers had gone back to their posts with barely more than a slap on the wrist; if anything, from the way Henry was couching his words, it seemed more likely than not that those researchers were *rewarded*.

For attacking their boss, because Kestel had been looking out for the delve team under him.

There had been a low thrum of anger through their group. Even Rekka, sitting in, looked disgusted. But there was nothing they could do about it, at least not *here*. Not when their points of contact were the nobles that had created this system to begin with.

But that information would filter back. Just because there was nothing they could do *now* didn't mean they would do nothing about it forever. It was just another process they had to get started.

Vex had left the meeting feeling frustrated but determined. He wasn't happy with the outcome, exactly, but he was eager to get started on his plan.

"What was all that about?" Misa nudged him as they walked away from the meeting room; the nobles had opted to stay and partake in the food the Guild offered, which was a fairly transparent attempt at using the Guild's resources instead of their own.

"The thing about nobility?" Vex smiled a small smile. "You'll see. I want to go get some food distributed first. Can't put that off too long, right?"

And so they did.

It didn't take them that long to get back to their caravan and recharge the mana-engine that went into it; it had already recharged mostly from the ambient mana in the city. Though now that Vex was paying attention . . . that seemed a little higher than normal.

"Where to first?" Sev asked, standing at the controls.

"I've got a location," Vex said. He walked over to input their destination into the controls, and the quiet rumble of the caravan slowly took over. Vex almost wanted to speak, but he didn't. Instead, he walked over to a seat and stared out one of the windows.

He hadn't quite been paying attention before. Elyra had looked the same, and Vex had been distracted by the way they'd been treated by the guards and the absolutely enormous building the Guild had transformed into.

Even then, he'd noticed how things were different. It was only now that it sank in *how much*. No one looked like they were starving, exactly, but they were thinner than they should have been. The loud conversations and friendly banter he remembered—the screaming children, even—were gone. People spoke to one another quietly, in whispers; food stores no longer displayed their food out in the open, though they still *existed*.

When he'd left, the people of Elyra had been . . . happy, for a given value of *happy*. There were problems, certainly, but it hadn't been too difficult to *live*.

Not anymore, it seemed.

It was odd how the smallest things changed a city so much. The quiet was almost disconcerting for Vex, who felt the urge to break the silence with chatter, and yet even that seemed disrespectful.

Instead, he remained silent until they reached the first of the merchants that had helped him so long ago, when he'd left Elyra.

The store was old and run-down—a far cry from when he'd last seen it. Once-polished wood gave way to splinters and cracks, and the sign outside the door was dirty and dusty; rust flaked off the once-proud symbol of this small blacksmith, a metal cast of a dagger outlined in silver. Vex was almost worried that the store was closed entirely and permanently, but the warm glow of firelight beyond the door told him otherwise.

"Hello?" Vex called out, pushing the door open. He winced when it creaked at him, signaling his arrival with a high-pitched whine that echoed through the smithy. The shop was filled with its traditional rack of weapons, with a special display for the daggers that were the smith's favorite. Even this one, Vex saw, was now mostly empty. He'd once said he'd never sell any of those daggers.

The most important one of them was still there, at least.

"One moment!" a voice called back—Vex didn't recognize it. A man emerged from the back a second later, dusting his hands off on his apron and giving them a tired smile. "Sorry, it's been . . . well, it's been. Honestly, I can't say it's been busy. Just . . . trying to keep myself busy. You know how it is." He let out a small laugh, and then when Vex and the others didn't join in, he blinked and looked at them again.

"Oh, shit, you're new to Elyra," he muttered to himself. "Uh, hi! I'm Ingress. Welcome to— Welcome to Dagger Superiority. Um. How can I help you? You're adventurers?"

"Is Victor here?" Vex asked politely, looking around the shop. He didn't see any trace of the man that had helped him.

"Ah." Ingress winced slightly. "He's . . . not doing very well at the moment. Not able to work. I'm sorry. I assure you, though, I can do anything he can—"

"Is he okay?" Vex interrupted, unable to keep the worry out of his voice, and Ingress paused.

"You knew him?" the young man asked. "Ah, shit, I'm sorry. I shouldn't have broken it to you like that."

"He helped me a while ago," Vex said quietly. "I wanted to see him again. And ask for his help, uh . . . since he probably has more connections than I do here."

Ingress sighed. "He liked helping people," he said with a small smile, and then at the look Vex gave him, quickly corrected himself. "He likes. *Likes* helping people."

"He's . . . not okay, is he?" Vex asked. Sev learned forward, touching his arm, and Vex shook his head; he would *not* ask Sev to heal another person and strip away another part of himself.

"He's alive," Ingress said. He glanced around and found a chair to collapse into, gesturing to the other four to take a seat, too; a lot of his energy seemed to drain out of him, all in an instant. "Dad's always been a bit too stubborn. Got a touch of rustbite a bit ago, and we didn't have the shards or the gold to get it cured. He just kinda kept working."

"He kept working with *rustbite*?" Vex asked. "In a smithy?"

"We told him it was stupid," Ingress shrugged. "But . . . he loves this shop. It's everything to him."

"Those daggers were too," Vex said, glancing at the half-empty shelf he'd noticed earlier.

"He told you about them, huh?" Ingress's smile was wry. "Yeah. He's the one that sold them, though. Not even for a rustbite cure; can you believe that? He did it because one of our neighbors was starving."

"That sounds like him." Vex hesitated. "Is he . . . here?"

"He's upstairs, but I don't think you want to see him." Ingress winced. "Rustbite . . ."

"It's not pretty, I know," Vex said quietly. "But he helped me out when I needed it. I feel like I *should* see him . . . No, you're not coming with me, Sev."

"But I can—"

"Sev." This time, it was Misa that spoke. She put her hand on his shoulder and shook her head. The charm saved Ingress from having to hear what they were saying. "Just . . . spare yourself. Late-stage rustbite can't be healed, and if you do it, you're going to take an even-bigger hit than you did healing Lendel."

Misa was right, of course.

Vex headed up the stairs with Derivan while Sev tried to argue with Misa—argued and argued poorly, in fact. He knew she was right too. If Vex had to guess, Sev felt it was necessary to at least see who he was refusing to heal, to remember them and carry them with him, because it was someone he could have saved.

It was a noble thought.

Noble but not at all healthy.

The steps to the upper floors of the smithy were remarkably clean, compared to the exterior of the building and even compared to the shop; there wasn't much to the upper floors. Two doors leading to two bedrooms, and a living room of some sort in the back. Vex didn't bother looking. He could spell the tangy, metallic smell of rustbite practically radiating from one of the rooms.

"Rustbite's a degenerative malus," Vex said quietly to Derivan, just before he opened the door; he knew the armor was curious, and he needed something to break the silence and distract himself. Derivan was probably not asking questions because he wanted to stay respectful. "It's metal accumulation, basically. The name's not entirely accurate. You get clumps of metal building up in your body, and eventually, it starts to grow out of you."

"That sounds . . . unpleasant." Derivan paused. "Should I be coming in with you?"

"He's most likely too far gone for it to matter," Vex said quietly. "The way Ingress was talking about it, I can't imagine it would. But your metal won't have a big effect on him either way, as long as you don't touch him directly. Especially since you're made of enchanted metal."

He pushed open the door.

There was a cruelty in rustbite, in that it was a magical disease that produced results that were grotesque and picturesque all at once. Small filaments of rust forming a miniature forest would have been beautiful had it not been growing on an old man's body—a body that was nearly a corpse. Vex barely recognized Victor beneath it all, and he had to suppress the urge to flinch away.

Instead, he approached Victor, albeit slowly.

"I'm sorry this happened to you," he said. The words felt wholly inadequate. "And thank you for what you did for me."

He wished there was a way to know Victor *heard* him underneath it all. There was the slow shift of his chest as he breathed; that was the terrible interaction between rustbite and health. Unlike a lot of degenerative maluses, rustbite didn't cause a reduction in health. If anything, it *increased* your health. It was strange. But the metal that grew was a physical impediment, and as the malus progressed, victims lost the use of their limbs.

There was a case here to be made for a merciful death. Many of those with rustbite would choose that option if they didn't have the means to cure it. But Victor...

"Oh, I'm never gonna die." *The old man grinned at a younger Vex, handing him the materials he'd requested; manaforged metal shaped like a dagger, and manashaped wood for the hilt.* "Trust me. Come back whenever, and you'll find me."

"That seems..." Vex tried to find the words. It was a little arrogant? But he couldn't just say that.

"I just don't ever want to die." *Victor seemed quite firm about it, too.* "No matter what happens. I wanna stick around to see what the world becomes, ya know? As long as there's a chance I can keep going, I'm gonna."

Victor wouldn't have gone for a merciful death.

"I wonder," Derivan said softly, "if there is a way to truly speak with him."

Vex glanced at him. "[**Telepathy**] doesn't work," he said. "Rustbite eats into the parts of the brain that understand language."

Derivan traced a shape in the air in response, the looping letters of Communication. Vex stared at it for a moment, and then at Victor.

Sev had the ability to heal. Vex hadn't considered that *he* might be able to do something, because that had never been his role, but this... this was a start?

This was what he wanted to do anyway.

"Maybe we can," he agreed.

CHAPTER 52

THE PLAN?

Communication was only the beginning. There was still more to be done—the Communication glyph was not, on its own, able to mimic anything so complex as even the [**Telepathy**] spell, let alone surpass the physical limitations that rustbite imposed on its victims.

But the set of glyphs they had were limited. Given time, Vex would have loved to explore the glyph system on his own; he could have spent days diving into different glyph combinations, identifying everything that worked and why.

That wasn't the plan, though.

The plan was simple.

Nobility in Elyra ruled through a majority vote, with every House agreeing to do whatever that majority vote dictated; this was primarily enforced through House Julia and House Varil—the enforcers and the military, respectively. There was a rather obvious reason Wisfield had wanted the Guild to qualify as a single noble House. With a total of sixteen noble families that all mostly voted unanimously, they would be able to effectively control the Guild through their votes.

It was a blatantly obvious maneuver, made all the more obvious by the fact that they were willing to let go of the usual requirement that a single House be blood-related. Though that, too, was a rule that they often let slip . . .

Vex sighed.

The point was that there was an obvious hole in this plan that Wisfield never accounted for and had no real reason *to* account for. New noble families were few and far between for a number of reasons; the biggest one was that it was hard to come upon a discovery significant enough to become a House without the kind of funding and resources that came from nobility to begin with. The *second* biggest one was that it was easy to *sabotage* anyone that was about to hit upon any such discovery, and steal that secret for themselves.

A few noble families held more than one secret that could qualify as their Principle.

Vex had exactly one such secret—but the nobles didn't know that. The last time Wisfield had met them was before he'd even discovered glyphs, and in the most recent meeting, they'd already worked out Relay glyphs. Wisfield had never had the opportunity to find out that Vex had a whole new magic—

—which meant that what Vex had here was an *opportunity.*

He had eight glyphs and two Signs to work with, not including glyph combinations. One glyph to each family meant he could create eight new nobles; he needed another nine to overturn the majority vote, and many, many more if he wanted to actually affect the direction Elyra was taking. He didn't have enough glyphs to make the changes he wanted to.

But that was fine. He only needed to plant the seeds now; he needed only a single family that would help him.

"Let's go downstairs," Vex said to Derivan. The armor blinked at him, surprised.

"We are leaving?" he asked. "I had assumed we would..."

"We will," Vex said. "But Communication by itself isn't going to be enough. We're going to need Ingress's help, and I want to make sure he's the right kind of person. We need to *start* at the right place, at least."

He hoped his plan would work. There was every chance it could backfire spectacularly.

Vex and Derivan found Ingress, Sev, and Misa lounging in the corner of the shop. In the time since they'd left, the three of them had apparently managed to find something in common—all of them were fascinated by a particular "weapon" Victor had apparently come up with before he'd been taken by rust-bite. It was one of his last projects, in fact.

So really, "lounging in the corner of the shop" wasn't that accurate a descriptor at all; Ingress and Sev were both trapped in a corner, and Misa was poking at them with a massive stick.

"I feel like I should've known something like this would happen in the *five minutes* we were gone, but somehow I can't imagine how," Vex remarked.

"Vex!" Misa's eyes lit up. "Look at this. It's such a cool fuckin' idea. See, it's a really long stick—"

"I can see that."

"—look, you know what I mean. It's a really long stick, and there are these rotating hinged blades at the end that lock in place—"

"Please tell me this isn't a weapon used to cut people in half."

"Nope!" Misa grinned. "The blades are dull; all it does it trap someone at a distance. I can't believe something like this wasn't already in use by the Guild. We don't exactly have a lot of *melee* nonlethal options."

"There *are* problems with it," Ingress said. "Dad said it's an Earth invention, so it doesn't really account for the system. Someone with enough Agility could unlock those blades pretty easily. Or just jump out of the hoop. We need to account for those."

"You could probably solve part of the problem by using a mana lock instead of a physical lock," Vex said thoughtfully, and he saw the spark in Ingress's eyes; the blacksmith leapt up—"Before you leave," Vex added hurriedly, "I need your help with something."

"Oh!" Ingress looked surprised. "Do you need a new weapon or something? You guys look pretty kitted-out already, I didn't think you needed anything new from me. Though I guess some of your stuff does look a little out of date."

Vex grimaced a little at the unintended insult. "Not with weapons," he clarified, much to Ingress's apparent disappointment. "We need help with organizing people."

"What for?" Ingress frowned at them, suddenly cautious. "We've tried to organize protests before. House Julia shuts us down pretty quickly."

"Not with protesting," Vex said. He gestured toward the door—their caravan was still waiting outside, secured with a variety of spells and skills to keep the goods from being stolen. There were small, intentional security holes in those spells, in fact, but they were holes that would allow a thief to steal a loaf or two of bread if needed; nothing too egregious, and it stopped them from trying to break the whole setup entirely. "We need your help distributing food."

"Distributing—" Ingress's eyes went wide. "You guys came here with *supplies?*"

"Donations from the Guild, yeah," Sev said. "We were going to send it to the government for distribution, but—"

"Oh fuck thank the gods you came here," Ingress interrupted, his eyes still a little wide, but he seemed to be rapidly calming down. Vex could almost see him trying to figure out exactly how many problems he could solve with an injection of food and where those problems were worst. "Okay, I might need some time to get everyone together, but we can definitely help. You're going to need more people than what I can gather, though. You don't actually have enough food for everyone, right?"

"Not quite," Sev admitted. "We're working on figuring out the problem."

"At least someone's doing something about it," Ingress said. "I'm half-convinced it's another one of those fucking no— Never mind. Don't mind me; I'm sorry. You actually have to deal with those guys, so you probably have it worse off than me."

"You don't know the half of it," Vex muttered.

"Thank you," Ingress said, catching all of them off guard with his sincerity. "I— Seriously, thank you."

Sev watched Ingress for a moment. "... The problem's a bit worse than it looks, isn't it?"

"You don't know the half of it," Ingress said, echoing Vex; he shared a significant glance with the lizardkin. "The nobles aren't exactly fair with how they distribute food, and some of them don't like the thought of us *redistributing* that food, so some families are worse off than others. We try to help when we can, but..."

"What would you do if you had nobility, Ingress?" Vex asked suddenly. "This family, I mean?"

"I don't fucking want nobility." Ingress's tone gained a sudden sharpness to it, and he paused only when he saw the way Vex flinched. "... Sorry. That's a bit of a sore topic for me. For... a lot of us, actually. Not everyone. A lot of people still want it. But that's sort of the problem."

"The idea that you can just earn nobility is a trap, yeah," Vex said with a shrug, and Ingress seemed to relax a bit. "The fact that there are only sixteen noble families after all this time should say a lot on its own. That's why I'm asking what you would do if you were one of them."

"Nothing," Ingress said. "I mean, don't get me wrong, I'd try. But if you had any idea of how the nobles vote... one new family isn't going to do anything. No offense. I'd sooner quit and do the work where it really matters than play around at politics."

"And if there were more than that?" Vex asked. He was glad for Ingress's answers, but also starting to hesitate; Ingress's points were good ones. "Eight? Seventeen?"

"... You'd need to get that many of us *agreeing*," Ingress said warily. "I know you haven't met that many of us, but we argue a *lot* about what we think is best. The only thing we really agree on is that this system doesn't work. It might be a start, but..."

Ingress sighed. "Two major problems," he said, his tone suddenly serious. "One is that I'm not sure I should be trusted—you barely know me. I know you haven't *offered*, but this conversation is obviously going in a direction, and I'd rather embarrass myself a bit in a hypothetical than risk looking like I'm not taking this seriously. More than that, *I* don't trust me. I try to be a good person, but I'm not immune to the shit that goes on down there. I can't live here without being affected by it, you know?

"The second issue—and it's probably the bigger one—is that if you're planning on somehow making twenty different families nobles all at the same time, or even more than that, the nobles that are currently in power can and will change the rules on you. Remember, everything is enforced through Julia and Varil; the only reason they bend to the other Houses in a vote is because they agree the majority of the time, and because each House provides a service to *them* that's too valuable to risk losing. Introduce twenty Houses at once, and Julia is just going to sit down and refuse to act, no matter how we vote on it. Hell, they could declare us illegitimate and just go after all the new Houses, and not a single one of us could stop them."

"The Guild might be able to." Vex hesitated even saying the words; he wasn't sure they *could*. Maybe Ingress was right and this approach wasn't the right one after all; he could just show his glyphs to Karix and force his father to both let them into the Elyran dungeon and free Riss from following in his footsteps.

He'd still make that glyph for Victor, though.

"Maybe." Ingress voice softened a bit. "To be very clear, *I'm* willing to risk that. But I don't know that everyone will be. I'm just warning you ahead of time. You obviously have a plan, and I'm not saying it won't work, but..."

"I want to make everyone a noble," Vex blurted, and he colored as everyone turned to stare at him, not only Ingress but Sev and Misa and Derivan, too; the only indication of surprise on the armor's part was the slight widening of his eyes. "... Not just seventeen. It'd be the same as removing the idea of nobility entirely."

Ingress paused and narrowed his eyes slightly. "Are you saying you have a way to do that?"

"... Maybe." There was a sudden intensity in Vex's eyes.

"Right." Ingress frowned. "Let me ... get in touch with some others."

CHAPTER 53

GROWTH WITHOUT THE SYSTEM

Vex sat uncomfortably in the caravan. The windows were all locked and spelled shut—he could have dispelled it rather easily but chose not to. Ingress had said something about taking them somewhere secret, and was sitting in the caravan with them; it was a bit of a tight squeeze with five people, but Vex didn't figure it was a trap.

Or, well, they'd discussed it and figured there was a chance it was a trap, but Ingress had been genuine when he'd agreed to help with food distribution. Vex suspected this was a step that was even further than what he was planning to do initially.

"Ingress is kind of bad at keeping secrets," Misa said dryly, adjusting her Relay charm to hide what she was saying from him.

"He's bringing us to a meetup for some kind of rebellion, right?" Sev said.

"I think it's likely." Vex glanced at the blacked-out windows again, wondering exactly what was so secret about the route—there weren't many places to hide in the Kingdom. "I remember hearing rumors about a rebellion even back when I was living here. They never really seemed to go anywhere, but..."

"I imagine it would be hard to rebel properly in a place like this," Derivan said. "Power does not appear to be distributed evenly, for all that the system makes it easier to gain power."

"The Guild's the only means for most people to safely get into combat situations that will help them raise their level fast enough to matter," Vex said, nodding. "Probably part of why they want to gain the Guild as an asset. And even then, you haven't seen how the Julia enforcers fight. They're strong and *really* loyal. It's like the delve-team thing."

"Emotional suppression?" That was Sev; the cleric leaned forward, an irritated furrow in his brows.

"That's so fucking shitty," Misa grumbled.

"Yep." Vex sighed. "I hope there's something more we can do. Julia recruits people by promising them power and a lot of pay—a lot of people join them because it's one of the most consistent ways to get gold. They *know* they're going to be emotionally suppressed, but there's the promise of money going back to their families..."

"What about Varil?" Derivan asked.

"Same thing, more or less," Vex said. "The enforcers and the military do almost the same things—Julia and Varil even pretty much always vote together. The only reason they're separate Houses is because they have a different Principle; Varil's is the loyalty thing, and Julia has the enhanced leveling and training program that their enforcers and agents go through. And delve teams, when they decide to train one of those. They effectively function as a single unit with two Principles."

"Sounds like we need to break both of those Houses," Misa said bluntly. Vex winced.

"Don't let any of them hear you say that," he said.

"Will glyphs actually help the rebels?" Sev asked. "Assuming we're right and that's where Ingress is taking us, as opposed to some noble-operated trap."

Vex hesitated. "I'm . . . not sure," he said. "I think Ingress got some of the idea; he understands that I have a secret that can be applied broadly enough that we can make multiple noble houses out of it, enough to mess with the voting bloc."

"He also believes that won't work," Misa said. "And he's probably right. Sorry, Vex. It's a good idea, but in practice . . ."

"Yeah, I know," Vex said, sighing. "I got a little excited. I want to get this done with as little bloodshed as possible, but . . . I don't know. We'll see what they say, I guess. And then we can figure out what we want to do about it."

There was a small silence for a while.

"We need to get ahead of the game," Misa said softly. "We're keeping up for now, but if we get a chance—if we get to the dungeon, somewhere else where time is stretched out—we need to figure out everything we can do and make sure we're ahead for the next disaster. We're surviving for now, but we're doing it through tricks, and even if we plan on sticking with that plan . . . we should have more tricks. What would happen if we fought the Julia enforcers now, Vex?"

"We'd lose," Vex said firmly. "I hate to say it, but we would. None of them really have rare classes or anything, but they're all at least Gold in terms of level, and the sheer number of them on top of the raw stats—we can do a lot, but we can't do *enough*."

"The more we understand the system, the better," Misa said. "It's another reason to get into the dungeon as soon as we can. We need more time."

"I have many things about my status that I must study in detail," Derivan agreed.

"There's more I can figure out about glyphs," Vex said. "There's something about the way my sign works..."

"I feel like all of you guys have something," Sev said. "I'm not sure where I'm gonna go. Gain more levels?"

"You have your connection with Aurum," Vex pointed out.

"If only he would respond to me," Sev said with a sigh. "But... yeah, I'll try something. Maybe he's caught up in something. There's Onyx to worry about, too. I think the Guildmaster sent a message about Velykos going to investigate that. I'll have to keep up with what they're doing."

"So," Ingress said, startling Vex, who had sort of forgotten that Ingress was in the cabin with them at all. "Who are you guys, anyway? I mean, I know your names now, but not really anything about you. Why do you care about Elyran politics?"

"Vex is Elyran," Sev said, giving Vex a significant glance. Vex winced a bit.

"I'm from Ashion, actually," he said. There would only be problems if he tried to hide that; he would have mentioned it earlier, but he'd forgotten.

"You're what." Ingress's voice was flat, and his eyes turned flinty and hard; Vex saw his hands poised over an invisible keyboard, like he was ready to send off a message and call off the whole thing.

"Victor should've mentioned it, right?" Vex said, trying to head off the impending conflict; he saw Ingress relax slightly. "I was trying to get away from my House, and Victor helped me."

"Oh." Ingress deflated a little. "Right. He didn't exactly say that, but he said something about wanting to help your little brother."

"The practices of House Ashion are not... particularly pleasant on their children," Vex said. "Part of the reason we're a smaller House, really."

They could have partnered with Julia and created loyal mages; Julia had even pushed for that on a number of occasions. It would have made them a bigger and more influential House, even. Karix had refused. For everything else that was wrong with his father, even he disliked the emotion-cutting magics that Julia used to ensure loyalty.

"I see," Ingress said, and he looked down for a moment. "Not even their kids get away with it unscathed, huh."

Vex chuckled, though it wasn't a happy chuckle. "Not particularly, no."

The caravan rolled to a stop, suddenly, and Ingress glanced up. "We're here," he said. "Come on."

He pushed the door open, revealing a small, cramped room that the caravan had somehow maneuvered into; it was lit by a number of ghost-blue enchanted torches. Vex recognized the design, even; they were a fairly expensive brand of torches that enhanced illusory and anti-perception-based magic.

Which made a lot of sense, considering the amount of magic Vex sensed around them; it was cleverly obscured for anyone with basic [**Mana Sight**], because it was colored just the same way as the walls and distributed evenly through them. Anyone not paying attention would sense that they were like any other wall in the city. The entrance to the room was obscured with this illusory magic, making it look like they were in a dark, empty room lit only by flickering blue light.

"Kinda creepy lighting," Sev remarked. Vex had to agree. "Not very encouraging."

"Sorry," a light voice resounded; Vex blinked once, and realized that a tall lizardkin was standing in front of him, so tall her head almost scraped against the ceiling. He recognized her, even—it was the librarian that would often help him with his spellbooks. A snap of her fingers, and the ghost blue turned into the regular orange light of a torch, though [**Advanced Mana Sight**] helped him see the same blue still hidden in its flickers. "It is usually simpler to keep it blue."

"The magic's more effective that way, too," Vex said, and the older lizardkin smiled at him.

"I am glad you still remember your lessons."

"I paid attention," Vex said, preening just a bit, and the old lizardkin chuckled.

"You made some friends, I see," she said. "Came back to fix this broken old Kingdom?"

"Came back for a few reasons, actually," Vex admitted. "One of them is my brother. Another is to get into the dungeon. It's . . . a work in progress. Wisfield is kind of forcing our hand here, though."

"They want you to do something for them?" another person said—this one was a grizzled-looking orc leaning against one of the walls. He stood with his arms folded, a scowl on his face that looked like it had been etched into his skull. "And you got out of it?"

"We tried," Vex said. "Like I said, it's a work in progress. They want me back in the Ashion household and they want the Guild to join the nobles. Both of those things are—"

"Quite bad, yes," Ingress said with a frown. "They're angling to get the Guild as a puppet."

"Is this everyone?" Misa asked, frowning slightly. "This is some kind of rebellion, right? There's just three people here."

"I don't know if we're a rebellion, dear," the old lizardkin-librarian said with a kindly chuckle. "But we needed a place to meet up and discuss what was happening to our Kingdom, away from prying eyes . . . This seemed as good a place as any."

"You said you need a way to get into the Elyran dungeon?" the orc asked. "We can get you in there. But we'll need something in return."

"I assumed that was why you brought us here," Sev said. "You want to know more about Vex's plan?"

"Not exactly," Ingress said. "Like I said, it won't work—the nobles control too much already. But you must have *some* kind of powerful secret, if you were planning on creating so many noble houses."

"So we want to propose a trade," the librarian said. She smiled. "I am glad it's you, Vex. I was a little worried someone had tricked poor Ingress. He can be a little easy to fool."

"Hey!" Ingress protested.

"But if anyone was going to figure out some deep secret of magic, I would have imagined it to be you," she continued, completely ignoring Ingress.

"We aren't just going to ask you for your secrets for free," the orc said. "If you believe this secret can help us get a leg up on the nobles, then we will pay you for it. You need to get into the dungeon, yes? We have a way in for you."

"Wisfield thinks they have a monopoly on information, but they don't." The librarian smiled again, this time with a certain smug gleam in her eyes; Vex recognized that look, even. "They're too selfish about their Principle to have agents everywhere, and they only read surface thoughts. So if you think this will help us, we can get you in. That's our promise to you."

Vex was silent for a moment. Part of him was just a little bit stunned; they'd had the Relays to help them communicate without Wisfield rifling through their minds, and these Elyrans had just been . . . doing it, without even a skill to help screen their thoughts. There was always the chance that Wisfield *knew*, but they were arrogant; if they knew, they would likely have come down on the rebels already.

"I have the beginnings of something that will help," Vex said. "It won't be enough yet, but I think it will be, eventually."

"And what exactly is it?" Ingress peered at him closely.

"A way to gain strength without the system," Vex said. He almost added more—almost said that it might be a way to talk to Victor again.

But... no. No false hope; he didn't know for sure if he could do it. When he was sure, he would speak to Ingress again.

No sooner.

CHAPTER 54

DISTRIBUTION

Vex had been a little concerned that his words wouldn't be enough—but it turned out that he needn't have worried. The "rebels," such as they were, were strangely willing to trust him on his word, though they insisted on sending someone in with them to the dungeon. The new person wouldn't have to accompany them—he'd stay at the edges of the bonus room, hopefully away from the danger, and focus on studying the glyphs that Vex gave him. In the meantime, Vex could go out to identify new glyphs and expand his knowledge of this True Magic.

First, though, they had to finish with the food distribution. They left a cartload with Ingress and the librarian, each of them promising they'd find the right people to help distribute the food to those that needed it; between them, they could cover about a third of the city, which meant they still needed to find trustworthy distributors for the other two-thirds.

Vex still had the merchants he wanted to find, the ones that had helped him out to begin with—but the rebels had also helped by providing a number of names they deemed trustworthy. They weren't necessarily members of the rebellion, but they were people that were noted as being *kind*, the sort of people that would help as honestly and fairly as they could.

So that was who they went looking for. It wasn't a process that was anywhere near as quick as they wanted—but Ingress told them they needed time to set up a way to sneak them into the dungeon, too, so that gave them a few days to secure distribution of the food and to figure out what was happening to growth spells.

It was time they spent . . . as well as they could.

"Hey, hey, hey, it's all right," Misa whispered. Vex was standing beside her, his dagger brandished and his eyes narrowed; he kept his back straight and his tail still, every muscle poised to strike. He was the very picture of danger, even as his larger companion comforted the small child that was crying on the ground. "Shhh. We've got you."

"Get out of the way," one of the teenagers Vex was poised against said. He was a scruffy-looking human, his hair and clothes both a mess; there were holes in his shirt, and streaks of dirt along his arms, along with hints of blood, like he'd fallen and scraped his arms. He was holding a dagger, but the dagger was trembling; Vex didn't need Physical Empathy to see how much the kid didn't want to do this.

The child was holding a piece of bread, clutching it for dear life; even that piece of bread was stained with tears and blood and dirt. Julia enforcers were nowhere to be seen, because of course they weren't; they didn't *really* come to this part of town. Vex was starting to understand how the rebels were able to operate under Wisfield's noses. A lot of the nobles just didn't care enough to bother with what they considered the slums of the city, the slightly poorer outer circle that lived along the Kingdom's walls.

"No," Vex said, his voice steady. Derivan and Sev were off deescalating another conflict; they'd seen three separate fights as soon as they'd entered the district, and immediately split up to break up those fights. "Put your dagger down."

"Get the *fuck* out of the way," the teenager said again, gaining confidence. The two humans behind him, both smaller and younger—his brothers, maybe?—stared up at him with eyes wide, but they did nothing to stop him; they stood poised to fight instead.

"You don't want to do this," Vex said again, adding a note of warning to his voice.

"Why? What level are you?" the boy demanded. "You're just another one of Mydsa's thugs, aren't you?"

"What are you— You're the ones trying to steal bread from a child!" Vex couldn't keep the exasperation from bleeding into his voice. "You think *I'm* the thug in this situation?"

"You didn't answer my question," the boy said.

"You didn't answer mine!"

"It doesn't matter," he said, and he charged. It was a reckless charge, too; the boy didn't know anything about his level or his stats. This was pure desperation at work, and . . .

There were three of them charging at Vex, actually; the boy's two brothers, if that was who they were, were charging with him. And even with that, Vex didn't feel like he or Misa or the small child she was helping were in danger.

They were just too... *slow*.

It was hard to get away from the absolute *stat disparity* between them; the difference had been clear with the bandits, and they were even clearer now. Vex had plenty of time to step out of the way and push the offending daggers to the side, his tail sweeping down to knock the boy off his feet, and even arrange the subsequent fall so the kid didn't stab himself on the way down. Likewise, his brothers posed almost no threat...

They tried an [**Adjust Position**] on their daggers, to force them to strike him, but even that Vex could respond to; the recent flood of levels he'd gotten allowed him to step away from the mana-focused build, giving him more of the Agility he needed in close-combat confrontations. When the dagger appeared in front of him, he sidestepped, letting it bounce off his leathers harmlessly.

Normally, at this point, he would've cast [**Sleep**]. But this...

"Look, you just want some food, right?" he said to them—to their backs, really, as they lay groaning on the floor. He didn't comment on it. "We'll give you some bread. We're not looking for you, anyway."

"You're not one of Mydsa's men," the first teenager said, staring at him, eyes wide.

"No," Vex sighed. "Like I said, I don't even know who that is."

"She's the one that handles food distribution here." The words were filled with spite. He got back up on his feet, slightly hunched over and breathing heavily. "One of Julia's lackeys. She just gives out the food to the families she *likes*." He glared at the child, who still lay trembling in Misa's arms.

"... That doesn't fucking give you leave to hurt a *child*." Misa's tone was flat.

"Well what the fuck do you want us to do?!" the kid suddenly exploded, rounding on Misa with a hostility that surprised even himself. His eyes were wet, but he spoke with defiance. "My mom hasn't—she hasn't eaten in *two weeks!* The system's gonna take her—"

"We'll get you some food," Vex interrupted, trying to calm the boy down. "For your mom. Whatever she needs to break the status effect. Just... stop. We'll figure things out."

The boy glared. But he didn't pick up the dagger again; it lay on the ground where Vex had knocked it, sparking strangely with a hint of his magic.

"Fine," he said. Not because he was really giving up, or even because he trusted Vex to give them the food he said he was going to. He just saw that he didn't have a choice. He'd tried, and the stat disparity was simply too large; Vex saw the defeat in his eyes.

Vex sighed again.

Some victories really didn't feel like one.

—⚔—

"You don't fucking get it," the orc told Derivan, his voice rough. "There isn't enough for us to *share*. We share and we both die before the next shipment arrives. This is all we fuckin' got. Don't come down here and judge us if you aren't going to fucking *help*."

They'd set up a pseudo-tournament in this part of town, one orcish fighter against a human girl. She was smaller and faster than the orc, and the orc was clearly losing; there were bruises developing on his skin where the system failed to heal him properly, a side effect of the [**Hunger**] effect that lessened the protection of health.

The girl didn't seem like she wanted to fight, though. There were tears in her eyes when she did. But her eyes were determined, and her fists were clenched; she would not lose.

Derivan couldn't explain they *were* here to help; not *here*, where they were surrounded with an audience. He'd already tried that once before, in a different encounter, and the result had been the four of them getting swarmed by people desperate for food.

"I didn't know it was this bad," Sev said, his voice quiet. "People didn't look like they were starving. Are people dying already . . . ?"

"Of course you wouldn't see it," the orc scoffed.

"You'd only see this around the city edges," the girl told them quietly; she'd straightened, apparently deciding that the fight was over for now, and spoke with a sort of soft confidence. "Places the nobles don't really touch, because they don't really consider it a part of their city."

"Sometimes adventurers come on by and help us out," the orc said. "But they've been doing that less lately."

"Turns out there's a reason for that," Sev muttered, glancing at Derivan; the armor just bowed his head slightly. He'd seen the glimmer of [**Reinforcement**] on more than one person while they were moving through the city, and he'd broken it where he could; the soul-cracks that resulted would still take some time to heal. He'd even broken it on some of the nobles they'd come across.

"Look," Sev said, glancing around. Derivan heard the pain in his voice when he spoke, though he tried his best to hide it. "Fight's over. Stop . . .

watching this. It's not— Don't make a *game* out of this. You're going through a lot and I get it, but..."

"Judge us when *you're* the ones starving," someone in the crowd jeered, and Sev winced slightly—but he didn't say anything. He watched as the crowd slowly began to disperse; only the orc and the girl stayed, both staring at him.

"If you're breaking up the fight, I assume you have a solution," the girl said.

"Or food," the orc rumbled.

"It is both, we hope," Derivan said quietly. "But it did not seem wise to say so in front of a large crowd."

"No," the orc agreed; he squinted his eyes at Derivan in a leer. "They would've torn you apart."

Derivan disagreed. They wouldn't have been able to do anything to him. But he didn't respond, instead staring until the orc shifted uncomfortably.

"...What now?" he finally asked, the word emerging almost reluctantly.

"Now we get you some food," Sev said. "And you bring us to someone that can help give it out."

Some places were better than others. That one district in the southwest section of Elyra was probably among the worst, whether it was because it was located farthest from House Julia or for some other nebulous reason; other districts had smaller evils or smaller needs, but it was largely the same thing between districts—there were always people who were desperate.

For Vex, it was a bit of a shock; he'd always seen Elyra as a prosperous Kingdom, for all that he knew it had its faults. Yet it was clear now that it hadn't taken much for Elyra to start to fall at all—a single type of spell had stopped working properly, and already the Kingdom had started to fall apart. Only at the outer edges, sure, but given enough time...

It was sobering. And maybe what was worse was the fact that most of the nobles likely weren't aware of it, even ones that specialized in *knowing*; if most of them didn't bother to spend their time in the outer edges, they would likely just assume that everything was *fine*. People closer to the center of the Kingdom weren't exactly hale and hearty, but they weren't starving or desperate, either.

That was only happening where it could be hidden.

They'd given out a good two-thirds of the food by now, not distributing it by hand but giving it to individuals they felt could be trusted to give out food in turn; the orc that had been losing in the southwest district? He'd turned out to be fighting to win food for a smaller community of impoverished people in the area and not just his own family, and so he'd gotten a large chunk of bread and another chunk of preserved foodstuffs that would last. They'd watched as they left, and saw him give a loaf of bread almost immediately to the girl he'd been fighting; she'd clutched it tightly to herself—

"A lot of this is so much worse than I thought," Vex said, hugging his tail to himself. "I need to figure out what's happening with growth spells. And why it's growth-specific spells that are affected. The food we're giving out isn't going to last forever."

Derivan nodded. "Perhaps what we have learned from Teque will help?" he offered. "Or perhaps we could study this phenomenon from within the bonus room."

"I think that's gonna be our best bet," Vex said. He leaned in to Derivan, feeling a wave of exhaustion overcome him, and saw the armor look down at him in concern; Vex managed a small smile.

"Any news from Ingress yet?" Misa asked.

"Nothing," Sev said, shaking his head. He glanced at Vex and Derivan and gave them a small smile, then turned to Misa. "We still need to get another third of this distributed before we can do that anyway, so . . ."

"About four more stops," Misa said. "You guys see the people following us too, right?"

"Yeah." Sev glanced back through the windows, toward the rooftops. "Not sure if they're Julia enforcers or people in the city, but an ambush didn't work too well the last time someone tried."

"I had some kids try to attack me, too." Vex said, tapping his fingers listlessly on his seat. "Not a surprise that some people noticed what we were doing. The caravan's pretty noticeable."

"If they are enforcers, we must be prepared," Derivan said. "We cannot assume it will be an easy fight."

"No," Vex agreed. "They'll have magic items and raw stats. So we'll have to be careful."

And they were.

Which was probably why it was *two* more stops before they got attacked instead of one.

CHAPTER 55

OH, BROTHER

It started with a [**Fireball**], which told Vex two things: one, that this was almost certainly a noble house attacking them, and two, that they didn't care about casualties. The [**Fireball**] was packed with enough mana to level several blocks of houses, and was cast despite the fact that they were surrounded by civilians.

Misa blocked it, of course.

She snapped in front of the [**Fireball**] with a strange object balanced on her shoulder, a sort of cylinder decorated not with runes but with *glyphs*; Vex noticed this a split second before the presumable weapon flared to life and just... sucked in the [**Fireball**], along with every drop of mana packed into it.

"Run!" she shouted, startling the few people that had stayed to stare into running. It was almost remarkable how quickly the surrounding blocks cleared, in fact, and it made a distant part of Vex wonder if they'd had to do this before.

Part of Vex was also afraid that a member of his own House was here. That [**Fireball**] had been an expensive one, and it would take someone from Ashion to cast it without making themselves useless for the rest of the fight. He was *pretty sure* no one from Ashion was here, though; none of his siblings were the types to participate in battle without flashy House colors, and his father wouldn't have allowed any of his siblings to join Julia and partake in their so-called loyalty program.

More likely, this was a cooperatively cast [**Fireball**], which meant that the majority of enforcers they were fighting were *mages*.

Though his older brother Helix did like his [**Fireball**]s.

"Derivan!" Sev called. "Anything?"

"It is strange," Derivan answered. "I can see where the system places status effects now, I think. There is one in particular that is digging into all of them."

"You think that's the emotional suppression?" Misa asked, and that was all the time Vex had to pay attention to the conversation. Their four opponents were casting again, this time within his sight; he saw runes forming in the air as their spell flickered into being, too rapidly for him to modify, as he had done with Tibeus. It was still slow enough for him to *read*, though.

They'd accounted for what Misa could do and were in the process of casting [**Rapid Firebolt**]. Fun.

For the first time in a while, Vex reached for the [**Chromaturgist**] skills he'd been given—the discovery of glyphs had distracted him and led him down a new path, but he wasn't ready for Wisfield or Ashion to know what he had to work with.

A [**Rapid Firebolt**] spell was very similar to a [**Fireball**], with some minor differences. Vex had studied it before, because it was one of the standard arsenal of spells used by Elyran enforcement. He was almost glad he'd been made to study it.

One, the spell was a chain cast; interrupting it was pointless, unless you killed every single one of your opponents before the spell finished casting. The first rune triggered the second one, and then the third, and so on, without any input from the caster. It was a fairly clever mechanism he'd built into a number of multi-rune spells, though he rarely had the cause or the mana to waste on them.

Two, the first few runes in the spell created a single normal [**Fireball**], albeit heavily overcharged; runes that were later in the cast acted to split that single [**Fireball**] into several smaller ones, using a lesser-known artifact of magic—every piece of a completed spell was in itself the whole of the spell. It was a clever sort of way to circumvent spells that took time to cast. [**Rapid Firebolt**] created only one [**Fireball**] rather than several dozen, and skimmed pieces off that first [**Fireball**] in order to create all the others.

It saved a few seconds, and seconds mattered.

Three, the [**Fireball**]s that were created afterward needed time to be charged with mana—and that was where Vex had the time to interfere. Their downfall here was trying to create something powerful enough to take them all out at once. He needed one effect to break this spell.

[**Manaburn**].

But there was something odd about the mana that was going into this spell—Fire-aspect mana was in there, so why were the flames flickering *blue?*

... Vex made sure his counterspell didn't completely drain one of the [**Fireball**]s. Purple flickered into the threads of his own magic, darting out like snakes; each one struck unerringly into a still-forming [**Fireball**] and burned the mana out of it, making it dissipate like smoke. He drained only enough power out of the last [**Fireball**] to make sure that it wouldn't explode all over multiple blocks of the district.

"Dodge!" he called as the spell completed, and to their credit, none of his friends questioned it; they got out of the way of that remaining [**Fireball**] instead, letting the flames splash ghost-blue on the ground.

For a moment, the two groups stood at an impasse. Their assailants stared them down—Vex was tense, waiting for a follow-up, but none came. The only thing that filled the air was the crackling of that flame, burning away at nothing on the ground, fueled by raw mana.

"Who are you, and why are you attacking us?" Sev asked, his voice calm.

Derivan spoke behind him, his voice filtered by the Relay charm, directed toward Vex. "I do not think that the status effect on them has anything to do with emotional suppression at all," he said. "Nor are their emotions suppressed. I believe these are not Julia enforcers."

"We are from House Julia," one of the mages called back, contradicting Derivan directly, not that he would know. "You will surrender. Or not. It's up to you, really."

"Doesn't exactly seem like you're winning," Sev said. "Why exactly are we being... what is this? Arrested?"

"You're undermining the Houses," he said. Vex frowned; the voice was... familiar. Different from what he remembered, but only slightly. Maybe his initial assumption had been wrong. If House Ashion *was* involved...

Derivan had said that these enforcers weren't emotion-suppressed as far as he could tell. They wore the colors of Julia, but they didn't speak like their enforcers usually did.

So this was a different group, pretending to be House Julia.

"We're giving out food," Vex said. "I don't see why the nobility should give a damn what we do."

The main speaker on the other side paused, as though surprised, and that was when Vex *knew* it was who he thought it was. Helix stared at him through the hood he wore, his eyes hidden in the shadows generated by his cloak.

Literally generated, by the enchantments woven into the fabric. He probably should have noticed that before; that sort of thing was an Ashion staple.

"You're making us look bad," Helix said, his voice light and casual. "We can't have that. And you're an unauthorized distributor of food. These supplies haven't been checked through any official channels. We're going to have to confiscate it."

Vex stared, then sighed. "Why are you really here, Helix?"

Helix had the gall to *pout* at him. It was more audible through his voice than anything, since the shadows were still shrouding his face, but he could tell when Helix was pouting. "I just wanted to see how my little brother was doing."

"*Throwing a fireball* is not an appropriate way of doing that," Vex said, deadpan. "Even if it's not an actual [**Fireball**]." Misa stared between the two of them in shock, and Sev had one eyebrow slightly raised; Derivan, as he usually did, didn't react much at all.

He *did* step up beside Vex, taking hold of one hand and squeezing it protectively.

Vex didn't protest. He squeezed Derivan's hand back, almost defiantly, and stared straight ahead as if daring his brother to say anything about it. To his credit, Helix only stared for a second before grinning.

"*Damn,*" he said, his words a half-whistle. "Lotta time for things to change in a year, huh?"

"Helix," Vex said, sighing.

"Okay, okay," Helix said; he glanced around quickly to make sure that no one was watching them—and no one *was* watching them; the whole place had been cleared out by that initial fireball, real or not, and Vex wondered if that wasn't pretty much the point—then he pressed a hand against the ground, and a pulse of mana rang out from him.

A large, *dense* cloud of mana. Helix had been the one in their family that was able to endure the mana-enhancement treatments the most, and mostly hadn't come out worse off for it; golden child of the family he was not, though. He didn't care for magical study as much as Vex had. Karix had always treated him a little bit like a disappointment, and some of that bitterness hung around him like a dark cloud...

...not now, though. Vex didn't see that around him now. Whatever he'd done in the year and a half Vex had been away, he'd apparently managed to find some kind of purpose in it.

The mana was tuned to illusion. Vex didn't react to it, letting it pass over him harmlessly; he saw Misa gearing up to block it, but when nothing happened, she seemed to relax a bit. Around them, the fire seemed to glow a little bit brighter—and then in the edges of his [**Mana Sight**] Vex saw an illusion playing, one in which their fight continued.

"Ghostfire," Vex said, mouthing the word. "Illusion-enhancing ghostfire."

"Quite right," Helix said; he bounced on his feet, pulling the hood off his head and revealing a handsome older lizardkin, somewhere in his late twenties. "Can you believe I managed to figure out *ghostfire*?"

"Not too long ago you could only do big [**Fireball**]s," Vex said, chuckling lightly. "But why are you here? Why all this deception?"

"We need to put on some kind of show," Helix said, turning serious. "Julia did actually send enforcers after you; they just didn't know *you* were there, because the Houses don't like talking to one another. Otherwise they probably wouldn't have allowed me to volunteer."

"Are you actually . . ." Vex peered closely at his brother.

"Yes and no," Helix said, shrugging his shoulders. "We figured out a way to block their emotion-suppression thing, if that's what you're worried about, but it kind of does the opposite—enhances emotional reaction."

"Ah, *that's* why you're more in tune with yourself," Vex said, only half-joking.

"It really is." Helix was silent for a moment. "And if we had more time . . . there's a lot I'd want to talk to you about. But we don't. This illusion isn't going to last forever. Is Riss . . . ?"

"Riss is doing good." Vex smiled a small smile, glad that his brother had changed at least a *little*; whatever he was doing here said a lot. "You're with the—"

"Shh." Helix put a finger to his lips. "I don't trust my magic that much. Look, we're going to take over the food distribution, okay?"

"Why?"

"The nobles don't want to look bad." Helix shrugged. "And this makes them look bad, random adventurers going around and giving away food, when it's supposed to be their job."

"And you're going to help them look . . . good?" Vex raised an eyebrow.

"No." Helix laughed at the idea. "When I say *we*, I don't mean the nobles. You know exactly what I mean. We're still gonna make them look bad. But we're going to do it *intentionally*."

"Aren't you one of the nobles, boss?" one of Helix's men asked him, tentatively.

"What? No! Of course not," Helix said, pressing a hand to his chest in mock offense. "I'm very far from noble. You should know that."

"You shouldn't say that out loud, boss," the same man said.

"Relax, we're under illusion," Helix said, waving a hand and ignoring the fact that he'd only just said he didn't particularly trust his own illusions.

That was enough to tell Vex how much his brother had changed, really. When he'd left, Helix had still been questioning his place in the family; the sheer amount of mana he had wasn't exactly enough to elevate him to any special status when his spells didn't match up to the mana he had. He had the same basic spell list as a lot of the family did, but the spells were simply less effective in his hands unless he charged them with more mana; it was an artifact of runic casting. Understanding still mattered.

Like with glyphs, actually. There was a thought there that Vex needed to dig in to a bit more, when he had the time.

The Helix now seemed surer of his place in the world and spoke with a confidence that was real—not the fake, conjured arrogance he pretended at only a year and a half before.

A year and a half was a lot of time, it seemed.

Helix turned his attention to Vex. "We just need to put on a show. We need you guys to lose this fight—or at least to look like you lost this fight—so that the nobles don't keep looking for you once you enter the dungeon. Dad wants you back in the family, and we're doing our best to stall him—"

"He hasn't really changed, huh?" Vex said, and Helix sighed.

"Most of us have," Helix said tentatively. "You leaving... put a lot of things in perspective for us. But Mom and Dad stuck to their guns more than ever. I think they think that if you're right, then they're going to have to own up to what they did to us. And everything Dad's parents did to them. Mom's mostly trying to stay out of it, but it's not great."

"I wish you'd said something," Vex said quietly. "I just thought you all agreed with Dad."

"We were going to?" Helix hesitated. "But we were worried it'd just look like a ploy or something. And, uh, I'd love to have more of this conversation now, but that illusion isn't going to last forever, so let's do it after we get you into the dungeon?"

"You're ready?" Misa asked. "This is it?"

"Yeah," Helix said. "We would've given you more warning, but, uh, we wanted a realistic reaction before we got the illusions going. Sorry. We wouldn't have hurt you, probably."

Misa glowered at the *probably*, and Helix let out an awkward laugh. "We trusted in your capabilities?"

Sev grimaced a little bit. "Not *really* a good approach, but points for drama," he said.

"My brother would've spotted a fireball like that coming a mile away," Helix said, just a touch defensively, "... but maybe that wasn't the best plan."

"I'm more ashamed I didn't realize it was *you*," Vex said.

"Anyway." Helix paused. "This is the part where I ask all of you to climb into a cart so we can get you into the dungeon."

Sev blinked. "Uh."

"Look I didn't realize how this would come off until I had to say it," Helix said. "It'll be fine! Trust me!"

"We tried to tell him it was a bad idea," the same man spoke up from behind Helix, who threw up his hands.

"Everyone's a critic," he complained. "Just get in the cart! The cart's fine! It's totally safe and not a trap!"

"Not helping my confidence here," Sev said.

"Honestly, *I'm* starting to get worried, and I'm in on the plan," one of his men said.

"You should probably get in the cart before Helix makes it worse," another one added.

"*I'm not making it worse!*"

Sev sighed. "Okay, we're going to need like five contingency plans for this," he said. "Give us three minutes."

CHAPTER 56

WAGON

If there was anywhere Vex hadn't expected to be about an hour from when that battle started, it was being carted around the city in a wagon. Particularly not in a small crawlspace underneath the floorboards of a wagon, lit only by illusion-enhancing ghostfire.

All four of them were being carted around, in fact, piled together in the same cart. A tiny bit of spatial magic gave them just a bit more space than they appeared to have, but it was really only enough to make them *fit*, not quite enough to make them fit comfortably.

Probably because Derivan's armor was sort of stabby.

Which was a problem they were trying to solve, given they had nothing else to do while pressed together in the wagon. The tarp above them flapped about in the wind, an unpleasant reminder of exactly how flimsy this whole plan appeared.

Hopefully Helix had gotten... a little better at planning since the last time they'd spoken. He'd managed to grow in every other way that was important.

"How much more mana do you need?" Vex asked. He was tucked up against Derivan's chest plate, trying desperately to keep his tone as neutral as possible—a task that he was spectacularly failing at, so he was mostly just trying not to speak. He'd gained confidence lately! But not enough confidence for being pressed against Derivan.

It wasn't that he was being *shy*. He'd already spoken to Derivan about his feelings. But these particular circumstances—

Anyway.

"About fifteen hundred," Derivan said. His Slime stat was up to forty-nine; another level would bring it to fifty, which would *hopefully* come with something that would help him mold his armor into something a little more malleable. Golden Geas hadn't given him any bonus passives, but passives with stat-milestone requirements weren't a sure thing anyway. They were a function of your accomplishments and understanding more than they were a fixed thing awarded on reaching a milestone. If you accomplished something stat-related and had enough points in that stat . . . you would be awarded a passive.

The hope here was that Derivan already had what he needed for a passive except for the stat requirement, and that the passive he got would be something Slime-related and help Derivan dull his spikes somewhat. It was a dim hope, but it wasn't like they had anything else to do.

Vex nodded in response to Derivan. He tried to duck his head, and mostly only succeeded in butting his snout against the armor's chest plate, causing a dull *bong* to resound in their limited space.

. . . It was probably a good thing there was a soundproofing enchantment built in with the spatial one.

"I feel like I should tell you guys to get a room," Misa said, her back pressed up against the other side of the wagon.

"That's not exactly practical right now," Sev said. His back was pressed against Vex's—awkward, considering Vex had a tail that was taking up more space than either of them wanted—and he was stuck staring at the side of the wagon.

"Shut up, guys," Vex grumbled.

More time passed in silence—none of them really wanted to strain the enchantment on the cart. Derivan's mana slowly ticked up toward the next inevitable stat point. Part of Vex was jealous. The process had so many similarities to what had been done to *him*, except . . . Derivan didn't feel any pain. Maybe it was because he had the stat, and the Ashion family was forcing the issue.

Whatever the case was, Derivan's stat tipped over into fifty, and something *changed*. For one thing, Derivan was suddenly a lot more comfortable to press against.

"Whoa," Misa said.

"Did something happen?" Sev asked. "I can't see anything. I've been counting the grains in the wood for the past three days."

"Sev, it's been thirty minutes."

"Three days."

"Do I need to be worried about time magic?" Vex paused, distracted, and then refocused. "Wait, no. Deri, you're . . . soft. Did you—?"

"I have received a passive bonus," Derivan said; there was a touch of wonder in his voice. He flicked out a box to them, and Vex focused quickly on it, ignoring Sev squawking in indignation as the box presumably interfered with his grain-counting.

> **[Slime Adjacence] [Passive]**
> You are partially Slime. +50% pliability when choosing to be pliable. +100 units of slime generation per minute when choosing to generate slime. +50% slime-related mana-gathering.
>
> Slime can be used to store mana at 10 mana per unit of slime. Your slime is always a part of you.

Vex blinked. "That's . . . a lot."

"There are so many uses for this," Misa said, her voice vaguely muffled from where her face had sunken slightly into Derivan's back. "Do you think actual slimes have a similar ability?"

"They do, actually," Derivan said. He brought an arm around Vex, seeming to take a moment to absorb the feeling of having the lizardkin pressed against him; for a moment, he was silent, and then he spoke again. "This is . . . very different from what I am used to feeling."

"Your armor is *soft*," Vex said, wonderingly.

"It's kinda weird," Misa said, though there was a teasing smile in her voice.

"I feel like I'm missing out here," Sev called, his face still pressed against the side of the wagon.

"I liked you anyway," Vex confessed, a little bit of his shyness creeping back up on him. "But this is . . . nice? It's nice."

"It is," Derivan agreed. "And I cannot hurt you with my armor anymore, which I am pleased by."

"As long as you choose to be 'pliable,'" Misa laughed.

"This is really interesting, though," Vex said. "Can you generate some slime? I feel almost like we should do some testing . . . I mean, not now. But now I feel like we should've done more testing on slimes in general. There's an obvious link between slimes and mana."

"I can try," Derivan offered; there wasn't a lot of space for him to hold up a hand, but he managed to wriggle an arm free from underneath Vex anyway, and he held it up where there was space. A moment of concentration followed, his light-purple eyes flickering off as he focused—

—and a small wellspring of lilac slime began to emerge from his armor, waving about in the air.

". . . That's pretty cool." Vex watched the mini-figurine for a second; the shape of it was slowly changing, resolving itself into something shaped almost like *him*, down to his frills and a tiny tail. It was a fantastic display of fine control and the instantaneous understanding granted by the system.

It was also very cute.

[**Advanced Mana Sight**] offered him only a little more in terms of understanding; there *was* mana in the slime by default, and it was mana that was pre-aligned with an aspect he hadn't seen before. It rang with a certain familiarity, and he spent a moment trying to chase that familiarity down, but the manner of it eluded him; he only knew that it was familiar.

Potential infolock. He reached to note it down in his notebook—

—Well, no, he couldn't reach his notebook.

"Um." Vex paused, trying to figure out how to phrase his request. "Deri, can you get my notebook for me? I can't reach."

"Of course." The little mini-Vex standing in Derivan's palm shivered for a moment, then abruptly extended into a tendril of goo, slithering down toward Vex's tailpouch; the lizardkin kept himself as still as possible as it slowly pulled the clasp open, then the bag itself, and managed to navigate to his notebook.

"You're really good with that thing," Vex noted.

"It is . . . rather intuitive to use." Derivan brought Vex's notebook up to his hands, and gently placed it there; the tendril retracting didn't leave even a trace of lilac slime on the notebook. "Perhaps because the stat is already so high to begin with."

"It's not too weird, if you think about it," Misa said. "Some higher-level slimes can do that kind of thing."

"I still can't see any of what you're talking about," Sev complained.

"Well, you agreed to this plan, so deal with it."

"Bah."

"Shhh." Vex's tone was lightly reprimanding as Derivan handed him his quill and he made a quick note: the familiarity of Slime-aspect mana. He had a suspicion about it, even. Slime was related to mana capacity, and the whole Principle of House Ashion was *about* mana capacity. Maybe there was more to mana than just system stats . . .

The cart they were in shook to a stop, and there was the sound of a tarp being pulled off; Vex stilled himself, trying not to move, even though he knew it wouldn't make a difference. They wouldn't see anything even if he did. He'd tested the illusion spells on the wagon himself, as one of their many contingencies. He felt his anxiety spike a bit anyway, not quite used to being trapped in a small space and unable to act.

Outside, they heard the sounds of a soldier discussing something with Helix, who had schooled his voice into something monotone and emotionless.

Vex had to admit, Helix was surprisingly good at acting now. It wasn't something he would have expected of his brother.

It didn't take long before the cart began to move again, and Vex sighed a small sigh of relief; the soldier hadn't noticed anything untoward.

"Worried about the illusion spell?" Sev asked.

"I'm just worried we're going to have to fight." Vex's voice was softer than it had to be, and he saw Derivan looking down at him in concern. "My family's... more involved than I thought they would be. If a fight breaks out..."

"You're worried someone's going to get hurt," Misa said. She sounded sympathetic, and a hand reached over Derivan to pat him on the head; Vex, not expecting it, almost flinched away from the touch before he realized that the hand descending on him was just Misa's.

"I am," the lizardkin admitted.

"I believe it will not come to that," Derivan said. "Or I suppose I hope that it will not."

"It'll help once we're in the dungeon," Misa offered. "Right now our presence here is... disruptive? So that kinda fuckin' sucks. But without us—"

"There's still going to be a fight," Sev said, his voice slightly muffled from echoing against the wall. "They've been gearing up for one. The food problem is just pushing existing tensions over the edge; they're not coming back from this without some kind of rebellion, which means a fight, which means that some people are going to get hurt. I could *heal* them—"

"Sev," Misa said, a note of warning in her voice. Vex only made a small sound of hurt, and Sev sighed.

"... It's probably a good thing I have you guys," he said after a moment.

"Damn straight," Misa said. She squirmed a bit, flailing an arm, and then spoke again, this time *her* voice slightly muffled against Derivan's armor. "Pretend I just punched you in the shoulder. I can't reach."

"Agh," Sev said, his voice completely deadpan. "I think you broke my shoulder."

"... Thanks, Sev."

"You're welcome."

Vex smiled a little bit at the banter, though his attention was still focused on the idea of the *Slime stat*; Derivan was still playing around with a single tendril of the stuff, making it dance and coil around in his hand with wonder. Every so often he would make it take the shape of a glyph, forming that glyph almost instantaneously—and Vex could see tiny particles of mana begin to move toward that glyph almost the moment it formed.

It looked almost like Teque's form of casting—like the way they could just carve glyphs into objects and have the mana come to it, instead of having to use [**Mana Manipulation**] to start the effect. They didn't have an active mana river flowing through the world, but mana had acted on its own before, on the painting of the [**Starry Night**] skill, primarily, but also whenever it moved away from the activation of a rune, or when it gathered around the residents of Fendal as they had their agency taken away . . .

Vex wondered, briefly, if the mana had been trying to *warn* them.

Every time, Derivan changed the shape of the slime before the mana finished trying to gather into the glyph and cast a spell—probably because he saw the same mana-gathering phenomenon and wanted to avoid bringing attention to them.

"You'll be able to cast glyph spells faster now," Vex noted.

"I believe so," Derivan agreed. "Though I am unsure if casting it in such a way will change the effect . . . Perhaps we can find out when we are in the bonus room. We will have time to examine things then."

"I need to start testing out these glyph combinations." Vex paused. "Or, well, I told Ingress about the glyphs already, and it sounds like they're going to explore a lot of the basic combinations. We can let the rebels focus on the majority of the basic combinations. I want to discover more *glyphs* and figure out combinations for those."

"We do not yet have a way to discover new glyphs," Derivan noted.

"Anton didn't have much for us there," Vex sighed. "I tried asking, but they haven't discovered a *new* glyph in ages, and all the old ones are recorded in their libraries. If I just had a way to find new ones . . ."

As he spoke, the wagon rolled to a stop. Vex heard the sound of the tarp getting yanked off—and then the floorboards being pulled open, yanked out of place rather frantically. Helix's face appeared above them, vaguely worried, though his expression schooled itself into one of relief when he saw them.

"Oh, good," he said. "I was worried you fell through the bottom."

". . . You were worried we what?" Vex blinked, staring at his brother.

"I forgot to check the bottom of the wagon," Helix said. "It's fine! Don't worry about it. We're all safe. And we're here now, too! Look."

Vex decided not to question it.

Instead, he stared out at the familiar sight of the Elyran dungeon. He'd been here before, though he'd never been *inside*.

Now it seemed he would be—sooner than he'd expected, even.

CHAPTER 57

XOTHOK–WHO YOU WERE

This time, when his memories were once more torn away from him, Xothok was awake to see it.

In a way, it helped that he was choosing for this to happen. The Guildmaster was standing too close for comfort, for someone of her level, one hand hovering just an inch in front of his chest; Xothok was struck once again by that odd impression of familiarity, like this was someone he had once known. Not something intentional on the Guildmaster's behalf, he was pretty sure; she seemed to be a rather private person. Nor was it that he'd simply interacted with the Guildmaster before.

Had he known the Guildmaster before she'd taken on the role?

That train of thought was torn immediately asunder by a sharp pain in his skull; Xothok grimaced, nearly collapsing forward, and only Max catching him and helping him up prevented him from smacking snout-first into the corridor.

"I didn't need your help," Xothok grumbled. Max just looked at him; she didn't say anything. She didn't even give him one of her signature grins.

"Are you okay?" she asked instead.

"I'm fine."

He really wasn't. He felt empty. He was exactly who he would have been if a multitude of things hadn't happened—if he hadn't been born a noble, if he hadn't pursued the path of astronomy that he had, if he hadn't grown into his own as a leader of a small group of navigators.

There was a bitter sort of knowledge in knowing that without that bit of help from his birth, he would've been *this*. A bandit. A *failed* bandit, even, for all that they'd managed to survive for a little while; that was less than a year out on their own before they'd been captured.

And now that was all he was and ever would be, because the piece of him that had been those things was torn out. That other Xothok was standing in front of him now, as far as he could tell visible only to him. He was a little scrawnier, but he seemed healthier; less gaunt, brighter scales, a kinder smile. He wore strange, flowing garb that touched the ground, decorated with long stretches of cloth colored like the night sky, with tiny pinpricks of white and lines drawn between them.

Xothok hated him, almost instinctively. Or maybe he just hated what he represented.

"They're constellations," the other Xothok told him, noticing his staring. "Patterns in the stars."

"Do they mean anything?"

"Only historically." Other-Xothok, as Xothok now decided to call him, chuckled. "And I mean that very literally. The stars used to sing, you know."

"... How would we hear them?" Xothok was vaguely aware of both Max and the Guildmaster staring at him, curious; neither of them said a word, though.

"Through the mana." Other-Xothok smiled at him. "They sang about everything that had happened and sometimes about things that would happen. They were archives of history in the mana. We could visit them, even. There was so much to learn—that was what our House did. We went to visit those archives and drew what knowledge we could from them."

"... Fuck."

Xothok had never cared much for history—or at least, this version of him hadn't. But even he understood the implications. Other-Xothok spoke of the stars being a repository of information, and the fact that they were all gone reflected the spotty nature of their own history...

There was a more pertinent detail there.

The stars had *changed*.

They once sang through the mana, and at some point they had become nothing more than balls of burning fire; Xothok remembered how Derivan's spell had looked. That was presumably the version of stars that came about after they had started burning. Now Xothok imagined libraries in the sky, filled with the history of the universe, slowly burning out.

"We have just one left," Other-Xothok said, pointing up. It was more a symbolic gesture than anything; the only thing above them was the wood of the Guild's ceilings, but Xothok understood what he meant. Other-Xothok smiled again, this time a small, sad smile. "One more archive, burning in the sky."

Xothok might not have given a shit about their history, but he didn't want it *gone*. Not like this.

The Guildmaster saw the look on Xothok's face, clearly, because she seemed almost immediately concerned. "If there's anything important we should know," she said, "you'll have to be careful about how you tell us. You're still under infolock—it's just that you can bypass it while you're talking to your echo. And you'll need to remember that you *can* talk to your echo—the infolock is going to make you try to forget."

Xothok nodded stiffly, not trusting himself to speak quite yet. This was far above his pay grade—

—*but it hasn't always been,* a small part of him whispered. He saw proof of that right in front of him, in this gentler version of himself that once navigated the stars.

"I'm not sure what I can tell you," Xothok said. "But I think I'd like to join the Guild."

—⚏—

The decision had been an impulsive one, but Xothok didn't regret it. Not even when his men yelled and shouted at him, though some of them seemed quietly relieved; they had been afraid he would ask them to join him as he left, to return to a life of banditry or what have you. Those were the ones that had grown comfortable here, that secretly wanted to try this new life.

The ones that yelled and shouted—those were the men under Byrrhon, mostly. They led the charge by far, with Byrrhon himself being the loudest and angriest among them.

"Coward!" Byrrhon was hissing at him. Xothok watched, trying to keep himself impartial. There was a time when he would have lost his temper and slammed the man into a wall, demanding subservience, but in light of everything else he'd learned . . . no. All these problems seemed too *small* in comparison.

"He used to be one of us, too," his echo observed, looking at Byrrhon with no small amount of pity. "Not one of the most talented, but maybe one of the most dedicated."

Xothok swallowed his questions; it would be strange to ask them now, in full view of all his men. Other-Xothok seemed to sense what he wanted to ask perfectly well, though.

"You aren't all related by blood," he said. "The Principle our House was based on was in the method we used to get to the stars; we were quite happy to let anyone who was interested join, as long as they shared anything they found."

"Are you fucking listening to me?!" Byrrhon spat.

"No," Xothok replied bluntly; he ignored the outraged sputtering that followed, turning his attention instead to the way the rest of his men were looking at him. Half of them looked genuinely hopeful, and the other half looked like they were more worried about what was happening with Byrrhon—

Xothok faintly registered that Byrrhon was throwing a punch.

Other-Xothok moved before he did, surprisingly. He moved before Byrrhon even did, but as a creature of perception, he couldn't do anything to block or prevent that punch—he just showed Xothok what to do.

Traditionally, Xothok handled fighting by taking the blows, rolling into them with his body, and dishing them back; the way Other-Xothok fought was completely different. He slid between them like he saw them before they even happened, and Xothok found that while he didn't himself remember how fighting like this worked—

—his body did.

> **Skill Acquired: [Martial Navigation]**

Byrrhon couldn't hit him.

He *tried*. The man was getting increasingly furious, and it occurred to Xothok that perhaps he should have just *let* him have a blow; maybe Byrrhon would calm down if he could get a good hit in and work off that anger. But the other man had invested heavily into Strength, too, and regardless of health, taking that blow would *hurt*.

"Byrrhon," Xothok tried. "Listen to me."

"I'm fucking *done* listening to you," Byrrhon snarled. "I've been listening to you, and look where that's got us!"

"It's gotten us a place to sleep and food to eat," Xothok said calmly; he saw a few of his men agreeing with nervous nods, though all out of Byrrhon's sight.

"It's got us *workin' with the enemy*," Byrrhon said.

... That was really the way he thought, wasn't it? This version of him, anyway. Now that he thought about it, he'd only ever seen Byrrhon *angry*; he had no memory of the man being happy, except when he was taking joy in fucking someone up. The man was a sadist—

—he was a danger. A liability.

"And?" Xothok asked, just to test him. "We get to eat now. We're not sleeping in the grass. We aren't constantly hungry and waiting for a traveler to pass by."

"We're not *us* anymore."

"And you think 'us' is *starving*? Sleeping on awful, uncomfortable dirt beds? Always afraid of fucking *dying*? Some people in the Guild fucked us over, but clearly that was just the Elyran branch, and we know exactly how Elyra treats just about anyone that doesn't fit into their idea of *value*."

"It made us *us*," Byrrhon said, but he sounded like he couldn't further defend his position; even his own men were starting to look disheartened. "It made us stronger."

"Starving did not make us stronger." It wasn't even Xothok that answered; it was Two. Xothok blinked; he hadn't expected Two of all people to speak up. The man had been mostly taciturn for as long as Xothok could remember. "It just made us tired and weak."

Byrrhon just scoffed. "Cowards," he said again, but without the same heat in his voice; there was instead a resigned anger as he glared around at all of the crew. Xothok didn't think he was any less angry—he just wasn't willing to take all of them on at the same time. "You're all just cowards."

He stalked out of the room.

Morkar frowned after him. "If he's not gotten better 'bout bein' here by now..."

"He's not going to," Xothok said, finishing the thought. He glared at the door Byrrhon had left through for a moment, like he could summon the man back by glaring hard enough—but then he shook his head.

"Give him time," someone suggested.

"He's had time," Xothok said. "It's not going to help. But keep an eye on him. He's going to try something."

"And what're we gonna do when he does?" one of Byrrhon's own men said—he wore a scowl on his face, but it was a slightly worried sort of scowl.

Xothok shook his head. "Whatever we have to," he said.

Byrrhon was powerful. He was weak to spellcasters but in melee was second only to Xothok; Morkar was almost as good as him but still consistently lost their duels, and even Xothok had a hard time winning consistently.

If it came down to it, though... he could win.

It was telling that even Byrrhon's own men said nothing to this pronouncement.

"That man," Other-Xothok said, pointing to Two and providing a rather convenient distraction. "What's his name?"

"Two," Xothok said, causing Two to look up at him curiously.

"It used to be Twice-In-Starlight," other-Xothok said thoughtfully. "We didn't know where he was from; we thought he might be a planeshifted, but he never really confirmed it. He still doesn't talk much?"

"You don't talk much," Xothok said, both to Two and to his echo. Two inclined his head and shrugged slightly.

"I speak when I have to."

"He was always like that," Other-Xothok said with a small smile. "He spoke the most when it was about the stars. I hope we figure out what's going on."

"I do too," Xothok said softly. He glanced back to where he slept; a lot of the notes he'd left for himself were fading away, getting harder to notice. Even his echo looked more transparent than anything else now.

"You'll be able to call on me whenever you remember," other-Xothok said. "The workaround is a good one, but you still need to trigger it."

"It's a good thing I made a note, then," Xothok said; his gaze lingered on the ink drawing he'd made of the stars. It wasn't fading out of sight like everything else; it stayed solid in his perception. Had he avoided the lock somehow? His men were looking at him a bit strangely, perhaps because he'd been talking to himself, but he ignored them and went to pick up the drawing, then held it up. "Two—do you recognize this?"

Two glanced at the drawing, and his brows furrowed, just slightly. "The sky," he said. "It is . . . familiar. But not."

"Hey, I recognize that too," Morkar said. "What the shit?"

"This has a pull to it," other-Xothok muttered; his copy touched the parchment and seemed to solidify, just a bit. At the same time, the drawing deepened, the ink running into the darker black of the night.

Small gasps rose from his audience, and Xothok's eyes narrowed.

"Seems you've created something special," Other-Xothok said.

"We're joining the Guild," Xothok said to his men. "And I think we have a mission."

They were going to find out what happened to the stars.

CHAPTER 58

ELYRA'S PRIME DUNGEON

Vex knew that a dungeon to some small degree reflected the space around it when it first came into being. The Prime Dungeons, though—the dungeons that were the core of every Kingdom and powered most of their supply of mana crystals—those were the exceptions to the rule. Over time, they'd grown to reflect the Kingdoms they belonged to, though those Kingdoms had been built long after those dungeons appeared.

The dungeon that now stood before them was one example of three. Vex had no idea what the Anderstahl dungeon looked like; the Elyran one was the only Prime he'd had the opportunity to study. And even then, in the year and a half he'd been gone, it had changed.

The major details were the same. The dungeon was still underground, located in a crater in the center of a massive cavern. That crater was host to what was effectively an enormous chandelier that hung from the ceiling. A long time ago, that had been nothing but rocks and stalactites; the original dungeon had been one of earth and stone, and as the Kingdom of Elyra had grown...

It had turned into *crystal*. In some ways it seemed like a dedication to wealth and opulence, which caused no small amount of debate amongst scholars; in other ways, it simply looked like a reflection of Elyran society itself. The upper tiers of the chandelier were lit in the colors of the various noble Houses, casting multicolored lights onto the rest of the crystal. Crystals on the lower tiers of the chandelier reflected and refracted those upper-tier lights, bouncing light around until it struck the walls of the cavern.

Where it was *different* was the fact that some of the crystals that represented their noble Houses had cracks in them. Some of the crystals that represented the lower tiers of the chandelier had grown. And the thing it all hung on—a long string of indestructible metal—looked considerably thinner than Vex remembered.

Vex couldn't help but notice that the Ashion crystal was cracked nearly all the way through.

"Holy shit," Misa said, whistling. "I didn't think Prime Dungeons looked like this. *Damn*. It's actually kinda beautiful."

"Very deadly, though," Vex noted, trying to ignore what he saw of his own family's crystal. The dungeon wasn't a *predictive* force, he told himself; it was a reflection. And that reflection was ... not inaccurate, the way things were now.

The dungeon wasn't for low-level adventurers. Varil had more or less perfected the art of dungeon-delving, at least for this particular dungeon—they were familiar with almost all the tricks and traps the dungeon had to offer—and even then, they didn't have a complete success rate when it came to dungeon completion. The dungeon would often come up with something *new*, as if in a deliberate attempt to throw them off.

Fortunately, even without the dilation of a bonus room, this dungeon itself dilated time by about three or four times, fluctuating based on ambient mana levels. Which meant they'd at least have the time to be *careful*.

"I'd give you a tour, but I *really* don't have time," Helix said, glancing around nervously. "I think Vex knows everything he needs to get you guys into the dungeon. Try to avoid any delve or research teams you come across. There shouldn't be one scheduled right now—we got you in during a shift swap—but the research guys wander where they shouldn't all the time, and the delvers follow them around, so be careful."

"I'm kind of amazed you got us here at all," Vex said, then paused, giving his brother a hesitant smile. "I'm glad it wasn't a trap. Thanks."

"I wasn't that bad," Helix said. He pulled the wagon around, starting to cart it off back the way he came. "Uh, I mean, maybe I was. Sorry. We should ... catch up sometime."

Vex nodded, and his brother disappeared quickly around the corner. The lizardkin didn't wait before he started clambering toward the chandelier-dungeon; the glittering crystals scattered on the floor made traversing that terrain a challenge, but he picked his way across fairly easily. Derivan had an even easier time of it, where he would have had trouble before. His armor simply molded to the shape of the ground.

Sev and Misa ... tripped a few times. It was fine, probably, even if Misa grumbled a bit.

"Your family has that [**Reinforcement**] buff too, right?" Misa asked him quietly, as they were headed toward the chandelier.

"... Yeah," Vex said. "I've been trying not to think too hard about it. Most of them already bought in to Elyran philosophy in the first place, so I don't think it changed them too much. It might even have helped Helix and the others in the opposite direction. I'm hoping they didn't apply it to Riss."

"They did not," Derivan said. "I did not see evidence of that buff on your father, either, for what that is worth."

"... I was hoping that he *did* have it on him," Vex said quietly. "Would've been nice to have something to blame. I mean, *Helix* changed his mind after I left. The fact that Dad didn't—"

"He's not worth your time, Vex," Misa said. She softened a little bit when she saw the way the lizardkin sagged, and placed a hand on his shoulder. "If he hasn't changed by now, I don't think he's going to. And even if he does, are you actually going to forgive him?"

"I don't know," Vex answered honestly after a short pause. "I've been trying not to think about it."

"Well," Sev said, "you're going to have all the time you need to think about it soon. Because we're here."

The entrance to the Elyran dungeon sat right at the bottom of the massive, ethereal-looking chandelier; it was a small doorway carved into the very tip, a large crystal hanging just an inch off the ground and slowly rotating. Within that crystal was a room that was barely enough to fit four people, though Vex knew from experience that the internal space was much, much larger than it initially appeared. There was some debate about whether that first room simply teleported you to a different space or it was actually engaging extreme spatial compression, but with what he now knew of the system, it was probably yet another Shift.

"I don't see any research teams around," Misa said, glancing around quickly; [**Guard Stance**] flickered quickly over her body, along with a few other skills, as she rotated through the various forms of precognition she had. "Nothing in adjacent timelines, either. I think we're good. Once we go in, it'll close off the dungeon to others, right?"

"Yes," Vex said. "But we need to do it one at a time. The dungeon likes separating people that enter together; if you enter one at a time, there are better odds that you end up in the same place as someone else." He pointed up. "Once we get through the starting room, we'll end up in any one of those spires up there. We can meet up when we head toward the center."

"Any idea where the bonus room is going to be?" Sev asked.

"No," Vex said, then hesitated. "... But if it's anywhere, it's going to be in the Ashion wing."

He pointed to the colors of his House in particular, in one of the southwest spires of the chandelier. The cracks that ran through it were uglier from up close, and he tried not to look too closely at them. Maybe the cracks were there because of his bonus room and not because of anything related to his family.

"We should meet up in the center first, still, though," Vex said. "We'll appear in the lower tier and have to make our way up to the upper tier together, anyway, and then head for the Ashion section."

"What should we expect in the starter room?" Misa asked.

"It's a pretty simple puzzle. The point of it is mostly to make it take longer for people that enter one by one, I think," Vex said, wincing slightly. "It's just a maze. The faster you make your way through it, the faster the rest of us can get in. The time dilation works against it here, so you have more time to try to make your way through."

"But it does mean we have to stay outside the dungeon and wait," Sev noted.

"Yeah," Vex said. "It's not . . . the best plan. Worst case, we can head in together and just deal with being separated."

"We'll try the one-by-one strategy," Sev decided. "If the next shift starts heading over, whoever's left should just jump in. They might be separated from whoever went in before them, but that's better than all of us being separated."

"Then we better get started," Misa said. She stepped forward, through the barrier—

"Shift," Derivan noted with curiosity. He stared at the entrance to the dungeon. "And . . . hmm. I would like to be last, if that is possible. There is an oddity I would like to examine."

—⚜—

Misa, Sev, Vex, then Derivan. That was the order they settled on, mostly because Misa had gone through first before they could fully settle on a plan; otherwise they probably would have sent Sev through first. Vex would stay behind for his knowledge of the dungeon, if it was needed, and Derivan would be last so he could observe all three of them pass through the dungeon barrier.

"It'll flash with light when Misa is done with the starter room," Vex said. "And in the meantime, the dungeon will start summoning monsters outside. We don't have to worry about that, though. There are enchantments to automatically deal with the summons."

"So, entering the dungeon one by one is an intended mechanic?" Sev asked. "It doesn't even guarantee that you end up at the same place."

"*Intended* implies that dungeons have intent to them, and there's obviously some measure of intent, but I don't know if it's something that was explicitly *designed*," Vex said. "I'm of the opinion that most dungeon challenges are emergent. There are basically four possible locations we can end up. If we enter together, we each end up in a different spot. If we enter one by one, the odds that one of us appears in the same spot as someone else is *minimally* twenty-five percent. When people discovered that, the dungeon evolved a counter. It's not necessarily intended, but it *is* cooperative design."

"Which is weird for a dungeon that's trying to kill us," Sev noted.

"I'll give you that, yeah," Vex agreed. He glanced at the dungeon entrance again—there was no trace of Misa, still, though he knew that she was *there*. Derivan was half-paying attention to them and half-paying attention to the dungeon entrance. "How's Misa doing, Deri?"

"I can sort of sense her," Derivan said hesitantly. "Through Shift. But it keeps changing, like she's constantly moving— Oh. She's using her timeline skill."

The entrance room flashed with light; it had taken her all of a minute to get through the maze. Vex was fairly certain that was record-breaking.

"She has left markers for us," Derivan said. "Interesting. I believe Shift is used to *contain* her timelines. The dungeon is attempting to scrub her markers, but it is taking longer, as she has left them across many different versions of herself."

"Then I'll be quick," Sev said. He stepped into the entrance, leaving only Vex and Derivan standing behind; Derivan seemed focused on the dungeon, leaving Vex to stay on the lookout for anything approaching them.

The Elyran dungeon had many, many automated traps and enchantments built into the area, specifically to make this process easier. Vex could already feel the outpouring of mana into their environment as various traps triggered, interrupting monsters as they were created. There was a question there he wanted to answer.

What *were* monsters?

The opportunity he had there was unique. He'd wanted to answer this question for Derivan before, but they hadn't yet come across anything that could answer that question. There, though, was a unique opportunity—the Elyran dungeon didn't just call to monsters like mana nuclei did during crystal collection.

It *created* them.

The monsters that attacked when it was being entered came from spawn points that their researchers had identified and categorized. It was a predictable, reproducible response, and therefore it had been easy to create a defense against them; there'd even been some attempts to study how those monsters were created, though not much progress had ever been made in those studies. There was a gathering of mana around each spawn point but no apparent spell being cast.

Mana and monsters were *related*. But they weren't the same thing. If there had been a spell, then Elyra would have found it long before; if there was simply some way to turn mana into a creature, then Vex felt he would have detected that process in some way.

There was a secret here. What *was* it?

Vex felt more mana gathering, this time somewhere close by.

Slowly, with an application of [**Splash of Mana**] and his paintbrush, he began to draw his Sign.

CHAPTER 59

SEPARATED

######
[Dungeon Spawner]

Mental static ripped through Vex first. He'd forgotten that this was a product of the *system*, and it didn't tap into the same library of knowledge that glyphs were contained in; this was something he should have known. The lizardkin nearly collapsed as sudden pain ripped through his skull, and he only barely heard the alarmed sound that Derivan made as metal arms wrapped around him and caught him just before he would have fallen.

"Shit," Vex said, his own words sounding distant and airy to him; the mana in him was still *reaching*, tapping in to a different library of knowledge. Somehow Vex knew exactly what it was doing—it was trying to tap into the system itself. Wherever the system stored its knowledge, what it was doing—the mana was stretching itself across the wavelengths of reality, trying to tap in to it. He could almost feel the **[Reality Shard]** he kept in his tailpouch dissolving as *something* was drawn out of it.

"Vex." Derivan's voice was worried. "Tell me what is happening."

"Just . . . tried something I shouldn't have." Vex grimaced—his voice still sounded strange, the ringing in his head distorting it with a painful warble. His mana was being drained faster than he'd ever experienced, and *that* added an unpleasant sense of nausea to this whole experience. "But it's working. It's just—taking a second."

"There are people coming." Derivan looked around, still holding Vex steady in his arms. Vex wasn't surprised; the distortions in the mana would have drawn the researchers regardless. He'd been hoping they'd have enough time for all of them to go in one by one.

"Give me . . . a moment." Speaking was still a little more difficult than it should have been, but it was nothing he couldn't handle. Vex felt like he was dragging his mind through water or mud, struggling to stay afloat. "I need this spell to complete. Then just . . . carry us in."

"I do not know if there is time." Vex felt himself being lifted as Derivan got to his feet, staying just a step away from the dungeon entrance; his boyfriend kept glancing around, presumably using mana sense to find the researchers. Vex himself couldn't use his mana sense in this state, and his vision was blurry. He didn't *see* anyone nearby. He *did* see the entrance room flash with light, which was good. Sev had made it through. That technically meant it was his turn. "But I will give you as much time as I can."

"Good . . . good." Vex blinked a few times, trying to clear up his vision—not that it helped. His gaze flickered a bit as mana poured through him and into his Sign, going dark in brief increments; he was almost worried he was going to pass out, and clung to consciousness as closely as he could.

The spell would complete, as long as he stayed conscious. One of his hands found Derivan's, and he gripped it for comfort, trying to focus and steady his mind—

Something *clicked*. Like the mana had found the key to an old, forgotten lock.

[Dungeon Spawner]
Not all memories are desired, and not everything that is forgotten loses its mark on the world.
When something is erased, an echo is created. [Dungeon Spawner]s reach into those echoes, pulling into existence whole-cloth something that has been forgotten. These echoes are never quite complete and are largely a mere mockery of the creatures they once were.
[Dungeon Spawner]s are one type of spawner of many. Different spawners reach into different sorts of echoes; the creatures they bring in to being are always a reflection of something that *was*, but not always hostile, and not always angry. Dungeon-spawned remain connected to their host dungeon and act as outlets for the waste products created by a dungeon during its run.

Vex's only thought was *What does a dungeon do, then?* as the last of his mana drained out of him. He felt himself slipping out of consciousness—and he felt Derivan tighten his grip on his body and *move*. There was a sharp jostle, like they'd been attacked, or maybe Derivan had simply leapt into the dungeon entrance.

Then the strange sensation of *entering a dungeon* hit him, and though the effect was mild, it was the last thing his mind could take; he felt himself slipping into blessed unconsciousness.

—ɯ—

Derivan was relatively certain that the way Vex explained it, he should have appeared in the entrance room with Vex. What was *supposed* to happen was that they would appear in the maze and make their way through it together; once they got through the maze, they would each appear in one of the designated starting points in the dungeon.

This was not what happened.

Derivan was also relatively certain that what *had* happened was not part of the normal function of the dungeon—he could feel, through Shift and Patch both, the way the dungeon reacted as he entered. Vex had entered the dungeon a split second before him, and the moment his tail made contact with the dungeon barrier, the dungeon had reacted; the system descended on Vex, and something *Shifted* him away, in a way that was different from how Sev or Misa had been Shifted.

His reflex had been to hammer at the descending system with Patch. He'd even tried. But whatever this mechanism was, it was far larger than he was; his grip slipped off it like a glancing blow, and Vex was snatched away.

The rest of his momentum carried him into the dungeon before he could hesitate and step back, which was probably for the best. The teams that were rushing toward them seemed larger than standard research teams; an optimistic guess would be that it was just a research team *and* a delve team, and the less-optimistic guess would be that they had found Helix or that Helix had betrayed them.

But it was too late to stop him.

A moment later, Derivan found himself in the maze Vex had mentioned. Towering walls of crystal stood before him, each glittering internally with light; the design of it all reminded him of the extravagance of the dungeon design itself.

"I wonder if it has always been like this," Derivan muttered to himself. Then he shook his head—that was not his primary concern. His primary concern was Vex.

And, secondary to that, was what he had noticed as he'd stepped through the dungeon entrance and Shifted.

First, he opened his system interface and crafted a message to send off to the party. [**Vex attempted to use his glyph just before we went into the** dungeon,] he typed and sent. He tried to keep his worry out of his words. [**He collapsed, and I grabbed him and brought him in. The dungeon took him away as he entered. I do not know where he is.**]

[**Shit,**] Misa sent back almost immediately. [**I'm not with Sev either. You've got 50/50 odds on joining one of us. Vex isn't with me.**]

[**Or with me,**] Sev sent. [**What are the odds he landed at a normal starting point?**]

[**None,**] Derivan answered; he could sense the mechanism that "chose" a starting location for them, and while it was just as large and immutable as the one that targeted Vex had been, it was a very different mechanism that hadn't so much as moved. [**I believe Vex is most likely at the Ashion point of the dungeon, where he suspected his bonus room would be.**]

[**That makes as much sense as anything,**] Sev commented. [**Okay, if Vex is missing, we need to hurry. And Vex, if you see this, please let us know if you're okay as soon as you can.**]

[**Please,**] Derivan added. It was an unnecessary addition, but something compelled him to add it.

Vex was . . . fine. The party interface showed them his health, and Vex was *fine*; he wasn't conscious yet, probably, or he would have sent them a reply. But he hadn't been drained of health or forcibly kicked from the party, and so they knew he was alive.

But they were in a dungeon. Even if he was fine for now, there was every chance he wouldn't stay that way.

Derivan began to race through the maze.

Fortunately for him, he'd spent a good chunk of the time waiting for Sev and Misa examining the maze through Shift; the stat wasn't exactly the same as having actual sight, but he could sense the presence of the maze as a whole, and he could vaguely sense what the other two had been doing in the maze. Each time, the maze as a whole had changed slightly, to make it harder for the next person— but since versions of Misa had left markers on all the nearby wavelengths of reality, no matter what the dungeon changed, Sev still had markers left to follow.

Derivan wasn't so lucky—with Sev through, the dungeon was able to clear out the majority of the markers. But he could see the maze in his head, still; he knew all the nearby variations, and if he was right . . .

. . . the end of the maze was right in front of him.

He ran for it, as quickly as he could; this was the first time in a while he'd truly regretted the loss of his Agility stat. As he ran, his mind turned to what he'd noticed as he stepped into the dungeon and been brought over into this wavelength of reality.

The amount of "distance"—for lack of a better word—that he could sense through Shift had been slowly increasing, but for the most part, examining something with that sense was difficult. The further things got from him, the more everything dissolved into ambient noise. It was hard for him to distinguish one wavelength from another, stepped too far away from him.

When Misa stepped into the dungeon, though—and when Sev had stepped in—he'd been able to sense the ripples they sent through the dungeon's particular wavelength of reality.

And that had struck him in particular, because if his spatial sense was correct, the Shifted plane the dungeon existed on spread across all of the main Kingdom of Elyra. Not all of its territories—it didn't include Fendal, or the patch of land that Emily lived on, or anything like that—but the city they'd just been in? It matched the borders almost exactly.

It matched the strange chill he'd felt when crossing into the city, too. It was the same chill he'd felt when they crossed territories toward Fendal, and there had been one more when heading toward Emily...

The false dungeon created by Misa's bonus room had a reality anchor marked by a letter-number combination. The error message in Fendal had listed a letter-number combination, too, except that letter-number combination had clearly been referring to Fendal and the area surrounding it. So those letter-number combinations referenced... zones?

And every zone had a dungeon.

Derivan felt like he was starting to get an idea of what dungeons were—what reality anchors were. If every dungeon had a reality anchor, and one dungeon was present in every zone... if running a dungeon helped to stabilize reality anchors, and reality anchors stabilized *existence*—which was certainly part of what they did, evidenced by the return of Misa's village and family...

Derivan had a thought.

The assumption for a long time had been that the expansion of the wild dungeons on the edges of their continent had stopped, largely held in check by the remaining population of the three Kingdoms. Vex had explained to him that every skill that measured the size of those wild zones returned a result that said they were roughly the same size. But if the outer edges were also being lost entirely, dissolving into the abyss?

Then the continent as a whole might still be shrinking.

Derivan reached that thought right as he reached the end of the maze, and he plunged through the light there. He felt the dungeon's mechanisms reaching for him and grabbing him, spinning an invisible wheel to choose where he would go.

He reacted more on instinct than anything else. The wheel was about to stop, landing him in a third position, away from both Misa and Sev and not at all close to Vex; he reached out with Patch and nudged the needle so that he would appear with Sev. The light picked him up and took him away—

—And he appeared just in time to stop a sword from stabbing Sev through the back. The *clang* of that sword against his armor echoed through the room.

"Holy shit," Sev said, turning around and doing a double-take; the suit of armor that had been sitting quietly in the corner of the room had moved, and only Derivan's sudden presence had stopped that sword from skewering him. "The moment I turn my back... Um. Good timing, Deri."

"You are welcome," Derivan said. He glanced at the door and then sent a message through the system.

[**I am through,**] he said. [**We must find Vex. Let us proceed.**]

[**Way ahead of you, buddy,**] Misa sent back.

CHAPTER 60

HEARTBREAK

Vex woke up leaning against a door.

It was a nice door, at least. There were no splinters digging into the scales on his back or the leather on his armor, which was a wonderful step up compared to some of the doors he'd had the misfortune of sleeping against in the past. Those doors had all been old, decrepit doors in ruins he'd been investigating, though, so the bar wasn't exactly set high on him for the "sleeping against a door" category.

Part of that, to be fair, was because every time he fell asleep in an unusual or uncomfortable position, Derivan took the time to move him somewhere more comfortable, like he had just now—

—Oh, gods, he'd thought of Derivan as his boyfriend. That was the first time he'd thought of him as his boyfriend.

It was that thought that jolted him properly awake. Vex snapped to his feet, his dagger held out in front of him to ward off attack; his breathing came quick and fast, and his eyes darted around, trying to pick out attackers in the darkness.

But there was nothing there. Only the flickering of firelight greeted him, magical flames slowly licking away against wood without consuming it.

The space around him ached with a strange sense of familiarity. Vex knew, almost instinctively, what he would find if he turned around.

He turned around anyway.

His back had been pressed against the door that was a replica of the front doors of the mansion that House Ashion lived in. A shining emblem sat embedded in the stone just above that door, the logo of the House—a slightly abstract depiction of a lizardkin mage glowing with internal mana, represented by light-blue flames around the mage.

It was a reference to the pain they went through for their power, too.

Vex had never been here before. He knew where this was—it wasn't the true entrance to his home. The air around him was too heavy with strange mana, and the door to the Ashion mansion was *certainly* not located in the middle of a dimly lit room with no apparent entrance besides the door he'd been found sleeping against.

Which meant that this had to be the Ashion tower of the dungeon. Alternatively, it could be a *very* elaborate trap . . . but somehow, he doubted that was the case.

Vex brought up the system interface, scanning through it for any messages left by his friends—but something in his mind buzzed painfully when he tried. He could see that they'd left *something* for him, but his connection with the system seemed . . . strange. Fuzzier than normal. Some result of his magic trying to interface directly with the system, maybe.

He couldn't contact his friends.

The thought was less worrying than it should have been. Vex trusted them, and this was where they said they'd meet up anyway—he could stay exactly where he was, and they would no doubt come and find him with time.

And yet . . . he felt a pull toward the door. Something inside him, telling him to open it and go through it, telling him that he would be *home*, if he only took a step through.

Vex paused, reaching for the door handle . . .

. . . then sighed and rolled his eyes.

"Really? That's not going to work," he said, speaking to the air and yet somehow confident he would be heard. "This place isn't my fucking home. Don't even try it."

With that, he sat on the floor and pulled open his notebook.

If the dungeon wanted to confront him, it was going to have to come to him. *He* was just going to periodically check his system interface to see if he could contact his friends yet, and in the meantime study the system of glyphs. He was *pretty* sure he was on the verge of some kind of breakthrough.

It took about fifteen minutes before whatever dungeon presence had brought him here to begin with showed itself. It almost startled Vex, who had just started to really get into his research—he was several pages deep into his notes by the time the door slammed open, and he was so flustered by how sudden it was that his immediate reaction was less combat and more "Damnit, my notes!"

Which was about the moment he recognized that there was, in fact, a legitimate threat in front of him—because the man glowering in front of him was his father.

Not his *real* father. He was too large to be his real father, besides the base impossibility of the idea that Karix had somehow managed to make his way into the dungeon, compromise its spawning mechanisms, and sit in wait behind a large, ornate door just to discipline him or something. This was a dungeon creation, and it wasn't completely unheard-of for the Elyran dungeon in particular to do something like this; it was very much in tune with the peoples of Elyra.

But to find *his father* and use it against him? That seemed almost too person-like to be an act of the dungeon.

"What do you want?" Vex said. He tried to keep his tone measured and controlled. If someone *was* doing this, like he suspected, then giving them a reaction was the last thing he wanted; they no doubt knew exactly what they were doing.

"You should rejoin our house," the false Karix said. His tone was almost kind. "We've missed you."

"No, thank you," Vex said politely. His faux father narrowed his eyes, then, and Vex felt a gathering of power—

—Fifteen minutes was *a lot of time*. This seemed like the perfect opportunity to practice some of the magic he'd just recently acquired.

Karix was gathering fire magic. Vex spun the paintbrush he'd been given, imbuing it with [**Splash of Mana**] and letting colored mana stream out of its bristles; he didn't paint his response on any particular surface, just in the air, the same way Derivan had before.

The glyph for Water spiraled into existence just a second after he thought of it, the mana spreading through his brush. It channeled his thought; it didn't require physical movement. And then he added in a touch of Light—because light represented expansion and growth, in some manner, the idea of something that could be lit and touch every corner.

Glyph of Watermist
This glyph represents the first depiction of the Great Waterfall, in the continent of Hureat, where magic has carved a hole into the earth so deep that the bottom cannot be seen from the top. At the bottom of the caverns, though, light magic shines from a guild of mages that have established a presence there—and the glittering sight of their light reflecting and refracting through the mist at the bottom of that waterfall created

the Watermist, a prismatic fog that extends for miles around the Hole. Watermist is a magical countereffect that has exceptional power against fire magics, completely suppressing any attempt to cast fire within its radius. It also induces a mild hypnotic effect with its prismatic rays, though this hypnotic effect largely serves as a mild tranquilizer; it cannot be used for mind control or even for suggestions.

The mist exploded from his glyph. He'd tested it in smaller quantities before, channeling only a small amount of mana into the Watermist and observing what would happen; the tiny, prismatic cloud that emerged reminded him almost of rainclouds. He remembered back when he was a child, when the only phenomena of nature he could observe from his room were the things that happened with the weather...

The clouds he liked the most were the clouds that came after the rain, when they would shine brightly as the sun shone off their edges.

Now the mist that emerged from his glyph was thick and dense; Vex didn't hold back. For all that this glyph claimed to suppress all fire magic, Karix was a powerful mage—and the dungeon's interpretation of him was even more powerful. The amount of mana being used to fuel the spell was phenomenal. It was enough to almost make him take a step back.

But he didn't. He was confident in his magic.

Karix's spell formed, a runic circle appearing in the air blazing with fire magic.

Just as quickly as it spawned, the mist consumed it. There was barely a sound beyond a quiet *whff*, rather like the sound of a candle being snuffed out.

Vex took the opportunity to take a step back and close his eyes; Watermist did not discriminate with its so-called hypnotic properties. The mist absorbed the sound of his footsteps.

"Vex?" Karix's voice was suddenly kind again, no doubt an effect of the mist. "What was that? That was incredible. You didn't... You *did* discover a new magic on your own, didn't you?"

Vex didn't respond. This wasn't his real father. This was the dungeon, pretending to be his father, creating an iteration of him based on—

—creating an iteration of him based on Shift. Based on what they knew of the system.

Which meant that on some level, this was still real. Shift didn't create things from nothing; it plucked ideas from different timelines, different interpretations of current reality.

"You should've told me," Karix continued. "That was incredible. You have to come back to the House, Vex. I was wrong when I said you couldn't discover magic on your own."

How many times had he thought about his father saying *I was wrong*?

Except his father was still wrong, even now.

"I didn't discover it on my own," he said. "I had help from my friends. We found out about this together. I wouldn't have gotten this far without Derivan, either."

"Is that the armored fellow that was hanging around you?" Karix asked him curiously. His voice still hadn't moved—he was still speaking from the same position. Vex held no illusions about responding; every time he spoke, he was revealing to Karix where he was. He'd given in once, but . . .

. . . actually, he had a solution for this.

Communication and Water. The Glyph of the Bubbling Stream.

It created a small river in the ground near him, and he took several steps away from it; the idea behind it was simple. It was like a sound illusion—it was something he could speak through.

"And my boyfriend, yes," Vex said, speaking through the stream. He didn't know how his father was going to react to hearing that he'd chosen a partner. His *fake* father, he reminded himself.

"You know you could've found even more if you'd had our resources," Karix told him, speaking through the fog. This time, Vex saw that he was moving— he saw a vague shape shifting through the fog and could trace Karix's voice moving with it, toward the stream. "Imagine how much you could've found if you were doing it with *us*."

Vex *almost* reacted. Because that was his father dismissing what he'd done on his own, in a way—that was Karix saying he was still right. That what Vex had set out to prove—that Elyra's system was broken, that his brother didn't need to be treated this way—was wrong.

But this wasn't his father.

He had to tell himself that again. He could have responded—the words sat in his throat, ready for him to speak them—but he found that they stuck there, unable to come out; his mind was a whirlwind of thoughts.

"Vex?" Karix prompted. "I'm not trying to hurt you. I feel like you're hiding from me. I'm just . . . Look, we miss having you around in the House. We want you back."

Because he'd been their chance at additional glory. Because they'd pinned so many of their hopes on him, the child that had taken to magic like windbeaks to elemental storms.

Because they missed him?

There was a genuine sort of hurt in Karix's voice. If it had been anyone else saying those words to him, he would have taken them at face value; it was only his history with his father that told him otherwise. His father would say these things, and he would mean them.

But he would mean them in his own, twisted way.

"No, you don't," he said quietly, through the stream. "You miss what I could have been for you. For the House."

"I—"

And for the first time, Karix paused.

"Is that what you think?" he asked.

"You've never given me reason to think otherwise." The stream burbled. "You won't even listen to me about Riss."

His father flinched *hard*, like Vex had just done a physical blow to him; something about his pride seemed to collapse, but Vex was still talking. "I've been telling you for years that we don't need this stupid Principle. All it does is hurt our family. Lyssa trembles whenever she's wearing anything remotely tight. Helix likes pretending he's in charge all the time. Varon spends mana like it's water until he passes out. Xirra lashes out in anger at anyone that looks at her the wrong way."

"That isn't my fault—" Karix said, but there was an edge of desperation in his voice. Something was wrong. This Karix was *different*. But Vex couldn't help the words that came out anyway.

"You don't think so?" Vex asked. He didn't yell the question—he said the words softly, almost dangerously.

And his response was silence.

The mist receded. Karix stood there, in front of the door, looking somehow smaller.

And then Vex watched as a blade stabbed through that door, right through the center of Karix's chest.

CHAPTER 61

WHAT COULD HAVE BEEN

Karix staggered forward. His face twisted into a rictus of anger and betrayal—Vex saw that the wound wasn't healing. Did this version of his father not have *health*? The system shouldn't have been this broken down already; a dungeon-created monster, of all things, should still be connected to the system...

Unless this Karix *wasn't* dungeon-created.

It still wasn't the true Karix. Too many details were wrong for that, unless someone had captured and altered his father significantly, and the amount of power and resources someone would need to be able to do that without sending all of Elyra into a frenzy was too great to be worth considering. But if this Karix wasn't created by the dungeon or the system—

"Boring," someone said, yawning slightly. The figure that walked out from behind the door to House Ashion was just a regular human, as far as Vex could tell—but he felt a chill running through his body anyway.

The man held a crossbow in one hand.

They'd known he was behind some of this. He'd appeared in the door dungeon as if to taunt him, and Vex wondered if he'd been responsible for Noram running into that particular bonus room. He'd possibly appeared at the gates of Elyra—Vex was recognizing now that some of the guards *were* equipped with crossbows, and the fact that he hadn't detected one should have been a red flag on its own. He'd been responsible for the creation of [**Bond Familiar**] and, by proxy, [**Guild's Hope**].

Who was this man?

No. He wasn't human.

What was he?

Vex looked at the man, and he saw hatred in his eyes.

"I was hoping you'd have more of a fight," he said when Vex didn't speak. The lizardkin reached for both his dagger and his paintbrush, uncertain how to react—he didn't have the same defensive skills that Derivan and Misa did, nor did he have them to back him up. "I go to all the trouble of summoning a version of your father, and you just *talk* to him? Come on. At least try to give me a little more entertainment."

"Is *that* what that was to you?" Vex asked, his voice low. His father twitched on the ground—Vex tried to remind himself that version of his father wasn't *real*—

—but he was, wasn't he?

The past month or so had been more than enough to call into question his understanding of reality time and time again, but one thing they'd learned was that the system didn't really create things that weren't *real*; it drew from different timelines, different possibilities, different layers of reality.

This version of Karix wasn't his father. But he was still a person.

"Yes?" the man said, raising an eyebrow at him like his answer was the most obvious one in the world. "Why else would I go to all that trouble?"

"Who the hell . . . Is this . . ." Karix rasped. His voice gurgled a bit as he spoke, and Vex's heart broke a bit.

There was a part of him that was very, very angry at his father. There was a part of him that was fairly certain he wouldn't be able to forgive him, even if Karix *did* learn to change his ways, not that he thought his father would.

That didn't mean he wanted his father to die. Especially not like this.

"Oh, you're still alive." The man crouched to stare at Karix. "You should've just stayed quiet and died. Really, bringing attention to yourself. What were you thinking?"

Karix glared at the strange man, and mana began to gather, though his chest heaved and his arms shook with every small movement; the man laughed, stepping a half-step back and folding his arms in a smug, self-satisfied sort of way.

"You stay . . . away . . . from Vex . . ." Karix rasped.

"What're you gonna do about it?" the man taunted. His hand flicked out—

Vex had had enough.

A month before, when they'd encountered the first Overseer, he'd cast a massive spell to try to kill it: a spell loaded with Manaburn and all the power he could pack into it. It was a modified [**Ray of Frost**] spell, with the essence swapped out for Manaburn and the entire array designed to draw in ambient mana, so that every inch of distance it crossed it would keep drawing in ambient mana, growing in strength and power for every step it took. Back then, it had the power to smash even the Overseer against the walls of the Nucleus, and while it hadn't *killed* it, it had been enough to do significant damage.

This dungeon was full of ambient mana, too. There wasn't nearly enough distance or time to carry that amount of mana—

But he still had a [**Reality Shard**]. It was his last one. He hadn't used it with the system yet. He didn't know what it would do. But he knew the effect that he *wanted*, and he knew it was possible; he had a theory regarding the way runes and glyphs worked.

Runes were glyphs without life or art. They were the system's attempt at replicating glyphs, but without something *alive* to look at it, they were a mere copy; the reason they took so much more adjusting, and had so many more small details to control various elements of the spell, was because it lost whatever made it magic.

It wasn't a spell under the system. Not really. It was the system's best attempt at a copy—a program.

But that meant he could copy runes. Because runes were still based on glyphs; he'd seen the similarities between the runic circles for various fire spells and the fire glyph itself. The glyph made him realize the underlying similarity they all had.

So he cast his [**Ray of Frost**], modified it with Manaburn, then overlaid his own Sign of Research, with a slot in the middle of the book drawn for his crystal.

He wanted to know *who this was*, and he doubted the man was going to answer any questions.

So he was going to take them his answers.

With the increases to his Agility, he could do all this very, very fast—but even as fast as he did it, he could see the man reacting to what he was doing. He started to turn toward Vex and then, as if realizing he wouldn't have the time to interrupt the spell, began to weave his own defensive sigil.

Vex ignored him. Manaburn would burn through it all. He slammed the [**Reality Shard**] into the slot he'd created for it and watched as it began to gather every spare scrap of mana in the room and beyond. That was the whole point of the [**Reality Shard**], after all. The idea was for it to help the spell Shift into all those alternate wavelengths of reality, ripping mana away from them and fueling this one spell . . .

It helped, too, that Karix was gathering his own magic. The spell could draw directly from him, pulling mana away from his spell and wrapping it into Vex's own. What emerged from Karix's spell was naught but a small, ineffectual ball of fire, but that was fine; Karix had seen what Vex was doing and freely gave his own mana to the cause.

Vex saw the strange man's eyes widen.

But it was too late. The ray ripped across the room with a sound that reverberated like the air itself was being torn apart, and shredded the shield that the man had drawn up; it blasted into him and threw him backward through the door and then through the wall behind it—

—and just like that, as the spell tore into the man and ate away at his flesh, Vex *knew who he was.*

Irvis, Spectre of Mana
A product of a failed reality anchor. He knows nothing except hatred. For a Spectre, names have power. By discovering his name, you have made him vulnerable where he previously was not.

The name rippled out into the mana itself, resonating nearby, growing in strength. Vex *felt* it as the mana named him, felt the change in the very fabric of reality that made something previously immortal and invulnerable suddenly *vulnerable.* The spell grew in strength, and Irvis *screamed.*

It took a full minute for the beam to let up, and by then, Irvis's screams had stopped.

A pained wheeze from the lizardkin that was not his father caught his attention. He didn't exactly know what he was doing when he rushed over— he'd spoken with Derivan before, and they'd talked about how his magic didn't have to be limited to *combat*; with access to glyphs, he could reach into areas of magic that he couldn't before.

But he hadn't figured it out. Not in the fifteen minutes he'd had before Karix had shown up through the door, before Irvis had—presumably—gotten bored enough to trigger this whole scenario. He didn't even know if Irvis was *dead*; he was just more worried about what was happening to Karix, who was breathing unsteadily.

Karix, whose eyes were unfocused, whose blood was pooled on the ground in a volume that Vex was pretty sure meant he was guaranteed to die.

Vex's emotions were in turmoil.

He didn't like his father. That didn't mean he wanted to see Karix die *like this*, bleeding out on the floor in a dungeon. It didn't mean he wanted to see his father struggling to breathe, making pained efforts to get up—

"Here," Vex muttered before his brain could stop him. He reached forward and let his father use his arm as leverage, pulling himself up to his feet; Karix staggered unsteadily as he stood, but he didn't fall.

Somehow.

Karix stared at him, eyes still unsteady. "You got . . . strong."

"No shit," Vex said, channeling a bit of Misa. He didn't know what else to say. What was he supposed to say? That he forgave the man?

He didn't.

Did he *hate* him?

That wasn't a question Vex felt prepared to answer. He didn't feel like he hated him. He didn't really want to care. He just wanted his brother to not have to go through what he had.

"Good," Karix told him. He didn't seem to care about whatever internal struggle Vex was having. He seemed mostly pleased that his son had made it exactly where he thought he would. Proud, even. It felt oddly hollow. Vex didn't say anything, even as his father's gaze focused sharply behind him. "He's . . . still alive."

Vex's blood ran cold.

"Won't . . . die easily." Karix kept talking. Vex was fairly certain his father's level was in the eighties; he was *powerful* and had all the resources of the nobles to boot, but . . . this was a version of Karix that had had his connection with the system sabotaged in some way. He didn't know how much of that strength Karix still had. He was, frankly, amazed that his father was still standing. "Step back, Vex."

Vex paused, considering, and then slowly took a step back. He glanced in the direction Irvis had gone; there was a smoking ruin there, little remnants of the Manaburn effect eating away at the mana-saturated walls of the dungeon.

"I'm not . . . the real Karix, am I?" Karix asked, though the question was largely rhetorical. The lizardkin laughed an odd, bubbling sort of laugh, of the kind that made Vex take another step back. "Bastard summoned me to fuck with you. Doesn't know what . . . doesn't know *who* he's messing with. My son. *Powerful*. You found . . . a new magic."

Karix was proud of him. How many times had he wished for exactly this?

And yet now that it happened, it felt hollow.

His father seemed to realize that. Half-dead as he was, he didn't say anything else for a long, long moment, and when he spoke again, it was a little softer. "I'm . . . not a good father, huh?"

Vex wondered if he should lie.

"No," he said. Karix laughed again, a choking sound.

"I do... wish I could have been better." *That* seemed genuine. There was something he was missing, something in the way Karix had flinched when he mentioned Riss's name. His father stared up at the ceiling of the room, and Vex followed his gaze; there was nothing there but more mana-saturated stone. "Never knew anything different. Maybe if I had..."

Karix shook his head. Vex felt his father gathering mana for some kind of spell—Vex didn't recognize this one. He wondered how much his father knew that he kept from him, even now. "You gonna forgive him? The real Karix."

"I don't know," Vex answered honestly. Even this version of his father—one that was dying—hadn't apologized. He didn't want him to, really; he wasn't the father that had hurt him. Maybe this Karix understood that.

"That's fine," Karix said. His chest wasn't bleeding so much anymore. Vex didn't know if it was because he had some way of healing or because he'd just run out of blood. Probably the former, since Karix was speaking more clearly—but who knew, when the system was involved. "You don't have to."

"Don't I?" Vex's tone was almost miserable. "I feel like I'm *supposed* to."

Karix laughed. "Fuck that. Ashions don't do anything we're supposed to. You think I did when I was your age?" He smiled at Vex, not unkindly. "Live better than I did. Forgive him or don't. It's not even your responsibility to make sure he understands."

Why was *this* what it took to make his father understand? Did he have to be on the verge of death to acknowledge that there were flaws with his methods?

"It *is* my responsibility to make sure he understands," Vex said. On this, at least, his voice was firm. "Because Riss shouldn't have to go through what I did."

"Ah. Riss is still alive here... That's good." Karix's words made Vex's blood run cold, just briefly. Or the implications did. He understood suddenly why this version of his father had reacted so strongly to his little brother's name.

Part of him wondered what happened, and another part really didn't want to know.

"Okay. Do that. Take care of your brother," Karix said, and then he paused. "And take care of *me*, if you have to."

"What's that supposed to—"

Vex didn't get the chance to finish his sentence. A spark of magic flared where Irvis had been left—and this version of his father had been prepared for it, clearly, if the corresponding flare from Karix was any indication. This version of his father stepped in front of him, shielding him from whatever spell was being used, a runic circle snapping into place in front of him and scattering frost and ice; the beam of light from Irvis struck and promptly split into a dozen smaller ones. It was like watching light getting physically ripped apart by ice. It spread *into* the light, even, freezing it solid in blatant disregard for the laws of physics, not unlike most system skills.

Several rooms away, presumably where Irvis was, there was an enraged scream.

Karix sighed, the remainder of his body already turning into nothing but remnants of frost. "I did my best," he said. "He's still alive. I'm sorry. But that spell will buy you a few minutes. You've got this."

"I—" Vex said, and his voice was half-choked, half-horrified; somehow this seemed even worse. "Dad, you can't—"

"Sorry," Karix said. "No time left. Love you, kid. I'm sorry we fucked up. Maybe in another lifetime, we could've been a real family."

Those words hit Vex hard. He didn't quite know what he was saying when he responded. "I found a real one anyway."

Karix smiled softly, and this version of him spoke his last word.

"Good."

CHAPTER 62

CREATIVE USES OF POWER

Derivan paused, awkwardly, after the blade struck him in the back; he didn't know how to react. The monster that attacked Sev was . . . well, it was like him.

In a manner of speaking, anyway.

It didn't seem like it was intelligent the same way he was. Its sword struck him, and it did not react to the lack of damage; it simply stepped back and then moved again in a traditional stab. It didn't take much effort for Derivan to simply step to the side and move Sev with him, though he kept the cleric behind him.

In any other situation, he would have stopped to examine this being that was like him yet not.

But if Vex was in danger . . . he would leave this for later examination. It took him no effort at all to reach for Patch and snap the one link it held with the system—he remembered that link, because it was the same one he'd had. The same one that had taken all three of the others to break before.

The stat suffered a slight decrease from that action, but it was nothing he couldn't deal with.

"Let's go," he told Sev, who raised an eyebrow slightly and glanced between him and the monster that was attacking them. He nodded after a moment, appearing to understand.

"Are we just going to leave it?" he asked.

". . . As long as it does not follow us." Derivan glanced back at the armor. The monster had stopped moving, apparently confused without the routines it had been following.

Perhaps it was cruel, to awaken it and then leave it to fend for itself. It was strange that it was so similar to him at all—the armor was certainly different, but not by that much. But the one dungeon that had been created with all four of them as a template had been broken and scattered throughout the others.

It was surprising, but . . . maybe it wasn't *that* surprising.

Derivan sighed.

"If you are at all like me," he said, not at all unkindly; the armor he spoke to stared at him, uncomprehending but listening all the same, "then you will be confused. There was a time that confusion was frustrating to me, but I think . . . I think that it is okay to be confused, and to take your time. Once you figure your system out, you may use it to contact me, and I will help you where I can."

"We gotta go," Sev said, but gave the armor Derivan was speaking to a concerned sort of look—not *fearful*, just worried. "He's right, though. Be careful who you trust, but don't be afraid to ask for help or accept it."

The armor still didn't respond. Derivan and Sev took that as their cue to leave; it wasn't for several minutes, as they traveled along a surprisingly empty brick corridor, that Sev spoke again. "Also, Derivan, can you just . . . do that now?"

". . . I did it without thinking," Derivan admitted. "But it appears that I can, at a minor cost to my Patch stat."

"We could get through our section of the dungeon really quickly if you used that."

"I . . . Should I?" Derivan asked, hesitating. "It seems potentially irresponsible . . ."

"It depends, I suppose," Sev admitted, "on how it works. If you're creating a new person when you do that, then yeah, that's not very responsible. But if you're just *freeing* someone from being controlled by the system—"

"Ah. Yes." Derivan paused. "I see what you mean. That is . . . I had not considered that."

"You just acted?"

"It was like me." Derivan glanced ahead in the corridor to see if there was any threat there yet, but everything ahead of them was curiously empty. It was strangely hard to find the words to explain what he'd done. He'd felt a moment of kinship and reacted entirely from that.

Or maybe there had been something more than that. Maybe a part of him had latched on to small elements of something he'd seen in the way the other armor had behaved, and he'd sensed something that needed to be freed . . .

Or he was projecting.

It was hard to say.

"That's fair," Sev said, misinterpreting his silence as a lack of willingness to continue. The cleric sighed. "It would be so much easier if we understood why the system's doing all this. I feel like we have so many pieces of the puzzle, and if we just put it all together..."

"I have some ideas," Derivan said quietly. "But every one of them worries me. I worry that stating them will make them real."

"... Yeah, I get where you're coming from there." Sev's eyes unfocused slightly. "We're gonna put it all together soon. And we're not going to like what we find. We need to hold on to ourselves once that happens."

Derivan looked at his friend curiously. "What do you mean?"

Sev blinked. "I... I don't know." He wobbled on his feet slightly. "That was strange. I'm sorry. We should get going."

"... Indeed we should." Derivan almost pushed on the subject more, but as he did, something in Sev's version of the system pulsed strangely, almost as though it was warning him away—he sensed it through both Shift and Patch, and it gave him pause.

So, instead of saying anything, he quietly wrote a note to Misa and Vex.

Of the four of them, Sev was the one still most bound to the system and the one whose bonds they'd loosened the least. This felt like an indication that their time with that was coming to an end.

There was no response from either of them yet, but that was fine; he hadn't expected one. They were both likely going through their own brand of problems. He just hoped he and Sev would be able to catch up to them in time.

"Shit!" Misa let out an undignified sort of yelp as she just barely ducked out of the way of a descending blade. If there was anything she hated, it was traps—not because she couldn't block them, although the fast ones gave her a run for her money. She still needed time to *react* to attacks to be able to block them, after all.

But traps were harder to block than people. People were easy to read. Traps had very little in the way of warning, especially when it came to the more-advanced dungeons—simpler ones would have things like light-up sequences to show that a trap was about to go off.

Good trap design? No. Convenient? Very. Misa wasn't exactly complaining.

The Elyran dungeon was far from a simple dungeon, though. She was already using her skills to examine the corridor ahead of her to the fullest, and in every one of them, the traps were slightly different—the dungeon was changing the traps on her as her actions changed. It meant she couldn't cheat. If she reacted differently to a trap, the next trap would be different as well, so even copying everything that Misa-from-another-timeline did wasn't a guarantee—

A runic circle formed in front of her, and Misa let a half-growl rip out of her throat. *This*, at least, she had a concrete way to deal with. She'd spoken with Vex about it before, the application of [**The Blade Arcane**] to spell constructs. Arcane mana tended to take on the traits of other mana aspects it came into contact with, which meant it did an excellent job of hijacking other spells.

One straight line through the runic circle. Misa slashed a moment before the spell fired, watching with satisfaction as the circle fell apart; she didn't have the same knowledge Vex did and couldn't outright *hijack* a spell, but she could certainly destroy it.

Once Vex had told her the trick to it, anyway. She really hoped that little guy was all right.

"Well, well," someone said, and Misa froze, spinning to face the intruder. The voice came from *behind her*—there shouldn't have been anyone behind her. "We meet again. I see you actually survived."

It took a moment for her to parse who she was looking at. There was a man standing there, plain as he could be. Brown hair, black eyes, entirely too much stubble; *familiar*—

"Oh," Misa said, narrowing her eyes. "You're the piece of shit from the dungeon."

"Irvis, yes," the man said, giving her a mocking bow. There was a hint of distaste in the way the name rolled off his tongue, like he was angry he now had to name himself. "I would say *Well met*, but that would be a lie."

"Please stop talking like a villain for two fucking seconds," Misa said. "It's exhausting."

Irvis frowned at her and tutted his tongue. "Kids these days," he said. "No respect for the classics."

What the fuck were the *classics*? He gestured, and Misa tensed.

The timeline skill was . . . a complicated one to use. She could choose to do different actions in other timelines and see how they played out; she could see what *would have happened* if she had done something just slightly different a few minutes in the past. That was useful, but it was a lot of information to focus on.

Which made it all the more worrying when every single other version of her was blown back. Not *killed*—she was harder to kill than that—but more than half her health was gone in most of them, from attacks too fast for her to see and block.

Even more worrying was that nothing happened to her *here*.

"Something wrong?" Irvis asked her, mock concern lacing his voice. "All I did was move slightly. Why do you look scared?"

"I'm not *scared*," Misa spat. She wasn't. There was a low anger thrumming inside her instead, calling her to violence. Irvis's words were designed to make her angry, to fight at less than her best.

Like she'd fall for that.

She'd been feeling that thread of anger ever since she'd entered Elyra. It'd be nice to have something to take that anger out on. There'd been too many fights lately where she had to hold back.

She would have burned timelines... but no. Irvis could see into them, for some reason or the other, could even choose how differently he acted in each one. In some way he was aware of her skills and was using them against her. She had no doubt that he'd do the same if she tried to summon anyone from her village, but that didn't mean that her bag of tricks was empty.

She wasn't one to use skills *conventionally*, after all.

But first, a little test to see how Irvis reacted to conventional attacks.

Misa leapt forward, drawing [**The Blade Arcane**]; Irvis met her with a savage grin. She didn't even see him wielding any sort of weapon against her. He wore a standard, well-trimmed suit, and when his reaction to her attack was simply to reach for her weapon, she allowed it. It was clear that *something* would happen, and that something would give her information.

Arcane mana *twisted*.

The nature of arcane mana was that in some sense, it took on the properties of any mana type it encountered; this she understood in an abstract sort of way, from the half-dozen lectures Vex had given about it. It still surprised her when the sword compressed and warped, eyes and nails and *teeth* growing along its length in a way that looked unnervingly like Irvis—

It snapped at her, and she mentally released her lock on it. Strange mana-flesh faded away almost immediately, replaced once more with the serene purple-red arcane energy that normally formed the blade, and Misa leapt back before Irvis could retaliate.

Not that he seemed to want to. He merely smiled at her, infuriatingly self-satisfied. "Learn anything useful?" he asked, his voice still mocking.

Misa smiled back. "I did."

Irvis was a creature of *mana*. Just like the mana abomination they'd fought, way back when all this first started.

"Wanna know something *really* weird I can do?" Misa asked, her tone nonchalant.

"What's that?" Irvis's tone was almost bored.

Misa attacked with [**The Blade Arcane**] again, this time throwing it toward Irvis.

It was, technically, a mana-based *attack*.

The instant before it struck, she blocked it. Reality shifted, and her mace took on a set of rapidly shifting prismatic colors as she blocked her own strike with a *clang*, and in that moment—in that instant between her mace reverting into a normal mace, while her weapon existed as whatever was optimal for blocking a mana-based attack—

She *also* used it to strike Irvis, as part of the same motion used to block the sword.

The prismatic colors of the mace settled into a single solid tone of blue and rang like a bell; it sent her sword flying and, more importantly, burned into Irvis's flesh with a loud *crackle-pop*. The *thud* as Irvis's body struck the wall hit her a second later, followed shortly by an enraged scream.

It was, Misa decided, very satisfying.

CHAPTER 63

TRICKS AND ALCHEMY

"Two of you," Irvis snarled; his face twisted in a raw, sudden sort of fury that almost made Misa take a step back. "*Two of you!* The mage I understand, but *you*? You don't have any magic!"

Shit, he's hit Vex. Misa's first thought was worry before it resolved into a more-determined narrowing of her eyes. Irvis had *waited* for this. This man—or whatever he was—had known about them at least since she'd blocked his attempt at killing Elyra's delve team only a month or so back. Then he'd followed them through Fendal, all the way to Elyra, where it turned out he'd compromised the Guild there long before...

This was intentional.

He'd waited for them to split up, and that meant he didn't want to face them together. Vex had been targeted first, and she had been targeted second, from what he'd said. She wasn't sure what to make of that. Maybe he was avoiding one of the two of them, or maybe he just didn't want to face Sev and Derivan together.

Either way, he wasn't as invulnerable as he pretended to be. Of course, she could have figured that out from the bleeding wound she'd left with her mace, where specks of light drifted out from his skin. It looked raw and painful.

Misa smirked at him, spun, and *threw* her blade far into the corridor, past the traps. She could sense Irvis trying to attack her in that moment of opportunity—[**Guard Stance**] tried to activate to push her into the right position to stop him—but she deactivated the skill before it could and activated [Endless Echoes].

The world spun into a fractal. One version of her was more familiar than all the others, the one she used most frequently to block when she wasn't in the right position for it. It was some version of her that had acquired a

[**Teleporting Mace**], and it had become her favorite shtick there. She used it now.

Misa reappeared halfway down the corridor, "blocking" and then grabbing her sword back out of the air and ducking underneath the trap that sprang almost immediately; pure instinct, this time, from her observations of the traps this dungeon liked to throw at her. It was sort of uncomfortable that the dungeon was adapting to her strategies, including her use of Echoes, but that was a distant concern to the threat of Irvis.

He was already catching up.

She had to lead him toward the center of the dungeon, where Sev and Derivan would be headed. Part of Misa wanted to try to fight him alone, to take a stand and see exactly how well she could fare against this monster, but she quashed that impulse; it would've been the same kind of stupidity she'd been reprimanding Sev over. *No more of that*, she told herself.

Instead, Misa scanned ahead, looking for a good way to stay ahead of Irvis and lure him where she wanted him. She could use her blocking trick a few more times—she had more than enough mana banked for it—but Irvis would no doubt be prepared. He'd figure it out the moment she pulled out her sword.

The corridor ahead of her was uniform to the point of being almost boring. Perfect square tiles, each of which Misa knew from experience could either trigger a trap or *be* a trap; there was no telling what was behind any given tile, and they all seemed identical, besides in color; they ran in long white stripes and shorter black ones along the length of the corridor. There was nothing there she could use, as far as she knew. She cursed under her breath and glanced back.

He was already catching up to her, bastard that he was—he moved in an odd, flickering sort of way. She never quite caught him *running*. She'd see the initial moment of him starting to move, and then he'd fade out of her sight, only to reappear closer to her. Always in a spot of the dungeon without a trap. Always on one of those empty tiles along the corridor, where he would reorient and move again.

It was creepy. He was also almost certainly Shifting the way Derivan could—the way her own other selves touched on, albeit in a slightly more distant way. It explained how he could see those other versions of her...

Ah. *That* gave her an idea—a few ideas, even. Misa grinned again, and it wasn't a nice grin; she wasn't in a very good mood.

To start with, if the dungeon was going to adapt to her, then she would have to make it adapt in her favor, against Irvis.

"Stop *running*," Irvis hissed at her. The sound carried across the corridor, and it was only the tone and strangeness of how that sound carried that made her think to block. Her mace flickered into the appearance of a flute, and something in Irvis's words was sucked into it, a shimmering red mist expelled from the other end of the flute a moment later. Irvis growled in exasperation, and Misa wondered what exactly she'd just avoided.

No matter. She stopped, just like he wanted; Irvis almost seemed startled by it. He charged at her a second later, some sort of bolt appearing in his hand, and she activated [**Guard Stance**] in response. She just needed the instant of precognition it provided her—

There. Misa twisted on her feet right as Irvis appeared next to her, taking a single step forward and shoving her body weight in. She felt a grim satisfaction take hold as Irvis gasped in surprise, and she kept going. One fist wrapped around the stupid tie he wore with his stupid suit, and she yanked as hard as she could.

Which was pretty hard, first of all. She'd invested a fair number of points into Strength. Second, and perhaps something that shouldn't have surprised her, the man was *light*.

Irvis went sprawling.

She would have followed up, but she'd thrown him with intent. Her Echoes rolled the dice on the traps, stepping on a half-dozen different ones in the instant. Every physical trap that was launched she blocked, and every mana-based one she'd gritted her teeth and allowed herself to get *hit*; if she was right about what the dungeon was doing...

A hole opened up in a nearby wall, and the hair on her skin prickled as mana gathered. Misa couldn't see the process, but she saw the *result*—mana so concentrated that it glowed a deep blue. Two bolts launched out of the hole in a fraction of a second, at a speed so blisteringly fast Misa wasn't sure she could have triggered her block in time if she'd been the one to set off the trap.

Irvis certainly didn't react in time. Whatever his stats were—if he had any at all—they weren't oriented around speed and reaction; the lances of mana impaled him through the head and chest with enough force to send him flying back and into the wall.

In the instant before the lance struck, though, Misa caught a glimpse of him starting to smile.

She didn't wait to see what happened—she could guess. Conventional mana-based attacks wouldn't work on Irvis; she needed the specific anti-magic weapons she summoned when blocking magical attacks, or else she would be hard pressed to do any real damage to Irvis.

Better yet, she needed Vex. From what Irvis had said, he hadn't been particularly successful in his attack on her friend, but she still worried; there was nothing from him through the system yet. But the little guy was resourceful, she told herself.

Sure enough, in the corner of her eye—even as she ran and dodged the traps in her way, sometimes only barely—Misa saw Irvis pulling the mana lance out of his head and looking at it in what almost seemed like disdain; he clenched his fist, and the lance shattered with the sound of a ringing bell.

Not encouraging. But not, she reminded herself, the end of it.

This fight, as far as she was concerned, was an opportunity to gather information. Arcane mana didn't react well to Irvis, but there had always been the chance that that was just a quirk of arcane mana as a whole. Now she'd learned that he had some immunity to standard mana attacks, too. She doubted Irvis was very concerned about physical attacks—she remembered how the delve captain, Harold, had attacked him only to have his sword phase straight through.

Time to lean fully into getting to the end of this fucking corridor, then. She was getting a little tired of all the planning.

—⚬—

"We must hurry," Derivan said, glancing sharply ahead.

"Something up?" Sev looked over at his friend.

"There is trouble . . . somewhere. I suspect it is with Misa." Derivan could feel reality fluctuating wildly through Shift, in the exact way he'd come to expect when Misa used the upgraded [**To Fall Yet Hold the Line**]. [**Endless Echoes**], she'd said it was called, though she looked oddly embarrassed while saying it.

The two of them hadn't exactly been taking their time with the dungeon—their path had been methodical and careful but not particularly slow. The theme of the particular corridor they were going down seemed to be enchanted items and weaponry. Lining the sides of the corridor were little alcoves styled after different workshops, everything from alchemy labs to entire foundries and smithing stations.

Derivan thought Vex would have loved it. As far as he could tell, each individual alcove was a fully functioning workshop all on its own; the ingredients stocked on the shelves seemed genuine, and the half-complete items that lay scattered about made it feel like they were left there by real artisans. The only reason he knew it was dungeon-made was because of the way Patch screamed at him—all of this was linked to the system in some way.

He suspected he knew exactly what style of trap it was. Create something in these workshops, and whatever you created would then be pitted against you farther down the hall.

The problem was what happened when you *didn't* create anything in those workshops.

Every one of those half-completed projects left strewn about in them came to life if they just walked past without engaging, this time much less *complete* than the single suit of armor he'd broken the link of; these were smaller, mindless creations of the system that would fall to nothing if he snapped that link. It wasn't worth the ding to Patch to destroy them that way, and so he and Sev resorted to fighting.

Mostly.

Animated swords and axes and whips were fine. Animated *potions*, on the other hand . . .

They'd learned very quickly that the alchemy workshops were not ones to walk past, because stray alchemical effects were *strange*, and animated potions were not fun to fight when a single splash of liquid created wildly different effects.

"Ah, shit, we've got another one coming up," Sev said, glancing to the right. There was yet another workshop there, this time with shelves lined with an assortment of red potions and herbs. Derivan thought he recognized some of them from Emily's garden, even. "You wanna handle this?"

"Yes," Derivan said simply.

He was quick and precise.

He also had no idea what he was doing. He enjoyed the process, though—there was something about grinding random herbs and throwing them into liquid and watching the reaction that was fun—but there was a solid chance that the whole mixture would just *explode*, which had happened once or twice. After the first one, Sev had declared that Derivan would have to handle all the potion-mixing from now on, unless there were ingredients that he explicitly recognized from priesthood.

Sev had mixed *one* successful potion and kept it, at least.

The potion Derivan made settled and stopped drawing in mana after a second, and Derivan would have let out a relieved sigh if he'd been capable of such a thing. He simulated one anyway, glancing back at Sev and giving him a thumbs-up.

"Nice," Sev said. "Any idea what kind of potion you made?"

"I do not," Derivan said.

"Hopefully it's not anything *too* bad. It looks like that's the last workshop we need to work through." Sev gestured to the corridor ahead of them—it led to a big, central room of some sort, and there was the sound of a *very* familiar orc yelling something that sounded suspiciously like *Come and get me, fucker*.

Sev paused. "Okay, you weren't kidding. We better hurry— Hey!"

Derivan didn't bother waiting for Sev. The human got tired too easily, because Agility apparently didn't come with stamina, and because he hadn't put that many points into Agility to begin with. He just picked Sev up under his arm and started running.

CHAPTER 64

ELEVATOR FIGHT

There was a certain satisfaction that came with being proven right, sometimes. Derivan found that this was not one of those times. Animated potions attacking them were one thing; they'd chosen not to deal with them because the effects were chaotic and unpredictable, and that made them more dangerous than fighting animated swords and slightly malformed boots.

Animated-potion *golems* were ... a little bit more of a threat. The upside of it was that all the salves Sev had made with his "priestly knowledge" were all relatively harmless. The downside was that all the potions *Derivan* had mixed were unknown quantities, and he had no idea what any of them did.

And then there was the more pressing problem of Irvis.

"Any ideas?" Misa asked. She was panting slightly, her eyes focused just ahead at the almost ordinary-looking man standing at the other side of the circular room. His name was, apparently, Irvis. "I can scratch him, but it takes some fuckin' work to do it. Also I don't want to lose my sword and he's probably going to try to grab it. You got magic, right, Deri? I could block that."

"That could work," Derivan agreed. Misa had explained what she'd determined about Irvis's strengths and weaknesses mid-battle—no mean feat, considering Irvis never quite stopped harassing them—and even with the Relay charms they still wore, Irvis seemed to be able to tell they were *talking*. He didn't seem to be able to hear what they were saying, but he was certainly aware something was happening.

It seemed to piss him off.

"You lot are really stubborn about just dying, aren't you?" Irvis said, his voice cold. He'd stopped at his side of the room, silently observing them while the potion-golems stalked toward them. "Even that little friend of yours."

"What did you do to Vex." It wasn't even a question—the words emerged from Derivan before he'd even processed saying them, and he was distantly aware that his grip on his sword had tightened.

"Oh, nothing much," Irvis said with a laugh. His eyes darkened. "I wouldn't worry about it."

"He's baiting you," Misa said quietly. Sev nodded beside him.

Derivan had Physical Empathy. He *knew* Irvis was baiting him; the man was pretty good at controlling his emotional cues, but the stat was high enough now that it was feeding him information without him even trying. There was almost nothing physical left about that stat. He could see the anger and hatred in Irvis's eyes, a hint of what almost seemed like anxiety in the way he carried himself. He saw the way Irvis's gaze flickered upward every so often, like he was trying to check in on something.

It didn't stop his eyes from narrowing. It didn't stop him from launching himself forward, a small cloud of [**Barrier**]s forming around him like shards of glass.

He wasn't angry, exactly. At least, he didn't think he was. He'd never really known anger. There was a part of him that knew that rising to Irvis's bait was exactly what Irvis wanted, but at the same time—

One of the potion-golems lunged for him, as Irvis no doubt knew it would. Derivan had been anticipating it too, but the golem moved faster than he expected. Liquid snapped out at him from the center of its chest, avoiding every single one of his [**Barrier**]s, and Derivan reacted more out of instinct than intent.

From within his armor, slime surged.

Derivan hadn't had a lot of time to try to learn more about his Slime stat. He had some understanding of Slime theory from discussions with Vex, in particular its relation to mana. He understood, in the abstract, that this was a new part of himself that he would have to learn to control.

Lesson one about his Slime aspect—it seemed to have a bit of a mind of its own.

It was strange, feeling a part of himself stretching out and then flattening into a shield. For as long as he could remember, his body was characterized by rigidity and inflexibility, save for the limited movement provided to him by the joints in his armor. Now there was a part of him that could move and shape itself almost freely, and would do so with barely a thought.

The golem tried to whip its potion-lash around his makeshift shield, to no avail; it struck the surface of his slime, and he *understood*.

The golem was a slime too.

Sort of. An advanced one, with a shape impressed upon it like a shell around its form—not unlike his own body. It was imbued with the properties of one of the potions he had created, and he almost laughed when he realized what it did.

He didn't, of course. All that had happened in less than a fraction of a second, and while his mind was processing what had *happened*, his legs had already carried him past the golems and to Irvis. Irvis's face sat somewhere frozen between surprised and mocking, but he caught himself before Derivan actually reached him.

"Worried about your friend?" he asked, his tone still mocking.

Derivan responded by flaring mana into the glyph that he'd etched into the back of a [**Barrier**]. It was a simple glyph—the glyph for fire—but Irvis still hadn't been expecting it; he was prepared to respond to a *spell*, but his expression changed into one of puzzlement when the mana moved past him and infused itself into a [**Barrier**] that hovered just over his shoulder.

Fire burst out. There was a moment of smug satisfaction from Irvis, no doubt because magic didn't do much to him.

Then Misa appeared, her mace sucking all the fire into it in an instant. She smashed that mace directly into Irvis's face while it was still in the process of blocking that attack, and Irvis yowled in pain as he stumbled backward.

"Surprise, fucker," Misa said calmly, and then turned to Derivan. "You should warn me when you have a plan next time."

"I did not want him to think I had a plan," Derivan admitted. "He is astute. And he was expecting me to be angry."

Really, he was mostly just worried about Vex. But they had to deal with the threat here and now before he could help their wizard—and that was if Vex actually needed help at all.

"You're lucky I know you," Misa said, smiling slightly. Derivan simply nodded in response.

"I am."

"You . . ." Irvis interrupted both of them—one hand was clutched against his face, and the rest of his expression was twisted in a frighteningly hostile grimace. "You have access to *Signs*."

Irvis knew about that form of magic, then. There was something personal about it, too—he wasn't just *surprised*; he was . . . There was a complex set of emotions there, far more than he'd felt from the man in the entire time he'd known him, though that admittedly hadn't been for very long.

Anger, still. There was always anger and hatred there, persistent in him like it was a part of his very self. A touch of *nostalgia*, strangely enough. A small spark of something that seemed almost like hope, but ruthlessly squashed. Grief, strangely enough.

Followed by a second wave of anger, more intense than the first.

"All right, then," Irvis said. "You're more dangerous than I thought. Means I can't play with you as much. A pity."

He genuinely thought it was a pity, too.

Irvis took a step forward and then began to *melt*.

Put more accurately, Irvis pulled his hand away from his face, where Misa had struck him—and long strings of flesh followed his hand, sticking to it like tar. In the gaps between those strings of flesh where there should have been blood and bone, there was instead a strange, pulsing gray matter. Irvis brought his other hand up to his face and began pulling away more clumps, letting more of his skin melt into a disgusting slurry—

"Hey, guys?" Sev said. "This is really gross and all, but we're not really going to just . . . stand here while he does whatever that is, right?"

"Oh, *fuck* no," Misa said. "Derivan?"

"Yes," Derivan said, and brought forward another two of his shards.

Fire and light. An easy-enough glyph combination to make on the fly; Derivan imagined a burning ray of light, and the pseudo-glass of his [**Barrier**] was the perfect medium for it. Misa bounced off that ray of light again, her mace this time flickering into what seemed like a *claw* that she slashed through Irvis's still-melting body; he didn't even try to *dodge*.

He didn't seem hurt by the attack, either.

Instead, Misa hissed in a mixture of bewilderment and pain as the Irvis-residue on her claw-weapon began to crawl *up* the weapon and toward her. Derivan hastily canceled his spell, and the claw flickered out of existence just before that residue reached her—she took several steps back, and her face went slightly pale.

"That version of me is gone," she said. It wasn't clear if she meant *dead*, or if it was just that she could no longer access that version of herself.

"I sense it too," Derivan said, his tone grim. Shift had rippled strangely for a moment—was *still* rippling strangely. A lot of those ripples were coming from the half-melted blob that was Irvis, and the three of them took cautious steps back, because maybe this was a process that would be dangerous to interrupt.

This was, of course, the moment the potion-golems decided that this was their time to shine and began to attack in earnest.

"Shit," Misa muttered—she blocked an attack almost reflexively, her mace turning briefly into a transparent shield that absorbed a potion-golem's whip into a flicker of color. "Any idea what these do if they hit us?"

"The red one will cause you to sparkle," Derivan said, pointing at the golem he'd blocked on his way to Irvis; even now, the potion was swimming within his system, though it didn't seem to affect him as long as it was contained in the slime portion of him. "It is largely harmless."

"How do you know that?" Sev gave him a strange look, and Derivan shrugged helplessly.

"It is an interaction with the Slime stat, I believe," he said. "The golems operate in a similar manner—"

The now-formless blob that had previously been Irvis *lurched*, and with it, the entire floor of the room they were on did too. Unprompted, the floor began to rise, lifting them up toward the fog above them.

And before they could respond to *that*, spikes lanced out of Irvis's body, piercing every potion-golem in the room. Three of them came for Derivan, Sev, and Misa as well, but a well-timed block shattered each spike, and this time, there was no residual matter that took out yet another timeline—the sword Misa had conjured seemed resistant to that.

"Good to know my skill's still *working*, at least," she muttered to herself. The potion-golems each sagged suddenly, like something vital had been drained from them. Then all at once, almost too fast to see, each of them was sucked up into Irvis, his spikes acting like straws through which he drained everything else from them.

And the Irvis-blob was suddenly much, much larger. Even as Derivan watched, it split into two and then slowly resolved into something that was very much man-shaped once again; Irvis's face peered out at them, though this time with no real attempt at looking human.

Almost perfectly on time, the floor of the platform flashed beneath them, flickering into a series of perfectly square tiles. They seemed to form a pattern on the floor that Derivan didn't quite recognize, though he understood it to be important.

And then, echoing from the fog above them, came the sound of music.

"Thank you for waiting," Irvis said, in a way that didn't sound thankful at all. If he was surprised by the change in the dungeon, he didn't show it. "Let's begin, shall we?"

CHAPTER 65

MUSIC

Irvis began by exploding into action.

Derivan saw Misa open her mouth, presumably to respond to Irvis—but she abruptly tensed instead, her expression flashing into focus in an instant. No time for banter. The two Irvis-creatures lunged toward them, their bodies flattening and spreading into a mess of flesh and teeth in a fraction of a second. Misa flashed forward once in a block, her body distorting slightly—Derivan felt the intensity of the *Shift* as she flickered through more realities than she normally had to.

She found one eventually, her mace morphing into something that looked like a cross between a whip and a cage of fire—but Derivan saw the exhaustion in her face, even as Sev hurriedly hit her with a heal. Misa staggered back to her feet as the two Irvises were thrown back, coughing slightly.

"That was . . . more than two attacks," she said, looking slightly ill. "Thought I could block it. Drained all my mana, half my health."

That explained some of what was happening but not all of it. Derivan felt for Irvis's connection with the system, but Patch didn't find anything—there were these occasional threads that would reach out from him and connect with the greater system, which was so far different from how everyone else connected with the system that Derivan had no idea what to do with it.

He still snapped those strands when he could. He just wasn't sure that it was *doing* anything. Irvis certainly didn't react to it when he did.

Sev looked like he was about to say something, but Irvis had already recovered and was launching yet another dual attack; this time, all three of them dove out of the way, with Derivan creating [**Barrier**]s in layers to protect them from the pieces of Irvis that snapped forward and threatened to consume them. His forms twisted and wove around those constructs, but it still slowed him down.

"We need a plan!" Misa shouted. The *sound* Irvis was making was a crackle of groaning teeth, overwhelming the music that played on through the room they were in. Irvis flowed over Derivan's [**Barrier**]s, his body distorting around each one with a disconcerting sound that was not unlike the *snap* of bone. Derivan hurriedly worked his Sign into each of his [**Barrier**]s, trying to make something broader—

No, there was something more he could do here. If he used the combination Sign with Vex, he could at least let his lizard know that something was wrong. He hadn't tested his own Sign in isolation yet, and while this was a good time to do so, this was also a way to reach out to Vex without relying on the system.

Derivan just hoped it would work.

A flare of mana into his [**Barrier**]s brought that book-shield into being. Irvis's eldritch forms slammed into his magic and then almost seemed to recoil, as if burned. Derivan took the opportunity to move his [**Barrier**]s and begin linking them up. It took him only a second—each [**Barrier**] acted as an anchor point for a hexagonal section of a greater glyphic shield, creating a faintly glimmering green dome of shields around them, each imprinted with the faint impression of an open book.

Irvis slammed back into that shield a moment later, uncaring for the way the magic flashed and reacted against him, burning small parts of his flesh. Gnashing teeth spread small cracks into the dome, and Derivan felt a small part of his soul respond, tiny flashes of pain resounding inside him with every small crack.

"The shield will not last," he said, though his words were redundant. Sev and Misa both could see the cracks spreading for themselves. Derivan was more concerned about the possibility that he had trapped them. Irvis had spread *around* the shield so that the only source of light left was from the magic itself.

But he'd had little choice, he told himself. Irvis was faster than any of them, and Misa's blocks would not last.

... Still, he almost regretted the magic. The shield lit up Irvis in a particularly disconcerting way, insofar as it was disconcerting to have a flesh-monster surrounding them.

"We're missing our major damage dealer," Sev said grimly. "We don't really have a backup. Derivan?"

"I have made an attempt to communicate with Vex," Derivan said. "And ... I do not know if I can hurt him. His anatomy is different."

Which was an understatement if there ever was one.

"There's more." Sev hesitated. "The dungeon's . . . playing music. That's not normal, right?"

"The potion golems were part of our path," Derivan said. "Was the music part of yours?"

"I . . . don't know." Misa shook her head. "I didn't pay attention. My section of the dungeon was just a shitload of traps, but *maybe* there was a musical element to it?"

"If we can use the dungeon against him, we should," Sev said. He glanced up at the protective dome. "Assuming we last long enough."

"We can't stay like this forever," Misa agreed. "I can push him back again."

"Do you have enough mana?" Sev glanced at her. Misa winced.

"Nooo," she said.

Derivan understood, though Misa didn't elaborate further. Her manasharing trick required her to cut into the mana supply of the reality anchor, and that wasn't something she was particularly willing to do. Not when the integrity of that reality anchor was still supporting the existence of her entire family.

Her entire village, even.

The cracks in his shield began to spread, and Misa let out a reluctant breath. She'd practiced this maneuver and a few others with her village, Derivan knew. All she needed to do was send a message.

It happened quickly. Gabriel appeared and disappeared, having prepared the [**Trade**] before he'd even fully manifested; he wasn't one for combat situations, and Misa didn't want to keep him there. The moment she was ready she gave him a nod, and Derivan let the barrier go. Glyphic magic flashed back into the [**Barrier**]s producing them, and those [**Barrier**]s shattered an instant later. Irvis surged forward—

Misa *blocked*.

Like before, Irvis was disguising multiple attacks in what was apparently a single one. Derivan could sense it through Patch and Shift now that he was watching for it—there were small threads of Misa's skill reaching out, testing with spiderlike limbs to identify the exact vector of attack. And there were a dozen hidden small attacks in what Irvis was doing. Every individual tooth coated in a different poison, slightly Shifted limbs, and even *sounds* that could damage them.

Without the extra mana, Misa would have died.

Even with it, she struggled. He saw the immensity of the skill as it connected with some greater structure, and a massive *Shift* followed, flooding her weapon with something that seemed alien even to the system. Her mace pulsed into a beacon of light that, very briefly, pushed Irvis back, splattering sections of his flesh against the walls. The slowly rising floor almost seemed to help Irvis here; as it scraped against the walls, it pulled clumps of Irvis-flesh with it, leaving him in puddles on the floor that moved surprisingly quickly to recoalesce.

This was still an opportunity, Derivan recognized.

As Irvis tried to recover, the armor slashed forward with his sword, cutting into the pseudo-flesh that was closest to him. He was mindful of what had happened to Misa when her own weapon had made contact, but there was always the chance that what happened with him would be different, given how he interacted with health.

The flesh split under his blade, but it did nothing else differently. He was lucky in that it didn't start crawling up his sword, like it had with Misa's mace. On the other hand, it didn't look like Irvis had been hurt at all.

He even chuckled. "Was that your best shot?" he asked, his voice mocking. It resonated in the arena around them, a half-dozen mouths speaking the words from the little globs of him left all over the room that were slowly crawling together.

Derivan didn't respond. Instead, he paid attention to the music. The first plan hadn't worked, so it was time to move on to the second; he could feel the way the system itself was threaded through every note. The only question was exactly what kind of challenge this was supposed to represent—

Irvis didn't give him much time to think. He surged together all at once and launched himself at Derivan, a broken sort of laugh emerging from his mouths, and Derivan instinctively held up his sword to block. No [**Barrier**], and he'd acted too quickly for Misa to even react.

She was there a second later, but not before Derivan had already taken the brunt of the hit. For the first time he felt his metal twisting terribly, a long, serrated gash tearing open along the length of his arm. It was sheer luck that the poison did nothing to him, that Irvis had chosen to attack him like this.

But even that wasn't an advantage they kept for long.

Irvis recoalesced into a humanoid form. He seemed to be getting better and better at recovering from Misa's blocks, and she looked more and more exhausted every time she blocked one of his attacks. Derivan almost wanted to check in with her, but . . .

They had more pressing problems. Sev would keep an eye on everything he needed to.

Irvis once again wore an immaculate suit, though this time he didn't bother looking particularly human. He kept himself just human enough to affect a fake, thoughtful frown. "Now that's unexpected," Irvis said, looking at Derivan. "You're a monster, aren't you?"

Derivan's hand immediately went for the amulet the Guildmaster had given him. It was gone, crushed in the weight of Irvis's attack.

"I am who I choose to be," Derivan replied, taking an almost immediate dislike to Irvis's label. Irvis just laughed.

"Oh, that's rich," he said with a chuckle. He paused, scanning Derivan thoughtfully. "You don't know what you are, do you? You don't know what *we* are."

Irvis was a *monster*? "Enlighten me," Derivan said, trying to keep himself from sounding too eager. It wasn't an answer that he *needed*—but it was an answer he'd been searching for for a while.

Irvis could tell, evidently. He watched Derivan for a moment before smiling carelessly. "No. I don't think I will."

He was mocking him.

Which was all well and good. Derivan was interested in the answer but was perfectly willing to wait if he had to; right now, it was more important that they find a solution to the situation they were trapped in, before Irvis decided to stop toying with them. Derivan had no doubt that he could have obliterated the three of them if he really wanted to.

But there had to be *something* they could do, or Irvis surely wouldn't have waited for them to split up before attacking them. Unless he was confined to the dungeon somehow.

The dungeon music washed over him again, and this time, Derivan paid close attention. It was related in some way to Misa's section of the dungeon, he knew, but all it seemed to be was music. Nothing was *reacting* to it—

—but maybe nothing was reacting to it because someone was already solving every puzzle the dungeon threw at them in real time.

Derivan opened up Shift a little bit more, searching for everything Irvis was doing. Irvis was clearly aware of these shifted realities to some extent—every variant of him was acting with deliberation, and Derivan realized for the first time that some of them were *singing*.

Nothing obvious. Low, pure notes, in time with the dungeon music that poured over them. And yet . . .

Each time, the dungeon reacted, pulsing. And each time, the foundation of the whole place shook, like it was building up to something.

"Nothing to say?" Irvis raised an eyebrow at him. "A pity. Especially since you're like me."

If Derivan had had a mouth, it would have pressed into a thin line at that statement. Instead, he just readied his sword and kept a mental finger on the building music.

Something was about to happen, and he needed to be ready.

He just hoped Vex got his message.

CHAPTER 66

MAGICAL STUDIES

Vex was in the Ashion section of the tower, doing his damnedest to ignore Irvis's frozen body.

Something about it was unnerving. There were times he looked away and could swear that Irvis's eyes were following him somehow—those eyes remained full of *hate*, in a way that made him shiver. But anything he did to interfere with his father's magic might also free Irvis early, and Vex wasn't ready to deal with him.

The more time he had to study Irvis, the more uncertain he was about whether he could deal with Irvis at all. Even if Derivan, Misa, and Sev had all been here with him...

His mana sense told him a lot of things. Irvis's entire body was made out of exactly one mana aspect, though whatever aspect it was, it was nothing Vex had ever encountered before. It was more alive than any form of mana he'd seen before; every piece of Irvis showed individual, identical reactions.

His... his not-father's freezing spell was far more complicated than he'd thought, too. There was a reason it had taken his entire being to cast. This was a propagating stasis spell that was alive, in its own way, the mana imbued with bits of Karix's soul; every time Irvis tried to break free, the ice-infused energy reacted, attacking that piece of Irvis until it was once again frozen solid—imbued with too much ice-aspect to be able to move.

But even that was fading away. It would take a while—Karix had definitely managed to buy him time—but the spell that would have lasted for centuries on anyone else was only going to last for about an hour on Irvis.

The problem was that he'd studied just about everything he could through the ice. His glyph couldn't make it through the potent ice to understand what was going on with Irvis in detail, which meant he couldn't spend his time probing for a weakness.

Vex turned his attention back to the rest of the tower instead.

Behind the broken rubble was a mess of books; the Ashion section of the dungeon was constructed like a library, no doubt a reflection of his family's propensity for study and magic. There were traps here, he knew. He'd heard plenty of tales from others that had been here. Sometimes delvers would bring materials out of the dungeon and to him, and it was from this dungeon that he'd gained some of his study material...

Having access to this library would have made him happy in nearly any other situation.

Instead, Vex searched. His bonus room was probably somewhere here—but trigger conditions for bonus rooms were strange. His room had been <A World Without the System>, and so he could only guess that the trigger conditions were in some way related to that, the same way Misa had gained access to her room by replicating the conditions in which she had lost her village...

... except he had no such event in his past. He'd never been disconnected from the system. The closest he'd ever done in that regard was when he'd helped Derivan break free from it, and that had happened *after* the dungeon had created the bonus room...

... What type of magic *had* he used back there?

Vex paused, struck by the thought. He'd never considered it—too relieved that he'd been able to help, and then too caught up by everything that had happened afterward, maybe. That didn't feel like it was enough to explain his completely forgetting to explore this branch of magic. It didn't explain the fuzziness with which he remembered that notification that had appeared when he'd cast his spell.

> **WARNING: ###### aspect magic is not allowed—**

He'd known what that aspect was.

He'd understood that magic when he was casting it, but that knowledge had been taken away from him at the same moment the box had appeared. It was part of the reason he hadn't focused on it with the intensity he otherwise would have. A magic that could interact directly with the system, that allowed him to act on it maybe the same way Derivan could with Patch and Shift—having access to that would have changed everything for him.

No wonder it had been locked away.

Even now, the memory was blurred and fuzzy to him, but now that he knew where to begin...

Vex felt his feet taking him to a particular section of the tower's library. It was a small, shadowed section in a corner that was uncomfortably close to Irvis's frozen body, but Vex did his best to ignore it; instead, he scanned the books. More than half of them were traps, if he remembered what the delver reports had said correctly; the Ashion tower tested knowledge and perception and *magic*, all aspects that their family purported themselves to be experts in.

Half of the books were layered in just the faintest shimmer of Illusion—those were easy enough to dismiss as fake. Another few books appeared not to be magical at all, but they were bound in a way that Karix would never have allowed in their personal library, and so Vex dismissed those as well. He'd come back to those later, but he suspected it was the sort of detail he was *supposed* to notice.

It got harder from there. He picked out an older-looking tome, glancing at the cover: The Origins of Magic, embossed in gold letters onto green leather. He frowned at it and put it back. The capitalization of the title wasn't correct.

Another book he rejected for having inconsistent kerning, and a third one he put back because he noticed the book didn't have a shadow. Vex went through them like this one by one, until he found a book that didn't have any flaws by his father's standards.

He took a breath, sat down, and opened the book.

Aspects of Magic

You may access more of the contents of this book by channeling different aspects into it.

Vex couldn't help but raise a brow. A magic test, after all that? Why not just start with the test to begin with? It was an easy-enough test, though—his class as a [**Chromaturgist**] had given him a particular affinity with even the most esoteric of aspects. Irvis's aspect aside, it wasn't difficult for him to channel a whole spectrum of the different types of mana he had access to.

Fire, water, earth, air, light, and dark; all the same elements he had access to in the form of glyphs. Arcane, for the esoteric, to represent a type of mana that would change and adapt. Necrotic, to represent rot. Life. Plague. Blood. Stranger aspects like one that, as best as he could tell, represented English, though he'd never been able to craft a useful spell out of it.

And then, like a fireblossom, text bloomed on the page in front of him.

If you can see this, you will likely have already realized that mana aspects are largely arbitrary. There are a few great secrets about magic, and here is one of them: *aspects do not exist. The lines are not as distinct as the mind makes it seem, though thinking about it in that way certainly makes your spells easier to understand and cast.*

The truth behind aspects is simple: they are small facets of a conceptual sphere. Anything you can conceive of is likely to be an aspect within the mana, though many of them are redundant and overlap with one another. Yet all of them are useful, and specificity can be immensely beneficial. To find an aspect of roads, for example, would be to craft a spell stronger for traveling on roads than any spell using an aspect of travel could be.

Vex paused in his reading there, his brows furrowing in thought. Here was a realization spelled out for him that had already been percolating in the back of his mind, perhaps for years: why *did* mana divide itself into aspects? The categories seemed so arbitrary, and the elements themselves were based on an archaic understanding of the world ...

This explained a lot about why the elements existed as they did.

And if aspects were simply a representation of any conceivable idea— then could there be an aspect for the system? Or was the system an outside element, something that mana couldn't intrinsically represent?

... There was still the question of how glyphs fit into all of this. Vex thought he could see the bits and pieces, the holes in the explanation where glyphs would have slotted in if all knowledge of them hadn't been erased. Glyphs represented art, and art represented what the book called the "conceptual sphere," the breadth of ideas that all living people had come up with.

If that were true ... then magic was much, *much* broader than he had assumed. He hadn't even considered an aspect of roads, and yet reaching for it with [**Multichromal Mutation**] was as simple as thinking about it, now that he knew. Many of his other attempts to use that skill had been difficult, requiring a thorough understanding of the aspect he was trying to reach, but understanding what aspects *were*—

—well, it didn't make using the skill completely trivial. But it certainly made it easier.

Vex wanted to start iterating through all the ideas he had—and he had so many now that he understood more about how these aspects came about— but something gave him pause, and it wasn't just the fact that Irvis was beginning to thaw.

It was the information he received, in a very familiar sort of way, of an attack. Of a *multitude* of attacks. Vex had to put down the book to parse the rush of knowledge, because the flow was stronger than it had been the first time Derivan had used their combined Sign to block an attack. A small part of him managed to mentally reach out and call out the system menu again, to see if the interference had faded, but he stumbled and had to lean on the wall to steady himself before he could read the chat.

Instead, he focused on his mind. If Derivan was using their Sign, he was trying to tell him something; if he was just blocking one of Misa's attacks or something...

But he already knew that wasn't the case. Derivan wouldn't have used it for something as trivial as that; the circumstances under which he would try to contact Vex in this way were few and far between, and Vex had no reason to think this was anything less than a real attack.

He was, of course, right. But more interesting—and more alarming—was the nature of what was attacking his friends. He felt a part of his mind chugging along, automatically sorting the information he'd gathered, and parsing it together with what he'd just learned.

Aspect of Hatred, Irvis
A physical manifestation of a single aspect in the mana, given life through a concentration and manipulation of Reality. This particular form of manifestation allows him to manipulate aspects of reality that are not normally accessible without the use of a [**Reality Shard**].

Poison Fang, (26)
A poisoned bite. The specific poison varies but is almost universally drawn from Shifted realities that have been rendered uninhabitable, usually due to the actions of poison mages in Elyra. Plague aspect variant.

Discordant Sound, (32)
An infectious sound, gathered from an unpatched Bard class. The sound does physical damage through a quirk in system-assisted physics and possesses a quality that will cause listeners to sing along, damaging themselves in the process. Sound aspect variant.

Biting Sight, (47)
A broken image of something that has been erased. To look upon it is to wipe away any memories that would otherwise be associated with that image as the associated infolock spreads to any memories that are "contaminated." Mental aspect variant.

Vex swallowed. That was probably why he'd struggled so hard to process everything—over a hundred distinct *attacks*, even if many of them were the same ones; he wondered if that was related to why Misa's health costs were per-attack. Perhaps the system had to process each one individually, the way he'd had to.

More importantly, this meant his friends were *also* being attacked by Irvis ... and a more-powerful version of him, if this was any indication. Vex glanced at Irvis's frozen body, feeling a slight chill come over him that had nothing to do with the ice magic that kept the living Aspect in stasis.

If there was more than one of him, he wasn't necessarily *safe*.

And with Derivan and the others in trouble, he had to decide what to do, and quickly.

CHAPTER 67

A LOSING BATTLE

Derivan was more hurt than he had ever been.

He was still *alive*, crucially. His chest plate, where the runes that kept him alive were etched—that was still entirely intact. But it was only intact because he'd made sacrifices elsewhere. Because when Irvis forced him to choose between damage to his chest plate and damage to something else, he'd always chosen *something else*. He was fairly certain he'd survive even if Irvis managed to take off his head.

Not that he wanted to test that. Being deprived of sight along with his limbs didn't sound like a good time.

Derivan had taken on almost half of Irvis's attacks, trading places with Misa whenever he could. She was still blocking him successfully, but it was taking something vital out of her. There were dark circles under her eyes and almost a gauntness to her frame that hadn't been there before. She was spending more mana than she ever had.

Patch told him, too, that the reality anchor she held with her was straining. It wasn't about to be destroyed, exactly, but it was a reminder that there was more at stake here than their own lives. If Misa died... Well. That was one of the reasons he was taking as many hits as he could.

Sev was healing them. He'd tried to tank a couple of hits with his [**Barrier**]s when he could, but most of the time, he was saving mana to keep Misa healed; he could do that for less mana than it took to block one of Misa's attacks.

All of that was to say that the fact remained that they were *losing*.

Irvis surged toward him, using one of the *three* bodies he'd created; Misa was dealing with the other two, and Irvis seemed to be studiously ignoring Sev, for whatever reason. There was something there, though Derivan didn't know what. There had to be a reason he wasn't attacking their healer—

Fangs crashed toward him, and Derivan tried to pull out of the way as best he could. He twisted, and he felt a part of his body turn *into* slime, affording him just a touch more flexibility than his metal usually offered. He was almost out of range—

But Irvis could freely change his form the same way Derivan could, and he adjusted easily, his entire body *unfolding into a mouth* so it could snap shut around him. Derivan wasn't used to fighting like this, and the Slime stat wasn't second nature to him the way Physical Empathy was. His sword was out of position, and the best he could do was bring his left arm up to stop Irvis's teeth from just biting through his chest plate, even as he shoved backward as fast as he could with his feet.

It worked, mostly. Just like most of Irvis's attacks before, his armor was strong enough to withstand the direct hit—but it wasn't strong enough to withstand whatever it was Irvis had on his fangs, that drooling liquid that was so much more than a simple poison. It began eating into his metal almost immediately.

Derivan didn't hesitate. His left arm was mostly useless from the forearm onward anyway; the metal was chipped and torn from the bits and pieces he'd been forced to hack off from Irvis's other attacks. One quick cut was all it took.

It was fortunate his sword was strong enough to slice through his own metal.

The remnants of his left forearm fell to the floor. The saving grace here was that it didn't *hurt*. There was, at most, a dull throbbing that Derivan interpreted as his version of pain. He heard Misa shout something that was muffled by the still-rising music and the sound of Irvis's own eldritch taunting. She sounded angry.

She would be. Derivan almost smiled at the thought.

"Derivan!" Sev was closer to him and his voice clearer; Derivan saw the way he started forward, only barely stopping himself from running right to Derivan's side. He looked lost, desperate. "Shit, I'm—I need to heal you. I'm going to try. I know we were talking about avoiding it but—"

"Do it," Derivan said. He understood the need for it. The worry was that he would get the health stat and lose the advantage his lack thereof gave him in fights, but this was— His lack of a Health stat wasn't helping him against Irvis. He still didn't know if Irvis had Health.

Sev shut up and *cast*. Derivan felt that rush of divine magic flowing over him, something he hadn't experienced since he'd first lost the stat. Irvis was attacking him—he hadn't stopped to wait—but transforming the way he did seemed to take something out of him, and he'd turned back into his humanoid form, reshaping one arm into a blade instead.

That was . . . more manageable. Irvis was still faster than him by a long shot, but Derivan was better with a sword. This was familiar ground for him. He could *survive*.

Though it didn't give him much of an opportunity to check his stats and see if he had actually regained Health. His metaphorical heart sank, though, when he realized his arm wasn't healing.

This would qualify as a status ailment of some sort, a malus. Sev had the ability to heal those, but if he hadn't already—

He saw Sev shake his head slightly.

If he hadn't already, then he'd probably tried and failed.

It didn't matter. There were other ways to get his arm back. The problem here and now was mostly the fact that losing an entire arm threw his balance off, and it limited his options. His options were already limited, and using the dungeon against Irvis wasn't going as well as he hoped.

He'd managed to work out more about what they were supposed to do, partially through Patch, and partially through an observation of what Irvis did in different variations of their reality through Shift.

The room they were in was a sort of hexagonal column, and each of the six walls had a different pattern painted on it. Every wall corresponded to a different instrument, and specific parts of each pattern corresponded to a different note. In the *normal* case, the elevator would begin rising, and music would begin playing; the potion-golems, or whatever monsters had been triggered or created in the other sections of the dungeon, would spawn and fight until whatever song was playing was "completed" by the delvers. *Completion*, in this case, was defined as participating and guiding the song to an end point. Different song completions led to different outcomes, whether it was a buff for the delvers or a malus for the enemies.

And the dungeon didn't recognize Irvis as an enemy. It thought he was one of *them*. That was a problem for them if they wanted to try to use the dungeon against him; anything they did would affect him, too. There was something Derivan thought he could do there—Irvis wasn't connected to the system in the same way, and so buffs and maluses would probably affect him differently, in a way he could affect with Patch . . .

But it was all a lot of conjecture. The possibility of damaging the stat wasn't a concern for him at this point, at least. There was too much danger here for him to restrict his options.

"Performance issues?" Irvis smirked at him, mocking. He'd relaxed a lot once he'd stopped restricting himself, like he wasn't worried anymore. Derivan wondered why he'd felt the need to restrict himself in the first place. He kept doing *this*, though, pausing the fight just so he could mock them. Normally they would have ignored it and kept fighting, but...

They needed the break. If Irvis was going to give it to them, even if it was to mock them, so be it. Derivan used the opportunity to surreptitiously check his status.

The good news was that he didn't have Health, still, though he didn't know if that news was *good* exactly. The... not-good-but-*neutral* news was that he had gained two new stats, which he'd sort of suspected was the other thing that might happen if Sev tried to heal him.

So, one stat from Sev, and the other was likely from Irvis.

Grace: 1
Intensity: 1

... He could tell nothing from the names. He couldn't feel any new sense like Shift and Patch, but then Shift had taken some time for him to really understand. It didn't mean much that he couldn't sense anything now.

But it also meant it didn't give him anything new to use against Irvis. Not yet, anyway.

"If you're not going to answer me," Irvis prompted, "you might as well die."

"I have nothing to say to you," Derivan said evenly. "You wish to see me angry. I am uninterested in giving you that satisfaction."

Also, he wasn't sure he was capable of feeling anger.

Irvis, on the other hand, certainly was.

"DERIVAN!" Misa called out, something in her voice worried and desperate, and Derivan glanced toward her only to see that both of the Irvises she was fighting had disengaged and were now heading directly for him; they moved too fast for him to dodge, and the third one joined in, his body morphing into another mess of endless teeth—

—Misa appeared in front of him, trying to block, though he saw her system connection pulsing through Patch, as though it was being strained; vast swathes of mana were being pulled through her to power her skill, and if it had *completed* successfully he wasn't sure what would have happened. But that didn't happen, because before the block could complete, Sev threw himself in front of them both, a divine barrier lighting up in front of him—

—And Irvis stopped.

He didn't hit Sev's barrier. He pulled his own attacks back, all three of them in all his forms, and recoalesced into one being that stared with undeniable anger at Sev.

But he didn't attack.

"Move," Irvis said. Sev narrowed his eyes.

"You won't attack me," he said. "You've been ignoring me for most of this fight. *I'm the healer.* I'm the first target for almost any group." Sev stalked forward. "If you're not attacking me, there has to be a reason."

"Sev, get back," Misa said, her voice tense. "You can't just make that gamble."

"Even if you're right," Irvis said, his tone almost conversational, "do you really think I can't get around you? I've been doing that this whole fight. You are *nothing*. An exceptionally good healer at best."

"That's a lot of words you're spending talking and not a lot of time you're spending on *doing that*," Sev retorted. He didn't move—but, to his credit, he didn't step closer, either. He took Misa's words into account and took a careful step back, but kept himself between Irvis and the others.

Irvis sighed and clicked his tongue.

Then he launched himself forward, his body splitting apart and going *around* Sev and his barrier, straight toward Derivan and Misa. Derivan stepped forward, intent on not letting Misa spend yet another block, but this time Irvis seemed determined to take them both out all at once; he somehow sped up even more, faster than Derivan could react, and though he tried to block with his arm again he'd forgotten that his arm just *wasn't there* anymore.

Irvis formed a spear of flesh, aimed at Derivan's chest; Derivan saw a similar set directed at Misa, except it was a hundred disparate spears. He doubted she had the mana to block that, even with the [**Trade**]. Not with all the blocks she'd managed so far.

Derivan told himself to do *something*.

But he didn't know what to do.

CHAPTER 68

LAST-MINUTE RESEARCH

Vex was working with an increasing sense of impending doom, not that he knew exactly what was going on. He'd regained access to his system interface a while back, but that didn't do anything for him—none of his teammates were responding, and there wasn't any way for him to get into contact with them otherwise. He'd tried everything, from using the Communication glyph (which required an anchor and thus still didn't work) to contacting the Guildmaster directly, but even she didn't have anyone with the ability to look inside dungeons while they were active like this.

That skill was, as far as anyone knew, exclusive to Derivan and the Shift stat. Trait. Whatever.

The only small comfort he had was that he knew they were still *alive*; none of them had dropped off from the party interface, though Misa's stats seemed dangerously low. If she was low, he didn't want to imagine what state Derivan was in. At least Sev still seemed to be all right...

Though that was strange, now that he thought about it. Was there a reason Sev in particular wasn't being targeted? He was the healer, and normally he would have been the first target. Vex couldn't imagine why Irvis wouldn't try to take him out first.

But he was letting himself get distracted.

He could, in theory, have run down the Ashion tower toward wherever this battle was taking place. If Derivan, Misa, and Sev were all embroiled in the same battle, then more likely than not they had managed to meet up; either they had appeared all at the same starting point, or they were at the central room that would take them to the upper tiers of the dungeon.

But that wasn't a bet he was willing to take. If they were in separate fights—or, worse, if Irvis was the level of threat that Vex thought he was, and even Vex's presence would do nothing to help them except perhaps delay the inevitable—then he needed a different solution, and he needed it fast.

He had the beginnings of an idea percolating in his head.

Irvis was, somehow, a manifestation of a mana Aspect into a living, conscious being. Vex wouldn't pretend that he understood how that was possible. What was more important was what the book had told him—the idea that Aspects were just reflections of facets of something the book called a *conceptual sphere*. The full gamut of potential ideas and concepts, filtered through the lens of every living being that existed on the planet.

So—if they were to go to a different world entirely—wouldn't its conceptual sphere be different? Even if Irvis *followed them there*, he wouldn't be able to stay the same. Hatred was a very specific sort of emotion, but it was directed, and perhaps that direction would be different if they were in a different world.

There were books in the library that had studied the phenomenon of planeshifting. Some of them, Vex suspected, he wouldn't have been able to find if he hadn't already known what he had about Shift and reality and the oddness of Misa's skills with the way they interacted with different timelines.

All of their world was contained within a set of limited set of wavelengths: Shifts. Every potential timeline, every possibility that sprang from their world—all just an infinite set in a larger set of infinite sets. There was a baseline wavelength that all of reality existed upon, and any distance that one took from it was a little bit like stretching a rubber band; other timelines, possibilities, and realities could exist so long as the baseline was stretched over it, but it was otherwise something virtual rather than real.

Which was all mostly just a very complicated way of saying that their world was *real*, and all those other timelines that Misa pulled from weren't; they were possibilities that existed in the ether that the system somehow let them pull from and make into reality.

Planeshifting was a step further than that. Planeshifting was still a *Shift*, but it was a much-larger hop than anywhere Misa could stretch. Even the realm of the gods wasn't as far away as a whole other reality; the phenomenon of planeshifting, therefore, was still far from being understood. The abstract realm of the gods and demons was like an isolated island within their set of infinity, while other realities sat entirely outside that set.

Bonus rooms, too, operated in a similar way. At least, the large ones that contained entire villages or kingdoms or worlds did. The system wrapped a whole localized realm into a smaller set of infinity; the experiments that had been done to confirm this were complicated, and—strangely—seemed to have been done by researchers in Elyra. That point confused Vex. None of their noble houses had done research that extensive on planeshifting, as far as he knew, and the book itself seemed to be older than the history of their Kingdom.

Not that he was surprised that their history was a little bit chronologically broken, at this point. The actual experiments were interesting, and Vex would have loved to spend some time delving into it. They had asked clerics to reach out to the gods outside a dungeon, *inside* the dungeon, and inside a bonus room; they'd measured the amount of subjective time it had taken for a response and the amount of energy that had been spent on that connection—

It was around here that Vex shook his head and pulled the tendrils of his Sign back, letting the Research magic fade away. He'd learned what he needed to. He knew his bonus room was the type that they needed; if the name of the dungeon wasn't enough, they'd seen proof of that back in Fendal and Teque.

It was convenient that Research magic let him read books much, much faster than he would usually have been able to. It was like having a virtual version of himself write down all the pertinent notes after going through the book thoroughly.

The next question was how to activate the bonus room—and how to get it to drag Derivan, Sev, and Misa in as well.

If nothing else, he was relatively sure he knew where it *was*.

In the time he'd spent looking for the relevant books in the library, Irvis had melted a little more; the aspect was able to move his head around slightly, and if glares could kill, Vex was pretty sure he'd already be dead. More importantly, though, that little bit of melting had introduced a lot of mana-rich water to the floor, and that water had soaked into the carpet. Vex *almost* hadn't noticed how the water soaked into the floor in a very specific pattern, but he'd recognized one spike that was particularly familiar to him as the outer edge of a runic circle.

There was a circle cut into the ground beneath the carpet.

It took more work than he would have liked; if Irvis hadn't been frozen next to the circle, Vex would have made use of a controlled burn to get rid of the carpet and preserve the books. Instead, he was forced to use a variety of cutting spells to rip up sections of the carpet, distantly aware that Irvis was watching him the whole time.

Uncomfortable. Vex was a little worried he'd be able to do something with the circle as well. Irvis *was* a living aspect—Vex had no doubt that he knew more about magic than he did, both the true, glyph-based magic and the system-enforced mockery of it that was runes.

After a moment of consideration, he grabbed some of the pieces of carpet he'd already cut up and placed them over Irvis's head as a makeshift blindfold.

Then he finished what he was doing and took a second to survey his work.

There was a door built into the ground—one that wasn't dissimilar to the one in the dungeon all the way back in Fendal, albeit much larger and also on the floor. At the center of the circle was something that Vex now recognized as a [Reality Shard]. Had that always been there? Or had the system adjusted now that it knew about [Reality Shards]?

He recognized some of the other components of the circle from the research he'd already done on spells, and from the work he did on runic circles in general; he understood them well enough to know how to modify a lot of them. *This* circle was, strangely, not unlike the runic circle that represented a [Fireball].

Funny how so many spells came back to that. Vex supposed there was a lot of use in the idea of packing mana into a ball and launching it, whatever aspect that mana happened to be. [Fireball] was just a common one.

The *launching* aspect of the circle was different, though. It was similar enough that Vex could recognize the pieces that represented position and momentum, but there was an extra variable baked into the vector that described *direction*. That was probably for the Shift element of it all.

The door was set to pull mana from the user as soon as it was opened. With a normal individual's supply of mana, there would only have been enough to transport one person. Vex's supply was enough to take their whole party, if only that party were *there* . . .

Vex tried to quell his rising panic, and thought.

The amount of mana he had was enough, essentially, to cover the room. If he wanted to get greater coverage—something entirely unintended by the system, as far as he knew—he needed a bigger supply of mana. Misa's reality anchor would have been a source, but she wasn't here; he couldn't rely on that.

The only other source of mana he had here was . . .

Vex glanced at Irvis, then looked at the runic circle again.

As far as he could tell, this circle didn't do anything to the mana going through it except use it to power the spell; the aspect he used wouldn't change the nature of the spell in any way. The possibility that Irvis's hatred aspect would corrupt the spell was no more likely than fire-aspect mana would end up creating a version of Teque that was literally on fire—there wasn't a way for that to happen within the circle.

But Vex had to be cautious, because Irvis *was* the hatred aspect. Even if the spell as it stood wasn't affected by the type of mana used to power it, there was every chance that Irvis would be able to change the nature of the spell somehow, either in the process of being used to fuel the circle or afterwards, when the spell was actually being cast.

Cautious or not, though, there was a more pertinent question.

Did he really have a choice?

He could have run back to try to fight with his friends—Manaburn could do damage to Irvis; he knew that much. But his father had died just to stop— *stop*, not kill—this version of Irvis. If the list of attacks he'd received from Derivan's spell was any indication, then the version his friends were fighting was much, much stronger.

... There was a risk no matter what direction he took here. Derivan had given him information, which meant he trusted him to make the right decision, and to Vex, the answer was plain.

As they were right now, they couldn't beat Irvis. They had all the tools, but they hadn't spent enough time exploring the full potential of that set of tools. They had plenty of *reason* for that; they'd been tossed into one situation after another and had simply responded the best they could, but...

They needed time. The bonus room was their best bet at that. Vex had the ability to give them that time, and more importantly, he had a powerful version of [**Mana Manipulation**] that he could use to stop Irvis from doing anything strange. Besides, the danger that Irvis potentially posed here was just that: a potential danger.

The danger Irvis posed to his friends was very, very real.

Vex didn't waste any more time. It took a small spell to buff his strength, but he dragged Irvis's body over to the door, making sure the carpet was secure around his head; he didn't want to give him any more of a glimpse at the circle, in case that helped him compromise it.

For a small moment, Vex hesitated. "... Sorry about this," he said, though he wasn't sure why.

Then—albeit awkwardly—he pushed the frozen statue of Irvis forward so that one hand was wedged into the door handle, and *pulled*.

Part of him was worried Irvis's arm would simply snap off.

But no. The circle flared to life and began to work almost immediately; the small bit of mana that touched the handle activated the siphon, and Vex could almost *feel* the flare of hatred from Irvis. It pulled more and more mana, unpacking the sheer *density* that was packed into just this iteration of Irvis.

It was here that Vex knew he'd made the right choice. There wasn't a chance in any of the realms that he or his team would have been able to beat

Irvis as they were. The amount of mana packed into him was beyond even that reality anchor they'd stolen.

It was too much mana, even. This wasn't just enough to grab his party—this would grab hold of the entire dungeon and snap it into the realm of his bonus room. Elyra would be missing its Prime Dungeon for the entire time that Vex and his team were gone, and all the infrastructure that relied on it would collapse for as long as they took to complete the objective in the bonus room.

Hopefully the time dilation was significant.

Vex kept an eye on the spell as it was cast, but Irvis didn't seem to be able to do anything to change it. He was, in this case, as helpless against the system as all the rest of them had been. A surge of mana followed, and the door began to open, all on its own. Vex saw a pulse reach out, grabbing on to as much in this reality as it could, packing it into a dense bubble of information and possibility—

—and then he saw nothing, as the whole world Shifted.

CHAPTER 69

RECOVERY

Derivan regained consciousness in the exact same room he'd passed out in.

He wasn't exactly sure when he'd lost consciousness. That was not, as far as he had known, something that was even possible; the closest he'd gotten to passing out was the strange semi-meditative state he had ended up in all the way back when his link with the system had first been destroyed and then rebuilt so that he wasn't recognized as a monster. The dreams he'd had back then were strange—Derivan was almost certain now that he was thinking about them that they had mentioned the stars, and for the life of him, he couldn't remember if the stars had *existed* at that point in time, or if they had only been in his dream—but he'd never been able to replicate the event.

It took a moment for him to gather his bearings. The others were still unconscious, and Irvis was nowhere to be seen; the floor itself had long stopped moving, having reached the top of the corridor it had been traveling up. Derivan didn't know what to make of it all, but . . .

Vex had probably done something. Derivan checked the system, just to make sure Vex was still *alive*, and saw a whole host of messages that had been left in their party chat—no doubt while they'd been caught up in the battle with Irvis.

[Hey, sorry, I lost access to the system for a bit,] he had sent. [**Are you guys okay? I'm in the Ashion tower. Irvis showed up here—it was really messy. Some fucked-up shit happened, and I don't say that lightly.**]

A small pause, and then later, another message: [**Respond if you get the chance, please? I'm worried.**]

And then: [**Shit, I can see Misa's health going down. You're in a fight. Do you need me to come find you?**]

No messages after that; Vex had no doubt figured out what was going on once he'd used their joint Sign to stop Irvis from killing them all. And then he'd done ... something?

[**Vex?**] Derivan sent, tentatively. He didn't like using the party chat very much; it was all very unintuitive for him, and his fingers didn't fit well on the keyboard. It was even worse now that he had only one hand to type with. Everything was a lot slower. [**We are alive. In the central room. You did something?**]

Derivan waited, but ... no response yet. Carefully, he dragged himself to his feet—he was still very much *hurt*, he was aware, and missing half an arm threw off his balance in ways he hadn't anticipated. The runic circuitry linking all his armor together had perhaps been damaged too, because he found moving to be ... sluggish. Slower than he was used to.

Maybe he just wasn't used to being this hurt, though.

He went up to Sev first. The cleric would probably know what to do and be able to heal any damage that Misa had sustained; very gently, Derivan turned him over so that he was facing the ceiling, and tried to examine him for injuries. He hadn't spent a lot of time learning how to do first aid—having a healer had made it sort of unnecessary—but there had been *some* mandatory classes in the Guild. He was glad for them now.

No major bleeding from environmental damage causing a status effect. Nothing was blocking his airways. Derivan saw Sev's chest rise and fall. *Moving him* wasn't too much of a concern, since Sev would almost certainly be able to heal his own maluses away, but Derivan didn't want him to do more healing than he needed to, so he tapped Sev on the shoulder instead.

To his credit, Sev started awake almost immediately. "What happened?" he asked, his eyes scanning the room. "Is Misa okay? Where's Irvis?"

He didn't even wait for Derivan to answer his questions—Sev's eyes landed quickly on Misa, and he almost leapt to his feet; it was only Derivan's hand on his shoulder that stopped him. "Check your statuses first," Derivan said gently.

Sev stared at Derivan instead. "Oh, gods, Deri," he said, letting out a breath. "Your arm ..."

"It is fine," Derivan said. "It does not hurt."

Which was a slight lie—it *did* hurt. But the pain was minor, and nothing like the kind of pain he suspected organic life could feel. It was an irritating sort of buzz on the edge of his perception, like something that should have been there ... wasn't.

"I can't heal it," Sev said. "I tried. I'm sorry. Maybe if we find the Guildmaster—"

"Sev," Derivan interrupted. "Check your status first, please. And then check on Misa."

Slowly, Sev nodded; Derivan saw the panic that had flooded into him ebb away as the cleric tried to center himself. There was all too much going on for him, and Derivan suspected that something else had changed, too, something deeper that was related to the way he'd previously been restricted by the system. Patch showed a small change there.

But there would be time for that later.

Sev glanced at the air, at his status, and then let out a small sigh of relief; nothing dangerous there, apparently. He got up with Derivan's help and jogged over to Misa, popping a quick [**Triage**] to check on her condition.

"She's fine," Sev said for his benefit. "Just unconscious and... very tired. I think her skill started to eat into her somehow."

"That is not supposed to happen," Derivan said, somewhat unnecessarily.

"You're telling me." Sev sighed. "We need to let her rest for a bit. System's not built for us to strain our skills to that degree, I guess... I don't see why it would eat into *her*."

"It was probably not doing that," Derivan said quietly. "It was likely eating into the reality anchor."

"... Which is a part of her right now." Sev cursed slightly under his breath. "Do you have any way of checking on that? Do you think her family's... you know, *okay*?"

"I cannot observe the anchor directly," Derivan replied honestly. "But I do not think it is irreparably damaged. We simply need to find a way to repair it."

"And we know it can be repaired," Sev muttered to himself. He looked down at Misa, and Derivan saw something in him crack, just slightly; the cleric took one of her hands in his own and hugged it to himself. "You're gonna be okay," he told her.

"Do you have reason to think she will not be?" Derivan asked, a note of worry entering his own voice.

"What? No, I just..." Sev looked down at her and fell silent. He sighed. "... I think this reminded me of something," he said quietly. "Don't know what. But it feels like it's something sad. Like I lost someone important, just like this."

Derivan didn't know what to say to that. He went up to Sev and put a hand on his shoulder, and Sev gave him a small, appreciative smile.

"I'm not Vex, you know," he said. "That doesn't help me as much as it does him."

"But it does help," Derivan said.

"... Yeah." Sev leaned against Derivan. He didn't say anything else.

They sat like that for a while. Derivan didn't move, not wanting to break the moment; Sev was clearly embroiled in his own thoughts, and Derivan had all kinds of worries of his own swimming about in him. More than anything right now, he wanted to go look for Vex—but he didn't know which of the sixteen passages represented the Ashion tower, and he wasn't actually sure that Vex would be there besides. All he could do was wait and see if Vex would respond.

Fortunately, he did, about ten minutes later; Misa still hadn't stirred. [**I got us into the bonus room,**] Vex sent. [**And, uh ... I think the entire dungeon, too. Are you guys in the center tower?**]

[**We have ascended to the second tier,**] Derivan confirmed. [**We are waiting here for Misa to awaken. Would you like me to come find you?**]

[**No, I'll, uh ... I'll come to you guys.**] Vex hesitated slightly, then sent a second message. [**I'm glad you're all okay.**]

Derivan didn't respond to that last message; he didn't know how to. He wasn't sure that they *were* all okay.

But they were alive, and that was what mattered.

The pitter-patter of Vex's feet came down one of the sixteen corridors not more than twenty minutes later, though Misa still hadn't stirred in that time; Derivan was surprised it hadn't taken longer.

"Most of the dungeon doesn't seem to be active," Vex said with a slight frown as he emerged. "I guess that's not particularly surprising—"

He stopped, and his eyes widened. Vex ran forward, dropping the books he was carrying with him. "Deri— Shit, what happened to you? Are you— No, that's a stupid question, but—"

Vex stopped, seemingly unsure what to say, but the anxiety and worry and *fear* that filled his face was palpable; Derivan reached out with his arm, and the lizardkin practically flung himself into him, only pulling back at the last minute to avoid completely bowling him over when he was already hurt. Derivan appreciated the sentiment.

"Irvis happened," Derivan said quietly. "We were unprepared."

"I ... Does it hurt?" Vex's voice was soft and plaintive; one hand reached out to trace the ragged edges of the cut metal. He winced and pulled back when it threatened to cut him, and Derivan gently maneuvered him so that Vex wasn't near the side of his lost arm.

"Only slightly," Derivan admitted. He leaned in close, nuzzling his forehead against Vex's, and after a moment he felt Vex return the gesture; the lizardkin's heart was still pulsing wildly, but it was slowly calming down. He grabbed one of Derivan's hands, clutching at it like his life depended on it. "Sev tried to heal it, but he was unable to," he continued. "He did give me a new stat, though."

"You can't distract me with your new stats," Vex mumbled, burying his face in Derivan's chest. "We can . . . we can get you a new arm, right?"

"I believe so," Derivan said. "But I have never tried such a thing before."

". . . I'm sorry I wasn't here."

"It was hardly your fault."

"Then I'm sorry I couldn't be here," Vex said. He pulled back, his eyes glistening. "If you'd gotten more hurt—"

"—I did not," Derivan said gently. "And that was because of you, was it not?"

". . . I guess." Vex sighed, planting his face into Derivan's chest plate again; Derivan found the gesture comforting, though Vex was probably doing it to comfort himself. A win-win for both of them, really. ". . . What was the new stat?"

"Grace," Derivan said. "And Intensity."

"Intensity is from Irvis?" Vex asked, slightly warily, and Derivan managed a light shrug; he didn't know. They'd both appeared at the same time, more or less.

"I believe it is," he said. "Though I cannot be sure."

"Right," Vex said.

"I'm glad to see you too," Sev joked, smiling slightly to show he was joking; Vex paled anyway.

"Are you and Misa all right?" he asked. "I'm sorry, I got so focused on Derivan—"

"It's fine," Sev laughed. He'd moved back slightly to give Derivan and Vex space, sitting next to Misa's head instead. "You were worried about your boyfriend. Don't worry about it."

"But are you guys okay?" Vex insisted. "All of you." He looked at Misa— *really* looked at her this time, and Derivan saw his demeanor shift even more to worry; he squeezed the lizardkin's hand gently but didn't say anything. Vex needed to process this in his own time.

Next to Sev, the difference with Misa was even starker—like she'd lost something vital, with her sunken eyes and shrunken frame.

"I don't know," Sev answered honestly.

"But we will be," Derivan added, and Sev nodded slightly. He glanced over at Misa as he did.

And Misa, perhaps rather predictably, chose that moment to stir.

CHAPTER 70

JEROME-SELF-REVIEW

Jerome sat next to Kestel.

He'd taken to visiting the head researcher of the dungeon team every few days, just to see if he was doing better. Ever since he'd learned about what happened to him at the dungeon—his own men turning against him the moment he hesitated to report back, wanting to first ensure the safety of his men...

Harold and the others had left, last he'd heard. They were worried about Kestel too, but none of them were really aligned to anything related to healing and recovery. Like Derivan's team, they'd left to investigate something and were hoping to acquire the crystals needed to heal Kestel while they were away.

They had their own problems, he understood. He noticed it out of the corners of his eyes, when they thought no one else was looking. The way they'd reach out to scratch an imaginary itch and then flinch. The way they'd fold their arms and then wince slightly when the weight of it was different—when their bones didn't catch in quite the same way their arms once did.

"The Guild still keeps making me take those stupid classes," Jerome said to Kestel. The scientist, of course, didn't respond; he was either asleep or pretending to be asleep, but he still wasn't quite *there*. He wasn't even sure why he was talking to Kestel about his problems, but he continued anyway. He'd found a certain comfort in being able to speak to someone without judgement. "And now I keep noticing things I didn't notice before. It sucks. I wanna go back to not noticing."

Kestel still didn't respond, and Jerome took this as encouragement to continue. "You know what I would've done before? I would've just told them to suck it up. Or I would've said that being a skeleton is fuckin' *cool*, and I wish *I* could be a skeleton, and why don't they appreciate having status immunities and *elemental immunities* and not needing to sleep . . .

"And you know, the more time I spend with people that aren't in my own fucking bubble, the more I realize this isn't just a fucking game?" Jerome looked down at Kestel, and he felt frustration burn in his voice for a moment. He'd *had* his moment with Kestel. He'd met the guy, back when he was negotiating for access to the dungeon himself, going behind the Guildmaster's back to do so.

He'd been kind of a dick to him then, too. He'd said something about how he'd find everything they needed in the dungeon, and they wouldn't need other delvers, and how trying to study a dungeon was stupid, anyway; they should just delve it for the loot and be done with it.

It was weird how different that version of himself felt, even though it had been only a few months. Spending more time with people had a way of doing that to you, maybe.

"I *thought* of this as just a game, because it looks like games back on Earth, and you people—fuck, not 'you people,' just—the people that are *here*, whatever—you don't act like the people back on Earth. And I never thought to visit the *fucking hospital*, or look at any of the fucking orphanages back in Anderstahl, and I didn't even fucking *talk* to people except when I wanted something from them.

"And now I have, and it sucks! And a part of me wants to go back to that, because I didn't fucking feel like shit all the time back then, and *that makes me feel even more like a piece of shit*. And the worst part is that I *know* I'm taking all the wrong lessons from this. Everyone around me is *so goddamn fucking understanding* all the time, and I just want someone to be *angry* at me."

Maybe it wasn't fair to dump on Kestel like this. It wasn't like the lizardkin had any choice in the matter, but . . . it wasn't like he could hear him, either.

"Why?"

Never mind. Kestel had woken up at some point and *could* hear him. The lizardkin was just staring at him with a placidly interested sort of look on his face, and somehow that made Jerome even angrier.

Not at Kestel. Just at himself. He'd never invested any effort into skills needed to *heal*, or else he might have been able to do something about this. Everything had gone exactly as he wanted. He'd gotten rich. He'd gotten rare skills. Granted, the "rich" part hadn't gone exactly the way he'd envisioned— somehow he hadn't considered that gold might not be intrinsically valuable, when he'd pledged himself to the God of Gold—but he'd still gotten there *eventually*.

And the whole time, he'd still been pissed at everyone around him. He'd still wanted more. The few flashes of pleasure he ever got were from *gain*, whatever form that gain took, and that vanished in a matter of moments. Replaced by a desire for more still.

More strength, more wealth, more prestige.

Some of that, he was aware, came from the nature of the geas placed upon him—a feedback loop in his mind, telling him he was deserving of more. A feedback loop placed upon him in an effort to help him become more confident.

... So many things had gone wrong.

He didn't *really* want to go back. He hated being *like this*, and he spouted off about it sometimes, but he wouldn't go back. He couldn't. Knowing what he did now, going back would be a betrayal of all the progress he'd made—

"Why?" Kestel repeated again, and Jerome flinched slightly. He'd almost forgotten the lizardkin was there.

"... I don't know," Jerome answered after the moment it took him to even remember the context of the question. Why *did* he want someone to be angry at him? "I guess I feel like I deserve it."

"Why?" Kestel asked him again.

"I hurt a lot of people," Jerome said. "I didn't mean to, but I did. And it feels like I'm not getting punished for it, and I feel like I should be."

"Why?"

Jerome was beginning to sense a trend here. But he answered anyway. "It's just how I've thought about things for a long time," he said quietly. "You do something bad, you get punished. Actions have consequences, and all that. You shouldn't be able to just get away with it."

"Why?"

It was like talking to a broken— *No.* Jerome stopped himself before the thought finished, almost snarling at himself before he saw the way Kestel began to flinch back. *Don't dehumanize,* he thought to himself, and then he managed a wry smile at the irony of the statement, which coaxed Kestel into relaxing again.

Dehumanize wasn't a very applicable word here. But it was the closest one he had.

"We punish people so they don't repeat their actions, I guess," Jerome said. He'd never really thought this deeply on the matter before; he'd long since learned to stop asking *why*.

Kestel seemed to consider this for a long moment. Jerome almost thought the lizardkin had fallen back asleep, but then he spoke again, his voice contemplative. "Are you going to?"

"Am I going to what?" Jerome blinked a few times. "Like . . . repeat my actions? No. Heck no. I— Oh. I see your point."

Kestel cocked his head slightly; Jerome wasn't even sure if that was the point Kestel was trying to make, or if he was just asking questions. He had been getting better, or so the priests said, but there was no change in his status; he still had difficulty moving and speaking . . .

But that wasn't fair, he thought. Difficulty with those things didn't make Kestel lesser. Taking longer to express his thoughts might be frustrating for him and sad for the people that knew him, but it didn't make him not a person. He couldn't just assume Kestel was a child and asking questions for the sake of it.

Kestel just stared at him. "If I'm not going to repeat what I do anyway, then there's no purpose to the punishment; is that what you're saying?" Jerome asked, and Kestel nodded slightly at him. Jerome sighed.

"I guess that makes sense," he said, though he said it reluctantly. "I dunno. It doesn't feel right. I still feel like people *should* get punished."

"Why—" Kestel started, and Jerome held up a hand.

"No, I get it," he said, and to Jerome's surprise, Kestel managed a small grin at him. Maybe he *was* getting better. "I get what you're saying, and it makes sense. It just doesn't change how I feel about it. I want to come up with other reasons that it matters—like, if we punish people, it's going to deter other people from doing the same thing, right? Not everyone is going to be convinced by words."

"But no one's going to be repeating what I did." Jerome looked down and away for a moment. "And fuck, I'm sure there's other ways to deter people. I dunno. I've never really thought about it. Do we even want to deter people? Maybe deterring people isn't the best way to get people to not do things! There's too much stuff to think about." He threw his hands up in frustration. "I feel like this is for people smarter than me to think about."

Kestel took a moment to reply again, and Jerome just waited. "You're . . . thinking about it," he said eventually. "That is . . . more than most."

"Yeah, I guess," Jerome grumbled. "I don't *like* thinking about it. I'd like to go back to not thinking about it. I want a refund and to get off this thought train."

Another beat, and then Kestel chuckled. "Sorry," the lizardkin told him. "No . . . no refunds."

"Bah!" Jerome said.

But he found he was smiling.

They talked for a few more minutes before Kestel got too tired and had to go back to sleep—but before he did, he made Jerome promise to visit again. He liked having a young mind to guide, he said, and even though part of Jerome hated being called a "young mind," much less the implication that he needed guidance, he'd agreed. He'd genuinely enjoyed spending time with the guy, after all.

He wasn't a "young mind," though. That was patently ridiculous. Kestel couldn't have been, what, more than six years older than him? Maybe eight?

Bah.

Jerome got up from his seat and spared one more glance before he left the lizardkin's "ward"—it was still just a set of curtains in the temple, although the curtains had been magically augmented and enchanted to give Kestel privacy and comfort. It was a service the other Elyran researchers had provided to all the wards once it became clear that the temple wasn't really equipped to hold anyone long-term, and it was something the priests all appreciated.

"All done?" Eleisse asked him, and Jerome jumped.

"*God*," he said. "Don't scare me like that."

He wasn't sure how to feel about his elf companions now. They were still the only elves he'd seen here—elves were more common around Anderstahl than they were here, apparently, though that didn't explain the complete lack of them—and he wasn't sure if they were actually comfortable here?

There was a lot of things he was questioning now that he hadn't questioned before. Like why they kept following him around after he had rescued them. At the time, he'd thought it made sense, but . . .

"My apologies," Eleisse said, bowing her head slightly.

"Don't do that, either," Jerome said, feeling slightly uncomfortable. "Were you waiting on me for something?"

"No," Eleisse said. "I was waiting in case I was needed."

". . . Don't take this the wrong way, but don't you have your own things to do?" Jerome asked. "Syra too, wherever she is."

"She is resting," Eleisse said. "It is my shift."

Jerome felt a headache coming on. "You've been keeping shifts this entire time and I haven't noticed?"

"Do not take this the wrong way," Eleisse said, this time with a faint smirk gracing her lips, "but you are not very observant."

"Please tell me this isn't a stupid life-debt thing."

"Were that an actual part of our culture, we would be offended," Eleisse informed him. "But it is not. You simply needed our protection, so we adopted you."

"I what?" Jerome asked blankly. "How have we never talked about this— never mind. I know the answer to that question. More importantly, *what*?"

"You attempted to save us and were poisoned in the process," Eleisse explained to him. "Elven couples have a tradition. We will care for a person, if we choose to, and the person accepts. It is like parenting."

"You guys are a couple?" Jerome said blankly, and then the rest of his brain caught up. "Wait, did you guys *adopt* me? I feel like I should get some choice in that! I'm an adult!"

"Yes, you are," Eleisse said to him, very patiently, like an adult would to a child. "And we did. You accepted. We explained it more than once, in fact, though I am unsure you listened . . ."

Jerome buried his face in his hands. "Oh my *god*."

"We can leave, if you wish," Eleisse told him.

"No, I just . . . Okay, please explain it to me again. I'm sorry I didn't pay attention the first time; I was a fucking idiot."

"I will look for Syra, and we will explain it together. For the . . . twelfth time."

"Somehow the fact that you've been keeping track of that both doesn't surprise me and deeply horrifies me."

CHAPTER 71

GETTING READY

"I feel like ass," Misa grunted, pulling at her shoulder as she slowly sat up—she protested when Sev went to help prop her up, which in and of itself was already alarming, Derivan felt. "We still alive?"

"Barely." Sev took the initiative to answer there. "But we're safe for now."

Misa relaxed just slightly. "Good," she said. "Now why the fuck does everything burn so much."

"You might want to check your status," Sev said gently. "You took a lot of damage in that fight."

"No fuckin' kidding." Misa made a tiny, unnecessary flicking gesture to bring up the screen; she stared at it for just long enough to make Derivan start to worry. "... My status looks fine, but I can tell there's somethin' here you want me to find. Spill."

"Your anchor integrity," Sev said, and Misa cursed. It didn't take her too long to bring up the screen, and she flinched visibly when she saw it.

"... We've got two weeks," she said after a slight pause, and then her voice went firm and her eyes determined. "We'll figure out how to fix this thing by then."

"We already know how, sort of," Vex said quietly. "We managed to make the integrity go up before."

"When you were doin' magic, right?" Misa asked. Vex nodded.

"Which lines up with what we're going to do here anyway," he said.

"Good." Misa stared out into the distance for a moment, keeping her expression as firmly neutral as possible. "I don't know about you guys, but I *really* need a bed. And some time to myself."

"Are you doing all right?" Sev asked, worried.

"No," Misa replied shortly, and then softened a little bit when she saw the way the cleric was looking at her. "Look, I just need a little bit of time. I'll be okay, I promise."

Derivan didn't say anything. Her words didn't express quite the depth of emotions she was feeling—she was holding so much back he didn't have any doubt that both Vex and Sev could see straight through the transparent lie. But they didn't call her out on it.

She'd talk about it when she was ready.

"What happened to Irvis?" Misa asked, after no one said anything. Sev blinked.

"Um. I don't know." Sev glanced around. "Vex?"

"I have theories," Vex said, "but nothing concrete. Our best bet is to get out of here before he comes back, though, if he can come back."

"So he's not dead." Misa's expression darkened a bit.

"... No, he's not," Vex said softly. "We—we wouldn't have been able to beat him. So I brought us *here*, where everything is a little bit different, and in theory... in theory *he* should be a little bit different here, too."

"Okay." Misa nodded sharply, not giving away anything else about her thoughts. "Let's get out of here, then."

—⁂—

The trek out of the dungeon was... surprisingly eerie.

There was a small mechanism in the wall of the elevator room that would activate it and bring them back down. Once there, all they needed to do was head back to the start of any of the four routes; they opted to head down the path Derivan and Sev had already taken, on account of the fact that that route was largely cleared of potential enemies.

What was strange about it was how silent it was. Derivan hadn't really noticed the noise in the background when he'd been through the dungeon the first time; the sound of metal being forged, of fires being stoked, of cauldrons bubbling to life. It was only now that those workshops were inactive that he noticed the *lack* of it. And what a strange phenomenon that was. There was no word to put to it except one: the place sounded... dead.

Which he did not, he decided, enjoy.

The sound of ringing metal *did* return after a moment, however, and all four of them tensed slightly at the sound. Misa crept forward first, followed by Sev, then Vex, then Derivan.

And they found a strange sight: a single suit of armor, molded in the fashion of Elyra's standard guardsman set, sitting alone in one of the workshops. One of the fires had been stoked with clearly inexpert hands, given how it was sputtering and dying rather than roaring. The suit of armor sat there anyway, hammering away at a piece of vaguely hot metal with what seemed to Derivan to be frustration.

Misa paused. "Is it . . . a threat?" she asked, sounding hesitant.

"I do not believe so." Derivan eyed the other suit of armor for a moment, then decided to step forward. It paused and stared at him but returned to its ineffectual hammering a moment later. It didn't seem to mind his presence, but it didn't seem to care to acknowledge him, either.

There *was* a moment where its gaze lingered on his arm; Derivan didn't know how he felt about that. It was . . . uncomfortable? He'd noticed the glances his friends occasionally gave him, too, but he gave no outward indication of his thoughts on the matter. He was still getting used to the idea that he was missing an arm at all.

He walked over to the fire, and then the suit of armor *did* pay attention; it stopped what it was doing and turned to stare at him intently. Derivan wasn't sure if it was trying to get him to move away through the power of its gaze alone, or if it was simply curious about what he was doing. But what he wanted to do wasn't anything complicated—he just wanted to help.

He drew the Fire glyph that they'd learned just above the fire and channeled just the smallest amount of mana into it. He had to guide the magic as fire began to emerge, directing it *down* rather than letting it stream out in an ineffectual sphere, but it was a pretty good try for it being his first attempt at this, he thought.

And then the proof that they were in a different world came—because the magic didn't just end there.

Like Derivan had stirred up something that had just been lying dormant, the mana around them came to life and surged into the glyph; the fire that was simply being *produced* became something *real* in that moment—more real than just the product of a spell. Like he'd informed the mana that *this was supposed to be a forge*, and it had responded, just like that.

"Whoa," Vex said. His eyes were a little wide. "Did you—?"

"It was not me," Derivan said, shaking his head slightly and stepping back.

The armor was staring at the renewed fire in awe, and its hand was twitching slightly, like it was trying to remember the shape of the glyph Derivan had drawn. It still seemed a little hesitant to approach.

The moment Derivan stepped even farther back, though, going all the way back to stand by Vex's side, the armor scurried forward and placed its hunk of metal in the forge, and began watching it intently.

"Well," Vex said, "I'm glad he's got something to be happy about."

"Sometimes it's the simple pleasures," Misa said with a small smile, though it seemed just a little bit forced. "C'mon. Let's go."

Derivan spared the suit of armor a final glance. "You don't *have* to stay here, you know."

It looked at him, but it didn't quite seem to understand. It cocked its head, shrugged, and went back to staring at the hunk of metal in the fire.

Well... it was as Vex said, he supposed. If it was happy just doing this, then that was fine. Maybe it would get bored eventually and look for the way out.

The original room Derivan and Sev had appeared in—and indeed, the one they'd encountered the suit of armor in to begin with—was just as they'd left it, save for a small mess made in one of the corners where a vase had been toppled over.

"Is the exit supposed to be here?" Misa asked with a frown.

"There *should* be a portal..." Vex trailed off.

There was nothing there. Just an empty room.

"We might have to break out manually if the dungeon is inactive," Vex said slowly. Misa snorted.

And then, before anyone could say anything, she punched the wall opposite to the door.

Sometimes, Derivan reflected, he forgot about the number of points Misa put into Strength. She began ripping the wall apart like it was made of paper—and seemed to be getting in a good amount of stress relief, too, if the way she was baring her teeth was any indication.

In theory, the dungeon should have been protected against damage like that. Vex had given them many a lecture on why people couldn't simply tear their way through the walls of a dungeon, and he'd even tried it once or twice, back in his own dungeon. When the system was present, dungeons were simply immune to this kind of damage.

Apparently, not anymore. But then this was Vex's bonus room, rather aptly named <A World Without the System>. He shouldn't have been surprised. Now that he thought about it, though...

"I did not consider this before, but should we not have received a notification about this bonus room?" Derivan asked after the dust had settled from Misa's... deconstruction efforts. The hole was large enough for them to get through now, and it seemed to lead outside, for a certain definition of *outside*. It seemed more important to settle his final concerns about where they were before they went out there.

"... You're right; we should have." Vex frowned. "System *menus* are still working, and I think I can still send and receive messages, although there's a message about the time discrepancy. Is the notification system specifically not working?"

"It's not like the notification system worked with any consistency before," Misa said, a little dryly.

"It's going to be a problem if we don't know what we're supposed to *do* here," Vex pointed out.

"Add it to the list of problems we've already got," Sev said, though his words were hard to hear, partially whipped away from him by the wind as he glanced outside the hole. "We're kind of in the middle of nowhere."

The four of them gathered to look out of the hole. They were still suspended a good distance from the ground, though that distance wasn't much of a problem; [**Featherfall**] was a simple spell that Vex had used many a time. What *was* a problem was where they were.

The actual area they had appeared in was, surprisingly, on the surface—Derivan had expected otherwise, considering what they'd seen of Teque. Noram had only briefly mentioned that there were reclaimed sections of the world that existed above the ground, and he had *also* mentioned that those reclaimed sections often had physical oddities and didn't work quite right.

That seemed to be true here, too. The sky split into fractals that reflected the ground back at them, in a way that made it almost *seem* like they were underground; it was only the vaguely transparent appearance of the reflected image that told them they were outside. The sun shone at them through that reflected image, lighting up what seemed like miles of grassy plains around them.

There was nothing to even indicate that there might be civilization nearby—even the reflections in the sky showed nothing but grass.

"It's really not even going to give us a hint, huh?" Sev muttered. No one responded to him, and he sighed. "We might as well go down and look around; maybe there's something down there that we can't see from up here. Sky's pretty weird, so who knows."

No one had a better plan. Vex did his thing; [**Featherfall**] was a simple enough...

The rune sparked in the air and did nothing. Vex frowned at it, then tried again, only to get the same result.

"... System spells don't work here," Vex said.

"Well," Misa said. "Guess we better jump, then."

CHAPTER 72

FRACTALS IN THE SKY

Jumping was much easier said than done. Derivan peered out of the hole to see exactly how viable jumping would be—it was not. Sev, on the other hand, just stared at Misa with one brow slightly raised.

"What?" she asked. She managed a small grin. "We're a Gold-ranked team. We shouldn't be afraid of a little fall."

"It's not exactly a *little* fall," Vex said, peering out of the hole alongside Derivan and shuddering slightly. "Somehow that's so much worse when I don't have my magic."

"You *have* your magic," Misa pointed out. "You just don't have access to your system-granted spells."

"I haven't figured out a Glyph of Featherfall yet," Vex grumbled. "Coming up with new spells isn't that easy, you know."

"We're not guaranteed the system's protection from anything," Sev said. "Never mind that the system doesn't protect from *falling*—we can't take for granted that any system mechanic works the way we expect in a bonus room called <The World Without the System>."

"What about your spells?" Derivan directed his question to Sev. "Divine spells are likely not under the same restriction."

"Huh," Sev said slowly. "No, you're right. They're a conceit of the system, as far as I know. They work like regular system skills, so if the rest of our skills are still working—and I know they are, because [Triage] worked earlier—then there's no reason my 'spells' won't work."

He tested it by flicking out a hand; a gleaming, golden barrier appeared a second afterward, floating in the air.

". . . I guess we could use these as steps," Sev said. "Somehow this feels vaguely blasphemous."

"I'm sure Onyx won't mind," Misa said dryly.

"He'd probably find it hilarious." Sev stared at the gleaming barrier for a moment, his brows furrowing slightly. "I hope Aurum's okay. I still haven't heard from the kid."

Misa glanced at him and softened, just a bit. "I'm sure he'll be fine," she said. She didn't say anything further.

They made their way down the makeshift steps in silence, pausing every so often to let Sev recover his mana. The whole process was arduous and took far longer than a simple [**Featherfall**] would have, but they didn't really have any other options.

The process did, at least, reveal to them that there was more to the world than had been immediately obvious from their perch in the dungeon.

The illusory mirrors in the sky weren't *just* in the sky; those were just the most obvious ones, because the light shining through them from behind made it clear that they were merely reflections of the ground. There were, however, scattered mirror-like planes all over the place, reflecting just a small fraction of the ground. The more they descended, the more it became clear that they had no idea what the ground looked like.

Or indeed how far down the *ground* even was. They passed the first layer where they thought the ground had been soon enough, only to find it was another wall of reflected ground, catching on to some piece of grass who knew where.

"I'm starting to notice that a lot of these patches of grass look the *same*," Vex mumbled, reaching out to let his claws drift through one illusory patch; it drifted apart on contact with his scales and came together again once he pulled away. He frowned slightly. "I can't even tell if this is a mana-based phenomenon. I can't *control* any of it . . ."

"Noram said something about the surface being strange," Sev said. He glanced around, casting another barrier just a little bit below theirs. "I didn't think it'd be this strange, though."

"I'd *really* like to find a fucking bed right around now," Misa grumbled. "Half-tempted to actually just jump for it."

"Please don't," Sev said dryly. "Even as a joke."

Misa glanced at him, then stared critically around them. "Anyone else think the grass is changing slightly?"

"They all look kinda the same at this point." Vex peered more closely at one of the panes in the air. "I guess the grass might be a bit more yellow?"

"Not yellow." Misa shook her head and tugged on Vex's arm, directing him to a different patch. "*Rotting*."

She had, in fact, discovered something that was best described as an illusory tunnel. The panes in the air formed a sort of circular path, but the farther down that path the panes were, the drier and blacker that grass was, very visibly rotting, maggots and all.

Vex paled. "Um. Let's not go down there?"

Misa seemed slightly skeptical. "I don't know that we have much of a *choice*."

They kept on going anyway. It wasn't like the panes stopped them from choosing a different direction to go in—they could just walk straight through them, and the collective decision to avoid the strange death hole in the sky seemed like a smart one.

It became clear relatively quickly that there *were*, in fact, other paths in the midst of them—each one seeming to lead somewhere slightly different. It wasn't always as obvious as what Misa had decided to officially deem the Death Hole; sometimes the grass just seemed a little brighter, or in other cases, there were flowers.

None of them, notably, seemed to have *people*.

At first.

The signs of civilization came slowly but surely. Panes where the grass was flattened, like many people had trodden over it; panes where there was glass or some other manufactured material lying scattered about. The path they eventually opted to follow was one that, at the end of it, seemed to have a *road*.

"Better than anything else we've seen so far," Sev commented, staring down the path.

"Let's not waste any more time." Misa gestured for Sev to start placing his barriers, and, after a brief pause to glance at her, Sev did so.

They didn't speak much while they walked down that path. Everyone that wasn't Misa exchanged slightly worried glances at one another, and Misa seemed content not to talk about whatever was on her mind.

So the time passed in silence, until they reached the end of the path and finally found themselves on solid ground.

In the middle of a town, no less.

No one seemed to notice them, though—or at least, no one seemed to be interested. A few people—shadow beings, it seemed, dressed in immaculate suits—glanced up at them and then went back to their own business, seemingly uninterested in the group of adventurers that had, for all intents and purposes, simply walked down out of the sky. The dungeon chandelier wasn't even visible from here, obfuscated by panes of light that each reflected a different part of the village.

If they hadn't come down here *from* the dungeon, they wouldn't have known that that was there, either.

"I'm beginning to feel like we should've left a tracker on that thing, just in case," Sev said, glancing back up at the sky in the rough direction of the dungeon.

"I believe I know where it is," Derivan offered. Sev blinked at him.

"You do? Using Shift or something?"

"It is not currently Shifted any more than we are." Derivan paused to find the words to explain. "I lost... pieces of myself in the fight with Irvis. Not my arm. It appears to be an intrinsic trait of Slime."

"You can sense where other pieces of you are?" Sev cocked his head. "Useful."

"To a degree," Derivan agreed, nodding. It was slightly uncomfortable, in fact—but it was nothing he couldn't get used to. Perhaps his connection to those pieces of himself would fade in time, even; it was still too early to say.

"Think we can get ourselves an inn here?" Misa said, glancing around. "Don't know what currency they trade in."

"[**Reality Shards**], if Teque was any indication, but I guess it might be different here," Vex said. He hesitated. "But we don't have any left."

"Let's just explore," Sev suggested. "We'll either find a place or we'll find someone we can ask about it."

The whole town itself was unremarkable. Derivan was rather uncomfortably reminded of Fendal, in a way, though the architecture didn't really resemble the other town all that much. Fendal was full of short, squat buildings, some of them divided into multiple storefronts, but most of them independent houses.

This place had *apartments*, but the buildings were almost unsettlingly close to perfect cubes, without any real flair of life to them. What few stores there were were dim inside, with the glass so frosty that the products they were selling were only barely visible. One store was stocked with identical loaves of bread, and another was stocked with a variety of fruits that Derivan didn't recognize, though *variety* was a poor word to use, perhaps. There were about five different fruits Derivan could see, and every copy of a single fruit seemed perfectly identical.

It didn't help that as they progressed through the town, they saw not a single person that wasn't what appeared to be a shadow elemental.

"I'm not going to lie," Vex whispered as they walked through the town— he had one hand grasping Derivan's as he peered through the stores and tried to avoid the gazes of the people around him, not that it was difficult. "This place is kinda creepy. I was sort of expecting a lot more ... life here."

"Perhaps we simply picked a bad path," Derivan said, trying to be comforting. He wasn't sure it worked.

"We'll probably have to find our way into Teque or someplace similar soon," Sev spoke from his position in front of them. "Noram did tell us the surface is unstable. I didn't think it'd be like *this*."

"He mentioned some areas had been reclaimed, too, right?" Vex looked around. "I just don't know if this is one of them."

"Just because we find it a little strange doesn't mean this place is bad," Misa said. She glanced critically at yet another one of the perfect-cube buildings; this one had a window that displayed, of all things, a bed. "What're the odds this is an inn and not just a place that sells beds?"

"About even odds, I'd say," Sev said.

"Fuck it," Misa shrugged, and pushed the door open.

The inside was surprisingly bright—so much so that Misa flinched slightly once she stepped in, having expected the interior to match the exterior. That wasn't the case at all—beyond the slightly shadowed display where the bed was, there was a beautifully decorated lobby. Bright red drapes adorned a window that was positioned perfectly at what seemed to be one of the few grass-reflecting panes in the town, creating an illusion of a bright park outside. Bright, warm flames licked at the upper corners of the room, each in small, perfectly controlled spheres.

The innkeeper—because this was very clearly an inn, there was even a wall of keys behind him—smiled happily at them as they entered. He, too, was a shadow being dressed in an immaculate suit, but he seemed perfectly happy to see and address them, unlike everyone else they'd met.

"Well, hello there!" he greeted. "I've never had any visitors before. How exciting!"

"You've ... never had any visitors?" Misa blinked and glanced around. "This *is* an inn, right?"

"Well, yes, but we don't exactly get any visitors here." The innkeeper let out a surprisingly warm chuckle and hopped up to sit on his desk. "It's a pleasure to meet you all. What brings you to the fine town of Aldea?"

"... Dungeon shenanigans?" Sev said, at a loss for what else to say.

"I'll mark that down in the guestbook." The innkeeper gave them a knowing grin. "The name's Clyde, by the way. You guys doing okay? Need some rooms?"

"We'll need four, if you have them," Misa said. "What types of payment do you take? We're kinda new here."

"Payment?" Clyde looked puzzled for a moment, and then brightened. "Oh! No. No payment. Stories, maybe, if you're willing to share them. But we don't work that way here."

"No?" Misa paused as Clyde swept up four keys from behind him and deposited them in her hand.

"Nah. Can't say when we dropped it, but I'd say we're all pretty happy here. I get that it looks kind of unfriendly from the outside, though." Clyde's smile vanished for a moment. "It's complicated. But here, your rooms—let me know if anything's wrong with them; I haven't checked in on them for ages. I'll fix it right quick."

"Sure," Misa said slowly. She tossed three of the keys to Vex, Derivan, and Sev, and then held up her own. "I'm gonna go pass the fuck out first, if you guys don't mind. Let's figure stuff out in the morning."

She vanished up the stairs without giving any of them a chance to respond. Sev, Derivan, and Vex glanced at each other.

"She's having a rough time of it, your friend," Clyde said suddenly, glancing up the stairs. His face was little more than two glowing eyes hidden in shadow, but he was able to emote well through it—not unlike Derivan, in fact. His face had softened somewhat. "Lemme know if you want me to talk to her, yeah? Or my daughter. She's pretty good at this kind of stuff."

"You're . . . very helpful; thank you," Sev said. Derivan glanced at him—the cleric was a little suspicious, and Derivan supposed he couldn't fault him. *Make sure Misa's okay*, Sev mouthed at him, using the Relay charm to communicate. *Give her space; just check on her through the system or something.* "Can you tell us a little more about this place? We're pretty new here."

"Of course!" Clyde smiled brightly. "Here, let me see; where do I start . . ."

Sev tensed slightly. Derivan watched as the system's strings around him suddenly pulled taut, like something was about to finally reach a conclusion.

He remembered, somewhat belatedly, that this bonus room wasn't just a bonus room—it was a recreation of the history of their own world if it had taken a slightly different path. If the *mana* had tried to fix whatever had gone wrong, instead of the system. Teque hadn't known what had gone wrong, but Teque was only a partial recreation.

Derivan realized with startling certainty that Clyde hadn't interpreted *this place* to mean their town at all; he'd interpreted it to mean *their entire world*. Clyde was old. This whole town was. It wasn't obvious, but . . .

> [**Intermediate Mana Sight**] has been upgraded to [**Mana Understanding**].

The mana here was *old*.

"Well," Clyde said thoughtfully, and Derivan's attention refocused sharply on the shadow elemental, waiting for the words that would change everything.

"I guess it all started when the universe ended, about . . . oh, 1400 years ago."

ABOUT THE AUTHOR

Silver Linings has been writing for over two decades and has finally decided to direct that creative energy into authoring complete books, preferably ones about kindness and compassion. He is also attempting to spread across all the clouds in the sky and give them a silver lining. This is not a metaphor. Do not panic, and stay indoors at all times.

DISCOVER
STORIES UNBOUND

PodiumAudio.com

www.ingramcontent.com/pod-product-compliance
Ingram Content Group UK Ltd.
Pitfield, Milton Keynes, MK11 3LW, UK
UKHW041304180426
11947UKWH00009B/675